Praise for *My Father's House*

"Ulf Kvensler skillfully and evocatively writes about Isak's growing anxiety, about the accident that came to mark his life, and about Grandpa, who became his most important supporter."

—*Dagens Nyheter,* Sweden

"High-level excitement in all areas."

—*Expressen Söndag,* Sweden

"Ulf Kvensler tells the story rapidly and effectively and manages to keep the tension alive throughout the book."

—*Ölandsbladet,* Sweden

"*My Father's House* jostles the reader and traps them little by little in a very oppressive atmosphere."

—*Télé Star Jeux,* France

"A merciless and Machiavellian game of life and death set against the backdrop of childhood trauma."

—*France Dimanche,* France

"A gripping novel until the final twist."

—*Elle France,* France

"After the success with *The Couples Trip*, [Ulf Kvensler] delivers another brilliant thriller."

—*Le Pèlerin,* France

My Father's House

A NOVEL

ULF KVENSLER

TRANSLATED BY PAUL NORLEN

HANOVER
SQUARE
PRESS

ISBN-13: 978-1-335-00038-5

My Father's House

Originally published in Swedish in 2023 as *Brandmannen* by Albert Bonniers Förlag, Sweden.

This edition published in 2025.

Published in agreement with Salomonsson Agency.

Translated by Paul Norlen.

Hanover Square Press
22 Adelaide St. West, 41st Floor
Toronto, Ontario M5H 4E3, Canada
HanoverSqPress.com

Printed in U.S.A.

Also by Ulf Kvensler

The Couples Trip

PART ONE

If I'd known then what I know today
I wouldn't have known it today.

Stanislaw Jerzy Lec

I DREAMED THAT IT WAS SUMMER, AND I WAS SWIMMING IN THE lake in the country at Grandpa's. It was just like when I was little but I was still me; I was grown-up.

I had that feeling that probably everyone has when they're little. You're in the moment in a completely different way than when you're an adult. Summer spread out in all directions, as far as you could see.

I was floating not too far from the shore, wearing a scuba mask with a snorkel. Peered down into the water, in that different, silent world. The bottom was furrowed; there were tiny, tiny sand dunes, like a miniature Sahara. And the light was shimmering. It was probably the ripples on the surface that caused that. Here and there scattered blades of reeds swayed slightly, back and forth. Small fish, almost transparent, fled when you reached your hand out toward them. The mouthpiece on the snorkel tasted like rubber, just like when I was little. With every breath I took there was hissing in my ears. It sounded like I was a deep-sea diver hundreds of meters below the surface.

That dream was insanely realistic.

I wasn't really swimming; instead I pulled myself forward with my fingers on the lake bed. Clouds of sand formed in the water, like a little explosion. It looked cool, I thought.

Then I floated quietly on the surface and looked out at the

lake. I shivered a little, because a little farther out the bottom disappeared, and the sunlight was swallowed by darkness. Grandpa talked a lot about there being a drop-off under the water a ways out. When I was little I was never that far from shore, because I didn't touch bottom before the drop-off either, but as an adult of course I've been up by the edge. The water reaches roughly up to your nipples, then you take another step and the bottom disappears. I think the lake becomes maybe five meters deep almost at once.

Grandpa drilled into Klara and me that we weren't allowed to go to the drop-off. As if we would have even thought of venturing out there, a six-year-old and a three-year-old. I was scared to death of it. And to be honest, even as an adult I feel a strange churning in my gut when I take a few steps out and my head disappears below the surface of the water.

Anyway. In the dream I felt a swath of colder water against my skin. Do you know how that feels? There are currents that bring water up from the deep part of the lake, I'm guessing. So I reached down toward the bottom to start pulling myself toward shore again.

But then I didn't reach all the way down.

I must have floated a while on the surface and drifted a few meters out without thinking about it.

I started to thrash and struggle desperately to reach down with my fingertips, but it didn't help. I could see myself thrashing in the water quite helplessly and slowly drifting out over the drop-off, to the deep part of the lake where the water was completely black and you had no idea what might be under it. Maybe big fish or eels were lurking down there in the depths—imagine feeling an unknown something suddenly rub against your leg. So disgusting.

In the dream I panicked.

Then it occurred to me that I could swim. Because I was the person I am today; I was an adult.

I paddled like a madman until I reached the shallower water, which in reality should have taken about five seconds. But in the dream I had to keep at it for at least fifteen minutes.

At last I could reach down to the bottom again with my fingertips, so I breathed out and pulled myself in the last bit. When it started to get really shallow the water felt so warm that it almost burned against my skin.

I looked up. The water was running over the scuba mask so that I didn't see clearly, but a little figure came running toward me up there on the shore. A three-year-old. Klara.

I haven't dreamed about Klara for years. But now I was happy. I pulled off the scuba mask and stood up out of the water. Klara was naked and rushed out into the water and started splashing me as much as she could. I splashed back, and she shrieked with delight.

The hair on half her head was burned off, half her face was black and cracked, one arm too. But she still had her eyes.

So that's where we were.

She didn't show it at all. That she was in pain or anything. She played and romped as usual. Me too.

There was something about Klara's face that made her always look happy. Or content, rather. As if she was always in a good mood. That is, not when she was sad or angry, of course. But it was like her basic mode was "isn't life just great." That was probably another reason I liked her so much. Klara was an extremely positive little person. Plus the fact that I was her idol, of course that was part of it. I was three years older and knew more than her about most things. But she thought I knew *everything*. She made me feel bigger than I was.

We kept splashing water on each other a while, then we went up on the beach and started building sandcastles. I showed her that the sand has to be wet enough to be stable when you turn over the pail. And that you should tap the pail with the spade so that the sand releases better.

Klara put a strand of her wet, dark brown hair in her mouth and sucked on it. She crouched right next to me, leaned against me, put her one hand on my leg, without thinking about it. A cozy feeling. Being almost joined together.

She smelled a little burnt.

I filled a pail with suitably wet sand, turned it upside down, tapped on the pail. Then Klara said, "Isak, don't go."

"What do you mean? What's this, 'don't go'?"

Klara patted me on the leg, leaned her head against my shoulder.

"Don't go."

Listen to this: When do you think I had this dream?

The night before the day my father called me and everything started.

The night before.

Isak, don't go.

It's as if she wanted to warn me. I mean, I get that it wasn't like that. It can't be like that. But still.

How sick is that?

Change of perspective.

I'm sure you've all seen that picture. At first glance it looks like an old lady. The next moment it looks like an elegant young woman with a long neck, turned slightly away.

I'm sitting on the ground in the recreation yard, in my little wedge-shaped space, and look up toward the sky. It feels like I'm sitting in a compartment in one of those Trivial Pursuit pies, but giant sized.

Confined.

But then I think, maybe it's the world that's confined. The whole universe. Only in this little piece of pie where I'm sitting can you move freely. Everything else that exists is confined.

Change of perspective.

Dad got me to see the world in a completely different way. For a few short seconds. That was no doubt his idea with the whole thing.

You could also say that for a few short moments I was just as crazy as him.

I can no longer see the world as I saw it then. But I remember the feeling anyway. And when it comes back I get dizzy and have to sit down.

The other day a raven came and sat on the wall up there. I think it was a raven anyway. It was big and black.

I wonder if it was her. What did she want from me in that case? Aren't we done with each other?

Please. Let us be done with each other.

I dream about my mother during the day and about Klara and Maddy at night.

The sky above the steel net is solid gray.

Just like it was the day when Dad called.

I was working as an aide in the home health care service before it all happened. I'd done that for almost four years. I was very content. Had a little work car and drove around to a gang of old folks who were still living in their own homes. Some of them lived in cottages in the middle of the forest. They would probably wither away and die in a few weeks if you put them in a nursing home.

People think that the worst thing about working in home health care is attending to the clients' personal hygiene. Changing diapers, wiping old folks' behinds when they've pooped on themselves. But the truth is you get used to that in a week. I did anyway. I hardly thought that it was disgusting any longer, didn't notice the smells like at first. It was just something that had to be done.

For me the administration was the worst. Writing reports, attending staff meetings, ordering consumables, everything that wasn't directly connected to the job. Boring as hell. Sometimes it made me think about changing jobs.

Many people think the stress is tough, that you never have enough time for the elderly, that you have to hurry on to the next one and the next one. Constantly feeling inadequate. But I probably had the best schedule in the whole municipality. It had to do with the fact that I'm big and strong and could move an old man, like Göte in Virseryd for example, into the shower all by myself. Göte had lost some weight in the past year but he still weighed well over a hundred kilos. If I didn't go to him two of my colleagues would have to go. If Göte was lying on the floor I was the only one who could get him up on my own. In that way you could say that I did the job of two nursing assistants and for that reason I had a really decent schedule.

It was the Tuesday after Midsummer. The weather was crappy, cold and rainy, the sky solid gray over the spruce forest. Summer in the province of Småland. Is it just as worthless anywhere else in this country? On this planet? I doubt it. In any event the weather meant that I was even more eager for the vacation that was supposed to start the following week. Maddy and I would go to Turkey, to Antalya, where we'd met the summer before.

That was the plan. God. It feels like a hundred years ago.

I'd already been driving around in my little car a couple of hours and it was almost nine o'clock. The roads were basically deserted that morning. I thought a lot about last night's dream about Klara. It had stirred up a lot of different emotions in me. Happiness at seeing her again, even if it was only in a dream. Sadness when I awoke. A worry that I myself didn't really understand.

Don't go.

I crawled through Tannsjö, the little community that old

Birgit lived on the edge of. An unmanned gas station, a small convenience store. Several storefronts that had been vacant as long as I could recall. The two-story apartment building, the only one in Tannsjö. No people out in the rain.

I parked on the driveway to Birgit's little yellow-brick, one-story villa. Once, long ago, it surely felt new and modern and fresh and practical. I knew that Birgit had been married and that her husband passed away many years ago. I had never heard anything said about any children.

When Birgit moved in here, did she know that it was for good? Or did she think that this was only a first stop on the journey that was the rest of her life? Did it feel as if she had endless time ahead of her, endless possibilities?

I went to the front door, unlocked it and went in. And discovered the wet spot on the hallway floor.

It wasn't the first time. Birgit had turned ninety last spring and was a little senile. Sometimes she pulled the diaper off at night. Then you might find one thing or another scattered around the house.

I went into her bedroom. She was lying there, snoring with mouth open. I took her bony, spotted hand in mine and squeezed gently.

"Birgit? Birgit? Will you wake up?"

She opened her eyes, almost in slow motion. She was far away. Looked at me with a sleepy and confused gaze.

"Good morning. It's me, Isak."

A cautious smile spread across her face, making her watery gray eyes look younger.

"Hi there," she said.

"Have you slept well? Are you feeling good?"

"Better than tomorrow," she peeped hoarsely.

I smiled. Birgit had a supply of retorts and jokes that she repeated every time we met. It was probably the dementia. But it didn't matter that you'd heard the jokes a hundred times before; they weren't what made you happy. It was the frisky look in her eyes when she said them.

I detected a suspicious smell. Yes, I hadn't become completely immune yet. I raised the covers, and discovered that Birgit was naked from the waist down and that she had pooped in the bed.

Not the first time for that either.

Just then the phone started to buzz. I picked it up and checked if it was someone from work, or Maddy. No. It wasn't a number I recognized. Probably a telemarketer. I clicked it away and went to work.

Half an hour later Birgit was sitting in the kitchen having breakfast. I had wiped up the pee in the hall, showered and cleaned her, put on a fresh diaper and a pair of light gray running pants, made coffee and a couple of cheese sandwiches. While she munched on the sandwiches and slurped coffee I tossed the soiled bedding in the washing machine and made the bed with clean, fresh sheets. Then I kept her company in the kitchen. When I came back into the kitchen she looked me over as if she was seeing me for the first time. Birgit had a stiff neck and couldn't bend her head backward, so she leaned her whole body instead, as if she was trying to see the top of a skyscraper or something.

"Oh, dear, here's someone who hasn't skimped on the porridge," she said, chuckling.

"No, exactly," I said and grinned.

This was the second time she'd said that this morning. If I knew her right she would say it a few more times before I moved on.

I took a cup out of the kitchen cupboard and poured coffee for myself, sat down on the chair beside her. I said, "Shall we take a walk later?"

"Shall we go out and walk?"

I leaned a little closer to Birgit and raised my voice.

"No, not out. I don't have time today. But we can walk around inside anyway."

"Yes, let's do that."

"You know, it's good for you to move. So your back doesn't hurt as much."

"No, no, my back doesn't hurt."

"That's good."

"I can lie down without a crutch now." She looked at me and laughed, her eyes became like half-moons, and I laughed too.

"Yes, that's good, Birgit. You go from strength to strength." I stroked her cheek.

The phone buzzed again, but it would have to wait.

When Birgit and I had walked around the house a few times, and I sat her in an armchair in the living room, I gave her a little hug.

"Bye now. Mia is coming this afternoon. I'll see you tomorrow."

"You are so welcome."

I closed and locked the front door and walked toward the car. At the same time I fished the phone out of my pocket. It was the same number that had called again, but now I had also received a message.

Telemarketers don't usually leave messages.

I checked voicemail and listened.

At first I heard a long silence, and someone taking a deep breath.

What was this all about?

Then: "Hi, Isak… It's Fredrik. It's Dad."

New, long silence.

"There's something I want to tell you. So…if you can call me at this number. Thanks."

Click. The message was over.

I unlocked the car, sank down behind the steering wheel, closed the door. Took a deep breath, stared at the phone.

I remained sitting on Birgit's driveway a long time, with my heart pounding in my chest.

That message affected me the whole day. I had a hard time getting it out of my thoughts.

At the end of my shift I went to the gym and did a really hard workout. Strained like a madman on the cross trainer, drove my pulse up to one seventy-five. I wanted to reach the point where you feel your heart pounding in your whole body, in your chest and throat and ears, even behind your eyes so that your vision almost gets a little blurry with every beat. Because something happens in the brain too when you push that hard. Maybe you're a little stuck in certain old ruts, in thoughts I mean, and then it's like a really hard workout resets the brain, and then you get back on the road again. Up out of the ditch.

The others at the gym stole glances at me. A girl that I'd seen there several times before—she's probably a few years younger than me, around twenty—looked a little worried, as if I might have a heart attack. But when I left I felt better. The worry had subsided a little.

On the way home to the apartment I thought about what I should do with Dad. There were only two ways to go, obviously: either get in touch or let it be. But the thing was that even if I didn't call back it wouldn't mean that everything would go on like before. He had called me; he wanted to tell me something. If I didn't get in touch I would still be wondering what it was he wanted.

He had made me face a choice, but I wasn't thrilled about any of the options.

Maddy and I lived in a little two-room apartment near the town center. It was a five-minute walk to the square with the old courthouse and a ten-minute walk to Ica Maxi, in the other direction. Close to everything. Or to nothing, depending on how you look at it.

New condominiums have been built along the river, big, fresh apartments with glassed-in balconies. The monthly fee is high but they sold out anyway like butter in sunshine. So there are people with money, even in our little town. Those apartments however were nothing for Maddy and me to think about. We found a shabby two-room rental of fifty-two square meters, fourth floor with no elevator.

When I happen to think about that apartment the pain washes over me like a powerful wave. I sit stock-still until it has subsided. It takes a good while.

Our lives, our future, all the hope and all the longing fit in those fifty-two square meters.

We still had an unpacked moving box in the living room. It's probably still there, by the way.

My God.

When I came in the front door I heard that Maddy was in the kitchen frying something.

"Hi," she called to be heard over the buzzing from the old fan.

"Hi," I called back and set the backpack with my workout clothes down on the hall floor. I continued through the narrow corridor, into the little kitchen. Maddy looked up at me and smiled.

"Hi there."

"Hi." I went up to her and put my hands on her waist. I leaned down a little, she stretched upward a little, and then our lips met in a kiss.

"My, your face is completely red," she said.

"I was at the gym."

I pulled her to me. She had a spatula in her hand, and in the frying pan turkey meatballs were sizzling. Water was boiling vigorously in a pan with pasta. I asked, "What can I do? Should I set the table?"

"Yes, please. And make a salad. There are tomatoes and cucumbers in the fridge."

I started setting the minimal kitchen table. A few times when Grandpa came to visit all of us sat in the kitchen and ate, but it was actually too cramped.

I looked over toward Maddy by the stove. She was extremely focused on food preparation and didn't notice my glances. Neither of us were good at cooking, or especially interested in it. At a flea market she'd bought a cookbook by Erik Lallerstedt, which said that you shouldn't feel guilty about using meal prep kits; sometimes you had to do that to get through the weekday. We'd taken that message hook, line and sinker, you might say. We also used meal prep kits to get through the weekends. When we didn't get takeout from the pizzeria or the Thai stand.

And I thought, as I often did, about how strange this was anyway. And marvelous. That this amazing woman was frying meatballs in our kitchen. That she'd moved from Stockholm, to this hole in the middle of darkest Småland, to live together with me.

Maddy was a few years older than me. Twenty-nine. She looked little in my arms but was actually of medium height. Her body was slender and well-shaped. She never exercised but looked fit anyway. I never understood how that worked. This evening she had on tight black jeans (I loved putting my hands in the back pockets of those jeans) and a white camisole that concealed the little tribal tattoo on the small of her back. She had fairly short, dark brown hair, which covered her ears and a little more, but showed her slender, fine throat and neck. It was cut in a special way; I don't really know how to describe it. You could see that it wasn't done at one of the salons here in town.

Maddy went to Stockholm more or less every other month and then she took the opportunity to get her hair done.

She had a beautiful face, *symmetrical* it's probably called, with high cheekbones and brown eyes. Always carefully made-up with a lot of mascara around her eyes and color on her cheeks.

But what truly made my blood rush were those things that didn't really fit with the image. Things that said she wasn't a rock star, but a person of flesh and blood. Her pale pink socks that had gotten discolored in the wash. How she scratched the top side of one foot with the toes on the other. Her slightly uncertain posture with the spatula in her hand, how she had to look carefully at the various knobs on the stove to know which one to use to lower the heat under the pasta pot.

She wasn't in her element here. And that was because of me. It was for my sake she subjected herself to this, to be together with me. And when I thought about it I felt that I loved her.

That evening, after Dad had contacted me for the first time in twelve years, I finished setting the table and sliced some cucumbers and tomato. Opened a can of corn and emptied it in the salad bowl. Maddy drained the pasta, put a coaster on the table and set out the frying pan and saucepan. I got ketchup out. We sat down and ate.

"So what have you been up to today?" I asked.

"Nothing in particular," Maddy said between bites. "I went in and checked the employment office website but there was nothing new."

When Maddy moved down last winter she worked for a while at Korseryd's Manor. Probationary period. They probably needed extra staff for the Christmas buffets and New Year's parties. But nothing came of it; she wasn't hired permanently. And then to be honest she hadn't seemed super eager to find anything else, even if she went online and checked the employment office every week. Or so she said.

I didn't have the world's biggest salary but I said that I could pay the rent and other things anyway, until she found something. But she didn't want to hear that. She would pay half; she stuck firmly to that.

Maddy had grown up in a wealthy family. Villa in Danderyd, summer house on the Riviera. On her mother's side the family had old money from some industry, and her mother worked as general counsel at a manufacturing company. Her father was a photographer and more bohemian but successful in his own way. Maddy was one of four siblings, second oldest, and generally considered to be the black sheep. Her mother she described as cold, power-hungry and unloving. As long as Maddy could recall they had argued. During her teen years there had been total chaos at home, a long, drawn-out rebellion. Maddy was truant a lot and got kicked out of the house when she turned eighteen. She had basically had no contact with her mother since then. Her father was gentler, more loving. He had secretly helped her financially over the years, and even let her stay in his studio sometimes when she was between subleases. She'd had every shit job there was in Stockholm, she said. And she had traveled a lot, backpacked around the globe. Sometimes she had to stay a few months at the same place to earn money for the next stretch.

"How was your day?" she asked.

"Good," I said. "Nothing special." I took more pasta and squirted ketchup over it. "That was good."

Maddy smiled a little wryly, self-ironic. She knew that she wasn't a master chef.

We ate in silence a while. My thoughts glided away to Dad, and to the dream about Klara. I didn't want to but I couldn't let it be. And Maddy must have noticed that I wasn't really there. I felt her eyes on me. Finally she said, "So, has something happened?"

"No, what would that be?"

"You seem a little… You look like you've got something on your mind."

"No, it's nothing. I'm just really hungry after the workout."

Maddy nodded and looked down at her food. She didn't seem convinced.

"Okay."

"Shall we watch something tonight?"

"Amen, let's do that."

I couldn't tell her that Dad had called, for an extremely simple reason. I had told Maddy that my mother and father were dead. That they died in a fire when I was little. Maddy hadn't asked for any details, out of consideration.

I thought it was simplest that way. What were the odds that Dad would get in touch after so many years? And in a way it wasn't a lie. He was dead to me.

I hadn't told her about Klara at all.

Maddy put her utensils on the plate; she was done eating. I fished up the last meatballs from the frying pan.

"You know," I said, "I happened to… I promised to help Grandpa with something. He's out at the summer house."

"I see."

"So I'm going to stop by there. After dinner."

"Okay."

"But it won't take long. We can still watch something later."

"Hmm."

It was true that Grandpa was out at the summer house, but not that I had promised to help him with something. I was simply forced to tell him that Dad had called and I didn't want to do that on the phone at home where Maddy could hear.

That time twelve years ago, when I last saw Dad, Grandpa said to me afterward that if Dad got in touch, then I had to tell him about it. I absolutely could not meet Dad on my own. Not under any circumstances.

I had made a solemn promise back then and that promise I intended to keep.

I took our beat-up old Nissan Micra and headed for Grandpa's cottage. Soon I was out of town and driving on a freeway with dense spruce forest on both sides. Just then the weather had cleared, but the asphalt was still shiny from the day's rain.

It's roughly twenty kilometers to the country place but it takes over half an hour to drive there. First there's a short stretch of freeway where you can really step on the gas; the road is straight and smooth and I usually go about a hundred and twenty. But then you turn off toward Rongaryd and it becomes a curvy highway a bit before you turn off again, onto a narrow gravel road between the spruce forest. It winds here and there and up and down and feels like it will never end. Grass and brush growing in the middle scrape against the underside of the car. Grandpa said once that somewhere near here, in the forest east of the big lake Lunnen, is the point in Småland farthest away from populated areas.

I have mixed emotions about the forest. I like the silence and the stillness among the thick trunks, the green moss that's like wall-to-wall carpet. It's a little like being in church. It calms you. But ever since I was little one of my greatest fears has been to get lost. I've always thought of it as drowning in the forest.

It started raining again. Fine drops pattered on the windshield as I wound my way ahead. A cloudy day like this it was almost like twilight in among the trees.

The forest thinned and you could make out the lake between the trunks. The next moment I was up at the house and parked the car. I got out and walked around the corner and looked out over the lake. Many of my finest memories were connected to this place. The worst too.

The lot sloped slightly down toward the lake edge and our own little beach. There was an old stone pier that Grandpa had thought about replacing with a modern floating variety, but instead he repaired it so it would last a while longer. Certainly as long as Grandpa was alive anyway. Reed beds framed in the shore. You had to work to keep it from getting overgrown. Every spring Grandpa and I each took a scythe and cut a broad trail out to the drop-off under the water.

It was down here by the lake edge that I sat with Klara in my dream.

Don't go.

The wind had picked up and the lake was dark gray, but there weren't any "white geese" on the waves yet, as Grandpa liked to say. On the other side of the water the spruce forest was black and dense. Lunnen is a big lake, which extends far to the north and far to the south. But it's only here in front of Grandpa's cottage that there is much open water. Otherwise it's divided up into a lot of bays and fjords that barely hang together. It's actually like several lakes in one, and there are ever so many islands. Three hundred sixty-five of them, they say, one for every day of the year. But no doubt that depends on how you count.

The old house was a croft. Once Grandpa showed me that there had been fields too. In the middle of the forest there were remnants of a stone wall and an old root cellar. What enormous toil it must have been to clear the forest and carry away a lot of stones so that you got a little patch to cultivate. Grandpa's paternal grandmother grew up here. There were seven siblings. One year the harvest was bad. They managed through the winter but when it was spring the food was almost all gone, so the parents told the children that they couldn't be outside playing during the day, because then they got too hungry. They had to lie in their beds until summer.

And this was like a hundred years ago. Maybe a little more. Life was so much harder then.

I never would have seen the traces of the old fields if Grandpa hadn't shown me. The forest had taken back all that my ancestors had toiled so hard to cultivate. Maybe it's always like that: nature wins in the long run.

I turned and walked around the house again, since the front door faced toward the forest. The new house stood in the same place as where the croft had been. It was one of those summer houses you buy as a kit. The style wasn't super modern; it could just as well have been built in the eighties or so. But that was how Grandpa wanted it.

I opened the front door and went in. It was nice to come inside from the damp and cold. As I kicked off my shoes I called, "Hello?"

"Hello," I heard Grandpa answer from inside the house.

I knew that Grandpa would be out here puttering, because Maddy and I had visited over the weekend, and then he'd told us about what he would start on next: insulating the attic with fiberglass.

I went through the hall and came into the kitchen, which was connected to the living room in an open floor plan, and just then Grandpa came down from the ladder leading to the attic.

"Hi there," he said, smiling.

"Hello there," I replied. He came up to me and we hugged. He almost disappeared in my embrace, like a little boy.

"It's nice that you come and visit."

"Yes, I thought that I have to see how you're doing. So you don't put the insulation in the wrong way or something."

He smiled again and chuckled. My grandfather Anders had just turned seventy-four. He was energetic for his age but walked a little bent forward, could never really straighten his back. He had always been skinny and sinewy. One knee gave him trouble so he limped a little too. He was on a waiting list for an operation. His hair was white and uncombed, the locks stood in all directions, especially when he was involved in something and had worked up a sweat, like now. His beard was white too but short and well-groomed, at least compared to his hair.

On some people you can see on their face exactly how they feel. Happy, irritated, sad, worried. Maddy is like that. Something happens with her eyes, their size and shape. Other people have roughly the same facial expression all the time. Grandpa is more that type. He has small, peering eyes, always looks like he's squinting a little. He almost never smiles. And when he laughs it looks tight and uncomfortable around his mouth. It's as if his face has also stiffened with age, just like his body. But I know him so well that I can read exactly how he's feeling. Almost better than Maddy, actually. I see it in his eyes, or I hear it in his voice. Small differences that maybe no one else would notice.

We talk every day. Sometimes several times a day. Meet at least a couple of times a week. So it's not so strange that I can read him.

And every time we talk, every single time, it feels like it makes him happy to see me, happy to hear my voice.

He has never said that he loves me; Grandpa doesn't use such words. But I have never doubted for a second that he does.

Well, yes, a couple of times. And then my whole world was about to fall apart. But I'm coming to that.

"Would you like a cup?"

"Please."

Grandpa took the old filter out of the coffee maker and threw it away, put in a new one and filled four scoops of coffee. Turned on the faucet, ran water into the carafe and poured it into the coffee maker. Switched it on. I took a mug for each of us from a cupboard, set them on the table.

"I miss the pantry in the old house," Grandpa said. "The kitchen faced north, and then there was ventilation straight out through the wall. Always cool."

"There's something I have to tell you."

"Yes?" Grandpa looked up as he placed some almond cookies in a woven basket. My heart was pounding and my mouth felt a little dry.

"Dad called me today. He left a voicemail message."

Grandpa set the almond cookie he had in his hand in the basket, but then it was as though everything came to a halt. He set aside the bag and straightened his back. Stood there quietly.

"So..." I continued. "I wanted to tell you that."

Grandpa stared out through the big windows, down toward the lake, with a strange gaze that didn't seem to see anything. His mouth was half-open. He stood like that a while.

"I wouldn't have believed that," he said at last. Pulled out a chair and sank down at the table. Suddenly he looked older and more tired, I thought.

"I haven't called back," I said.

Grandpa sat quietly, simply stared down toward the water. I looked out too. The lake had turned rougher; the waves were a darker gray now.

Grandpa said, "What did he want?"

"He didn't say."

The only sound was the coffee maker hissing and thrumming.

"So I don't know..." I fell silent, didn't know how I should complete the sentence.

"After all these years," Grandpa said, and it sounded as if he was talking more to himself than to me.

The coffee maker bubbled and puffed even louder, and then it was silent. Just one last, discreet hissing. I got the carafe and filled our cups, pulled out a chair and sat down across from Grandpa.

"What do you think I should do?" I asked. "Should I call back?"

Grandpa sighed. Shook his head a little.

"I can't say that," he said. "You yourself have to..." He didn't finish the sentence. Raised the cup to his mouth, blew on the coffee, took a small sip.

"I know," I said. "But I really want to hear what you think."

I saw a lot in Grandpa's face in that moment. I saw fatigue, I saw resignation, I saw pain, but mostly worry. I almost regretted having told him; it didn't feel good to cause him this.

But I did promise that time twelve years ago.

I could see that Grandpa was thinking about what he should say. His gaze was still fixed on the lake below the yard. The open water, like a big field of iron. But now you saw the "white geese." The waves had started to foam. At last he said, without taking his eyes off the lake, "No. I don't think you should call back."

He fell silent again, but I could see on his face that more would come. He swallowed, bit his lip. When he started speaking again his voice was a little hoarse and rough.

"You do know that he had a breakdown after the fire. That he was committed to a mental institution for a time."

"Yes."

"But..." Grandpa cleared his throat. "The thing is, he was mentally unstable already before that. He behaved very strangely. And..."

Now Grandpa looked right at me, with a naked gaze. His voice trembled.

"You're a good person, Isak. I don't want you to..." Grandpa fell silent again and looked down at the tabletop.

"No," I said. "That's what I was thinking. If he calls again I'll text him and say that I don't want contact."

Grandpa nodded slowly.

We finished our coffee and talked about other things for a while. Grandpa would order pressure-treated lumber for a wooden deck we would build together when Maddy and I were back from Turkey.

I said goodbye and gave Grandpa a big hug. I held him a little longer than usual. He asked me to send his greetings to Maddy.

Then I hurried out to the car. It was both raining harder and windier than before.

Soon I was crawling on the gravel road through the dark forest. The car rocked from side to side when the tires climbed over roots and sank down in puddles.

I thought about when I last saw Dad.

I started practicing soccer when I was eight years old. It was Grandpa's idea, not mine. He thought I needed a free-time activity. Some guys on the team had been practicing soccer since they were five, and played at every recess at school, year-round, in sunshine and snowstorms. So I was truly not the star of the team. But when I started practicing I also started playing at recess. And I never missed a practice. So I quickly got better, and at the same time I became less of an outsider at school, which was probably what Grandpa had hoped for from the start.

When I was about eleven or twelve I started growing faster than the other kids, both in class and on the soccer team. As a thirteen-year-old I was almost six feet tall, the biggest and strongest on the team. I was fast once I'd picked up speed and my technique was decent. Pontus, our coach, who was the father of one of the other boys on the team, made me a midfielder. That wasn't something I asked for. Like ninety percent of all guys who play soccer I wanted to be on top and score goals. But I soon discovered that I was a capable midfielder, and then of course it became fun too.

We started playing eleven-man that year. We were one of the better teams in the series and had the ball for the most part, and pressed on to score goals. Some of our opponents made it a tactic to go on defense, try to intercept a wrong pass or the like and then boot the ball up on our half of the pitch to some fast little guy who rushed solo toward the goal. But I was vigilant about that, stood by the midline and kept track of the other team's players. Usually I saw the danger in time and when the long ball came I'd already started running homeward. I was really not the fastest at the start, but over long stretches no one could catch me. And I didn't lose a one-on-one during the whole season. Shoulder to shoulder there was no one who had a chance.

I also played some with under-fifteens, you know, the guys who were two years older, and didn't embarrass myself there either.

This was a Sunday evening toward the end of August. It had been warm and sunny during the day, as I recall it, but now it was cooler. The long summer evenings were over. The match started about seven or so and you felt that twilight wasn't far off; it would get dark before the match was over.

It was an away match against Lunneberg, which had a pretty good team. They battled against us at the top of the series. Their A-team played in division four at that time, I think, maybe even in three. Grandpa drove me to the gathering and would stay and watch the match. Lunneberg's athletic facility was right at the edge of the big forest. Like at many old sports fields there were running tracks around the pitch. The long jump pit was dilapidated, with a cracked plank and tufts of grass in the sand. There was a little wooden stand that looked like it could collapse at any moment, and an old clubhouse with small, rundown changing rooms that reeked of sweat. The grass field was uneven and full of holes.

On Lunneberg's team there was a guy I knew from before. Viggo.

When I was six, after the accident, I moved down from Stockholm to live with Grandpa and Grandma. It wasn't at all easy to come from the capital to a school class in the country where everyone knew each other from daycare. I wasn't doing so well then either. Mostly kept to myself and played my own games.

Viggo was in my class and one of those who played football

every minute we were outside. Often he took the ball with him inside and kept at it in the corridor too, until the teachers scolded him. Extremely good feeling for the ball and technique already then. "Viggo's going to play on the national team," the other guys in the class said admiringly. He was number one in the hierarchy. So when he started calling me "fireman" the rest of the class latched on.

Was I bullied? Maybe. That's what you'd probably say today. But to be honest, at that time it wasn't my biggest problem. I lived so much in my own world that the taunts and shunning didn't really reach me.

Sometime in elementary school Viggo's family moved to Lunneberg and he disappeared from the class. When we were going to play this match I had just started seventh grade and Viggo had shown up at school again, because there wasn't a secondary school in Lunneberg. They were bussed into town. He wasn't in the same class as me, and I was happy about that. There was something about Viggo that made me uneasy. And now I can see what that was about. When Viggo left my class I was still a complete outsider, a strange little kid who sat by myself and often cried. Gradually that changed. I was feeling a little better and no longer as much of an outsider in the class, even if I didn't exactly have any friends. I started playing soccer and got better and better at it. I grew past my classmates. Girls started to be interested in me, which took me a very long time to grasp; it seemed unbelievable that anyone would think I was good-looking. I was invited to parties in middle school. Rojda and I became a couple, and she explained that when you kiss you put your tongue in the other person's mouth.

I had become someone different than I was when I came to town as a six-year-old. I had risen in the ranks. But then Viggo showed up again, and he hadn't been part of that journey. To him I was still that strange new kid who lived with his grandpa and grandma and totally panicked when one of the teachers read out loud from "Mamma Mu and the Crow," screamed and cried like a three-year-old. What if he told people who I really was?

When we'd faced Lunneberg the summer before Viggo wasn't there for some reason. But now he was on the pitch. He was the star of the team; that I understood. He played on top. He was the one I should keep track of.

Me against Viggo. A match within the match.

Before kickoff he stood on their half and jumped in place, stretched the front side of his thighs, clapped his hands and encouraged his teammates. One time our eyes met, but neither of us said anything of course.

On a soccer field, during the seconds before the referee's whistle starts the match, you're nervous, impatient, excited. You have so much energy inside you that simply must find an outlet. An awful feeling, a marvelous feeling.

My gaze ran along the sideline. There stood the parents, eight or ten of them, the same gang as usual, Grandpa among them. And there stood Lunneberg's parents, a few more. Two groups, each a little spread out, but still with a clear gap between them.

On Lunneberg's side there was also a group of little boys who'd come to check out the match. Plus a man who was standing by himself, with the little boys between him and the others. Rather tall, with sunglasses and cap. There was something about him that made me sense he didn't belong with the other parents. Maybe the clothing.

Can I really have thought all this when the match would begin in just a few seconds? I was completely focused on that; the adrenaline was rushing in my blood.

Maybe I've added on a bit with hindsight, but I really think that already then I knew who was standing there. I was just not aware that I knew.

The signal sounded, Tor kicked the ball home to me, Viggo came rushing at top speed to put pressure on and I placed a long ball out on the left edge, which went to a throw-in for Lunneberg, fairly high up on their half of the field.

So far according to plan. Only twelve seconds had passed.

After a few minutes came the first duel between me and Viggo. We had the ball in the middle of their half of the field, but their sitting midfielder stole it, looked up, and at the same moment Viggo ran deep. I hung with and picked up speed. When the long ball was kicked I was ahead of him and felt really sure that he wouldn't be able to get past. The pass was a little too steep besides. My task now was simply to protect the ball so that Viggo couldn't get at it before it had rolled over the endline. I braked with the ball a step or two in front of me, knew that Viggo would come rushing. He tried to go left but I moved over and he ran into me, shoulder against shoulder. I had foreseen the impact and pressed back from my direction.

Viggo flew down like a mitten in the grass. The ball rolled slowly over the endline.

"Good, Isak!" my teammates shouted and clapped their hands. I ran up to the ball, passed it to our goalie, Sebbe, turned up toward the field again, got ready to receive the rollout. Felt satisfied with my effort.

Viggo was already on his feet, and he jogged homeward. As he passed me he spit onto the grass and said, without looking up, "How's it going, fireman?"

I didn't reply. I didn't like trash talk, not because I thought there was anything wrong with that, but it just wasn't for me. I was simply bad at it. Couldn't get those withering comments out in the moment, always had to think about it.

We took the lead with 1–0 on a corner kick, the kind of tangled situation in the penalty area where the ball travels like a pinball and at last goes into the goal. Then we made it 2–0 on a beautiful attack that started on the right edge, perfect long-range pass to Kendal, who pulled his fullback and passed at an angle in backward, which Hampus met with a controlled broadside that sat unplayable at the top of the net. I promise, Real Madrid couldn't have done it more beautifully.

Then we felt that we had control of the match. Everything felt good.

Viggo continued trash talking as soon as we came anywhere near each other. The whole time it was "fireman" this and "fireman" that—"Are you still as disturbed?" "Are you still making your sick drawings?"—one thing after another. I didn't respond, just let him carry on. He hadn't gotten anywhere during the match; I was the one who had the upper hand. I understood that he was mad.

But then, right before the break, Lunneberg got a corner kick. They ran a rehearsed variation where Viggo ran and met the corner kicker, passed back on a shot, continued running in an arc into the penalty area, got the ball back, adjusted with a good first touch and fired. Somehow the ball worked its way through the mess in front of the goal and sat in the back of the net.

A scream of jubilation from the Lunneberg players, who gathered around Viggo. Their coach also howled out loud.

Our goalie retrieved the ball from the netting.

Was the goal my fault? Not exactly. But I was a little passive when Viggo got the ball back. I could have come out at him faster and covered the shot.

Viggo released himself from the clump of his teammates, ran up to me and screamed right in my face, "Don't break down now, fireman! Don't start crying or anything!"

He stared at me, his gaze completely wild with aggressive triumph.

The referee, a kid about sixteen or seventeen, heard him and blew briefly on his whistle.

"You. Calm down."

He glared at Viggo, who jogged away with his teammates in a group after him.

"Now let's turn this around!" he shouted, certain that we would hear too.

A minute or so later the referee signaled the end of the first half and we slouched off the field.

Pontus encouraged us, said that we'd had a perfect first half, apart from that crappy goal that trickled in at the end. These things happen. But we still had the match under control. It was just a matter of going out in the second half and doing the job.

"They talk so much trash," said Sebbe. "Especially that little guy on top. He's out of his mind."

"That may be," said Pontus. "Let him talk. Focus on what you have to do on the field instead. That's the best response."

Sebbe glanced at me, probably wondered if I wanted to say something. I was the target of Viggo's trash talk after all. But I didn't say anything.

The referee blew his whistle. We jogged out onto the field, formed a circle with our arms on each other's shoulders, shouted that we would play our hearts out now and clapped our hands. Lunneberg was already waiting for us. The ball was on the centerline, where Viggo stood with his right foot on it. The referee blew the whistle. Viggo kicked the ball back to one of the midfielders.

He kept on with his endless bullshit.

"What's with you, fireman? Did someone light a fire under you?"

"Shut up."

"Wow, the freak can talk! Ha!"

At last he'd gotten to me. I was biggest and strongest on the field but he made me feel small.

Unconsciously, even though it was contrary to everything Pontus talked about in the break, we tried to protect our lead. Got scared of exposing ourselves backward, made mistakes. We gave away the initiative. And then it went the way it often does. Kendal played homeward, there was a misunderstanding between our holding midfielder Adde and me, neither of us went wholeheartedly after the ball and their number ten took it and placed a perfect ball deep to Viggo.

I threw up my hand and shouted offside but actually knew that it wasn't; when the ball was kicked Viggo was on his own half of the field.

He had a head start of several meters. I felt a cold wave running through my body. No, no, no. *If Viggo gets free now, and makes a goal...*

I didn't like losing; I guess no one does. But I wasn't one of those who loses their mood completely, starts whining at teammates and moping the rest of the day. We had a few like that on our team.

I could take a loss against Lunneberg. But what I couldn't take was losing the match within the match against Viggo. That would make me that desperate six-year-old again. That would make me so little that I almost ceased to exist. I can't describe it better than that. This meant life and death for me.

I picked up speed, but Viggo was faster on shorter stretches and extended his lead.

My teammates, the coaches, the spectators, everyone was screaming.

I started to close in on him, but realized that I wouldn't catch up to him in time. And that insight opened an abyss in me.

There was only one thing to do.

I braced myself, threw myself forward and clipped him.

A scissor tackle, like out of an instruction book. If it hadn't been that scissor tackles are prohibited on a soccer field and aren't in any instruction books. But apart from that. Purely technically it was perfect.

Viggo fell headlong forward. One second he was running toward the goal, and the next moment he was lying with his face pressed down in the grass. He probably didn't even have time to understand what was happening.

It felt really damned good. I must be honest and say that. Viggo wouldn't get free and have the chance to score a goal. I felt relieved. But I also thought it served him right, for his uninterrupted trash talk, because he reminded me of who I was when I was little, because he tried to draw out that little six-year-old that I had deep inside me.

Lunneberg's coach howled. He even rushed onto the field.

"You, referee! What the hell!"

Viggo flew up from the grass. Clearly he hadn't hurt himself too bad. He rushed at me, shoved me with both hands on my chest, his eyes wild with fury.

"What are you doing, fucking freak!"

The ref came running; he already had the yellow card in his hand.

"That has to be red!" Lunneberg's coach screamed.

Viggo's teammates were also on their way toward us. Viggo was still staring at me, then he screamed, "You should be locked up! Is it my fault that your fucking mom burned up?"

I clenched my right hand and hit him as hard as I could right in the face.

The referee hurried over, shoved me away. His teammates screamed and rushed up to Viggo where he was lying in the grass, for the second time in half a minute.

Lunneberg's coach ran up to me and screamed something—I didn't hear what. I was a little out of it at this point; it was as if I was experiencing it all at a distance.

The referee dug in his chest pocket, got out the red card and held it up in front of my face. Pontus came up, put his arm around me, hustled me off the field.

I cast a glance over my shoulder and saw Viggo sitting on the grass crying, with his hand on his mouth, blood running over his fingers. His teammates stood in a circle around him.

"Go into the changing room—we have to talk after the match," Pontus said. "But that was damned far from okay."

He sounded cold and grim. The scissor tackle he had forgiven; I was pretty sure of that, even if perhaps it was unnecessarily brutal. But that I hit Viggo and knocked him down was something else. There was no excuse at all for that.

I walked off the field, and Grandpa came walking toward me. His facial expression at that moment I will never forget. He looked sad, and worried, but it wasn't just that. It was as if there was also a film of something else over his face. I can't really describe it. But what that film told me was that I had done something he didn't understand, and that he didn't like. I was like a stranger to him.

I had never seen that expression before. I've seen it one other time since then, out at Ajkeshorn.

Grandpa put his arm around my shoulders and we walked toward the changing room. Behind my back I heard Lunneberg's coach shout to Pontus, "He has no damned business being on a soccer field!"

"You—let the referee decide!" Pontus shot back, he too with an angry voice.

Grandpa held open the door and we went into the changing room, leaving the agitated voices behind us. I sank down on one of the worn wooden benches. Grandpa sat down beside me.

"What happened?"

I started sobbing. Because I was so very, very ashamed. I had lost control and done something unforgivable in front of a lot of people, many that I didn't even know, like Lunneberg's players and parents, some that I knew a little or at least knew who they were, like our team's parents, and a few that I knew well, like the guys on the team and Pontus.

Could this ever be washed away?

All that was bad enough. But what truly crushed me completely was that I had disappointed Grandpa. That distancing I'd seen in his face, that scared the shit out of me. Because Grandpa was still everything in my world when I was thirteen, truly everything, my only fixed point, and if he no longer liked me, then it was truly over for me. So fucking over. If even he turned away from me, then I just wanted to die.

And I got that awful feeling that the world had been shaken loose from its foundations, everything was about to capsize, the shame grew and grew beyond all control and it threatened to take over everything, I just cried and cried. Cried so that I was shaking.

Grandpa put his arms around me, a little uncomfortably and at an angle where he was sitting beside me on the bench, since he was smaller than me too. But that meant nothing. I leaned against him. Felt his warmth and special scent. He stroked my hair.

"Listen…it's not that bad."

I sobbed. "Yeah…"

He took my hand in his. Grandpa's hand was sunburned and spotted. There were only two kinds of hands I knew of at that time: children's and old people's. I thought that all adults' hands looked like Grandpa's.

I don't know how long we sat there, Grandpa with his arms around me, and me crying uncontrollably. It was a long time anyway. At last I calmed down a little.

"Did he say something to you, that boy? Or why did you get so angry?"

I nodded. Sniffled.

"Hmm."

There was a brief silence, but then I told him.

"He said that I was disturbed, and that it wasn't his fault that my mom had burned up."

Grandpa stiffened abruptly.

"He said that?"

Grandpa drew a breath, a deep breath, and blew out the air again with a hissing through pouted lips. It wasn't like him.

"Then I understand why you got angry."

Grandpa's voice was hoarse and quavered a little. I understood that he was upset too.

Neither of us said anything for a while. I felt calmer, the shame subsided a little and the world got its right proportions back. It started to feel as if maybe everything wasn't completely over for me anyway. My nose was running and I wiped the snot with the back of my hand.

"Wait a moment, I'll get some tissue."

Grandpa let go of me, went to the toilet and got a rough, unbleached paper towel. I took it and blew my nose. It felt harsh against my nose.

"I'll go out and talk with the coaches. About what he said. They have to be told that. Will you be okay on your own for a while?"

"Yes."

"But even so you mustn't fight, you know that, right?"

"Yes. Sorry."

Grandpa smiled, and tousled my hair before he left the changing room. When he opened the door the sounds from the match reached me. The panting and shouting, the sound when the ball was kicked. The applause and the cheering from the little audience.

The match had started again out there, almost as if nothing had happened. I felt consoled by that. It told me that the world would keep on turning, even though I'd hit Viggo on the jaw.

The door slowly closed with a thud and the sounds from the match were dampened again. Here in the changing room it was calm and quiet and cool. I leaned my head back against the concrete wall and closed my eyes. Sat like that for a while. Opened my eyes again. On the bench on the other side of the room, between two steel hooks you could hang clothes on, was a sticker. I think it was for Halmstads FC. I looked up at the ceiling, where several dried *snus* pouches were stuck.

Then the door opened, and Dad came in.

★ ★ ★

I hadn't seen him in seven years, more or less, but I knew immediately that it was him.

You might think I should have been really shocked that Dad suddenly showed up, in a changing room at Lunneberg's IP on a Sunday evening, far away from everything. But I really wasn't. And that's why I think I actually recognized him, standing on the sidelines before the match started, even though I wasn't aware of it.

He took off his sunglasses and put them in the chest pocket of his jacket.

"Hi," he said. "Do you recognize me?"

I didn't think about it then, but now I realize that I take after Dad a lot in appearance. He was tall and looked athletic, there was something about his straight posture and how his arms hung and his shoulders rose up toward his throat and neck. Blond curls poked out from under his cap in back. His face was very tanned.

He had strange clothes. I thought so then anyway. He was wearing a suit, but in the kind of rough cloth that carpenters' pants are made of. Blue, with obvious white seams where every stitch was visible. The jacket fit rather tightly on his upper body and emphasized his muscles. Under it, a white shirt, open a bit down on the chest. Around his neck he had a scarf in some light gray, slightly glittery fabric, dapperly tied. He was wearing tennis shoes with the thickest soles I'd ever seen; they looked almost comical.

And then the cap. A baseball cap with bent brim, also blue, but so worn and bleached from the sun that it almost looked gray. A red *C* in the middle in front.

People his age didn't wear caps, in any case not a cap like that, not in this part of Småland. Not that kind of scarf either, so elegantly tied around his neck.

Dad smiled at me. His eyes shone blue.

Did I recognize him?

"Yes," I said.

"I didn't recognize you at first," said Dad. "Although I knew you'd be on the field. But then I thought there was something familiar about that blond beast on defense."

I got a little embarrassed. Didn't say anything, just looked down at my hands. Dad continued.

"So what happens now? With you, I mean?"

"Well..." I hesitated, didn't really understand what he meant.

"Will you be suspended, or what?"

"I suppose so."

Dad nodded. There was a brief silence.

"He said something to you, didn't he?"

"Hmm."

"What did he say?"

I didn't intend to reply to that. It was a really personal thing, wasn't it? Dad hadn't been in touch in seven years, and now he suddenly showed up in this changing room and wanted to talk as if he'd been the most present father.

Wouldn't think so.

I was silent and stared down at the floor. Then Dad said something that really surprised me.

"That was one hell of a right hook you got in."

His voice sounded like he was smiling, but that wasn't possible, was it? I looked up, and sure enough, he was smiling broadly at me. And it wasn't a consoling smile, one of those smiles that doesn't come from the eyes. No, it was a quite open and frank smile. Dad truly looked happy. And proud.

I had punched an opponent on the soccer field and Dad was proud of me.

"And when you tripped him...so damned beautiful."

I was too surprised to answer. There was silence for a while again. Then Dad crouched down in front of me.

"They're going to tell you that what you did was wrong," he said, and his voice was subdued but nonetheless firm and clear.

"That you should be ashamed. Maybe you already feel that way. That you embarrassed yourself in front of everyone. I say: ignore them. How did it feel when you did it? It felt damned good, didn't it?"

I didn't reply. Dad put his big hand on my knee.

"You didn't even think about doing it—you just did it," he continued. "When you do something without thinking about it, that's when you're most yourself. You showed who you really are tonight. Hold on firmly to that."

At that moment the door opened, and Grandpa came back into the changing room.

His expression when he saw Dad sitting there with one hand on my knee. Shock. He truly looked as if he'd seen a ghost. An instinctive aversion, something that almost resembled hatred.

Dad looked at Grandpa and said quite coldly, "Hello."

He remained in the same position, crouching with his hand on my knee, and I felt, in some slightly diffuse way, that it was a kind of demonstration from Dad's side. There was defiance in it. He knew that Grandpa didn't like what he saw but he intended to ignore that.

"What are you doing here?" said Grandpa. His voice sounded strange. And I sensed something more than anger and aversion in it, a faint secondary tone that he tried to conceal: fear.

Do you remember the first time you saw one of your parents get scared? The first time you felt that they didn't completely control a situation, or themselves? Maybe this never happens to some people, I suppose. But it's really frightening. At least if it happens when you're young and counting on the parents to hold the world together for you.

It had never occurred to me before that Grandpa could even get scared. But now I both saw and heard that in him.

"Watching soccer," said Dad. "And consoling my son."

Still crouching, his hand on my knee.

"You can't just show up at any time."

"Yes. I can." Dad stood up and turned toward Grandpa. His voice sounded cold and controlled. "Or is there a restraining order?"

Grandpa simply shook his head.

"Do I have one, Anders? Is there a restraining order? In that case show it to me."

Grandpa extended his hand toward me.

"Come, Isak."

Sometimes completely crazy thoughts come. Like when you're out practicing with the road bike and you meet an eighteen-wheeler with a trailer that comes thundering at high speed from the opposite direction and you think, *Maybe I should turn right across the road and crash into it.* It's almost so that you ride down into the ditch in the other direction because you get scared of yourself.

And I remember that a thought flew quickly through my mind, there in the changing room, that I should get up and take Dad's hand instead. What would have happened then?

But there was only a moment's hesitation. I stood up, went over to Grandpa and took his hand. He pulled me to him, put his arm around me. I felt his body trembling.

"We want you to go now."

"We?" said Dad. "Maybe we should hear what Isak thinks."

"Please, Fredrik."

Dad didn't seem to be listening to Grandpa. He turned to me instead.

"Do you want me to go?"

Yes, I wanted that. I wanted this painful situation to end. It was really tough to be standing in the middle of a tug of war between Grandpa and Dad. But I didn't say anything. I just stared down at the floor.

There was silence, and it felt like an eternity.

At last Dad changed tack and said to me, "Think about what

I said, Isak. Don't let them make you feel ashamed. Least of all him."

"Just go now," said Grandpa.

Dad turned and went out of the changing room. Then he disappeared from my life again.

Grandpa stood there with his arm around me for quite a while, almost convulsively. Then he suddenly relaxed, let go of his hold on me and sank down on the wooden bench. He sighed deeply. His sinewy, spotted hands were shaking.

If a large bear had come into the changing room, nosed us a little and then turned and gone out, I think Grandpa would have reacted similarly. That was the image I had in my head anyway. It was as if we'd both been lucky to get away in one piece.

When we came home that evening it was almost as if Grandpa had forgotten that I'd punched Viggo. While I showered he made warm sandwiches and tea, and then we sat at the kitchen table and ate. I had a bathrobe on and my hair was wet. Grandpa wondered what Dad had said to me when he wasn't there. What did he mean when he said, "Think about what I said, Isak"? I told him that Dad didn't think I should be ashamed about hitting Viggo.

Grandpa's face darkened, but he kept quiet. I took a big bite of my warm sandwich with melted cheese, ham and ketchup. I was hungry after the match.

"You know... I don't want you to be ashamed either," he said at last. "I saw how sad you were when you were ejected. That made my heart ache. But... I think that we're ashamed for a reason. It's the shame that teaches us not to make our mistakes again. It's like..." Grandpa fell silent, searched for words. "If you burn yourself on the stove, it hurts like heck," he continued. "And you remember that pain—that's why you don't set your hand on the burner again. Isn't that right? And if you do something stupid to other people, then you should be ashamed. It must feel unpleasant so that you don't do the same thing again. Do you understand?"

I nodded. "I think so."

There was silence for a while again. Grandpa took a sip of tea.

"But… I'm really not surprised that Fredrik said that. He's not a person who feels ashamed for no reason. I actually think he hasn't felt ashamed of anything in his whole life."

I took the rest of my warm sandwich in two big bites. Grandpa looked at me.

"Has he called you?"

"No," I said in surprise, with my mouth full of toasted bread.

"Certain?"

"Yes."

"I wonder how he knew that you would be playing a match at Lunneberg's IP."

I wondered that too, but I didn't say anything. Grandpa sat silently again for a while, looked thoughtful. At last he said, "If he calls you, just hang up. Don't talk to him. Do you understand?"

"Hmm."

"Or if he sends a text, or leaves a message. Don't reply."

"No."

"And then you must tell me that he's made contact. Do you promise that?"

"Yes."

Grandpa reached over, took my hand and smiled. It wasn't a smile that said that he was happy; it was a smile that was supposed to comfort and calm me.

I was suspended from soccer the rest of the season. From the matches, that is; I could still practice with the team. I know that Grandpa called Pontus and told him what Viggo was referring to when he said what he did. I eavesdropped on the whole conversation. I don't think Pontus knew about that before. At the next practice he was a little extra friendly to me. He smiled more often and his voice was gentler than usual. Patted me on the back.

Grandpa also contacted Viggo's parents and arranged a meeting between me and Viggo, at their home, so that I could apologize for hitting him, and Viggo could apologize for what he'd said. Viggo's parents didn't seem angry at me. Maybe they remembered my story from the time when we were in the same class.

It didn't feel good to go to school on the Monday after this happened. I thought that everyone would look down on me, think I had a screw loose, that I was a freak. But I didn't hear anything like that. I was actually really surprised. It was almost the other way around; my status rose from this whole thing.

A few days into the new week we met in a corridor. I had my friends around me, and he had his. Everyone fell silent as we approached each other. But Viggo's gaze wandered and he looked away.

It's pretty strange when you think about it. Adults say all the time what's right and wrong, the official version. It's called "friend rules" when you're in preschool. It's called "shared values" when you work for the county. In principle the same thing. Any child can rattle off the official version in their sleep: this is good, this is bad, evil and good, the whole package. But any child also knows, without anyone telling them, that there are other rules, and those are the rules that really count. Where does this come from? Is it inborn?

Strong. Aggressive. Good-looking. Outgoing. Verbal. Funny, to some extent. If you're like that, then you're the one who's right. Then you're king of the hill. It applies in every schoolyard all over Sweden. It's the law of the jungle.

In the adult world it's a little better. Then there are more that follow the official version, so to speak. But to be honest there are many adults too who silently follow those other rules.

I continued playing soccer next season too but was never as good again. Or else the others developed faster—I don't know. But when we played a match it was as if I didn't really want to go into the situations a hundred percent. I no longer used my physique in the same way. I think I was afraid of losing control again. Grandpa still came and watched every match. It was as if I saw myself with his eyes the whole time; I didn't let myself go.

At the end of summer I told him that I wanted to quit soccer. He didn't protest all that much. Actually I think he was content with that, but he said that in that case I had to start with a different sport. Must keep going, it was important both for your body and your mind. So I started track and kept at it for a few years, but never became a star.

I was thinking all this as I drove home from Grandpa's place, that Tuesday evening after Midsummer. It felt nice to have made a decision. I would keep Dad away from my life.

That was one hell of a right hook you got in.

His eyes had glistened appreciatively at me.

When I came into the hall at home I was met by Maddy and I could immediately see that something had happened. She looked worried. A little confused.

"Grandpa says hi," I said, taking off my shoes.

"Okay," said Maddy. "Listen. Someone called. He said that he was your dad."

Steps are approaching in the corridor outside the cell; it sounds like several people. I hear that one of them is Soraya. Only her heels strike so brightly against the concrete.

I sit up on the cot. Hear the key in the door. Per opens it and lets her in. He closes the door again.

"Hi," says Soraya. "How's it going?"

As usual she doesn't smile. She just gives me a penetrating look, as if she's trying to look right through my eyes and into my brain to find out what's moving in there. I thought it was awkward at first. Never a smile, no warmth in her voice, she seemed like a robot that didn't care. But now I'm starting to almost feel the opposite. That total straightforwardness feels sincere. It's just the way she is.

No bullshit. That's probably a pretty good quality in an attorney.

"Quite okay," I say.

"Are things good with Per?"

"Yes, he's nice."

Soraya could sit down at the foot end of the cot, but she doesn't. She remains standing.

"You're not allowed to be in the workshop with the others because you're on full restrictions. But you can do tasks on your own. In the laundry, for example."

"Hmm."

"Think about it. Might be nice to get out of the cell a little. Do something. Think about other things for a while."

"Hmm."

"You do know how to run a washing machine? From the home health service?"

"Yes, sure."

"Of course you do. I'll bet that you're a wizard at doing laundry."

Soraya glares at me with her stone face. I can't keep from smiling.

"You don't need to decide now," she continues. "But do think about it."

Soraya paces around a few steps on the floor.

"The prosecutor wants you to have a psychiatric evaluation."

"Yes?"

"Because you've confessed it can already be done now."

Psychiatric evaluation. Yes. I understand what the prosecutor is thinking.

"If the conclusion is that you suffered from a serious mental disturbance when you committed the crime then you won't be sentenced to prison. It will be forensic psychiatric care instead."

"Okay."

"What's relevant now is a so-called paragraph seven examination, which is actually just an interview with a psychiatrist. A screening, you might say. Takes about an hour."

I nod to show that I've understood.

"It will only say if they should proceed with a major assessment. In that case you'll be taken to Huddinge and be there for a few weeks. But we'll deal with that if it becomes relevant."

"Yes."

"I haven't got a date and time yet. I'll get back to you as soon as I know more."

Soraya's heavy, exotic perfume lingers in the cell long after she's gone. I get a tiny, tiny headache from it.

I understand from the way she talked about the psychiatric assessment that it's a big deal for some.

On the one hand it probably doesn't feel so cool to be labeled a mental case. On the other hand it doesn't sound so bad to be treated instead of sitting in prison. Maybe easier to get out early.

Or not.

Prison or forensic psychiatric care, it doesn't matter that much to me.

I still intend to leave as soon as I can.

Maddy and I sat down on the couch in the living room. I had a few things to explain.

"Is that true?" she said. "Your father is alive?" Her voice was subdued. She didn't sound angry, more like inquisitive and sad. She had pulled her feet up under her. She sat turned toward me with one elbow on the back support, leaned her head on her hand. I sat facing straight ahead. It felt best like that. I thought it was awkward to look at her.

Of course I was ashamed. We'd been a couple for almost a year; we lived together. I lied to her and said that my father was dead. Now I sat in silence. Didn't know at which end I should start. It was up to me to say something but it was like my tongue was paralyzed. I hardly dared breathe. My body had stiffened. I felt constricted.

It still smelled like fried meatballs in the apartment. Someone was walking in the stairwell.

"Listen," Maddy said gently, "I'm not mad at you." She touched my arm. "But you can tell me."

I took a deep breath, and then I said, "Yes. He's alive."

So. Now the hardest part was over. I had admitted the lie.

Maddy stroked my arm. Waited for me to continue. I was still staring straight ahead. At last she said, "Is your mother alive too?"

"No."

New silence.

"So why don't you have any contact with your dad?"

"He left when I was little."

There was more to say. Much, much more. But if I started telling, where would I end? I couldn't tell her everything; I was sure of that. That terrified six-year-old had been dead and buried a long time and so it would remain.

"And he hasn't been in touch since then?"

"No," I said.

Yet another lie. A little one, but still.

Maddy's hand on my arm, her gentle voice.

"Did he say why he wanted to talk with you?"

"No."

"Okay. Because he told me. He has cancer. A brain tumor. He's going to die soon."

"I see."

"So he would really like to see you."

I didn't respond to that. Maddy was still sitting close beside me, and now she took my hand in hers.

"Shouldn't you call and talk with him?"

"No. We have nothing to talk about."

There was silence for a while again. Then Maddy said, "Although…you probably do."

"I don't owe him anything."

"No."

Maddy released her hand but still sat with her body pressed against mine.

"But maybe you ought to talk with him for your own sake."

I didn't reply.

"It sounds like you're angry at him."

"No, I'm not angry. But I don't care about him. I don't want him in my life."

"If I were you I'd be angry at him. He left you, didn't he?"

But you're not me, I thought. *You don't know what I'm feeling. Who are you to say anything about that?*

This was probably the first time that I felt really irritated at Maddy. But I didn't say anything. We had never quarreled, not a single time. Never argued. Obviously we thought differently about things sometimes. She wanted to do this or that; I wanted to do something else. But every time that kind of situation arose we both backed off, said, "We can do what you want instead, it's just as good." Then we coaxed each other a while until we figured out what we would do. Usually it was Maddy who broke the loop, so to speak, and then we did what she wanted. But she always gave me the opportunity to decide and I felt secure in that.

I was scared to death of conflict. I'd been with a couple of other girls before Maddy but never argued with any of them. Grandpa and I hadn't quarreled or argued either. I simply didn't know how to do it. In school or on the soccer field it was a different matter; there I could stand up for myself. But in a relationship? What would happen if we were at odds? Where would it end? Would Maddy realize that I really was an idiot and leave me?

I felt panic faced with starting something that I had no idea how to stop. So I kept my mouth zipped sitting there on the couch. Irritation was bubbling in me but I just clenched my teeth even harder. Maddy must have sensed my anger; she sat facing straight ahead on the couch, pulled away, just a little bit but enough that we would no longer have physical contact.

The silence filled the room like a sluggish, thick mass. It was barely possible to move.

"I think you'll regret it when you get older," Maddy said at last.

I don't need a fucking psychologist, I thought. I had enough of that when I was little.

"Grandpa didn't think I should call him," I said, and regretted it immediately. How old was I? Eight? Now it was obvious that I wasn't at all independent and only did what Grandpa said all the time.

"Why not?" Maddy asked.

"You don't know my dad."

"But why?"

"Or my Grandpa."

"I just think it's a strange piece of advice."

"I'm going for a walk." I got up from the couch, went toward the hall.

"Listen… Isak…"

I didn't answer, simply continued out of the room. Maddy got up from the couch behind me.

"Sorry."

I threw on my raincoat and pulled on my shoes. Pulled the hood over my head. Maddy came out in the hall.

"I have nothing to do with this. I know. Sorry."

"No, no, it's fine. I just… I need to think."

Maddy came up, put her arms around me, spread her fingers out over my shoulder blades. She looked carefully at my face to make sure I wasn't angry, and I met her gaze. Smiled faintly.

"I love you," she said quietly.

"Me too," I said. We kissed, a bit dutifully. I opened the door and stepped out into the stairwell, and my sense was that I was fleeing.

I dreamed about Maddy last night.

I was lying in bed in our apartment, in the dark, and heard her fussing in the bathroom. She was probably removing her makeup. She kept at it a really long time in there, but it didn't matter; I knew that she would come at last, and I was longing for her.

At last I heard the sound from the handle when she unlocked, the door opening, the click from the switch when she turned off the lights in the bathroom and then light footsteps. She climbed into bed and crept on all fours over to my side, I held up the covers and she disappeared into my embrace. I put my arms around her and felt a little like the Beast in *Beauty and the Beast*—don't know why but it wasn't a bad feeling.

Her face was cool and still a little damp after she'd washed it. My eyes were used to the darkness and I saw her like no one else. She was just as beautiful when she didn't have makeup on but in a different way. Vulnerable, somehow—I saw the little girl in her. A warm wave traveled through my body, and my mouth almost got a little dry, I felt so much love. I ran my hands into her hair, let my fingers spread across her head, held it as if it was the most precious thing in the world and kissed her. I put my nose against her shoulder, took in her marvelous scent. My skin had longed for her.

Then I woke up on the cot in my cell. It was the middle of the night, dark and silent and still. But it was as if I'd had Maddy in my arms just now. Her scent was in my nose, the warmth from her skin in my palms. Closed my eyes and tried to lure her back. I wanted to go back in the dream again, fall asleep with legs and arms intertwined.

But I lay awake a long time.

Thought about that time last winter when we were down at Ritz partying with some old buddies of mine. It was the first time they met Maddy, and she wrapped them around her finger. She was pleasant and funny and looked quite smashing. At the same time I noticed that among the girls in the party, and a few besides who weren't part of our group but that I knew a little and who came up and wanted to exchange a few words, I also evoked a great deal of interest in the opposite sex, if I may say so. A few couldn't quite conceal their possessiveness. When Maddy noticed that she clearly marked her territory and was borderline unpleasant. She didn't care for a moment if the atmosphere turned bad. That made me completely warm inside.

If there was a power couple at Ritz that evening it was me and Maddy.

When we skidded home through the snowdrifts we were pretty drunk, both of us. With my arm around her I asked what she really saw in me.

Sure, maybe I was fishing a little for a compliment. I felt strong and handsome and attractive that evening. But this was also something that I really had asked myself several times. What made her move from Stockholm to live in this hole, as it probably must be in her eyes? Was I really so exceptional?

"It's the four *H*'s, you understand," said Maddy.

"The four *H*'s?"

"Yes. You're Handsome, Hunky, Humble and Humorous."

"Aha. The four *H*'s. Because I'm so humble I'll be content with that." Maddy raised her face to kiss me. I bent down, but at the same time we continued staggering ahead on the sidewalk so the kiss turned out a little awkward; our lips only met halfway.

"I forgot Hot. Five *H*'s."

We stopped and kissed again, properly now, a kiss that said she wanted something more, just like me.

When I thought about that kiss I started crying.

That evening, when I left the apartment to do some thinking alone, I walked away from the town center and our little residential area. It was still raining, softly but persistent and cold. The soil in the town flower beds was soaked and black. Bushes and trees almost looked fluorescent green. The asphalt was shiny, and water rippled in the storm drains. I passed a closed day care with a deserted playground. A jungle gym with a little slide, all in bright colors. Three small concrete hippos that hunkered in the rain.

It kept coming down and the light gray soft cotton hoodie was starting to get soaked; I felt it up on my head and ears. The rain jacket also had a hood but I didn't want to pull it up. Wanted to feel the damp penetrating.

I came up to Herrmann's Park. Don't know why it's called that, have no idea who Herrmann was. When I was little Grandpa and I came here often anyway. Then there was an ice cream stand and a miniature golf course here. They'd been gone a long time but the water-spouting sculpture in the middle of the park, with a pond around it, was still there. The grass looked freshly mowed, the gravel pathways free of weeds. The municipality maintained the park perfectly. The big trees with hanging branches—weeping willows, I think they're called—still harbored their secrets. I had always liked those trees. If you went to the trunk it was almost like a grotto under the branches.

The phone started buzzing in my pocket.

My stomach churned.

Was it Dad who was calling again?

I took out the phone. It was Grandpa. I felt a wave of relief, clicked open the call and brought the phone to my ear.

"Hi," I said.

"Hi," said Grandpa. "Are you busy?"

"No. I'm just out walking."

"In this rain?"

"Yes."

"Are you dressed for the weather?"

I smiled.

"No, I couldn't find the snow pants."

"A summer cold is no fun, take my word."

"It's cool."

"Well…" There was silence on the line as Grandpa paused. I could hear his breathing.

"I was thinking about what I said earlier. That you shouldn't call Fredrik. That was dumb. Of course you should call him and hear what this is about."

I was silent for a moment.

"Maybe," I said at last.

"I'm so affected by what he was like before. He was actually crazy then. But that was a long time ago."

"Yes."

"And even if he's still crazy you're an adult now. You can handle it, I know that."

I didn't say anything.

"I forget that you're not a little kid any longer." Grandpa chuckled into the phone and I laughed too, almost embarrassed.

"No… I guess I'm not."

"You do as you wish. But I think you should call him."

"Hmm. I'll think about it."

I promised to be in touch and tell him what I'd done, and then we ended the call.

But I remained standing under the hanging branches of the weeping willow for quite some time and didn't know either in or out.

I had decided to not call Dad back, to not let him into my life. When Grandpa advised me against contact I felt relieved. I didn't want to open the door to the past. But now Grandpa had changed his mind, which meant that the two people I cared most about in my life—to be honest, the only people I cared about—both thought that I ought to call Dad.

I understood that they were right, actually. I ought to talk with Dad before it was too late. But I was afraid, and I was proud. Above all in relation to Maddy. Didn't want to appear indecisive.

The tree subdued both the rain and the light. In the green grotto it felt like twilight. I was a bit sheltered from the world, and I needed that just then.

If I were to call I must do it before I went back to the apartment. Not a chance that I would talk with Dad when Maddy was listening. But the cold and the rain were at last starting to get to me. The hood was damp, and my pants were damp. A cold stream was running down my back. Soon I would start shivering seriously.

I thought about what different directions a call could take. Wanted to prepare myself for all the alternatives, think through what I should say. But soon realized that was impossible. Instead I clung firmly to this thought: I could call Dad and simply listen to what he had to say. If he asked anything I wasn't compelled to answer. I could hang up, think it through, call back. Or block his number, never talk with him again. That way I could maintain control, I told myself.

If you must say to yourself, *You're in full control, you're in full control, you're in full control*, then you probably aren't, right?

But the decision was made.

I took the phone out of my pocket, scrolled through the list of received and missed calls. Found the number that had called me when I was at Birgit's. My heart was pounding in my chest and my mouth was dry. Didn't know if I would manage to keep my voice steady. But I was simply forced to do this now. I took a deep breath, clicked on the number and brought the phone to my ear.

Silence. Then the ringtones started. One, two, three, four.

What if he doesn't answer, I thought. *Maybe his phone is turned off. Then I've tried anyway.* I hoped desperately that it would be that way, that the call would be pushed into the future, and that it wouldn't be my fault.

There was a click. Then I heard his voice.

"Hi, Isak," said Dad. He cleared his throat.

Was his voice trembling a little? Was Dad just as nervous as me?

"Hi," I said. Concise, neutral, almost cold. I didn't intend to let him sense what emotions he tore up in me, how I was shaking inside.

"How nice of you to call back."

I didn't say anything. Dad cleared his throat again, and now his voice sounded steadier, more like I remembered him from before.

"How's it going?"

"Good."

"What are you doing?"

I didn't answer that, let there be silence for a moment. Then I said, "What do you want?"

Dad sighed on the other end.

"Have you talked with your girlfriend?"

"Hmm."

"What's her name, Malin?"

Forget about what her name is, I thought. There was silence for a moment again, until Dad understood that he wouldn't get an answer.

"Anyway," he continued at last, "if I should take the short version… I'm sick and I'm going to die soon and would really like to see you before I die. To explain myself. But above all to say sorry."

I heard steps approaching on the gravel path outside the tree. And I thought that if I say something now, suddenly hearing a voice from inside the weeping willow is going to scare that person. What if there's some fucking creep lurking in there? So I was silent.

Why did I even care about what a complete stranger would think? That person wouldn't see me, wouldn't know whose voice they heard. And I was in the middle of a phone call I would probably remember the rest of my life.

That makes me wonder how much we simply do on autopilot. At least I do.

"Isak?" said Dad. "Are you there?"

The steps passed outside the hanging branches and faded away.

"I'm still here," I said in a subdued voice.

"What plans do you have this summer?"

It was on the tip of my tongue to say, *I'm going on vacation next week*, but now it was crucial to stick to the plan. As little information as possible. The less he knew about me, the better.

"Hello?" said Dad, and now he almost sounded pleading. "What are you doing next week? Are you working?"

"No, I'll be on vacation," I said. "Maddy and I are going to Turkey."

Did I fold? Was I unable to withstand the onslaught of questions? Maybe a little. But I wanted to make it quite clear to Dad that it was impossible for me to see him next week. It wasn't in the cards.

"I'll compensate you for the trip if you come here to my place instead. On Gotland."

"No."

"You're welcome to bring Maddy with you too. I have a very nice place here. By the sea. It will be like vacation for the two of you, although you and I will talk a little sometimes. And then you can take a week abroad later in the summer. Wherever you want. When I'm dead and buried."

"No. We're going to Turkey next week."

Go "wherever you want"? What did he mean by that?

There was silence on the phone for a moment. Then Dad asked, "Do you have the Swish digital payment app?"

I didn't reply.

"Of course you have Swish," he continued. "If you don't want to, you don't want to, Isak, I respect that. But you can at least ask Maddy what she thinks about my proposal."

My head was spinning. Even though I had decided to maintain control over the conversation at any price by revealing as little as possible of myself, he'd gotten me off balance. I swallowed hard.

"I have to hang up now," I said and heard for myself how pitiful that sounded.

"Isak, please, listen to me." Now I heard that pleading tone in Dad's voice again. "I understand that you're angry at me."

Now it was Dad who sounded pitiful. He actually sounded sad.

"Bye now," I said and clicked away the call. I felt cruel and hard, completely ice-cold around my heart. And it was great. At that moment anyway.

I put the phone in my pocket, parted the branches of the tree and went out into the rain. Out into the dark summer evening.

I came into the hall at home in the apartment and closed the door behind me. Kicked off the wet tennis shoes. I didn't hear a sound from inside the apartment, which made me a little disappointed, because I'd pictured that Maddy would come out into the hall as soon as she heard the front door open, look at me with loving and worried eyes, still with a guilty conscience because she'd meddled in things that had nothing to do with her. Give me a hug. Be horrified at how wet I was. Ask if she should make a pot of tea.

None of this happened. I called into the apartment, as a signal that I was home again.

"Hello."

"Hello," I heard from the living room. I perceived it as rather quiet and neutral.

Was it Maddy's turn to be mad at me now?

I hung up the rain jacket and pulled down the damp hood. My neck felt cold. Then I continued into the living room. Maddy was sitting on the couch with a cup of tea in front of her on the table. She gave me a look. Guarded, questioning.

"I called him," I said, sinking down on the couch beside her. Maddy's face softened once I'd said that. She smiled a little, let her hand run through my hair.

"You're completely soaked."

"He wants to meet me."

Maddy nodded.

"I thought so."

Her hand felt warm against my cold, wet head. It was nice.

"But I said that it won't work."

"No?"

"He wanted me to come to his place on Gotland next week. But I said that we're going to Turkey."

I didn't mention that Dad had invited Maddy too. Yet another half-truth. Maddy looked a bit confused. She took out her phone.

"I got a text message."

"He texted you?"

"Yes..."

"When was that?"

"Just now. Fifteen minutes ago maybe." Maddy tapped open the message and read it out loud.

"'Hi. Nice talking with you today. Ask Isak to check Swish. Regards, Fredrik.'"

He tried to put pressure on me by dragging in Maddy. Damned old man.

I had no choice other than to tell what I'd left out earlier: that Dad said I was welcome to bring Maddy to Gotland too, and that he offered to compensate us for the canceled trip. Maddy didn't say anything, just listened. But she looked thoughtful. And I understood of course what was going through her mind: Why hadn't I told her from the start that she was invited too? Why had I said that Dad wanted to meet just me?

It wasn't exactly a lie. It was me of course that Dad wanted to meet to start with. But it wasn't the whole truth.

I should have said sorry and explained that it didn't feel good to let Dad so casually into my life again, after all these years. That all this tore up old wounds and that I needed time to think. But I didn't say anything else; no apology came across my lips. I sat and stared like an idiot down at the coffee table.

At last Maddy heaved a quick sigh and said, "So, are you going to check Swish?"

I took out the phone and opened Swish. Clicked on History.

"Uh…" I said.

"What is it?"

I just stared at the screen.

"There must have been some mistake," I said.

Fredrik Barzal had made a deposit of a hundred thousand kronor.

Had he added a zero by mistake? Had he intended to transfer ten thousand?

My brain was fumbling for explanations while I sat on the couch and stared at my phone with the Swish app open.

"What is it?" Maddy asked.

He had said that he would compensate our booked trip if we went to Gotland instead. But he must understand that you can't get a trip to Turkey for two for ten thousand kronor.

"He deposited a hundred thousand," I mumbled.

"What?" Maddy frowned, took my hand and turned it so that she could see the phone screen too. "You're joking."

It was probably no mistake. Dad had deliberately deposited a hundred thousand kronor in my account.

Maddy looked at the screen.

"Holy moly," she said at last.

My first thought, or perhaps feeling rather, was: *That bastard. Now he's using his money to take control over the situation, in order to take control over me.* I started tapping to send the money back at once.

But at the same time a very different thought came: *A hundred thousand kronor. That's a lot of money.*

To think that some numbers on a phone screen can evoke so many physical reactions in your body. Your stomach churns, a tingle of expectation and hope, a feeling that resembles hunger and thirst, you try to swallow it away. Your heart beats a little faster. Because money isn't money, actually; money equals things you've dreamed about and longed for, which suddenly and quite unexpectedly can be reality, and then it's probably not so strange that you get excited.

Maddy and I were basically living on my salary as a home care aide. Besides that I guessed she got some money from her father occasionally. We weren't exactly swimming in cash. A hundred thousand kronor would make a difference for us. A big difference.

The Turkey trip cost twenty-five thousand, more or less. What could ferry tickets to Gotland cost? At most a few thousand, I thought. We would easily have seventy thousand kronor left for other things.

All this ran through my mind in just a few seconds, at the same time as I mechanically kept tapping in the Swish app to transfer the money back to Dad.

"Is your dad made of money, or what?" Maddy asked.

I didn't reply. Entered "100,000" in the amount field. Dad's phone number was already in the field for recipient. I clicked on Swish and the app for BankID opened. Maddy asked what I was up to.

"Sending the money back," I said, and started tapping in my six-digit code for BankID, but I was moving slower now. With every digit I slowed down a little more.

At last I was done anyway. My thumb over the sign button. If I lowered it two millimeters the money would be on its way back to Dad.

"Wait," said Maddy, and her hand took hold of mine. "Wait. Think it over now."

I am never going to admit this to her. It's hard enough to admit it to myself. But when she took hold of my hand I felt relieved. Maddy rescued my self-respect. And the money.

For the sake of appearances I quibbled a while. Said that this was Dad's way of trying to take control over me, the money was in reality a bribe. He shouldn't believe that he could buy a place in my life. Maddy held my hand, stroked my cheek, spoke gently. Said that she understood how I felt, but that I mustn't see it that way. You could also see it as Fredrik truly doing all he could to get to see me before it was too late. You could see it as a sign of how eager he really was to reconcile. And sure, money couldn't take away the fact that Fredrik had abandoned me when I was little. But couldn't I feel somewhere that I deserved this money anyway?

Maddy painted up image after image of what I could do with it, all the time careful to point out that it was my money, I should use it however I felt like, without thinking of her. I could buy a better car. Or travel to New York and see the Rangers play hockey at Madison Square Garden, which I'd said at some point that I'd dreamed of since I was little and Henrik Lundqvist was the King of New York. Invite a few friends along. Or, if it felt better, do something for Grandpa that he would truly appreciate. Maybe something nice for the summer house? Or invite him on a trip—wasn't there some exotic place he dreamed of visiting?

I could even take the money and donate it to the Red Cross; then I would have done a really good deed. Certainly something much better than if Fredrik kept it, in Maddy's opinion.

She made it sound as if the only immoral thing in this context would be to send the money back to Dad. She gave me a way out.

I said that *if* I were to keep the money, *if* that is, then we would do something with it together. Take a really great trip, or buy something nice for the apartment. It was important to me that the money in that case was for Maddy too. Sure, Maddy said, if that's important to you, and now it was her turn to act reluctant.

What a charade. We were both putting on a show, we both saw through each other, but we kept on anyway. It's really comical if you think about it.

Pretty soon, however, we set aside our reluctant facade and started fantasizing about what we could do with the money. A week in the Seychelles? That would work. A new double bed from Hästens? An Italian espresso machine?

Look me in the eyes and say that you would have reasoned differently.

We had no travel insurance on the Turkey trip, so that money was lost. It was harder than we thought to find ferry tickets to Gotland, at least if you wanted to bring a car. I thought those boats went in shuttle service. But it worked out at last.

I told Grandpa that I'd talked with Dad, that he was sick, and that he had invited me and Maddy to come and see him on Gotland. That we intended to go. Grandpa nodded, but was silent for a long time. At last he smiled faintly at me.

"I think you're doing the right thing," he said. But his facial expression said something else.

The night before we left I couldn't fall asleep. Maddy snoozed beside me in bed, but I lay awake staring at the ceiling. It wasn't just ordinary travel excitement, which is about feeling jittery and expectant. No, I felt worried, wondering what I'd gotten myself into. Grandpa's reaction when I told him about my plans was part of that. I was so used to always being in sync with him that I felt discomfort as soon as I did something that disturbed his peace of mind.

But it wasn't just that. It wasn't even mainly that.

I hadn't seen Dad since I was little, if you didn't count that short conversation in the changing room at Lunnebergs, IP twelve years ago. And I was afraid of what demons from my childhood our encounter would bring to life. I understood that I ought to deal with this, try to figure things out with Dad before it was too late. But I didn't know if I would manage it. Was afraid that I would break down.

Don't go, Klara had said in the dream. *Don't go.*

I felt something that resembled panic: my heart raced, my temples were pounding, I had difficulty breathing. Wanted to cancel the whole thing, send a text to Dad and say that we wouldn't be coming, I could say that I'd gotten sick or whatever. Send the money back. Go out to Grandpa's cottage and stay there a few days with him, feel the calm and the security.

But what would Maddy think of me then?

In principle we had already decided that we would take a last-minute trip after Gotland, to the Seychelles or Mauritius or Florida or Mexico, find a really deluxe resort and just enjoy ourselves.

She would be so disappointed. Maybe even break up with me. No, that wouldn't work.

She was still sleeping peacefully beside me, had no idea how shaky I was, what despair and terror were raging in me. And I intended to see that it remained that way.

I had to bring the CDs with me.

Carefully, carefully I pulled back the covers and rose to a half-sitting position. There was some creaking from the bed frame, which couldn't be avoided. I sat stock-still and looked at Maddy, until I was sure she hadn't woken up. Set my feet quietly on the floor and then stood up slowly. There was a little creaking again and Maddy twisted under the covers, turned toward me, reached out her arm toward my side. I was sure she would wake up. But she burrowed her head into the pillow again and I could tell from her breathing that she was still asleep.

Which corner should I start with?

I padded carefully over to the dresser beside the window, stood on tiptoe and reached to the very back of the top shelf, under a thick knit sweater I never wore anymore. I felt something smooth under my fingertips and pulled out the disk just as quietly as I could. I set it by the foot of the bed on my side.

Then I continued to the corner beside the door. There was an air vent high up on the wall, with a round cover you could screw in or out. Fortunately it didn't squeak at all. Had I greased the screw to avoid that? I couldn't remember. The CD was still where I'd set it, on the backside of the cover. I picked it up, set it on the bed with the other one and replaced the cover.

The third disk was in the drawer on my bedside table which I had pushed into the corner. There was a narrow gap between the bed and the table. Once when we were cleaning, and Maddy had taken the bedroom, she'd moved the table so that it stood next to the bed. I slept poorly several nights in a row, until one night I discreetly pushed the bedside table back into the corner.

The last disk was the trickiest to get out. I had placed all the disks during one of the times Maddy went up to Stockholm for a few days, just to be able to do it in peace and quiet. Fairly close to the corner, on the outside wall next to the window, was a poster. A reproduction of an old French poster that advertised a ballet in Paris. It was put up with tape on all four corners. Carefully I loosened the top left corner and folded down the poster. The CD was taped on the back side. Slowly and patiently I picked at the tape with my fingernail until I could get the disk loose. I folded up the poster, attached the tape again and everything looked like before.

I padded out into the hall, opened the zipper on my bag as quietly as I could and placed the disks in an inside pocket. Straightened up, took a deep breath and exhaled. Now I felt considerably calmer.

I went to the kitchen and drank a little water. Through the window I could see that it was already starting to get light over the wooden tables and swings in the courtyard. A bird was singing and got a distant reply from over in the forest.

I sneaked back to bed and it didn't take long before I fell asleep.

PART TWO

if it is so that you feel departure in you
like a crack or a thought
if it is so that you long to be changed while
you travel
like the unripe fruit changes when it travels,
in the cargo holds, across the seas, under the Southern Cross,
a ship's skin from the water
if it is so and not some other way,
if it is so
then you have already turned off the lights in the house
and are on your way.

from "The Outer Hebrides" by Eva Ström

THE NEXT DAY WE WERE IN THE HARBOR IN OSKARSHAMN, IN LINE for the Gotland boat. The weather had changed to high summer heat, almost from one day to the next. The sun was broiling and it was insufferably warm in our little Nissan Micra. The windows were rolled down. Vapors from exhaust, oil and garbage that had been in the sun too long drifted into the car. There were at least ten lines of cars, if not more. The ferry looked big but it still seemed impossible that there would be room for all of us.

In the next line over was a Volvo station wagon, with its windows rolled down too. A little terrier looked out the window and sniffed the air. It was sitting on the lap of a blonde woman with big sunglasses and her hair pulled up with a clip. She looked sullen. Behind the wheel I glimpsed her husband, I assumed, also wearing sunglasses, and in the backseat the kids, two or three of them. Through the windows to the luggage compartment baggage could be seen that reached up to the ceiling. Suitcases, pillows, blankets, boots, *padel* rackets, all piled together. I could picture that when they opened the luggage compartment a torrent of things would pour out on the ground.

It seemed stressful to have responsibility for a family. Maddy and I only had ourselves to think about, and even though our car was much smaller it was far from fully packed. A suitcase and a bag with our clothes, swimsuits and shoes. That was basically about it.

Maddy sat and smoked with one sandal up on the dashboard. She had black velvet shorts on and the sun was roasting through the open window on her bare legs. Her brown skin was covered with small gold-colored hairs that you never saw otherwise. I thought they were fine. With a simple white camisole and Gucci sunglasses she looked like a movie star. Even if I knew that the sunglasses were knockoffs. I was sure that she would be the best-looking on the whole Gotland boat, and she was my lady.

I probably didn't look too bad myself either, I guess, in jeans shorts and a peach-colored, worn polo shirt. Bare feet stuck in a pair of Converse. Ray-Ban aviator sunglasses, actually genuine, that I got from Grandpa as a present when I turned twenty. I loved those sunglasses and guarded them with my life. On my head a beige baseball cap with a bent brim, old and worn and bleached by the sun.

Maddy sat up, looked out the window toward the line ahead of us.

"Now," she said. "It's moving."

The taillights on the car ahead of us came on. I turned the ignition key and soon we could start creeping ahead. Our line coiled nicely up onto the steel ramp. A steel plate thudded and then we were on the incline, the tires buzzing in a special way. We drove in through the opening in the side of the vessel. It felt dark in there, after the broiling sun outside, with the echo from engine sounds and screeching rubber tires against steel. Men in light yellow uniforms directed us into the right lane and stared at our bumper as they waved at me to pull a little closer to the car ahead. Then a palm in the air, *Stop, that's enough*. I turned off the engine.

"Can you go back to the car when we're crossing?" Maddy asked, pushing her sunglasses up onto her hair.

"Don't know," I said. "I don't think so. Best to take what you need with you."

I gathered up my things and got out of the car. I looked forward to seeing the boat embark, getting something to eat on board, maybe having an ice cream or a coffee later. A lovely vacation feeling. There was no reason now to think about what was coming later. I could deal with that then.

I was so happy that I had Maddy with me.

We went up on the sundeck and watched the ferry put out. I held firmly onto the railing and looked down. The gap between the vessel and the dock grew slowly, and the water whirled and bubbled as the propellers drove us out into the harbor basin. The ferry's movements made several car alarms down on the deck go off. The cars were like a herd of cows; when one started mooing the others followed suit. Brisk winds chased a few cumulus clouds across an intensely blue sky. Soon we were on our way out toward open sea. The ferry picked up speed.

We went down to the restaurant deck and regretted that we'd stayed on the sundeck so long. The line to the restaurant was both long and wide; it filled up almost the whole walkway between the tables and made it hard for folks to move ahead.

"Are you very hungry?" I asked. "Or shall we go and sit down for a while?"

We had seats in the front cabin. Maddy shrugged.

"No. Let's go and sit down."

Next to reception was a room that seemed to be a children's movie theater. There were benches to sit on, at three or four different heights. Full of little kids crowding the benches, the smallest were only two or three and couldn't sit still. The oldest were maybe seven or eight years old, and they looked big by comparison. All except the smallest kids looked intently toward the same wall, where I assumed there was a screen showing some cartoons.

All were looking in the same direction. All except the smallest kids.

Among them Klara.

She was sitting in the second row, in the midst of a sea of other children. I didn't see her at first. And in contrast to the other three-year-olds she wasn't climbing around and shrieking; she sat still.

Her face was turned right toward me. Her hair was burned off on half of her head, the skin black and cracked, the naked flesh shining pale red in the openings.

She had no eyes. Two empty, bloody eye sockets stared mutely at me.

So that's where we were now.

My feeling was that she reproached me, that she was reprimanding me.

I told you not to go.

I turned my eyes away, gasped for breath. My ears started ringing and I was forced to stop so as not to fall down. I bent forward to get blood to my head.

"What is it?" Maddy's voice sounded like it came from far away. I was separated from her in both time and space. Enclosed in my own body, in my own experience. It was burning in there. Everything accelerated.

I got an image in my head that Maddy placed her hand on my back, but it didn't feel like my back, and not like her hand. I heard someone moan and realized that it was me.

"Come, let's sit down here," I heard Maddy say, and she took hold of both my hands, led me over to a wall where I sank down on the floor. Small dots of light danced before my eyes, faded in and out. Maddy crouched in front of me.

"Isak? How are you feeling? What's wrong?"

I saw other passengers stop and look at me. Curious, attentive, worried. Total strangers. They hesitated. Should they go over and help out?

I bent my head down between my knees. Must get blood to my brain so as not to faint. Felt nauseated, was afraid that I would vomit.

"I got a little dizzy," I said, and could hear for myself that I slurred my words. I heard a stranger's voice, a woman, ask Maddy what had happened, and if she needed help.

Maddy hesitated.

"I just need to sit a little," I said in a slurred voice. "It feels better now." I looked up and tried to smile, but Maddy didn't look convinced.

"Are you sure?"

"Hmm."

I let my head sink down between my knees again, and soon it actually did feel better. The dots of light stopped appearing before my eyes and the buzzing in my ears slowly faded away. Cold sweat broke out on my neck and forehead.

"My God, you're as pale as a corpse," Maddy said the next time I looked up.

I'm lying on my back on my cot, staring up at the ceiling.

Thinking about when I saw Klara on the Gotland boat.

Maybe it wasn't Klara, maybe it was a little girl that resembled her, maybe she just had a birthday that day and wanted to have her face painted so that she looked like a zombie, maybe she shivered with delight mixed with terror when she saw herself in the mirror and barely recognized herself.

Maybe. I only looked for a second or two, then I instinctively turned my gaze away. Didn't dare look again.

Sure. It could be that way.

But I know.

Now I hear steps approaching in the corridor, then three quick knocks. The key rattles in the lock, and the door opens.

"Hey there, Isak," says Per.

"Hello," I say, and sit up on the cot.

Per is a little shorter than me but still tall. Beefy tattooed arms and broad bull's neck, a stomach that pokes out a little over his belt. Big beard and thin steel-rimmed glasses. Maybe ten years older than me.

"You've got a meeting now, huh?"

"Yep."

It's time for my psychiatric evaluation.

The sun was still broiling when we drove off the boat in Visby. After the dimness on the car deck we were almost blinded, and we started reaching for our sunglasses at the same time. Mine were hanging on my shirt collar but because I was sitting behind the wheel Maddy helped me put them on.

We had the glistening sea to our right and Visby to the left. A short ways out from land a big cruise ship was anchored. Slowly we wound our way out of the harbor area, a kilometer-long snake of cars, up a long hill, in a wide arc around the city itself.

Dad's summer place was on Fårö, the island immediately north of Gotland. Maddy had Google Maps open and guided us through roundabouts and past shopping centers. We never came into Visby itself but instead moved on the outskirts. But soon we left all the urban development behind us and drove on a fine highway toward Fårösund. The landscape was flat, with large fields on both sides of the road and farms surrounded by leafy trees. Here and there a tractor at work. On the roadside there were clumps of flowers growing with the same color as the sky. Everything was green and yellow and blue, besides some scattered poppies like red dots. In the smallest village we passed there was a massive old stone church.

"How nice this is," said Maddy. "Looks like Österlen."

"Uh-huh."

I registered the beautiful summer landscape around us but couldn't enjoy it. The shock I got on the boat, when I saw Klara in the children's theater, had receded but left behind a sense of discomfort that wouldn't let go. It was mixed with worry about seeing Dad for the first time in twelve years.

I felt a bit like when you're going to ride a roller coaster, and the car you're sitting in slowly chugs its way up the first incline. The insight that it's too late to back out now. You are where you are. You look up toward the peak, halfway to the sky. You look down on the side of the car, although you know you shouldn't. You feel dizzy, shit, considering how high up you are already.

That feeling, but many times worse. My stomach was like a hard knot. I realized that my teeth ached and that it was because I had clenched my jaw without thinking about it.

The long line of cars from the ferry thinned out little by little as people turned off to their summer homes. We passed Lärbro. The landscape gradually changed. The smiling, open farm landscape was replaced by one more barren, more closed. The extensive fields disappeared. Light green foliage became dark, dense bushes of juniper and pine. The narrow roads that stuck out to the sides were white with lime gravel, dry and dusty in the blazing sun.

We cruised into Fårösund, the biggest town we'd seen since Visby. Here there was a gas station and an Ica store. We drove straight down to the ferry terminal. The line wasn't long and the sound was served by several ferries, so we wouldn't need to wait long. But Maddy took the opportunity anyway to slip into a shop and get an ice cream. I didn't want any.

Soon a ferry berthed. It was completely full, with a mixture of personal cars, RVs and some trucks. I had heard that Fårö had nice beaches, so there were probably more people driving away from the island than to it at this time of the afternoon. People were returning home after a day at the beach. We drove on board, the whole line of cars was swallowed easily and when the ferry put out it was only half-full.

I put on my old beige cap and then got out of the car. The wind blew nicely on my face as we headed out into the sound.

The smell of sea was mixed with the odor of diesel from the ferry. Maddy put her arms around my waist, pulled me next to her.

"How does it feel? Are you nervous?"

"Maybe not nervous exactly, but…"

"You're not saying much."

"No. Well, I guess I'm a little tense."

Maddy stroked my cheek, pressed her lips against my neck.

"I'm here."

Without you I never would have done this, I thought. But I didn't say that. Maddy might get the idea that she was indispensable to me. But the warmth from her body, her lips against my throat, the tenderness in her voice, all that put me in a slightly better mood.

I put my arm around her and thought that this would probably be fine.

Soon we could see the harbor on the other side of the sound and the line of waiting cars. We hopped into our Nissan Micra again. The ferry berthed, a boom opened and we could drive on land on Fårö.

The landscape was not so different from north Gotland, but the vegetation looked even more barren and windswept now. The highway cut a straight incision through the forest of stooping pines and junipers. No fields as far as the eye could see, but pastures framed by stone walls or fences. Large flocks of sheep wandered around, grazing in the meager vegetation.

Here and there along the road were old-fashioned barns, with pointed roofs covered with dried reeds. All the buildings were stone or wood and seemed gray or dark brown. It felt as if Fårö welcomed us with a gloomy expression. An old man who took life seriously.

We passed a church, and immediately after the road came very close to the sea. Glistening waves, dazzling white sand and dazzling white cliffs. An aroma of rotten seaweed.

Dad had instructed us to take the main road north across the island and pass the turnoffs toward Sudersand and Ava. For the last stretch he had texted me a detailed route description. "Google Maps doesn't work up here," he'd written.

Around Sudersand there was denser development. Summer houses and bungalows lined the road. We saw signs for both cabins and camping. But we continued, and soon the houses were more scattered. Dense spruce forest started, but it wasn't the tall, magical sort we have in Småland. These were short trees that stood very close together.

There was the turnoff to Ava. We were getting closer. I felt butterflies in my stomach and gave my phone to Maddy so that she could read Dad's directions out loud.

"After a long curve to the right you'll glimpse a house a short ways into the forest on the right-hand side. Shortly after that house turn right onto a small gravel road."

There had been several curves to the right and to the left one after the other—how would we know which one he meant?

"There's the house, right?" said Maddy. "Or what?"

"Hmm."

Sure enough there was a house out by the road, but Dad had written that we would "glimpse" a house "a short ways into the forest." That description didn't really seem to fit. And there was no gravel road immediately after either.

We drove farther, both of us eagerly staring out the side window on the right side.

The curves were replaced by a straight stretch, and then one more.

"If you come out on a straight stretch you've gone too far."

I sighed, braked and turned around. After a little backtracking we were on our way back toward Ava and Sudersand. Maddy said, "It must have been here then anyway."

"He's not great at giving directions."

After a little while we saw a gravel road to the left. A short distance farther ahead was the house by the road.

"Can it be here?" I said.

"Let's try it," said Maddy. "There aren't that many roads to choose from."

I turned onto the gravel road, which didn't look like much from the highway, but a short ways into the forest it divided in two. The one road almost looked newly paved. Smooth and nice with macadam, no middle string of grass.

"Left, huh?"

"Yep. Left."

The forest again changed character, or else we simply hadn't seen it from out on the road. The ground billowed, as if it went in big waves. The straight, close-standing spruce was replaced by knotty pine. The road coiled ahead between the hills but it was still smooth and nice to drive on.

The trees thinned out. I felt more than saw that we were approaching the sea.

"Now we're close," I mumbled.

And then the road ran out onto a gravel driveway, which glistened white in the sun. Beyond it was Dad's house. Ajkeshorn.

A broad, low building in modern architecture, with different levels so that it would follow the billowing sand dunes. It looked pixelated, if you understand what I mean. No rounded soft corners. Everything built up at distinct angles. As if someone had taken the first sketch from a really bad graphics program and reproduced it exactly in reality.

The whole thing was a bit Minecraft-ish.

Maddy just stared.

"Wow," she said at last.

Beside the main building was another low building. The garage. How did I know it was the garage? Well, because parked in front of it was a Lamborghini and a Koenigsegg.

I pulled up a little more and parked the car by the edge of the turnaround. We got out. Maddy looked at me.

"Who the hell *is* your father, really?"

Now the door to the house opened, and Dad came out. He was smiling broadly.

"Welcome! Was it hard to find?"

Dad came to meet us. He was dressed in black linen shorts and a tight black T-shirt, washed out and bleached by the sun. Birkenstocks on his feet. He was very tan, his skin a reddish brown.

"A little," said Maddy. "But we made it."

"Hi. I'm Fredrik." Dad extended his hand toward Maddy, who took it. A firm handshake, they smiled at each other. On the inside of his forearm Dad had a tattoo with some strange signs and curlicues.

"Maddy. Nice to be here."

He let go of Maddy's hand and turned toward me. He smiled, but his gaze was searching, a little uncertain.

"May I?" he said, taking a few steps toward me and opening his arms, as if for an embrace. I met him halfway, and we put our arms around each other.

He was thinner than I remembered him. Hard to say if he was consumed by the disease or just fit for his age. *He must be fifty-seven now,* I thought. The blond hair was darker and sparser than the last time, and cut shorter. His body felt bony but muscular in my arms. He smelled good from some expensive aftershave.

"How nice that you came," he said in a subdued voice.

Was his voice a bit unsteady too?

We let go of one another, Dad took a deep breath and cleared his throat.

"Well now, what shall we do? Should we have a cup of coffee first, then I can show you where you'll sleep?"

"Coffee sounds good," said Maddy.

"Do you have guests?" I asked, with a look at the sports cars.

"No, no, both of those are mine. We can go for a drive to-morrow."

I had decided to keep my distance from Dad. Be correct, not unpleasant, but not warm either. Not show any emotions. But the thought of taking a spin in one of those rides put a smile on my face before I was able to stop it.

I've always been interested in cars. I could tell that this was a Lamborghini Aventador and a Koenigsegg Regera, two of the most extreme super-sports cars that have ever been manufac-tured.

Dad looked at me, noted my reaction, looked content. Damn, how bad I was at keeping a straight face. *Shape up, Isak.* Dad said, "But let's do this. First we'll have coffee on the patio."

He went ahead toward the entry and we followed.

"What an unbelievable house," said Maddy.

"Do you think so? How nice to hear," said Dad. "I'll show you around later."

We went in through the front door, which was tall and wide and seemed to be made of massive wood, maybe oak. The entry hall wasn't especially large but corridors extended in three direc-tions from it. And none of them went straight; there were little twists in them that meant you couldn't see where they ended. Besides that, differences in height, a step here, a step there. A large skylight meant that the hall was lit by daylight from above. The floor was laid with some kind of light gray stone.

"You can keep your shoes on."

We followed Dad in the corridor that went straight ahead from the front door. The walls were painted in a pleasantly soft white shade. Here and there artworks were hanging, maybe Dad's own. But what you mainly noticed were the wall lamps. They looked like they were made from remnants of an explo-sion, maybe an airplane crash. The metal around the bulb was bent, twisted and cut, half-melted and discolored, as if it had been dipped in corrosive acid or something.

You hear what I'm saying. It looked really disgusting. Why anyone would want such things on their walls I didn't understand. But of course I wasn't surprised that Dad did.

Along the corridor were doors both to the left and right. We passed an area with a large glass sliding door. Outside was a small courtyard, framed in by the house on three sides and a sand dune. A twisted pine stood in the middle, and a hammock was set up between the pine and a wooden pole. The crown of the pine shadowed the hammock.

"Wow," said Maddy. "Check out how nice that is."

At last, after a few steps up, the corridor ran out in a large, modern kitchen with a gigantic stove, a kitchen island with shiny black marble countertop and a dining table with room for at least ten people. Floor of polished and waxed concrete or stone. All the things that rich people like to have in their kitchens. Stripped-down and minimalistic, as it's called, in subdued colors. Dad turned toward us.

"What would you like? Brew coffee or espresso?"

"I could go for a flat white with oat milk," said Maddy, looking innocently at Dad.

He looked bewildered. Three seconds of uncomfortable silence passed before she cracked a smile.

"Just joking. Brew coffee is great."

"For me too," I said.

"Are you sure? I'll gladly make espresso otherwise. I think I have soy milk."

"No, no," said Maddy. "For real, brew is perfect."

"Okay...go out on the patio for now, then I'll come out with the coffee."

The one long side of the kitchen faced out toward a large patio, and the sea. Windows from floor to ceiling, open via yet another sliding wall of glass. Maddy went out and I followed.

The patio was gigantic and had the same light stone flooring that we'd seen in the hall. Here was another dining table with eight places, and in the other corner a large, low lounge group: a corner sofa and some armchairs with a ridiculously low coffee table in the middle. The lounge furniture was shadowed by the biggest parasol I'd ever seen. A low stone edge framed it all in. There were openings both to the sides and ahead.

We went up to the edge that faced toward the sea. A stone stair led down to where a path with wooden planks started. It sloped gently downward and coiled ahead between sand dunes overgrown with what looked like reeds, and violet and yellow wildflowers. Knotty pines on both sides. Maybe fifty meters farther down we saw a bit of dazzling white beach, and then the sea—light green closest in, turquoise after that, farther out dark blue with white foam on the waves.

We stood quietly a moment and just gaped.

"Wow," said Maddy at last. "Absolute fucking wow."

"Hmm," I said.

"I have to stop saying 'wow' all the time."

"Yes."

"How many times have I said it since we got here?"

"Four or five, I think."

"Awkward."

"Come on now, really. That's enough now." I smiled and put my arm around her.

"But isn't it all just unbelievable? What a place!"

"Hmm...maybe not quite my style."

"Not your style?" Maddy looked at me.

"Doesn't it feel a little like you're at a museum or something?"

"I like it anyway."

"It is beautiful."

"And the view. You can't complain about that."

"No."

"Your dad must be loaded. I didn't think you made that kind of money being an artist."

That was more or less all I'd told Maddy about Dad, that he was a modern artist. Now I felt a sting of worry, a light pressure across my chest, a premonition about things that Dad and I would need to talk about during the coming days. We stood silently a moment. Maddy leaned her head against my neck.

"We have to swim later."

The beach and the sea below looked almost ridiculously inviting. After a few boiling-hot hours in a Nissan Micra without air conditioning a dip would be nice. I told myself that I must try to be in the present, enjoy it. The rest I could deal with later.

Dad came out from the kitchen, carrying a tray with coffee and milk and some biscuits.

"Let's sit in the shade, okay?"

We sat down on the lounge furniture. Dad placed a mug in front of each of us.

"There's milk here."

Maddy took her mug, took a sip of coffee and said, "Isak tells me that you're an artist."

"Hmm..." Dad nodded, and then he looked at me, once again with that slightly questioning, defensive gaze.

"I don't know how much you've said...?"

I tasted the coffee, let the question hang in the air a few seconds.

"No more than that," I said. Short and tight-lipped.

This was going to be hard, I felt it immediately. Being so taciturn, borderline unpleasant, not helping the conversation to flow—it was so against my nature. But I was forced to exert myself. Especially now, when in principle I'd been knocked out by the sports cars, by the house, by the seaside location. *It mustn't stand out. Don't thaw out after twenty minutes. Must maintain control.*

"No," Dad started, staring down at the table before he continued. Probably didn't know how much detail he should go into. "I'll give you the short version then."

Dad told her that he'd had a breakthrough as a painter almost twenty years ago. Was discovered at the art fair in Basel by an international gallerist, who took him to London. This was at roughly the same time the city was filling up with Russian oligarchs with piles of money. He'd had luck with timing, Dad stated soberly. Since then it had rolled on. The Russians loved him first, then came the Asians and the Americans. He mostly had private clients but gradually more and more institutions. Nowadays his work was in many of the world's most renowned art museums. To help him he had a staff consisting of five or six permanent coworkers. The main studio was in London but he also had a small one here on Fårö. At the moment his art was being shown at separate exhibitions in Bilbao, Shanghai and Phoenix.

"There are usually a number of people with me here. But now they all have time off over the summer. And it's a little uncertain if they'll come back in the fall. Don't know if there's any sense in that."

"Do they know about your illness?" Maddy asked.

"I've told my closest coworkers. But for the others it will be an unpleasant surprise."

There was silence around the table. It was Maddy who had interjected questions and comments during Dad's story. Now she left the field open for me to say something. I felt an expectation both from her and from Dad. But I sat silently. Sipped my coffee, peered out toward the sea. A faint rustling was heard when the wind passed through the crowns of the pine trees.

Such an uncomfortable atmosphere.

At last Maddy heaved a deep sigh and said, "It truly is lovely here." Dad smiled and nodded.

"Are you two in the mood for a swim?"

★ ★ ★

We retrieved our luggage from the car, and Dad showed us where we would sleep. We followed him through one of the winding corridors. At one point we passed the entrance to another corridor which was closed off with plastic barriers and duct tape. Dad stopped.

"I thought that you would sleep in the guest rooms," he said. "But we've had water damage in this part of the house. The roof leaks. So I'm waiting for the handymen to come and fix it."

"Okay," said Maddy.

Dad shook his head.

"Architects...they always present ingenious new solutions that haven't been tested before. 'Yes, we'll let the roof slope in toward the middle, so when it rains it will be like a waterfall in the house, then we avoid having gutters and downspouts on the outside. What could go wrong?' Quite a lot, it turned out."

We continued through the corridor, to yet another hall. Or I could call it a cloakroom. Here was an entry door, here were a couple of sturdy racks made of wood and steel to hang clothes on and here was a bathroom door. Same light stone on the floor, same skylights opening toward the sky above.

But what really attracted your attention was a sofa that stood along one wall. I don't really know how to describe it so that you understand. It was the sickest thing I've ever seen.

At the left end it looked like a typical waiting room sofa. It was upholstered in black leather with a lot of buttons. Tall, straight seat, not particularly thick padding, square lines. The kind you often see at airports. But gradually, the farther to the right you came, the sofa started to be transformed. The padding swelled up and became bulky. Soon you couldn't even sit on the sofa, the padding swelled and swelled out of control, like a gigantic dough that poured out over the sofa legs and up onto the wall and all the way up to the ceiling, a big black cloud of leather and buttons that brooded over the room.

"I had this part built to be able to have small viewings here," said Dad. "Some of my private clients like getting a little special treatment."

Neither Maddy nor I said anything. We just stared at the sofa.

"Pretty special, isn't it?" said Dad.

Maddy nodded.

"It's IKEA, right?"

"Haha, yes, exactly," said Dad.

"This model is probably called Mardröm."

"It actually started when I bought an Italian sofa from the seventies at auction," Dad told us. "Extremely large sofas were in then, they almost look swollen. I thought that I must have that sofa here. Then it occurred to me that I could redo it, and draw out this design ad absurdum. So I sketched it, but then came the next thought, to proceed from a sofa with a completely different design, something strict, severe that was in during the fifties. To get a bigger development."

"Yes... I don't know what to say," said Maddy. She turned to me. "Should we get one like this for our little one-bedroom?"

"Rather not," I said. "Only one person can probably sit on it."

"Hmm," said Dad, nodding. "It's actually an armchair."

What a fucking idiot, I thought. *Buying a sofa and then remaking it, probably for a whole lot of money, so that only one person can sit on it. What a waste.*

"In any event," Dad continued, "it's part of the story that I got the idea, made a drawing and let my people start constructing this in the studio. And at the same time I started to have headaches. It was like it never went away. So at last I went to a doctor and had a lot of tests done, and they determined that I had a brain tumor."

Dad fell silent. Maddy and I contemplated this, waited for him to continue.

"So... I think that somewhere I knew, even if it was unconscious, that I had this tumor growing in me. Completely out of control. This was my way of portraying my subconscious."

There was silence again. Maddy and I continued staring at the sofa.

"Incredible," Maddy said at last.

"You don't need to sleep out here anyway," Dad said, smiling at me. "Come."

At the opposite end of the hall, seen from the entry door, there was a double door which he opened, and we now came into a larger room that resembled a gallery in a museum. At the far end was a high, narrow window that faced toward the sea, and in the ceiling was a smaller skylight that let down a square of daylight in the middle of the room. But it was mostly in semidarkness. A mute collection of strange figures waited for us in the shadows.

Dad pressed a button beside the double door and discreet lighting, inset in the ceiling, clicked and blinked on. Along the walls stood a lot of sculptures of wood and stone and clay. They looked like idols from some ancient civilization. Smiling and laughing gods, some male, others female. Some with animal heads, others with animal bodies. Hanging on the walls was a collection of large masks, the kind that I think medicine men in some cultures use in their rituals. They looked wild, with staring eyes and gaping mouths, furious or full of terror, it was hard to decide which. There were dragons and tigers and birds, many colorful and decorated with feathers and straw and leaves.

In the middle of the floor, right under the skylight, was a large double bed with a headboard on either side, and two floor lamps. The bed looked luxurious and inviting; it was that high kind with the bed frame on several levels. Bedded with glistening sheets and pillows in sober colors.

Dad said, "So this is actually my exhibition room. But I use it as a storeroom now. I collect old sculptures and masks, maybe you remember that?" Dad looked at me.

"Yes," I said. I remembered that he'd had a number of such things in his studio in Stockholm, where Klara and I visited sometimes when we were little.

"The collection has grown a bit since you were little," Dad continued. "But I hope it's okay that they're in here. In any case, this is the nicest room in the whole house. The climate control system in here is the best you can get for the money."

That was actually true. The room felt cool and nice compared with the rest of the house. Maddy went up to the bed, stroking her hand over the sheets.

"Here we're going to sleep like a king and queen," she said, smiling. She set her bag down on the floor beside the bed.

"You can see the starry sky through the window, if you want," Dad said as he went over to the double door. "Or...if you want it dark..." Dad pressed another button on the wall, and a horizontal curtain started being drawn in front of the skylight with a discreet hum.

"Perfect," said Maddy.

Dad looked at me, and now his gaze was a little more challenging.

"Does it feel okay? Does this work for you?" I thought I heard a slight, slight acid tinge to his voice, a lack of patience. *Why did you even come here if you're just going to be silent and sullen*, more or less. Maybe I was only imagining it. In any event I nodded and answered, "Of course."

"The bathroom is in the hall, you saw that?"

"Hmm."

"That was probably it." Dad looked at his watch. "Shall we say that we meet for a drink on the patio in a couple of hours? At six? Then we'll have dinner?"

"That will be perfect," said Maddy.

"Sure," I said.

Dad nodded and smiled broadly at us.

"Nice to have the two of you here."

He disappeared through the double door and closed it quietly behind him. Maddy stood stock-still, as if on tenterhooks, and listened for his steps that disappeared through the hall. When they were no longer heard she took a big jump, up into the air, and landed on her back on the bed.

"Woohoo!" she shouted. The bed frame creaked worrisomely. I laughed and went up to the bed, set my bag on the floor, climbed up and lay down in Maddy's open arms. My cap fell off my head. We kissed each other, rolled around, hugged, kissed again.

"Heavens, what a lovely bed," she said. "There'll be fucking here."

"Do you say so?" I had her under me, and she put her hands on my buttocks and squeezed.

"Yes, I say so." I kissed her on the throat, my hands went in under the camisole, and I spread my fingers out across her back.

"Imagine lying here and seeing the stars at night," Maddy mumbled. "Wait a little." I rolled off her and she wriggled up out of the bed. She went over to the row of buttons beside the double door and started pressing them to find the right one. Soon she found the one that pulled away the curtain in front of the skylight. I lay on my back and looked up. A shaft through the rather thick ceiling, and above that, an almost unreal bright blue square.

"Sweet," I said, and waited for her to come and keep me company in the bed again. But the room had aroused her curiosity. Or rather, the collection of statues and masks had done that. She walked slowly along the row of figures, stopped and looked extra carefully at some, lightly touched another with her fingertips.

"What kind of old guys are these?"

"Don't know. Ancient gods, maybe."

"This one doesn't look jolly." Maddy observed a sculpture of completely black wood. It was just a little taller than her and had its hands crossed over the chest. The eyes stared, while the mouth was open with exposed teeth, like a wolf.

Maddy took it by the ear.

"Hey. Cool down. We're on vacation."

I got an impulse to ask Maddy not to touch the sculptures. Somewhere in the back of my mind a dark recollection lurked that Dad had been extremely careful about that when I was little and visited his studio. But I didn't say anything. I probably didn't care what happened with his old sculptures.

Maddy moved on. Now she had raised her eyes to the row of masks hanging on the wall behind the sculptures. And there was one in particular that captured her interest. Carefully, so as not to knock over any of the figures that were on the floor, she squeezed her way in between them and took the mask down from the wall.

It was a big, black bird mask.

"Listen… I don't know if you should…" I didn't finish the sentence.

Maddy held the mask up in the air and slowly passed the sculptures until she was standing out on the floor again. She turned the mask toward her, looked at it in fascination.

"Check this out."

The mask was truly stimulating to the imagination. The bird head itself was roughly the size of a human's, with a long grayish beak, and two shiny black eyes that appeared to be made of some type of polished stone. It looked very natural. The plumage was dense, certainly made of real feathers, and glistened black. Unlike some of the other masks this mask did not appear worn; you could almost believe that it was recently made.

I sat up in the bed. My heart was pounding in my chest. Maddy weighed the mask in her hands.

"It's heavy. Come and feel."

"I think you should hang it back up."

Maddy didn't seem to hear me. She was completely enchanted by the mask. Now she turned it.

"Maddy. Listen."

She bowed her head forward and carefully pulled on the mask. The plumage concealed her throat and fell down over her shoulders. Then she straightened her neck and turned her head toward me. The big, black eyes stared cross-eyed right at me.

I felt dizzy and nauseated.

"Isak? What is it?" I was looking down at the floor but could hear that Maddy pulled off the mask.

"I probably just haven't had enough to drink," I mumbled. Maddy set the mask on the bed, sat down beside me on the edge of the bed and put her arm around me.

"I understand… Shall I get you some water?"

"Please. If you can."

She stroked my back.

"Of course. You stay here and rest for now."

I nodded silently.

"Shall we go and take a dip then?"

"Yes." Maddy kissed me on the cheek and got up from the edge of the bed. From her bag she took out a plastic sport bottle, and then she left the room. I immediately heard water running from the faucet in the bathroom in the hall.

I felt the mask's presence on the bed, sensed it in the corner of my eyes. I didn't dare take the risk of looking right at it.

What if it blinked at me?

I hate how birds blink. That film that is quickly drawn up over the eye and then just as quickly down again.

"How would you say you're feeling, right now?"

Karin is about forty, or maybe closer to fifty. Good-looking. Athletic. The blond hair tied up in a little ponytail, some kind of activewear with a short zipper in front, tight jeans, Birkenstocks. She doesn't look like a typical psychiatrist and that's probably the idea, I guess.

"Good," I say.

She nods. Her gaze is friendly but neutral. She has a laptop on the table in front of her.

"Are you sleeping well?"

"Yes. I think so."

"I see that you've seen a doctor so you get sedatives."

"Hmm."

Karin looks down at her screen briefly before she continues.

"And before you and your girlfriend went to your dad's place, how were you feeling then?"

"I was feeling fine."

"You didn't have any contact with psychiatric care? Didn't seek help for anything?"

"No. That was a long time ago."

"Hmm… I've spoken with your employer back in Småland. And they confirm that you've managed your job very well, there are no signs of ill health or anything."

"No."

"But then you and Madeleine—that was her name, right?—went to…"

"Hmm."

"You went to Fårö to visit your father."

"Yes."

"Tell me how you were feeling when you were there."

"Not so good."

"Why not?"

I squirm, but sit silently. Stare down at the table. Feel Karin's eyes on me.

"Is this hard to talk about?"

"A little."

"I understand that. But can you say anything?"

I'm so used to keeping my thoughts to myself, at least the past fifteen years, that my whole body resists starting to talk.

During the police interviews the first few days I talked and talked. I was just completely exhausted and had no energy to think about what was smart to say and not. On the contrary, it was a relief to just set all the cards on the table.

This was that way. That went like this.

But now a week has passed and I've started to be myself again. Pulled myself back into my shell.

"How did you sleep when you were at your father's?"

"Not good."

"No...did you sleep poorly the whole time?"

"Uh...almost. But the last few days, more like not at all."

"No."

"And I was drugged too."

"You didn't take drugs, but instead they were put into you involuntarily?"

"Yes."

I look down at the tabletop. That's almost true.

Maddy and I walked along the wooden walkway down toward the beach, each with a towel in hand. It was late afternoon now, but the heat was still unmerciful. The air stood still among the sand dunes. Spiders, sluggish from the heat, sunned themselves on the planks and refused to move as we approached. A big dragonfly with shimmering wings whizzed soundlessly past us.

The walkway ended and we were down at the beach. Here there was a slight breeze, but the air was so warm that it almost wasn't at all cooling. We kicked off our flip-flops and stepped out with our feet in the sand, fine-grain as flour. The soles of our feet burned. We tiptoed until we'd come closer to the water, where the sand was rinsed by the waves and was smooth and damp. The beach was fairly long, maybe a hundred meters, and curved like a crescent moon. We were about in the middle and there were no other bathers close by, but toward either end we saw a few people. Some families, a group of young people.

One group was busy with surfboards at the water's edge. Maybe someone was giving lessons.

We had changed up at the house, and now Maddy dropped her towel on the sand and pulled her batik-patterned tunic over her head. She had on a white bikini with thin straps, which showed a lot of that body that I longed for all the time. I took off my cap and tennis shirt and unbuttoned my shorts. I wanted to get down in the water really fast.

Maddy went before me down toward the water's edge. The first wave rinsed her feet.

"Aaaahhh," she moaned and pulled her arms against her body. "It's really cold!" She stepped up on the shore again. I went out in the water—it reached a little over my ankles—before the next wave rolled in and splashed across my shin.

Maddy was right; it was cold as hell.

"It's probably not that bad," I said, trying to sound unconcerned.

"Are you joking? It's below freezing."

"Now let's swim."

I continued out in the water, which soon reached to my knees. A wave reached me far up on my thigh. Involuntarily I got up on tiptoe and sucked in my stomach.

"Isak," Maddy said imploringly. I turned around toward her and smiled quickly.

"Come on in, it's nice and bracing!"

I was actually not a cold-water swimmer. If you grow up in Småland and are used to swimming in lakes, that's what happens. The water may feel cool when you glide down into it, but after a second it should be nice; that's my standard. This water was so cold it would probably never be pleasant. But the bird mask had exposed my weakness; I almost fainted. This swim gave me a chance to turn the tables. I could be the braver one.

I know what you're thinking. So damned infantile. Well, I

think you've had similar thoughts many times. If you're being completely honest with yourself.

Maddy ventured down in the water again but she still looked very hesitant. I turned out toward the sea and took a few more steps. The water now reached roughly to my waist. I understood why the beach wasn't packed with families with children; it was anything but shallow. My body screamed at me to immediately get out of the water, this was madness, but I was focused on how I looked in Maddy's eyes, and simply continued to walk quite calmly out until the water reached a bit over my navel, when I put my hands together over my head, fell forward and dived in.

It was one hell of a shock. Ice-cold over my whole body. I took a few blind swim strokes under the surface, tried to shake myself warm before I popped up with my head again and set my feet on the bottom. Quick, shallow breaths, right under the jugular notch. I wiped the water out of my face.

"Cold, huh?"

"No...r-really nice..." I was breathless, could barely talk, and my teeth were almost chattering. Maddy laughed out loud.

She shouldn't have done that. I ran toward land, waded in the waves.

"You just wait."

"No," Maddy shrieked, but too late, I was already close enough to be able to fill my hands with the sea and throw an ice-cold shower over her.

"Stop!" Maddy ran away, up onto the shore, but I ran after her. She turned to the side but too late; she got another shower, and now she turned around and ran out in the water herself to splash back. I got some over me but it was nothing compared to what she got. She got a whole scoop of water over her back, and when she realized that there was only one thing to do, she ran out, tried to raise her feet over the surface of the water but soon stumbled and fell headlong into the sea. She immediately flew up again.

"Fuck, fuck, fuck. Oh, how fucking cold."

She sank down under the surface again, and I dived in too. Crawled a little. The cold wasn't nearly as shocking this time. I swam up to her, took her in my arms.

"Isn't it nice though?"

"No, not at all, really."

We kissed each other. Her mouth tasted of seaweed and salt.

Soon we were lying beside each other on our towels, drying out in the sun. The cold from the sea lingered in our skin. But it was rather nice. The sun wasn't quite as sharp as in the middle of the day but the air felt dully warm, like in a sauna, and the sand was blazing hot. Our feet and shins were covered by the fine, fine grains.

Maddy turned toward me, put one leg over mine. We were lying with our faces close, close up. I took a strand of her wet hair and put it in my mouth. She caressed me across my chest, kissed my neck, and continued down toward one nipple. I got hard, and she noticed that and let her hand slide down in my swimming trunks.

"Listen..." I whispered. "We can't do it here."

Admittedly it was a long ways to the nearest group, but someone might come by on a walk along the beach.

"No, I know," Maddy mumbled, pulling out her hand. "We have to go back to the room."

After a minute or so I stood up, pulled on my shorts and held the towels and tennis shirt in front of me. Maddy took her towel and her dress over her arm, and then we walked up toward the house with our arms around each other. Eased our feet into the flip-flops where we'd left them. Maddy looked over toward the group that was surfing at one end of the beach. They had now come out in the water, lying on their boards and waiting for a wave. When it came they paddled and tried to stand up, but almost all of them fell in the water immediately.

"Have you ever tried surfing?"

"No," I replied. "It looks hard."

We started up the walkway toward the house, Maddy first and me after.

"It's really hard. But it's a little like riding a bicycle—once you've learned you never forget."

"Are you good?"

Maddy told me that she'd learned to surf on a train trip when they stayed a week in Biarritz. She was lying in the water uninterrupted the first two days, but on the third day it was as if her body suddenly simply got it.

She had now reached the stone steps up to the patio.

"Maybe your dad has a board somewhere," she said at the same time as she stopped and waved one foot over the ground. I didn't understand what she was doing. "Or else it's possible to rent for a day. Would be cool to show you."

Now she was holding her other foot in the air, and I saw that there was a little nozzle on the side of the steps, a few centimeters above the ground. It sprayed water over her foot and sandal. When she took it away it stopped running.

"This was smart," I said. Held out one foot and the sand was immediately rinsed away. Now I saw that there was a little photocell under the nozzle.

Maddy was silent, didn't seem to have heard my comment. She went up the steps to the patio.

We hurried back to the room, took off all our clothes and dried each other so as not to get the bed wet. That was also a nice bit of foreplay, enjoying each other's nakedness. She lay on her back and finally I could come into her.

Maddy had hung the mask back on the wall before we went down to swim, and I almost wasn't thinking about it at all now.

I was aroused enough not to be afraid. That was probably also a healthy sign.

★ ★ ★

A few hours later we were sitting on the lounge group on the patio drinking frozen melon daiquiris with Dad. Maddy and I sat together on the sofa, Dad in one of the armchairs. It was early evening but the occasional breeze still felt warm against your cheek.

I had pulled on a clean polo shirt, light gray this time, and dark blue linen shorts. Dad was wearing a tight black T-shirt in some shiny fabric, which emphasized his fit, tan upper body. Wide black linen trousers to go with it. I've never understood that thing of wearing black clothes when it's hot. It's as if they draw in the heat.

Dad apologized for offering daiquiris before eating.

"They're actually much too sweet. Sabotage your taste buds. But I'm childishly delighted with these. Cheers."

Maddy and I raised our glasses, and then we drank. We had no objections. The drinks tasted lovely in the heat. Fresh, not all that sweet, and with a little warm bite from the rum that lingered in your mouth. But above all—the cold stream through the esophagus when the frozen, mixed watermelon ran down into your stomach.

"Did you go down to swim?"

"Yes," said Maddy.

"I'm sure it was warm and nice."

"Haha, no."

"That's how it is here. By the end of August it will start to be a decent swimming temperature."

Fredrik told us that the beach below the house was called Ullasand and was unknown to most tourists. The water got deep rather quickly, so it wasn't popular among families with children. When it was windy and the waves were big, hazardous undercurrents also formed that could pull you down under the water. But surfers liked the beach, and they kept watch over it like a well-guarded secret.

We continued chatting about nothing in particular, and it was probably here that a little of my defensive wall fell. I wanted to keep Dad at a distance, but the drinks were too good and the sofa too nice and the weather too lovely and the view too marvelous. The nearness I felt to Maddy, my love for her, was too intense. A crack appeared.

And did I really want to keep him at a distance? Deep down? Why then had it felt so good when we met in front of the house a few hours ago, and he looked at me with love in his eyes and gave me a hug?

Like something I'd longed for without knowing it myself.

Dad filled more of the light red daiquiris from a misty pitcher. The smell of food worked its way out from the kitchen. Meat, garlic and herbs, sweet grilled tomatoes. From inside the kitchen clattering was heard, and I cast a glance in that direction. The glass wall reflected the shoreline forest and the sky but I saw someone moving behind it.

"Are you two starting to get hungry?" Dad asked.

"Yes, a little," I said.

"Okay then. Let's go in and sit down."

For a second I felt a little unsteady when I stood up. I don't think either Maddy or Dad noticed it. It wasn't as if I staggered; it was mostly a feeling inside me. But all the daiquiris I'd had clearly had an effect. I decided to abstain from wine, or whatever would be served now with the food. I didn't want to get drunker than this.

We followed Dad into the kitchen, where an older woman was waiting for us. I would guess she was in her seventies, maybe a little younger. She looked stiff, almost standing at attention. Her dress was black as night and looked old-fashioned. It was buttoned high up on her throat and reached all the way down to the floor. Hanging over one arm was a neatly folded kitchen towel.

"This is Barbro," he said with a gesture toward the woman. "Barbro, this is Madeleine and Isak."

"Nice to meet you," said Madeleine, extending her hand. Barbro took it and bowed a little, without saying anything. Then it was my turn. I said hello and took her hand in mine. It was little and bony and the nails were long; one of them scratched me a little on the wrist. Once again she made a little bow that looked subordinate but mechanical. Then she returned to her stiff position, her hands folded in front of her stomach.

"Barbro has been with me for many years. She's amazing... but you should know that she's mute. So she's not going to answer when spoken to." He smiled at Barbro. She didn't smile back.

"No, no," said Maddy. "Now we know."

"What would you like to drink? There will be lamb fillet."

"I'll have whatever you're having."

"I drink red. Isak? What would you like? There's red, white, rosé, lager, IPA..."

"Uh...sorry... I'll have red."

Yes, I was distracted. I couldn't stop sneaking glances at Barbro. And at first I didn't understand what it was; she didn't look that unusual anyway. Sure, the dress appeared to be from the seventeenth century or something, but apart from that... Her face was almost commonplace and insipid.

Maybe that was the thing. That her expression was so totally empty of all emotional expression. Completely neutral. No warmth, no coldness, no joy, no irritation. Nothing.

We sat down at one end of the big dining room table, set for dinner. Thick linen napkins, heavy tableware in modern design. A whole row of glasses at each plate, with a wineglass big as a small bowl at one end. I felt that I needed an instruction book to know which glass should be used for what. But Barbro served the drinks so I didn't need to worry. She uncorked a bottle of red wine and poured in a splash for Maddy to taste.

She swished the wine around in her mouth, seemed to truly be sensing whether there was anything wrong with it, but then nodded happily at Barbro.

"Mmm...really good."

Barbro poured wine into Maddy's glass, then in mine, last in Dad's. He raised his glass.

"Cheers. And welcome. Once again."

Maddy and I raised our glasses, and my gaze met Dad's. I smiled and took a sip of the wine.

Yes, it was probably quite okay. To be honest I mostly thought it tasted sour. Maybe Dad was right; maybe all the melon daiquiris had sabotaged our taste buds. But on the other hand I usually think that the more expensive the wine, the more sour it tastes.

Barbro set out pans from the stove and casseroles from the oven: lamb fillet with more side dishes than you could count. Oven-grilled new potatoes and plum tomatoes, a sauce that looked like bearnaise but didn't really taste as usual, several different sauces and something crisp that may have been roasted chopped almond. It was good anyway. Really, really good.

Dad said that the food came from a restaurant down at Storlandet which was run by a friend of his. To find a better chef he would have to fly in someone from London, Dad maintained.

That sounded a little boastful to my ears. As if it really was an alternative to fly a chef in for our sake. I still hadn't fully understood what kind of world Dad lived in.

I took a sip of the wine.

Oh boy. What was happening now?

Together with the food the wine was quite different. Now it tasted sour and sweet and salty at the same time; gentle and heavy, it rolled like a mighty wave through my mouth. There was a beginning, a middle and an end. I'd never tasted anything like it before.

Must hold back now, I thought. *Not get too drunk.*

"So tell me now," said Dad. "How did you two meet?"

★ ★ ★

We helped each other tell the story. Talked at the same time.

Last summer we had both, completely unaware of each other, booked charter trips to Antalya in Turkey the same week. I with an old group of friends from school. Maddy on her own. She was coming out of a failed relationship and simply wanted to be by herself and sunbathe and swim for a week. She didn't have a thought about meeting someone new. For my part the sun and swimming during the days alternated with dancing and parties at night. Maddy strolled around in the old city in the evenings, had dinner at some cozy neighborhood restaurant, went back to her hotel and got to bed early. When the thumping bass from the outdoor discos down by the beach started up after midnight she closed the balcony door and put in earplugs.

My buddies and I found a restaurant near the hotel where we usually had a late dinner before we went out, and one evening Maddy was sitting there by herself in a corner. I noticed her immediately. She was immersed in a well-thumbed, salt-drenched paperback. Don't remember which one exactly—it may have been something by Jens Lapidus. In any event I understood that she was Swedish. She was done eating but she had wine left in her glass. My buddies and I sat down and ordered food and drinks. I couldn't keep from stealing glances at her, and once when she looked up from her book our eyes met. Her look at me was unlike any of the others I'd gotten from women since we'd come to Antalya a few days earlier. I'd had many flirtatious glances, and I had that look turned on too, as if on autopilot. Smiling, a little superior, interested but aware of my own worth.

Maddy's look wasn't flirty. It said rather, *What are you up to?* Not irritated, but as if...adult. I felt a bit like a slobbering sixteen-year-old. Exposed.

As I told this, that first evening with Dad, Maddy laughed, reached across the table and placed her hand on my arm.

"You know, I have no recollection of this at all. I was so involved in the book. I simply looked up without even seeing you, I think."

"Nice."

"But it was a stroke of good luck that I did. Because it made such an impression."

At the restaurant in Antalya I was the one who turned his eyes away first. My buddies and I finished our food, ordered more beer and started planning the rest of the evening. Which club should we go to? The same as last night? Or should we try a new one?

Maddy disappeared from my field of vision for a moment, my attention was on other things, but when I looked in her direction again she had company. A guy my age had sat down on the chair across from her. Tottenham's match jersey fit tight across his stomach, his face was red as a crab after too many hours in the sun and sunglasses were pushed up on his hair. Loud and slurring his words a little when he talked. Brit, judging by the accent. His buddy, who was probably more sober, was standing next to the table, and he looked a bit guarded.

Now the guy on the chair laughed loudly and put his arm on Maddy's shoulders. She looked extremely uncomfortable and moved his arm away, but there he was again, with his hand on her shoulder, in her hair.

I stood up and went over to them. She saw me coming and her gaze told me that I was welcome. I asked, "Is he bothering you?"

"Yes."

I turned to the Englishman on the chair.

"Guys. She wants to be by herself."

He looked up at me, his gaze hazy and a little confused.

"Yeah?" The guy sounded defiant, set for confrontation.

"C'mon, Eddie, let's go," his friend said. "Let's get out of here." He took his buddy by the arm and pulled him up from the chair. When Eddie noticed that he came up to my collarbone, something went out in his eyes. He turned toward Maddy, on slightly unsteady legs, and bellowed, "Have a good life! Enjoy life! That's...life!"

Maddy nodded, as if she received this bit of wisdom like a great gift. Eddie took his half-full beer glass from the table, and then he and his friend staggered away toward the exit. Maddy looked up at me and smiled in relief.

"Thanks... May I treat you to something?"

It was the first time I saw Maddy smile.

"No need," I said.

"But you can at least sit a little anyway?"

I retrieved my beer and sat down. Maddy ordered a pitcher of the house red. When my buddies wanted to move on I checked with Maddy and asked if it was okay if I stayed there a while longer.

"Please, do that." She put her hand quickly on my arm.

We sat there for several more hours. Went from red wine to coffee drinks. We joked that we should have Eddie's final line tattooed on our arms—"Have a good life! Enjoy life! That's life!"—and then we laughed so that the tears ran. Every time one of us came back to the table, after having been at the bar or in the restroom, we ended up a little closer to each other.

I followed her back to her hotel through streets and alleys that were filled with a ravaging army of partying young people. Lusty glances, sweaty bodies, pounding bass from the clubs, buzzing and shouting. A drunken chaos. At one point there were so many people on the street that we had to force our way ahead, and I took Maddy's hand. She put her other hand on my wrist.

Don't let me go. Never let me go.

Her hotel was in a slightly calmer neighborhood. A cooling breeze passed through the alleys. After the pounding and clamor in the city center our ears enjoyed the quiet. Outside her hotel's entryway she stood up on tiptoe and kissed me with her arms draped around my neck. We discovered that our bodies fit as if made for each other. I was surprised, she was surprised and we rejoiced wordlessly and at the same time. We fell in love in that second.

I know that I did anyway.

It's like a chain reaction. You trigger each other, one thing leads to another and you experience a loss of sense and control which is marvelous. The feeling resembles what scared me so much as a child: that everything is coming loose from its foundations, it accelerates, faster and faster it goes and soon the whole thing is going to explode. But just in this case, when you're falling in love, there is no better feeling. Just in this one case.

I really wanted to follow her up to her room, but Maddy said that if I went with her now maybe I wouldn't want to see her tomorrow. I said that was idiotic, of course I would want to see her again tomorrow, and we kissed and hugged a while longer, but then Maddy released herself, and we exchanged phone numbers and promised to call each other the next morning. She disappeared into the hotel, and I floated back to my own, a few centimeters above the ground.

She texted me a series of hearts before I'd made it halfway. I texted back, Have a good life!!! Enjoy life!!! That's life!!! followed by kiss emojis. I got three crying/laughing emojis in return.

The next morning we had breakfast together in the old town. Then she asked if I wanted to see her hotel room. We slept with each other for the first time.

"You still had some croissant crumbs around your mouth," I said, emptying the last bit of wine in the glass. Maddy laughed.

It was Dad of course who'd wanted to hear how we met, but somewhere along the way he seemed to have lost interest. Maybe Maddy and I were too long-winded when we told the story. Now he looked a bit absent.

Barbro started clearing the main course, and I noticed that she had a tic—at regular intervals she turned her head to the side, away from us at the table. A bit like when your neck is stiff and you're trying to get the vertebrae to crack. After a few seconds she turned her head back. It actually wasn't a startling movement, but once I'd seen it I simply sat and waited for it to come the next time.

Outside it was starting to get dark. In the shoreline forest around the house lanterns had come on, a warm and gentle glow that resembled candlelight. As the twilight deepened, the lanterns were seen more clearly.

Barbro served dessert wine, golden yellow and very sweet. It smelled like fresh strawberries. We each had a little glass with parfait made with milk chocolate and some kind of berry, raspberry or blackberry, I think. It was good anyway.

I was full and pleasantly drunk. Checked the time—it was just past ten. Was it too late to call Grandpa? No. He would probably want to hear how this first day went. I pushed out the chair and stood up.

"Excuse me, I'm just going to make a call."

Dad didn't look at me, just said a bit dryly, "Say hello from me." Then he emptied his dessert wineglass.

I went out on the patio. The evening air still felt warm rather than tepid. I now saw that the lanterns in the woods extended both to the left and to the right. Took out my phone and called Grandpa. He answered almost immediately, as if he'd been sitting and waiting for my call.

"Hi," he said.

"Hello," I said. "How's it going?"

"I'm fine. How are things with you?"

I described everything in detail, how we'd had a little difficulty finding the house but that it worked out at last, and that there were two super-sports cars in the driveway. The big, luxurious and very special house.

I glanced in toward the dining room, where Maddy and Dad were sitting at the table, talking. Maddy had pulled one leg up on the chair and put her arms around it, leaned back. I took a few steps toward the sea, away from the opening in the glass wall, and lowered my voice a little.

"There was water damage in the guest rooms. So we're staying in a kind of storeroom, or exhibition room, you might say. And outside the room it's like a hall. With the sickest sofa I've ever seen."

"Really?"

"You wouldn't believe your eyes. But it's probably the sort of thing you find at the home of a modern artist, I assume."

I described the sofa, how it looked normal at one end but then swelled over all the edges, all the way up to the ceiling. That you could hardly sit on it. Grandpa chuckled. I grinned a little too as I told him. We found a mutual understanding in this, a connection, in how strange that sofa was. A slightly superior feeling—*Yes, yes, that's the way Dad is.*

I told about Barbro, Dad's mute housekeeper, with the old-fashioned dress.

A gust of wind passed through the crowns of the knotty pines, and the branches rustled, the lanterns swayed. The waves of the sea that calmly rolled against the shore were heard more clearly now in the evening than during the day.

"But we've had a good time," I said. "We swam, there's an amazing beach below the house. And now we've had a really good dinner."

"It sounds like you're having a good time."

Grandpa's voice sounded calm and content. Feeling his affection also did me good. We said goodbye. I ended the call and cast a glance at the dining room as I put the phone back in my pocket. Dad and Maddy were still sitting at the dining table talking. Behind them, in front of the kitchen counter, Barbro stood with her stiff posture, absolutely still, almost like a statue.

She was staring right at me. Her gaze was penetrating and completely expressionless.

My heart skipped a beat and the hairs on my neck rose. I felt exposed. It was as if she understood that I had talked about her with Grandpa, even if I realized that it was impossible.

I couldn't turn my gaze away. It simply wasn't possible. Barbro also kept staring, until finally she twisted her head and upper body away in her special way and the enchantment released.

I turned out to the sea, took a few steps back and forth. My heart was pounding violently in my chest.

That gaze.

As a normal person, if you're staring at someone in secret, and you're discovered, then you feel a little embarrassed, almost by reflex you turn your gaze away. But Barbro didn't do that. It could be about confrontation, that she wanted to send me a message: *I understand that you're talking shit about me.* But that wasn't the feeling I got. My impression was rather that she didn't understand how that gaze would be interpreted by another person.

That what played out between us wasn't fully human.

"Grandpa says hi," I said when I came into the kitchen again, even though he hadn't asked me to say that at all.

"Is everything okay with him?" Maddy asked.

"Yes," I said. "Just fine."

Dad showed a neutral smile.

"Would you like coffee and AVEC?"

I was actually rather content. Felt tired and longed to stretch out on the bed with Maddy by my side. But I could have a little AVEC.

"Sure," I said.

"Can the two of you manage to carry the cups a little ways?" Dad asked.

A moment later Dad went ahead of us across the patio, turned left and took the stone stairs down to the ground. He had a thermos of coffee in one hand and three bottles of liquor in the other: a single malt, a calvados and an amaretto. I was carrying three whiskey glasses and two coffee mugs. Maddy was carrying a little cup of espresso with both hands.

We now followed another wooden walkway that coiled ahead between the sand dunes. It ran parallel with the beach. Lanterns edged our way, but the summer night was still so light that their glow could barely be seen. Soon we came up to a wooden stairway that led along the twisted trunk of an unusually tall pine. Dad set the thermos down on one of the bottom steps and held on with one hand as he went up the stairs with the liquor bottles in the other. I followed him. The stairs led up to a wooden floor, and when Dad had come up he turned around and took the glasses and cups that I handed him. Maddy passed the espresso cup to me, and I passed it on. I continued upward and climbed over the edge. At last Maddy came up with the thermos in hand.

We were in a treehouse. It was roomy enough to fit four small homemade chairs, set around an upside-down wooden crate that served as a table. The chairs were made of unplaned planks, as was the floor that supported it all. Here and there wooden slats were nailed onto branches that twisted and coiled around us. Many lanterns lit up the treehouse, some of them colored. The trunk of the pine appeared red in the glow. Over us the crown of the tree arched like a roof.

It all looked rather crudely made. But I understood that it wasn't by chance. If the treehouse looked like something a couple of twelve-year-olds had nailed together from a little driftwood they'd found, it was because Dad wanted it to look exactly like that, give exactly that feeling. A boyhood dream realized.

I could imagine worse places to drink a fine single malt, on a light and warm evening that was starting to be night.

"Now I must say it again," said Maddy. "Wow."

We each sat down in a chair. They were more comfortable than you might think, with pillows that resembled the ones you see in old motor boats, dark blue or dark green with a white edge and white buttons. It was hard to determine the color in the dusk.

Dad poured whiskey for me and Maddy and took a calvados for himself.

"There is something special about being in a treehouse," he said. "You feel secure, don't you?"

He had a theory about this: millions of years ago, when our ancestors were living on the savanna and were prey for lions and other predators, it was easier to defend yourself up in a tree. Less risk of being bitten by poisonous snakes or spiders too.

I had no idea whether his theory was correct, but it was cozy to sit up there in the crown of the tree and chat in the glow of the lanterns, while you rolled a whiskey soft as velvet on your tongue—there was no doubt about it. You couldn't see the water, but you heard that it was near. A giant that heaved its chest with calm breaths.

"You'll want to sleep in tomorrow, I'm guessing," said Dad. "But then I thought we can take a tour of Gotland with the cars. You haven't been here before, right?"

No, we hadn't.

"There's a lot to see. It will be fun. The weather is supposed to be nice tomorrow too." He grimaced a little, straightened up in the chair as if he was trying to find a nicer position, breathed deeply. Maddy asked if he was in pain. Dad nodded.

"It's starting to come. I didn't take my medicine this evening, because I wanted to be able to have a glass of red and a calvados with dinner. But now it's starting to creep up."

There was silence around the table. Only the waves and the faint murmur from the crowns of the trees were heard. In the gentle glow of the lanterns Dad looked older, I thought. The creases in his forehead deeper, his cheeks more sunken. I said, "We should probably go to bed…but it's been a pleasant evening."

"Truly," said Maddy. "Magical."

Dad smiled at me, a little grateful and mournful smile.

"That's nice to hear, Isak."

The hall was dark when we came back to our part of the house. The sofa towered like a threatening cloud over me as I crossed the room to turn on the ceiling light. When the light fixtures blinked on I felt relieved.

We got our toiletry kits from the bags in the exhibition room and brushed our teeth in the bathroom out in the hall. Squeezed together in front of the mirror over the sink, spit and rinsed. When we were done we turned the lights off in the hall and closed the door behind us. Maddy raised the curtain over the skylight, while I drew the curtain at the narrow window down toward the sea. Then we collapsed in bed. Maddy turned her back to me and nudged her rump against my crotch. I put my arms around her, and she placed her hand over my hand.

"Good night, darling," she mumbled sleepily.

"Good night," I said and kissed her neck. Pouted my lips, let them linger against her skin. We lay there as if intergrown. No other position could give us more touch. Soon I was asleep.

I woke up because it was too hot. Released myself and rolled over on my side. Maddy also moved farther away, without waking up.

My eyes were accustomed to the dark. A little of the night radiance seeped in by the side of the curtain in the skylight. The idols stood lined up along the walls, in double rows. Murky shapes that glided into each other. On the walls the masks, like gigantic nailed-up insects.

I thought about the sofa. When I talked with Grandpa about it on the phone the grotesqueness of it stood out as something silly, almost comic. But now I'd been sleeping a while, and woke up, and it was dark around me. I remembered the shiver I felt when we came back to the hall and I passed below the overgrown mushroom of leather and stuffing to turn on the light.

Why does someone make a sofa that looks like that?

Something sick. Something that accelerates. That grows, faster and faster, beyond all control.

Barbro's gaze at me. Expressionless, but penetrating. Threatening in the way that nature can be. A steep cliff, or a whirling rapids. Total indifference to whether you live or die.

I wanted to call Grandpa, hear his calm and secure voice. Chat about everyday things that don't mean anything.

But it was the middle of the night and I couldn't call now. I knew that he was worried about me. I was grown-up, damn it; I had to manage this myself.

When I was little and couldn't sleep, or was wakened by a nightmare, I used to pad into Mom and Dad's bedroom and as quietly as possible poke at Mom.

"Mom, I can't sleep," I whispered.

Never poke Dad. It was pointless—that I'd learned. Either he didn't wake up or else he simply told me grumpily that I should go and lie down again.

Toward the end, by the way, Mom was mostly by herself in the bedroom.

She would raise the covers and I could climb up in the warm bed, press myself against her body. She put one arm over me and pulled me to her. I felt secure, enclosed in her warm and soft and slightly stuffy embrace. It was so cozy that I tried to stay awake a while, but it never worked. I always fell asleep right away.

After the accident I moved in with Grandma and Grandpa. The fire raged in me, day and night, and the only thing that could get the flames to go out was to sit curled in Grandpa's arms, in his old rocking chair, and listen to his quiet humming while we rocked, back and forth, back and forth. All through the night we sat like that, hour after hour. At last I fell asleep.

I remember that I thought it was an unbelievable thing about

Grandpa, that he could fall asleep anywhere and anytime at all. If we went to Herrmann's Park so that I could play a while, I only managed to run over to the swings and when I turned around and called to him he was sitting asleep on a park bench.

Not so strange. I kept him awake night after night, week after week.

About Grandma I remember that she was in bed a lot. Grandpa hushed me sometimes when I was noisy, said that Grandma was tired, she needed to sleep. Now I understand that she was deeply depressed after having lost her only child and one of her grandchildren. From what I remember she couldn't bear to even attend the funeral. She withered away and died only a few years later.

I have a memory from the kitchen at Grandma and Grandpa's. I think it's after the funeral, because Grandpa has a black suit on—it's the only time I've seen him wear one. I'm also dressed up in a shirt and dress pants. I've eaten too much cake and cookies at the funeral reception, so I'm completely stuffed. I understand that I've been part of something extremely sorrowful, because many of the grown-ups have been crying. Grandpa too. Everything has been rather frightening. I cried too. But I don't understand why. What actually happened?

"When is Mom coming back?"

"She's not coming back. She's sleeping now. In heaven."

"Klara then?"

"She's not coming back either. But she's in a very good place."

"And Dad?"

"Dad isn't feeling so good right now. So you're going to live with me and Grandma a while. But Dad is coming back."

The thoughts whirled faster and faster as I lay in bed, an incoherent stream of childhood memories and the sort of things that happened during the day.

What if I never got a wink of sleep the whole night? I would be more dead than alive during our outing tomorrow. Would I even be able to drive one of those cars? I sat up in bed, wide-awake and stressed, completely wound up. I knew what I needed to do.

Carefully I pulled back the covers and set my feet on the floor. Stupidly enough my bag was still on Maddy's side of the bed, so I tiptoed around it as quietly as I could. Maddy was lying with her face almost by the edge of the bed, only a couple of centimeters from where I stood. But her eyes were closed and her breathing calm and quiet. You could barely hear that she was breathing.

I bent down and started to carefully pull on the zipper to the side pocket on my bag, where the CDs were.

Suddenly Maddy sat up in bed by my side. She was gasping for breath. I froze in place and looked at her.

"Hi," I whispered. "It's just me."

Maddy breathed out.

"God, you scared me."

"Sorry. I'm going to take… I need a pain reliever."

Maddy sank down on the bed again, turned her back to me and pulled the blanket over her. I pretended to search in the bag for the pills, opened and closed the zippers discreetly but so that it could still be heard.

Best to play this charade a little while.

I went over to the door out to the hall, which I would have done if I was going to dissolve a tablet in water. Opened and continued to the bathroom. Cast a glance at the sofa, but I was wide-awake now. That feeling of threat I always have when I wake up at night had faded away. The sofa looked grotesque. Neither comic-grotesque nor horrid-grotesque, simply grotesque. That was a step forward.

I went into the bathroom, ran water into a glass and set it on the sink. Rooted out the tube from the toiletry kit and dropped two round tablets in the water. It couldn't hurt, I thought, when I fell back asleep. The tablets started fizzing. I put up the toilet seat and peed.

When the glass with the pain reliever started to settle down

I took it in my hand and went out in the hall. Stared at the sofa in the darkness and took a couple of deep gulps. Let my gaze run from the normal end, past the middle where the cushions started to swell, to the other end, where everything seemed to grow exponentially.

I took another gulp and thought about how this sofa had been constructed. Dad, who made drawings with measurements of width, height and depth. Someone in his studio who calculated what materials like leather and stuffing would be needed. The construction itself, which certainly required many days of work by skilled people. The installation on-site.

Much of the threatening magic disappeared when you thought about such things, I felt. I emptied the glass, set it back in the bathroom and returned to bed. Maddy was sound asleep on her side. I lay on my back with the covers a bit up on my stomach. I was much calmer now. The square in the ceiling looked a bit lighter. *Dawn is coming early*, I thought, but maybe it was just imagination.

I turned on my side and soon fell asleep.

When I woke up I was lying on my stomach in the middle of the bed, with my head submerged in the pillow. I could barely see with one eye. At the outer edge of my field of vision I sensed a figure by the side of the bed. I tried to raise my head to get a better look, but it was impossible; it was like I was paralyzed. Conscious, but trapped in a dead body.

Based on the shape and color I understood that one of the wooden sculptures was standing right by the bed. And behind it I sensed more.

It was as if these old gods had gathered around the bed and were now looking down at me.

I wanted to scream but my throat and tongue didn't obey.

Maddy was nowhere.

Were there idols standing on the other side of the bed too?

Behind my back? I tried again to raise my head, sit up in bed, but it was like trying to move a table or a car with your mind. I understood that it was pointless.

Trapped in myself. A cell I couldn't move in. The panic made my blood boil, a wave of terror inside.

What did this silent mass of ancient gods want from me? Who had placed them by the bed? Or had they moved there by themselves, by means of some long-forgotten power?

Maybe something was slumbering in these dead things that we didn't understand.

Maddy! I screamed in my mind. *Maddy!*

The room was silent. Not even the sea was heard.

In the corner of my eye I saw that one of the figures was moving.

Karin looks at the screen in front of her, opens a new document, scrolls.

"You tell about a sacrifice that needed to be made. Would you say that this was the background to the deed? Was that why you did what you did?"

I sit in silence and stare down at the tabletop. How should I explain? Is there even any point in trying?

Karin changes position in the chair across from me, leans back.

"You know, Isak, I have access to the medical records from pediatric psychiatry and social services… I know about the trauma you experienced when you were little. And one way that a child can react when something like that happens is with what we call dissociation…when the reality gets too awful you construct your own reality instead, as protection. It can express itself in different ways. For example, you may have hallucinations, that you see and hear things… You can become paranoid, you think that people are out to get you, that you're being manipulated… Magical thinking is common…compulsive thoughts… And so my question is actually: when you were with your father, did you feel that thoughts and ideas you had when you were little came back? Do you understand what I mean?"

"Hmm."

Sure, I understand. I understand exactly. But I don't say anything, so Karin continues.

"In part, you said in an interview that your father's paintings have magic powers, in some sense... Do you want to tell me more about that?"

Want to, I guess I want to.

But it's impossible to explain.

"A picture says more than a thousand words," the saying goes. And it not only says more; it also says something else.

When I woke up the next time Maddy was putting her arms around me and pressing her warm body against me from behind. She kissed me between the shoulder blades, and her hair tickled my shoulders.

I started and raised my head from the pillow. Yes, now I could move just fine. The room was still in semidarkness, but the light that sneaked in alongside the curtain was white and strong. It was probably full daylight outside.

The old gods stood where they should, in double rows along the walls. The masks were hung up. I sank back with my head on the pillow.

What was it I'd experienced during the night?

"Good morning, good-looking," Maddy whispered.

"Good morning," I said, turning and putting my arms around her. We kissed. Snuggled up against each other.

"It seems really nice outside," she said. "Shall we take a walk on the beach before breakfast?"

"You know... I think I'll stay in bed and rest a little."

"Okay."

"By the way, were you up last night?"

"Hmm...what do you mean?"

"I woke up last night and you weren't here."

"I was in the bathroom once."

Maddy climbed out of bed and took fresh clothes out of her bag.

"See you in the kitchen later then."

"Let's do that."

She put on the sandals and disappeared to the bathroom. After a few minutes I heard her shuffling steps fade away through the house. I stayed in bed a little while to be on the safe side. And because it was nice.

Then I got up and went over to the window toward the sea. Drew back the curtain. The sunlight was so strong that it blinded me. The sky was still blue, but here and there wispy clouds were seen. The dark green crowns of the pines hung motionless over the sand dunes, which shone so white that it was almost painful to look at them. I could hear the sea but not as strongly as last evening.

Last night, when I dreamed about the gods, I didn't hear the sea at all. That probably meant it didn't happen for real.

I went up to the wooden sculptures along one wall. Crouched down beside one specimen that appeared to be made of teak or a similar type of wood. The wood was burnt and the rings were visible as black lines. The face was dominated by a pair of thick lips. The eyes were closed. There was no nose, only two holes over the mouth. It was hard to say if the sculpture depicted a human or an ape. Maybe an ape god.

I looked at the floor where it stood. Could I see any signs that it had been moved? I got down on my knees, my face almost next to the floor.

I thought I could see a contour, a line that followed the base of the sculpture, but which was displaced a few centimeters. Yes, it had probably been moved. But what did that prove? It could have been last night, or last week, or five years ago.

I got up from the floor, went over to the row of buttons beside the entry door and drew back the curtain over the skylight. Took out the CDs from the side pocket of the bag and started setting them out. Three of the corners were quickly established—the sculptures stood along the walls there, and it was just a matter of setting a disk behind the one that was farthest back. The fourth was a little trickier. It was empty, only two white walls and the dark gray floor that met, nothing to hide a CD behind for several meters in each direction. There was a risk that Maddy would notice it, pick it up, maybe even ask Dad why he had an old Dire Straits CD lying on the floor. But a short distance away along the wall was a roll of lining paper, the kind you use when you paint indoors and want to protect the floor. I moved the roll to the corner and placed the CD behind it. I had to take a chance that Maddy wouldn't think that the roll had been moved.

I started pulling fresh underwear out of the bag. No longer felt tired, but instead intended to take a nice, long shower, and then go to the kitchen and have breakfast. My fingers felt among the clothes and suddenly touched something unexpected. Small, round, hard. I brought it up into the light.

It was a thin, black disk, maybe a centimeter in diameter. Appeared to be made of painted snail shell or clamshell. It felt hard but very light on my palm. When I angled it toward the light it shimmered faintly.

Where did it come from? How did it end up in my bag?

My pulse quickened. My mouth felt dry.

With the disk in hand I went up to the sculptures, slowly followed the long row of mute faces, looked carefully at each one, and at the decorations of the bodies. But nowhere did I see any small disks resembling the one I had in my hand.

Until I came to the corner.

The figure was rather short and made of coal-black wood. It depicted a woman. She was very bowlegged, and from her vagina a little baby was forcing its way out; you could see a forehead and a pair of small eyebrows. The rear end and chest were grotesquely large in relation to the rest of the body. The eyes on this figure were also closed, and she looked peaceful; you could sense a smile.

The figure was some sort of fertility goddess.

The large swelling breasts were covered by small, round, black disks that shimmered in the light and drew your eyes to them even more.

Disks just like the one I had in my hand.

I bent forward and looked more closely. Yes, I could see several places where disks were missing. I felt an impulse to fit the loose disk in, but decided to keep it.

If during the night someone had moved this statue up to our bed, the disk could have come loose and fallen down in my open bag on the floor.

It hadn't been a dream.

What did it mean? I couldn't grasp it.

As I approached the kitchen through the corridor I picked up the marvelous aroma of fresh bread and coffee brewing from far off. Dad was standing by the kitchen counter putting ingredients in a large blender. What I saw on the table didn't disappoint me—a basket of fresh croissants and rolls, fresh-squeezed juice, boiled eggs, cheese and sausage and other toppings, sliced cucumber and pepper rings. The best kind of hotel breakfast.

"Good morning," Dad said happily. He gave me a friendly smile. "How did you sleep?"

"Good," I said.

"Are you hungry?"

"Yes."

"Perfect," said Dad, starting the blender. With a growl the ingredients in the glass container were transformed into a green slurry. Dad looked more tired than the day before, I thought. When he first met us in front of the house I'd had a hard time deciding whether he looked worn or fit. But now the signs of age were clearer. The wrinkles on his face, the bare patch on the top of his head, which wasn't as well concealed when his hair was a bit tousled, the liver spots on the tops of his hands.

The glass section toward the patio was open. Outside the sun was already high in the sky. The sharp sunlight fell into the kitchen too. Dad turned off the blender and continued.

"We can sit outside if you want, but it's not that nice. It's already too damned hot."

"It will be fine in here."

"Is Madeleine on her way?"

"She's taking a walk on the beach. But we can start."

Dad nodded.

"What kind of coffee would you like? I'll be happy to make a latte for you."

Madeleine. I never called her that. It sounded strange.

I enjoyed breakfast but still couldn't get that fertility goddess out of my thoughts. She must have been up by the bed, by my bag.

Who had put her there? Why?

Dad noticed that I was taciturn and wondered if I hadn't slept badly anyway. It wasn't strange in that case, he thought; he always slept restlessly when he'd been drinking. And last night he'd had pain before the tablets started to work.

Soon we saw Maddy come up on the patio via the stone stairs. She kept us company in the kitchen, a little breathless and warm.

"Good morning," she said to Dad. "It's really hot already."

She raised her tight camisole and fanned her stomach. Then she put her arm around me and gave me a kiss. Her upper lip was sweaty, tasted salty. Dad served her a smoothie from the blender and then started on another latte.

I wondered where Barbro was. She seemed to have gotten the morning off.

★ ★ ★

An hour later we were ready to depart. The Lamborghini and the Koenigsegg were waiting for us out on the turnaround. I felt a tingle of expectation in my stomach. Maybe I was a little bit nervous too.

Dad rooted in the pocket of his white linen shorts. He pulled out his hand and extended it toward me with an open palm. There were two car keys.

"Which one do you want?" he asked.

The one key had a little triangular gold symbol on it. I took it.

The Lamborghini.

I went up to the car. It was incredibly low; the roof hardly reached up to my waist. I pressed the open-lock symbol on the fob and heard an electronic click. Dad asked, "Have you driven one of these before?"

"Haha, no," I said. I was grinning from ear to ear and felt extremely uncool.

"It's a little different from a Nissan Micra," said Dad. "You open the door like this." He reached down and pulled on the handle. The door tilted the back end so that it pointed up toward the sky. The driver's seat looked like the cockpit on a fighter plane, more or less. Black leather and silver details. I eased myself carefully into the seat. It felt like I was sitting right on the ground, yet my cap grazed the roof. And the steering wheel was poking into my stomach. This car wasn't built for people my size. But Dad showed me how to push the seat back and adjust the steering wheel, both in height and depth. Soon I was sitting reasonably comfortably.

In the meantime Maddy had opened the door on the other side and squeezed down into the seat. She looked over her shoulder, to set her bag in a nonexistent back seat. She started to laugh. Dad reached his hand in on her side.

"Shall I take your bag?"

"Please."

Dad opened the hood and set the bag in a space there, and

went around to my side. Bent down to say something. Then I flipped up the little red control on the midconsole, the engine started humming rather modestly, but I changed driving mode to *Corsa* and now there was a different sound from the engine—impatient and aggressive, almost threatening. At the same time the digital speedometer changed color from chilly, cooling blue to fiery red-orange.

"Bloody hell, what a racket," Maddy complained cheerfully.

I looked up at Dad and tried to look unmoved. I think I almost succeeded.

"You wanted to say something?"

"You have driven one of these before?"

Now the charade cracked. I started laughing.

"Haha...no, but there is something called YouTube, you know."

"Okay."

"I've seen something like a hundred videos of test drives of these. So I knew what that was." I changed the driving mode back to *Strada* and the engine calmed down considerably.

"Then you also know that you shift gears with these paddles here," Dad said, pointing at two small disks that were on either side of the steering wheel.

"Yes."

"Well, all right then. Let's go. Just follow me."

Dad went over to the Koenigsegg and jumped in. The taillights came on and the engine started humming when Dad accelerated in idle, like a strong throat-clearing. I pulled down the side door. The Koenigsegg rolled away, slowly and nicely, and Maddy and I followed.

I was driving a Lamborghini.

One good thing about being in jail is that you have plenty of time to daydream.

It had been many years since I'd done that, like I did when I was little, and I actually believed I'd lost the ability. But it turned out I was just a little rusty.

I'm thinking about Mom.

After the accident Grandpa and the psychologists did tell me that Mom was dead, but it was something that I couldn't or wouldn't take in. I thought that she was alive somewhere and would soon show up again. The daydreams were about this. They were fantasies about what was keeping Mom from making herself known, and what it would be like when we were reunited.

Every afternoon when I came home from school I first had a snack, some sandwiches and a glass of milk. Then I sat down in one of the swivel chairs in the living room. The apartment was peaceful and quiet. Grandpa wouldn't come home from work for a few hours. Grandma was sleeping. I let my thoughts drift away. It was the nicest time of the day.

I still kept at this when I entered my teens. I was ashamed of how childish I was, tried to stop, but couldn't. And after Dad suddenly showed up at that soccer match the daydreams got new life. If Dad could suddenly appear out of nowhere, why couldn't Mom do the same thing?

But the years passed and one day it struck me that I hadn't daydreamed in a long time. Couldn't even recall when I'd last done that.

The summer after I finished high school I worked as a mail carrier. Tried to get used to getting up at four thirty in the morning, had no idea what I would do with the rest of my life. It was a feeling of freedom that bordered on terror. Everything was possible; everything was up in the air.

One day I was sitting on a park bench eating my lunch. Grandpa had made a sandwich for me, two thick slices of sourdough bread with a hard crust, butter and caviar in between, and sliced radishes. I thought about how much Mom liked radishes and that she must have learned that from Grandpa.

But I couldn't remember what she looked like. When I tried to summon her image in my mind it wasn't possible.

I had a vague feeling of what her hair color was and her physical shape, but her facial features were simply gone. I drew a blank however much I tried.

I started to panic.

I knew that the image must be somewhere in the folds of my brain, but I was blocked. The more I tried to force out the memory of her face, the blurrier it got.

My heart was pounding, and my legs were shaking. Couldn't eat a bite more of my sandwich.

"Calm down," I said to myself. "Calm, calm. Think about something else. Sure enough she'll pop up again."

I tried to concentrate on my job. Got back on the moped and continued my round. But part of my awareness was racing around in my head searching for Mom's face. Many letters probably ended up in the wrong mailbox that afternoon.

When I came home I rushed to the box on the bookshelf where I knew all the old photographs were, both slides and prints, grabbed a thick photo envelope and browsed until I found a picture of her. Exactly. There she was.

And when I saw the picture all my memories came back too. Hundreds of images in my head, maybe thousands. The whole card index.

Then I found the passport photos she'd had taken a year or so before she died and put one of them in my wallet. For a long time after that I would look at that photo several times a day, almost compulsively.

Since then I've never forgotten what Mom looked like.

It was late afternoon. The winding alleys in Visby were steaming hot after a whole day of broiling sun. My tennis shirt stuck to my back. Crooked old wooden houses sat in a row with massive rosebushes by the entries. Suddenly we came up to a cliff with a view over the whole city below us. Beyond the harbor the dark blue sea glistened.

Dad led us farther, Maddy and I followed a few steps behind, hand in hand. We stopped at an ice cream stand and I had an affogato, a double espresso with a scoop of vanilla ice cream. Dad had a scoop of pistachio ice cream in a cone. He asked if we were satisfied, or if there was anything else we wanted to see in Visby. Maddy looked at me.

"I'm pretty content," she said. "How do you feel?"

"I'm satisfied. It's hot here."

Dad nodded. "Then we'll drive to my friend's restaurant. It's a bit south of Visby, out by the sea. There's more of a breeze there. Thought we could have dinner there."

We returned to the cars, and soon we were out on the highway that ran near the coast heading south. Here and there we could get a glimpse of the sea.

On Fårö we had visited Langhammar sea stack field, amazing stone formations that the sea had carved out of the soft limestone. There were dozens of them, maybe a hundred altogether, along the water. I thought they resembled the big stone heads on Easter Island in the Pacific. Ancient gods that gazed toward a distant horizon.

We had also stopped for lunch at a fishing village on Gotland's west coast twenty or so kilometers north of Visby. There was of course lots more to see, but a long day in the sun, with a lot of fresh air and many impressions, was starting to make itself known. Likewise the driving position in the Lamborghini. Not the world's nicest if you're almost two hundred centimeters tall.

Dad turned right, and we followed. The road coiled down through a forest of pines. Soon an amazing view of the sea opened up, and there was our destination, the Granath restaurant. A big, modern slope building, with a parking lot on the upper side and extensive patios in two levels down toward the sea.

We parked the cars next to each other, got out and walked toward the entry.

"What a view," said Maddy.

Dad smiled broadly.

"Isn't it? But above all, the food is really good here. Yes, as you experienced yesterday. Peppe took silver in Bocuse d'Or ten years ago."

The building was a box covered with stone that resembled slate, black or dark gray. We went in through two open double doors of smoked glass. The same stone covered the walls in the foyer. The floor was in a lighter shade. It felt dark after the flooding light outside. Our eyes needed time to get used to it.

The only thing that was properly illuminated in the foyer was a painting hanging on one wall, which meant that your eyes were drawn to it as soon as you came in. The painting was large, perhaps two meters wide and one and a half meters high, like a fairly big rug.

I could see immediately that it was painted by Dad.

It depicted a sea of fire. Whirling, raging. The colors went from deep red, across orange, to spots of blinding white. What was burning was hard to see, since the flames covered most of it. Perhaps it was a building. Perhaps it was people. In one place I thought I saw a hand.

I went up to the big canvas, as if bewitched. The oil paint was so thickly applied that the surface looked furrowed and uneven when you got close enough. The picture seemed to have been painted in an outburst of fury.

I was terrified. Yes, that's not saying too much.

I had experienced this. Once when I was little I had been inside this painting.

"Freddy!" I heard a cheerful voice call, and finally I could tear my eyes from the canvas. A burly man in his forties came walking toward us. He had dark, combed-back hair and well-groomed beard stubble. A round face, with a little double chin.

Big stomach, hidden under a thin jeans shirt that hung outside the light linen trousers. He opened his arms to an embrace and laughed.

"Hahaha…old man, how nice to see you…"

Dad smiled too, and hugged his friend.

"Yes, the same…how are things?"

"Very good." Dad turned to me and Maddy. "This is Isak. This is my boy."

Peppe extended his hand.

"Peppe. How nice, welcome."

We shook hands.

"Thanks, nice to be here," I mumbled. I was still shaken up from having seen the painting but I managed something that resembled a smile.

Dad continued. "And this is Maddy, his girlfriend."

Maddy and Peppe shook hands too.

My boy. Dad had said "my boy." I felt distaste at that.

Peppe looked at me and said, "I saw that you were checking out the painting. Isn't it special?"

"Hmm."

"I've helped Peppe a little with the art here," said Dad.

"Not so little either."

"No, but I felt that if I'm flying clients in from London or Tokyo, then I want to have somewhere to take them to dinner," he explained to me and Maddy. "Then you want it to look a bit representative. So I said to Peppe, 'I can pick out a little art for you.'"

Peppe grinned.

"Yes, and how did that go?"

"Ended up hanging my own paintings here."

Peppe took Dad by the arm.

"And I'm very happy about that. But this, then…" Peppe looked up at the big canvas. "Sometimes when I'm the last one here, closing and locking up for the night, then I hardly dare look at it."

I nodded silently.

"It's a very different thing to see it at night than during the day."

I met Dad's gaze. I saw something searching there. He sensed of course what it did to me to see that painting.

"What would you like to drink? Champagne? I've brought home a couple cases of Jacques Selosse."

"We can start with that," said Dad.

We headed toward the dining room, where the colors were a little lighter than in the foyer. Cognac-colored leather on the chairs, cream-white tablecloths. There weren't any guests in the dining room yet but the staff scurried back and forth between the tables getting everything ready. On the walls several artworks by Dad were hanging, but smaller and not equally as striking as the one in the foyer.

Peppe showed us out to the terrace via large open glass sections, like at Dad's house.

We came out in the sun. Only now did it strike me how cool and pleasant it had been in the dining room we just passed. But the view of the sea was magical and each table was shaded by a big parasol.

At the far right on the terrace were three lounge groups. We sat down in one of them. Peppe said that the champagne was already on its way, he wished us a pleasant evening and then disappeared into the dining room. In one of the other lounge groups two men and a woman, all in their fifties, were sitting and talking. Expensive sunglasses, pink shirts, linen shorts. Even, nice suntan. The woman had well-groomed hair and elegant makeup. Gold watch. Yes, you get the style.

This was Dad's world. These were the environments, with these kinds of people, in which he moved. Maddy and I, we were only on a visit. I felt sticky and unwashed after a long hot day in the car and in Visby, wondered if I reeked of sweat or if my feet stank. Resisted the impulse to stick my nose in my armpit to check.

A waiter came out from the dining room and set a course toward us. He was a guy in his midtwenties, rather slender, with short dark hair and a perfectly trimmed little mustache. He was carrying an ice bucket with a bottle of champagne in it and three rather large glasses, like a big bouquet, in the other hand. When he caught sight of Maddy he lit up, and said, "Hiii!"

It was dead silent around the table. Maddy looked quite perplexed. With skilled movements the waiter set down the champagne bucket and placed the glasses in front of us. It took a second or two before he noticed that he didn't get any response from Maddy when he looked at her still with an open smile.

"Have we met?" said Maddy. She sounded truly uncomprehending.

The waiter's facial expression in that moment. The smile that melted away. How he tried to come up with an explanation, but didn't succeed. He looked completely lost.

"Uh..." he said.

"I've never been here before," said Maddy.

The waiter's eyes wandered a little before he took hold of the neck of the champagne bottle and started opening it with quick, practiced movements.

"Sorry," he said quietly. "I must have mixed you up with someone else. Sorry." He stared down at his own hands, as his face turned bright red.

"It's cool," Dad said with a slight drawl, turning in the chair, placing one leg over the other. "It's cool."

Several seconds passed, maybe half a minute, without anyone saying anything. It felt like an eternity. A heavy silence. The waiter twisted the cork out of the bottle and poured a little into Dad's glass. He took the bowl of the glass in his hand and brought it to his mouth to taste. Maddy said to the waiter, "Do you work in Stockholm too?"

"Absolutely," he said. "In the winter. This is from May to September."

"I lived in Stockholm before. Then I've probably seen you there."

"Certainly," he said. "That must be what it was. I apologize again." The waiter did not meet Maddy's gaze; he looked as if he simply wanted to make himself disappear.

"Mmm," Dad said, smacking his lips with eyes closed. He had tasted the champagne. "This is so damned good."

"Sorry, now I've completely lost it here," the waiter said nervously. "I didn't even tell you what it is you're drinking."

Dad raised his hand dismissively.

"What was your name again?"

"August."

"August, take it easy, breathe. I know it's a Jacques Selosse."

"Exactly, this is one of his *lieux-dits*, produced entirely from grapes from the same village. This one is called Le Bout du Clos."

"Chardonnay?"

"No, actually not, but you might think that. I thought so too when I tasted it the first time...but it's actually pinot noir."

"Whatever," said Dad. "It's good anyway. Fill away."

August filled our glasses, exactly the same amount in each, without spilling a drop.

"Sooo...it doesn't seem to be my day today," said August, placing the bottle back in the ice bucket on the table. "But I hope you have a very pleasant evening." He looked up at us and smiled, an apologetic and humble smile, before he disappeared into the dining room again. Maddy took a deep breath, exhaled, stuck out her tongue.

"My God... I got really nervous..." She laughed, and put her hand on mine. Dad smiled and shook his head.

"A little shaky, that."

"Why did he make such a big deal out of it? Was it because it was you?"

"Maybe."

"I need a damned smoke."

"Let's taste the champagne first. Cheers."

He raised his glass to us, and we raised ours in response. I took a sip.

It tasted sour. Of course. Champagne does.

I'm not much for bubbly wine in general, but I've had Prosecco a time or two, that Italian variety, which tasted really decent.

I know how you drink fine wines. You take a sip, swish it around in your mouth, look thoughtful, as if you're searching for the right word to describe what you're experiencing.

As far as champagne goes I know the right words. You know them too. *This is so sour that my jaws just locked.*

Talk about the emperor's new clothes.

"Isn't it incredible?" said Dad.

"Yes, truly," I said. "Just incredible."

"Yes, it was good," said Maddy. "May I smoke now?"

Dad raised the bottle from the ice bucket to refill our glasses, but I raised my hand dismissively.

"I'm good."

"For real? Didn't you like it? A little too sweet, or what?"

"No, but I do have to drive home."

"You don't need to worry about that," said Dad. "I've thought of that." He filled my glass, then Maddy's and finally his own, which was the only one that was already empty.

We smoked, and drank champagne, and the sun sank in the sky.

After a while we moved indoors, which had filled up with guests without my noticing it. There were only a few vacant tables left. One of them was in the first row facing the terrace, with an amazing view of the sea but still in the shade and with the slightly cooler air in the dining room. The best of two worlds. And it was ours. Dad pulled the chair out for Maddy and we sat down.

What followed was a tasting menu with seven or eight courses; I don't remember exactly. And that still doesn't count any in-between plates, like a mint sorbet consisting of little white balls stacked like a miniature snow lantern. All the courses were rather small, which was fortunate; otherwise you never could have finished the last few. Toward the end of the evening I was stuffed anyway.

Each course looked like a little work of art. Several times I hesitated to put my fork in the food. It felt crazy to destroy what someone had spent so much time and energy creating. Each course also had its own drink. Just a few drops. It could be rice vodka or hefeweizen, or white wine, or red. Port wine, brandy from Georgia.

I had decided to hold back on the alcohol this evening, but I still wanted to taste all the various beverages that arrived, feel how they interplayed with "their" course. And because there were many sips I got a little tipsy anyway. Maddy was probably at about the same level as me.

Dad, on the other hand, he wasn't exactly restrained. He quickly knocked back each new drink and often asked for a refill. The night before he'd been rather subdued, asked a lot of questions, let us talk. Now he did most of the talking, louder and more intensely than I'd heard him previously. But maybe it was just because he wanted to make himself heard over the buzz in the dining room.

He talked about the artist's role in society. Everyone actually has a lot of strange thoughts and ideas all the time, in his opinion. That's how consciousness functions. And when you're a child you capture those ideas, you register them, do something with them. Draw a picture, tell a story, ask a grown-up something. But gradually as you get older those thoughts and ideas are no longer valued. You're conditioned by school and work to become a part of the social body, a cog in the machinery. You stop noticing that constant flood of thoughts and ideas. But the artist keeps playing, the way children play. And in that way shows everyone else that another world is possible. It's possible to break loose; you don't have to just be an insignificant little cog. And that gives people who experience art a feeling of freedom.

Something along those lines, I think he meant.

Suddenly he got up from the table, almost in midsentence, and asked if we would be fine on our own a moment. He wiped his mouth with the thick linen napkin, and his forehead too. His face was red and shiny. The eating and drinking and talking had made him warm. The air conditioning couldn't really keep down the heat in the dining room. He left without waiting for a reply.

I reached my hand toward Maddy and smiled.

"I'm so stuffed."

She smiled back and took my hand.

"Hang in there now, there are only two courses left," she said, giggling.

"Do you know that? Are there two more courses?"

"There can't be more than that, right? A little cheese and then dessert."

I moved my chair so that I was sitting right next to Maddy and could put my arm around her. She leaned against me, put her hand on my leg. We kissed. Then she rested her forehead against my neck.

"God, I could go lie down and fall asleep right away," she said.

I cast a glance over toward the bar. Dad was behind the counter talking with the bartender, a sinewy guy with dark hair in a perfect wave, well-groomed beard and tattooed arms that shot out of the short-sleeved shirt. Dad was leaning toward his ear.

The bartender listened and nodded, while he mashed something in a drinking glass.

I emptied the last of an extremely good white wine that had come onto the table three courses or so ago. It tasted salty and sour and was still cool. My arm rested over Maddy's shoulders, and my hand hung loosely in the air in front of her breast. She took my hand in both of hers, squeezed and pulled on my fingers. I turned my body toward her and put my other hand over her crossed thighs. We kissed again, deeper now. It wasn't a kiss that was appropriate in a restaurant. But we didn't care about that.

I heard the sound of a chair being pulled out and our kiss ended abruptly. Dad tumbled down at the table. Maddy and I let go of each other, straightened up. I looked at Dad, and he gave me a strange, slightly aggressive gaze that looked very different than anything else he'd shown so far. Did he want to show me that it wasn't okay to make out in a fine restaurant like this? Was he ashamed that I didn't know how to behave?

Maybe. Or else he'd simply had too much to drink. In any event, his facial expression changed quickly. He heaved a deep sigh and gave us a hazy smile.

"What an evening, huh?"

"Truly," said Maddy. "What an evening."

"Would you like more wine? Are you thirsty?"

"No, I'm good," I said.

Dad took hold of his shirt and fanned it over his stomach.

"Isn't it fucking hot in here?"

"Yeah."

"Hello? Can we get a little more water?" Dad turned and put one hand up in the air. Soon a waitress came with a big stainless steel pitcher. She filled Maddy's and my glasses first and asked, "Would you like more mineral water too?"

"Please," said Dad. "That would be great."

"Then I'll get it," the waitress said cheerfully, a stout little woman in her thirties. She was wearing black jeans and the same short-sleeved black linen shirt as the other servers. She went around the table to fill Dad's glass and stood right next to him.

"Sorry," he said, taking hold of the lower edge of the waitress's shirt, which was hanging outside her pants. He bent his face toward her stomach and wiped his sweaty forehead with the shirt. "It's just so hot in here."

The waitress stiffened, but Dad had a firm hold on the shirt and pressed his face against it. Now he was rubbing his cheeks.

"Sorry," he said again, letting go of the shirt and sitting up straight in the chair. "Sorry."

It all happened in a few seconds. The waitress bit her lower lip and looking anything but happy, but she turned and left the table without a word. Dad smiled at us.

"Now some cheese will be coming soon," he said.

Maddy and I were no longer touching, but I sensed in the corner of my eye that she had stiffened in her chair, and I did the same myself without thinking about it. My back got even straighter, and I pulled my hands back. As if we wanted to compensate for Dad's lack of boundaries by tightening ourselves up.

What a fucking unpleasant thing to do. Wiping off your sweat on someone else's clothes.

"I think we'll get a little amarone with it too," Dad continued. "And marmalade. You should put gorgonzola, amarone and marmalade in your mouth at the same time. I promise, it says 'Boom'!"

Maddy stared at Dad. Her gaze was so full of contempt at that moment.

"Why did you wipe your face on her shirt?"

"Why? I was sweaty."

"You don't do that sort of thing."

"No, but when I came back here I saw you two sitting here necking, and then I thought, 'Okay, I guess you can do whatever you feel like here.' Or what were you thinking?"

Dad almost sounded jealous. Or was it envy—he couldn't put up with seeing two young people who are in love and have their whole lives ahead of them, while he himself was old and in pain and would soon die?

Maddy didn't answer Dad's question; she just looked at me, sought my understanding.

What kind of idiot is your dad, really?

I held her gaze and almost imperceptibly shook my head.

Our eyes built a separate little room where only Maddy and I had entry. Dad was left on the outside. He fished a pack of cigarettes from his inside pocket.

"Maybe that wasn't so nice, to..." He waved in the air in the direction of the bar, where the waitress was. He shook out a cigarette and put it in the corner of his mouth. "I'll apologize later. And then I'll give her such a big tip that next time I come in here, she's going to hold her shirt out like this, 'Please, Mr. Barzal, please wipe your face.'" Dad grinned.

What a tasteless joke. You didn't get the feeling that the apology was honestly intended. Dad continued. "Listen, now let's forget about that, and then we'll go out and smoke. Or what? I see the two of you really need a smoke. You can't take your damned eyes off my cigarette pack."

Dad stood up, and without really knowing how it happened Maddy and I stood up too. We'd let it be known in some way that we thought Dad had behaved badly. Maddy did anyway.

And then we probably needed a smoke too. Dad was right.

We crossed the patio, where there were now guests sitting at all the tables. Took a stairway down to the ground and stood there to smoke. It was almost ten o'clock. The sun glowed orange and pink and was on its way down into the sea. It was a spectacle. At last the sun was just a ribbon of quivering light at the horizon. Then it was gone, but the reflection was visible over large parts of the sky. A few wispy clouds high above were an almost unreal shade of pink. This evening looked like kitsch.

★ ★ ★

We went in and sat down again and dinner continued. Each of us got a little plate with small pieces of cheese, five or six, dollops of marmalade, a few dates.

The waitress whose shirt Dad had used as a towel wasn't seen anywhere close to our table again.

Dessert came in too, mocha parfait with some sour berry sauce and crunchy bits strewed over it. It was good but I couldn't help thinking that a ball of Big Pack with a splash of O'hoj strawberry sauce and a fistful of Start on top would have been just about as good.

I hardly tasted the dessert wine at all. I was starting to get really tired. And Dad clearly saw how my chin and cheeks were drooping, because he asked if I was starting to fade.

"Yes, actually," I said.

Dad turned his head and raised his hand in the air until he made eye contact with a waiter.

"How will we get home?" I asked.

He didn't answer, so I continued.

"You said you'd thought of something."

Dad nodded.

"Yes, exactly... I was thinking like this..." He made a little stage pause and raised both index fingers in the air, as if he was going to say something decisive.

"We'll get the cars, and then we'll drive them home to Ajkeshorn."

I didn't have the energy to even smile at his joke. I was too tired.

"But for real."

"For real. We'll drive the cars home."

I sighed. Felt irritation bubbling up inside me.

"Please. I can't do it."

"Can't do what?" Dad sounded calm, not at all irritated or confrontational.

"No, but this nonsense… We've been drinking—of course we can't drive home."

"We haven't been drinking that much."

"Stop."

"Why can't we drive home?"

"Why?"

"Yes. Explain to me why. Why can't we drive the cars home."

He's not for real, I thought. Would he stick to this joke the whole night? But there was something in his tone that made me sense that maybe it wasn't even a joke.

"Are you serious now?" I said.

"Quite," said Dad. "Quite serious."

I turned toward Maddy, sought her eyes to find that mutual understanding again, our separate space with Dad outside, but her gaze wandered.

"He's right, we've all been drinking," she said, but it didn't sound convincing. On the contrary, she sounded quiet and defensive.

"Let Isak explain now," said Dad. "Why can't we drive the cars home?"

In my world it was totally forbidden to drive a car drunk. It was simply something you didn't do. And you aren't used to arguing for things that you think are completely obvious. I felt nonplussed by Dad's question.

"Because," I began hesitantly. "You don't drive when you've been drinking."

"And why don't you do that?"

"It's prohibited."

"So you might go to jail, you mean?"

"Yes."

"There are no police out on Gotland at this time of day, a weekday evening. If we avoid Visby."

"Doesn't matter."

"The risk that we'll go to jail is basically zero."

"No."

"Yes."

"I don't intend to drive, in any event."

"No, okay, I've understood that. But why? Give me an argument. You say 'You can go to jail,' and I say 'No, you won't.' If you take the back roads."

"There's a reason that it's prohibited," I said, hearing myself how my voice trembled a little. I knew that I was right but still felt at a disadvantage. Dad was so calm and so self-assured. He had a way with words, and he'd been in this situation many times before, certainly. Arguing for the sake of argument. It seemed like he was enjoying it. Personally I was upset, thought it was unpleasant. *I can't keep my damned voice steady either,* I thought.

Maddy had her hand on my arm but sat silently.

Why didn't she say anything?

"And what is the reason?" Dad continued.

"Yes, it's...pretty...obvious." I felt little beads of sweat break out on my forehead. "When you've been drinking then you have poorer judgment, and...well, the risk that you'll cause an accident is greater."

Dad made me feel like some kind of boring, corny moral police, and I hated that. Hated that.

"There are no people out on the roads this time of night. So we aren't going to crash into anyone."

"You don't know that."

"Sure. Statistically it's a lot more dangerous for us to drive here during the day, with a lot of other cars out on the roads, than it is to drive home now."

I shook my head.

"Whatever."

Again I sought Maddy's gaze, and there it was, remarkably neutral. Not questioning but not particularly supportive either.

"Everything in life involves risk, doesn't it?" said Dad. "Risk minimization isn't the right way to go if you want to have a good life."

I was on the verge of saying something to the effect that I'd had enough of risks early in my life; I'd lost my mother and my little sister and was extremely close to dying myself. It was easy for Dad to sit here and talk about risks, since he hadn't experienced what I'd experienced. But I didn't say anything. Felt that I would simply expose myself, reveal how shaken and upset I was. Instead I got up from the table. I stared at Dad. My voice was shaking a little with anger.

"You do as you wish. But I don't intend to get behind the wheel. I'll take a taxi and stay in Visby." I turned to Maddy. "Are you coming with?" She looked pleadingly at me, took my one hand in hers.

"Listen...take it easy."

"But how long do I need to listen to this drivel?"

"If you drive the Lamborghini home you can have it."

Dad looked up at me with a firm gaze from the other side of the table. I just stared at him. In the corner of my eye I sensed that our scene had drawn the eyes of the guests around us.

"Stop, for God's sake."

"You no longer feel drunk, right? This conversation has made you feel stone sober."

Dad was right about that. And the thought flew through my head, that maybe that was what Dad wanted to achieve by starting this argument.

"Drive the Lamborghini up to Ajkeshorn and it's yours."

Now Peppe came up to the table and set a leather-lined case in front of Dad.

"Maestro," he said. "Hope you all have had a fine evening."

"It's been super, as always," Dad said, smiling. He took a gold-colored card from his wallet and gave it to Peppe without looking at the bill. "Add on as usual. And there was a woman who was here with water…a little stout…she should have a thousand extra."

Peppe nodded submissively, almost like a little bow.

"Then we'll arrange it."

He was already moving away from the table when Dad stopped him.

"Peppe? Can you bring me a regular piece of white letter paper?"

"Of course," said Peppe. "One moment."

Peppe disappeared over toward the bar. Dad turned toward me.

"Now I'm going to write this down on a piece of paper, so you understand that I'm not kidding you. Say no if you want, I'll respect that a hundred percent. But in any case think this through before you answer."

Dad's tone was different now, more sincere. I heard none of that scornful and challenging tone that irritated me earlier. Maddy was still holding one of my hands.

I sat down on the chair again, without a word. Dad smiled.

"You love that car, Isak. I already saw it in your eyes when you arrived yesterday."

"And?" I said. "You don't drive a car when you've been drinking."

Peppe came back with a card reader, a pen and a white piece of letter paper. Dad's card was already inserted in the end of the device. He entered his code and the receipt started to print out. At the same time he pushed aside the plates and glasses and tableware from one part of the table, and folded up the tablecloth so that he would have a good foundation to write on. Peppe tore off Dad's part of the receipt and gave it to him. Then looked at me and Maddy and smiled.

"Did everything taste good?" His voice was subdued, as if he didn't want to disturb Dad in his important writing.

"Amazing," said Maddy. "Like the best I've eaten."

I nodded in agreement. Peppe winked at me.

"Nice to have you here."

Dad had finished writing, and his hand moved in quick, looping turns when he signed the paper. He looked up at Peppe and said, "Will you witness my signature?"

"Of course."

"And then you can ask one of the servers to witness too."

Peppe took the pen to sign his name below Dad's. He would actually only be certifying that Dad's signature wasn't forged. But I followed his gaze carefully, and saw that he couldn't help scanning through what Dad had written. He bit his lip and cleared his throat lightly. Then he wrote his name and civil registration number and signed at the very bottom of the page. He stared intently at what he'd written, as if he was afraid his gaze would slip and wander higher up on the page again.

When he was done he straightened up and waved August to him, the waiter who had served champagne on the patio and thought that he recognized Maddy. August came over and also certified Dad's signature. If he saw what was on the paper his expression didn't reveal it. He didn't look at either me or Maddy, and slipped away from the table as soon as he could.

When everything was done Dad stood up and gave Peppe a hearty hug, and both promised that they would soon be in touch again. Peppe disappeared from the table. Dad set the paper on the table in front of me.

"I'm going to the men's room. Think this over now in peace and quiet."

Dad went off. I felt an impulse to pick up the paper and scrunch it into a little ball, maybe tear it into small pieces. That would have been the most honorable.

Would Maddy have been impressed? Or would she have thought that I was crazy? And what would Grandpa think, if he'd been here? On the one hand there was nothing in the whole world that could justify driving a car with alcohol in your bloodstream in his eyes. On the other hand it was also an important principle for Grandpa not to act on impulse, to always give yourself an opportunity to think things over.

I will never know what either Maddy or Grandpa would have thought about such an action. Simply because I didn't scrunch the paper up, or tear it into pieces. Instead I quickly read through what Dad had written.

On condition that Isak Andersson (my biological son) drives my Lamborghini Aventador with registration number FUG 79R from the Granath restaurant in Ygne to my house at Ajkeshorn, Fårö, this night of July 6, 2023, he will receive the referenced car as a gift. Any gift tax will be paid by me, or by my estate.
Ygne, 07/06/2023.

Signed by Fredrik Barzal, signature certified by two persons.

"Your dad is out of his mind," said Maddy, and she talked quickly and quietly, as if she was in a hurry. "But I think you should take the car."

"Forget it," I said, shaking my head firmly. "Forget it."

Without thinking about it I had fallen into Maddy's way of speaking, soft-spoken, as if I didn't want anyone to hear us.

"How much is that car worth?"

"Doesn't matter. I'm not going to drive drunk."

"Four million? Or five?"

"But…is your hearing bad?" I glared at Maddy, irritated. She leaned against me, stroked my arm soothingly.

"Isak, Isak, listen…you can drive thirty kilometers an hour the whole way. We can take gravel side roads. It doesn't say when you have to get there, does it? We can take five hours. If you ask I'm sure we can get a big thermos of coffee from here. We can take a break every half hour. We can even stop and sleep a while if needed."

I squirmed uncomfortably in the chair, but didn't say anything. Maddy continued.

"It will be a really tough night, but tomorrow when you wake up you can be four million richer. Four million, Isak! And it's only because your dad is drunk and stupid and stubborn. Let him face the music, damn it."

"Should I go to work in a Lamborghini, do you think? People are going to think I'm nuts."

That's how easy it went from being a firm no to thinking about what the consequences would be if I said yes. Maddy saw the crack and continued to work me.

"Sell it then. Give three million to the Red Cross and keep a million for yourself. Don't you think Anders would be proud of you if you did that?"

This was starting to resemble the conversation we'd had when Dad Swished me a hundred thousand just over a week ago. And like then I had mixed emotions. Four million—that was an unbelievable amount of money for me. Such a sum could truly change my life and I felt excited about that. But at the same time I felt ashamed of myself, because I was so cheap; one moment I could firmly maintain that I wasn't the type who drove drunk, to the next moment seriously thinking about doing just that.

Why? Because of money. I was simply greedy.

Dad had already bought me once, and now it was about to happen again.

My God how weak I was.

But four million, that was a really big pile of money.

"You don't need a Lamborghini," said Maddy. "But you don't need to drive around in a Nissan Micra from the nineties either. You can buy a Nissan Micra from 2002, or something. Indulge yourself."

Maddy tried to joke, but I didn't crack a smile. Looked into the distance. Over there Dad rounded the bar and came walking back toward us. Expectation was written on his face.

"So…do we have a decision?" Dad leaned against the back of the chair he'd been sitting in.

"Just one question," said Maddy. "Can he hire me as a chauffeur?"

"No, he has to drive himself," said Dad.

I didn't say anything, just stared down at the table, at that damned paper. There was silence for a little while.

"Yes…" Maddy said carefully. "I think maybe we've thought it over a little?"

I was intensely aware that she was looking at me; her gaze burned on my cheek. Dad's too. My big body had locked up, it was like a big awkward thing that couldn't be used for anything, completely worthless. I wanted to flee out of myself. Be little and inconspicuous.

A thought occurred to me. *If I say no now. And then we make our way home to Ajkeshorn somehow anyway. I wake up early tomorrow in the bed in the exhibition room. Maddy is sleeping beside me.*

And I feel that I've said no to four million.

Dad claps his hands.

"Good," he said energetically. He took the paper, folded it carefully in the middle once, then once again and held it out toward me.

I didn't look Dad in the eyes when I took it.

When we came out of the restaurant it was just past midnight, the darkest point of the night, or rather its least light, and that felt good, I didn't want anyone to see my face. The crickets' song mixed with the distant murmur from inside the dining room. It had gotten cooler. A cold stream ran down my sticky neck and back. I was longing to take a shower.

We crossed the parking lot, toward the cars. Dad came up beside me, put one arm on my back.

"You feel like both a winner and a loser, right? You've won a Lamborghini, but lost a little of yourself. Is that so?"

His voice was confidential and warm in the night.

"I can tell you that I've made one hell of a big fortune—you've probably understood that—and the way to do that is that you figure out what the world wants, and then you throw yourself away, piece by piece, until you are what the world is longing for...that's how it works. Give yourself up, and be rewarded. The world is a whorehouse. But...a whorehouse isn't the worst place to be."

I didn't reply. I wanted Dad's Lamborghini, not his thoughts about life. Maybe he'd bought me, once and even twice, but I would still never be like him.

Still I couldn't keep from thinking about this, that Dad had thrown himself away, as he said, that he'd sold himself. Was that why he was eager to try to buy other people? To prove that everyone was just as wretched as himself?

I still had the key to the Lamborghini in my pocket. I took it out and opened the car. The lights blinked, twice in quick succession, as if to welcome its new owner.

But first I had to drive it through the night all the way to Fårö, with a high level of alcohol in my blood.

"Drive carefully," Dad said cheerfully and opened the door to the Koenigsegg. "See you at home. Then we'll have a nightcap."

Maddy and I got into the Lamborghini with me behind the wheel. When I started the engine the dashboard lit up in a cool blue. At the same time Dad backed the Koenigsegg out and pulled out of the parking lot. His taillights disappeared quickly along the winding road up to the cliff, and then he was gone. We would probably see no more of him before we were back at Ajkeshorn, I guessed. Maddy looked at me.

"So how do you want to do this?"

"Drive at thirty, along back roads. Like we said."

"You don't want me to drive instead, then?"

"No, it's cool."

The risk that Dad would discover that Maddy was driving the

car was probably pretty minimal, actually. But you couldn't be completely sure that he wouldn't stop and wait somewhere, along a stretch of road he knew we had to pass, turn on the brights and pull up alongside and check who was driving.

And it wasn't that if that was the case I'd broken our agreement and wouldn't get the car. Not primarily. It was more about being exposed as being dishonorable, trying to fool someone. The shame that would go along with that.

Yet another thing that meant I didn't want to let Maddy drive: my pride. My male pride, if you will. Didn't want to feel like a coward.

Maddy brought up Google Maps on the phone and found a way to cross going north without driving on the main roads. I backed up, turned around and drove out of the parking lot. Followed the narrow asphalt road upward. At thirty kilometers an hour.

Right away I felt that it was unbearably slow. Who drives thirty where the speed limit is fifty? In a Lamborghini? We would draw attention to ourselves. I realized that I must try to stick to normal speed, more or less, for the road I was on, if it wasn't going to look suspicious. I increased the speed to fifty. Maddy was staring down at her phone, zoomed out, zoomed in.

"So...if we're going to take back roads and avoid Visby, then that will be a good detour," she said. "We have to drive south first. In the wrong direction."

"Okay, if that's how it has to be," I said.

Maddy was silent a moment, squirming uncomfortably in her seat. I understood what was coming.

"We shouldn't... Anyway I think that if we just try to get past Visby, on the beltway..."

"No," I said. "We can't do that."

Me in a Lamborghini, stopped by the police. Asked to take a breath test. Convicted of drunken driving. My driver's license revoked. A fine, or even prison? Conditional to be sure, but still. Not able to do my job until I got my driver's license back.

The shame, the shame, the shame.

It irritated me that Maddy was constantly trying to get me to abandon what we'd agreed on. It felt like that anyway. She was the one who'd said that I could drive thirty the whole way, take breaks, let this take all night. She'd convinced me. Now I was sitting behind the wheel, and then it was as if she'd forgotten all that. *We're trying to get past Visby.*

Fuck no.

"May I look at the map?" I said.

Maddy held out the phone, showed how we needed to drive in order to avoid Visby. She was right; it was a serious detour. But there was nothing to be done about it.

We came up to the highway and I slowed down. A couple of cars heading south approached, I let them pass and then turned right. I increased the speed to seventy. We drove a short stretch on the highway, then we took off to the left, onto a smaller asphalt road. No other cars were visible, no houses either for that matter. Sometimes a moth flew into the car's headlights to be consumed by the darkness again a moment later. I stared at the road ahead of me.

In the restaurant I had felt disgust over the fact that Dad, and Maddy, were trying to get me to do something I really didn't want to. But I'd also felt excitement. To own a Lamborghini. To suddenly be several million kronor richer. But that excitement had subsided faster than I thought. Now I'd already gotten used to the thought, couldn't feel that there was anything special about it. Instead I felt a vague discomfort. Almost like loathing. This business of giving away a very expensive car, worth millions, when you're drunk after a dinner...it was so out of control somehow. So different compared with the world I'd grown up in and the values that had shaped it. You should live sparingly, take care of the things you own, cherish them. To waste was to undermine the very ground you were standing on. Digging your own sinkhole. I felt almost nauseated when I thought about it.

Maybe I was just tired after a long day in the sun with many impressions, and a heavy dinner with wine and alcohol too. I yawned. Maddy asked if I was tired.

"No, it's no problem," I said. "I'll drive a little more."

Of course we should have stopped and changed, there and then.

We cruised into a little village. The lights were off in the few houses and farms that edged the road. A cemetery wall with a row of trees, the crowns black against the deep blue sky. Behind them a threatening silhouette of an old stone church could be seen. Everything was silent; the world was asleep. Maddy's face, lit up by the phone screen, was reflected in the windshield.

The digital clock on the dashboard told me that we'd now been driving for about an hour. I turned off to the side and stopped, without turning off the engine. The idle uneven and jumpy, I got an image in my head of a pot with a little boiling water on the bottom, bubbles big and small that took turns breaking against the surface.

Maddy showed me how far we'd gone. We had made our way a fair distance eastward and were roughly in the middle of the island, but we were still only on a level with Visby, more or less.

And we'd been driving for almost an hour.

Fuck.

The tiredness washed over me. My eyes stung. I hadn't felt drunk since we left the restaurant, but now my temples were pounding and I was starting to get a headache—was it a hangover setting in? My back started hurting from the curled-up driving position.

"This isn't working," I mumbled. "It's taking too long."

Maddy looked quietly at me for a moment. Probably wanted

to be sure that she'd understood me right, afraid that I would feel pressured again.

"Shall we drive out to a bigger road?"

"Yes. Let's do that."

She showed me on the map. We could get to Highway 147 pretty quickly, then drive by way of Slite up to Lärbro, where we would come out on Highway 148 toward Fårösund.

"What time is it now? One, huh? There's zero traffic. I think we can be in Fårösund in an hour or so."

"Hmm. That will be good," I said.

She put her hand on my arm.

"Speak up if you want me to take over for you." Her voice sounded gentle and considerate.

"No, it's fine."

Soon we had reached Highway 147. I turned right and increased speed. Here I could drive ninety. I felt livelier again, more optimistic. Shifted position to relieve my back. We had the road completely to ourselves.

Maddy fiddled with the buttons on the midconsole and after a short time managed to turn the radio on. She tuned into *Awake* on P3.

"So you don't fall asleep, dear," she said.

I smiled and put my right hand on her knee.

We approached Slite and I saw the towering cement factory, like yet another gigantic stone church, bigger than all the others. A temple for a different god, perhaps. I felt a little worry in my gut. Slite was a town after all. Who knew if there was a police patrol on night shift that rolled through the deserted streets in search of anything suspicious. For example a Lamborghini sneaking along the house facades, trying to look invisible. But I didn't need to worry. The road never led into the town itself. Soon the buildings thinned out and we were back out in the countryside. I increased speed again.

By and by we came to Highway 148. I reduced speed as we passed through a deserted Lärbro. The road turned in to a long uphill climb and I accelerated. Soon I was up to ninety again. I didn't intend to drive any faster than that. As I recalled it we had maybe fifteen or twenty minutes left to Fårösund. Then there was the car ferry, where you had a chance to get out and stretch your legs, take in a little fresh air. After that approximately half an hour up to Ajkeshorn.

This would probably work out.

It struck me that I was well on my way to becoming a millionaire.

Now it came back, a little of that excitement I felt in the restaurant. It already felt like many hours ago. Strange.

The road was quite straight now, with dense forest on both sides. The sky was clearly a bit lighter over the pines, even if it wasn't enough to light up the landscape yet. The headlights cast their beams in the darkness. The dashboard lit up the interior in a cozy way, I thought, and here sat Maddy and I, on our way somewhere together. Whether in a Lamborghini or an old Nissan it was actually all the same; I was just as happy anyway.

You ought to drive more at night, I thought.

Something light fluttered on the roadside.

I stomped on the brakes with all my strength but too late.

BOOM!

A loud crash, Maddy screamed and we were both pressed forward by the sudden stop. The tires squealed, and the rear skidded and jumped, sliding on the asphalt until at last we stood still.

Everything was silent. It was as if the world had stopped at the same time as the car.

That light something, fluttering. It was a summer dress.

The shock hit me a moment or two after I'd stopped the car. A cold wave ran through my body, and my heart seemed to stand still, a tingling feeling in my face and scalp.

Damn, damn, damn.

I pulled my hands loose from the steering wheel; my fingers were crooked like claws. Unfastened the seat belt, opened the door and stepped out on the road. All I could hear was a quiet sighing from the forest and the crickets chirping. I went in front of the car and looked at the roadway in the glow from the headlights but didn't see anything. Then I searched farther, out on the roadside and down in the ditch on the other side of the road. It was dark and hard to see whether anything might be lying in the dark grass, so I went down into the ditch and paced back and forth, turning and twisting.

Heard behind my back how Maddy was getting out of the car. I came up out of the ditch, as there didn't seem to be anything there. Maybe I'd missed something on the road in any event. Went over to the other side and met Maddy on the road. She tried to take hold of my arm, but I didn't stop.

"Isak?"

Turned around, looked first in one direction, then in the other, then continued down in the other ditch and crouched to see if anything might be hidden in the grass there.

"Isak...what are you doing?"

"But didn't you see...?"

Maddy came down to me in the ditch, took hold of my arms and both hands. Her voice was firm.

"Isak! Calm down. Calm."

"We ran over something."

"Yes," said Maddy. "I heard the crash. It was probably a badger."

No, I wanted to say. It was bigger than that. Something had fluttered on the edge of the headlight beam, and it was a summer dress. I saw two slender, white legs that ran out in the road to get over to the other side before the car. A head with dark hair cut short.

Klara.

But of course I couldn't say that. So I kept quiet.

Sure, it was a badger.

I stood still, breathed deeply, with short, small breaths that didn't seem to be enough. My heart was pounding like when I was at maximum pulse at the gym. Stars danced before my eyes.

Maddy suggested that she should take over driving, and it was hard for me to say no without seeming ridiculous. We continued on toward Fårösund.

Gradually the shock and fear subsided. But I didn't feel calm. Instead something else started to grow in my gut.

Anger.

I didn't want to drive this car up to Fårö after consuming quite a lot of alcohol. I really didn't want to. I resisted. But she nagged at me, didn't accept my no. At last I'd given in, and she got what she wanted.

And then it went the way it went.

The shock I felt, that moment of terror, it was Maddy's damned fault.

The streets in Fårösund were deserted. The ICA grocery store closed, the parking lot empty. In the little harbor a lone car waited for the ferry. An information board with rolling, illuminated text told that the next trip would depart at 2:00 a.m., and it was by reservation. I didn't really understand what that meant but soon we saw a man come walking from a building on the pier and get on board one of the ferries. Lights were turned on and the road boom raised. Maddy drove on board.

We got out of the car and felt a cooling early-morning breeze against our faces. Out in the sound we saw the horizon to the west. A narrow ribbon of light over the sea. I suddenly felt dead tired, could barely keep my eyes open.

Maddy put her arm around my waist. She yawned.

"God, I'm so tired," she said.

"Hmm."

"Do you think you can manage the last bit?"

No, I thought. *Can't manage, don't want to, can't.* But I didn't say anything. Maddy stroked my cheek, looked up at me.

"We'll turn on the radio. And it's not that far."

Anger flared up again. *Don't talk to me as if I were a child.*

"Is that okay?"

"I'm really tired too," I said.

"Yes, I understand that..." Maddy fell silent. She was still looking up at me, with her warm, empathic gaze without saying anything, as if she truly understood how I felt.

But actually she was just thinking about the next argument. And she found one.

"But," she began cautiously, "I think we have to try to take turns...and now I've driven a ways—"

"Yes, yes," I cut her off abruptly. "I'll drive."

"Are you sure that's okay?"

Why the hell do you ask if you don't want to hear the answer? I thought, pulled myself free from her embrace and went and sat behind the wheel. Closed the door. Maddy understood of course that I was mad. She remained standing out on the deck a while longer. Crossed her arms over her chest and pulled her shoulders up a little—it looked like she was cold. The wind played in her hair.

When the ferry slowed down to dock at Fårö Maddy jumped into the car again, without saying a word. She closed the door. We were enclosed together. The silence in the car was very heavy. Zero resonance, zero love. The boom was raised and I drove onto land.

The trip up to Ajkeshorn took about twenty minutes and neither of us said a single word. My thoughts were whirling, and the more they whirled, the angrier I got. Maddy hadn't seemed tired when she was driving. Not before when I drove either. Was it simply a pretext? Did she want me to be sitting behind the wheel when we came up to Ajkeshorn, so that we could say to Dad that I'd driven the whole way?

So that I would get the car. The four million, which would definitely spill over onto her life too.

She pressured me, even though I was so tired that I was about to collapse. Because she wanted a little gold lining on existence.

She manipulated me and didn't think that I understood what she was up to.

I stared at the road, hugged the wheel, clenched my teeth.

When we came up to Ajkeshorn I parked the Lamborghini beside Dad's Koenigsegg and turned off the engine. There was sighing and crackling from the V-12 as it started to cool down. We got out, closed the doors. I locked the car, and the lights blinked a couple of times. We went up toward the entry. Maddy put her hand on my back.

"That went just fine."

Yes, I thought, *because you've riled me up so much that I feel completely wide-awake.*

Was she toying with me? Was she mocking me?

The door was unlocked and we went into the hall. The light was on and we heard footsteps approaching from the kitchen. Soon Dad came to meet us.

"That took a long time," he said. "Has anything happened?"

"We ran over an animal," said Maddy. "But it went fine."

"Then she drove for a while," I said. "We took turns."

Maddy stared at me. There was silence for a moment. Dad looked perplexed.

"I don't want that fucking car," I continued and gave him the car key. "I'm going to bed."

I left them without waiting for Maddy.

Soraya is visiting my cell again. She looks at me with her stone face, her absolutely fixed gaze.

"This thing of running over something. I wouldn't worry about that if I were you."

I nod. Feel relieved.

I asked her yesterday if she'd heard anything about a little girl getting run over, or reported missing, on Gotland the past week. Told her about the night when I drove the Lamborghini up to Fårö and collided with something. The summer dress that fluttered in the beam of the headlights.

"You're on full restrictions," she said then. "I can't tell you any news."

But I interpret what she's saying now as that she's googled it and didn't find anything. Maybe also asked around with the police. If it really had been a little girl I collided with it should have been reported as a hit-and-run accident by this time.

"Have you thought any more about what I said about the laundry?" Soraya continues.

I squirm on the cot, sigh.

"No, I'm not that excited about it."

"I think it would be good for you."

I don't say anything else. The silence speaks for itself. Soraya can't force me—that I know.

When she's gone I stretch out on my back on the cot and think about what it really was I ran over.

A badger, Maddy thought, but I don't buy that. Those white, spindly legs. But possibly a lamb. They escape from their pens sometimes. Don't they?

The summer dress in that case the wooly little body.

If I truly exert myself I can just barely accept that it was a lamb I ran over.

At seven o'clock Per comes with dinner on a tray. Breaded fish, mashed potatoes, a lemon wedge, green peas, a glass of water. I eat it all up but save five peas and the water. Then I start practicing. Put a pea in my mouth, then a sip of water, swirl it around and try to get the pea to end up at the very back of my mouth, between my cheek and molars. It's harder than it sounds. Try it yourself if you don't believe me. I don't dare help too much with my tongue; that will look suspicious. And the water is soon finished. I don't succeed with any of the first four peas but I save the last one and practice without water. Concentrate on trying to move my tongue in my mouth without it being visible from outside.

When Per comes back with tea and a sandwich, plus water and my tablets, my heart is pounding. Shall I make an attempt even though I couldn't do it when I practiced? Is he going to get suspicious, and then the opportunity is past?

I don't have time to decide before it's time for the strong sleeping pill, but I take a big sip and then my mouth and tongue move as if by themselves. The movement has in some way taken hold anyway, and the tablet slips out on the side of the molar where it isn't visible.

"Open wide," says Per. I open wide.

"Tongue." I raise my tongue.

Check. Nothing here, nothing there.

He nods and smiles briefly at me.

"Sleep well now, Isak. Then we'll see each other tomorrow."

"We will."

His steps fade away through the corridor. When I no longer hear them I open wide and pluck out the tablet with my thumb and index finger. The coating is a little chipped from saliva you can see that it didn't come straight from the bottle. But the active ingredients are probably not in the coating.

How many do I need to be sure of dying? Twenty? Thirty?

Thirty ought to be enough, I think.

One month.

I passed the hall with the threatening sofa and went into the bathroom. Stared at myself in the mirror over the sink. I could see that I'd been in the sun a lot that day. The skin on my face was a little red. And shiny. I looked just as sticky as I felt. The circles under my eyes were big and dark.

Must take a shower before I go to bed, I thought. *If I have the energy.*

I was completely done in.

Why didn't Maddy come, by the way? Was she still talking with Dad about me? That I was behaving strangely?

I felt darkness in my heart.

Then I heard her footsteps approaching in the hall. She came into the bathroom. I stared hard at the mirror. Our eyes met there.

"Now you have to tell me, why are you so mad?"

"I'm not mad."

"No? What was that thing with your dad then? 'I don't want that fucking car'?"

"No, I don't want it," I said. "I don't care about it."

"Isak..."

"What?" Now I turned toward Maddy, stared right at her. The anger welled up; it was surely visible on my face. Maddy didn't meet my gaze, stood silently a few seconds, wondering how she should phrase it.

A final attempt to calm the whole thing down.

"I just think...it wasn't a nice thing to say."

"I see."

"You ran over an animal, and you were shaken up by that. And I get that, but you've been in a bad mood since then... It really wasn't—"

"Yes, I got mad," I interrupted her. "Because you refused to drive the car."

"What do you mean, I didn't refuse..."

"Yes, you did, damn it! On the ferry!" I had raised my voice now, and that set Maddy off for real. She also raised her voice and leaned toward me.

"I said I was tired! Wasn't I allowed to say that?"

"I was tired too. I'd been driving the whole day!"

"Because you wanted to!"

"Yes? And?"

"Or was I the one who forced you to drive?"

"You want that Lamborghini more than me," I said. "You're so fucking hot for that car."

"Go to hell," Maddy grunted through tight lips and left the bathroom. I followed, didn't intend to let her off so easy.

"Why did you nag me then, that I should drive it home, even though I didn't want to?"

Maddy walked quickly through the hall, into the exhibition room. I chased after with my questions.

"I wanted you to think about it!" she almost screamed, half turned toward me, but without slowing down.

"Stop," I said. "You nagged and nagged until I said yes."

The first argument. Now it broke loose. There was something liberating in it, to finally say exactly what I felt without a thought for the consequences.

"And then you didn't want to drive the last stretch, because then maybe I wouldn't get the car anyway."

Maddy had reached the bed. She turned around and stared at me with a wild gaze, furious.

"I'm trying to help you, don't you get that?"

"No, I don't get that."

"You have such a disturbed relationship with your father..."

"You know what, I know that..."

"But can you be quiet and let me finish talking!" she hissed, and that helped. I fell silent. "He's going to die soon, and he's trying to reach out a hand, and I know one hundred percent that you're going to regret it if you don't take that hand, but it's like you constantly mistrust every little thing I do... I'm so fucking tired of tiptoeing around you!"

"Then don't do that, damn it," I said, and my voice was trembling now because I was so upset. "But listen to what I'm saying! Don't carry on, and like...manipulate and...nag..."

Maddy shook her head and laughed, bitterly.

"Manipulate?"

"And you know nothing about my relationship with Dad, so please, just shut up."

"You're completely paranoid, do you know that?"

Maddy was staring at me. I didn't answer, so she continued.

"I manipulate you, and your dad means you harm… So, listen to yourself…do you get how disturbed that sounds?"

Yes, I understood that, but the quarrel was an earthquake. The ground collapsed under our feet, there was no longer any rescue and then I could just as well let all the dams break.

To hell with all of it.

"Why did that waiter recognize you?"

"Who…?"

"At the restaurant! He said hello to you as if you were old buddies."

"He was mistaken! How can you not get that?"

"Have you been here before?"

Maddy gaped and stared, as if she had a hard time believing her ears.

"Please!"

"Just answer the question! Have you been here before?"

"No! This is just so crazy…"

"How did you know about that faucet where you rinse off your feet?"

Maddy put her hands in front of her face, seemed to hyperventilate.

"When we came back from the beach yesterday. We were talking about other things, and at first I didn't understand what you were doing, but you rinsed off your feet with that little faucet. Before we went up on the patio. How did you know it was there?"

Maddy took her hands from her face. She closed her eyes and breathed deeply, but didn't answer my questions.

"Isak..."

"But tell me then. Because I don't understand. That nozzle was really little, I never would have noticed it. But you used it automatically, as if you didn't even need to think about it."

Maddy bit her lower lip. She was struggling not to cry now, but couldn't keep the tears from welling up in her eyes.

"Coming here was a big mistake," she said in a shaky voice. "I've sensed at times that something isn't quite right with you... but that you should be so..." Her voice died away, and she shook her head.

"But that's really good, now you know it," I said and managed to make my voice sound cold and hard, even though I felt completely naked and little and worthless. "But we should probably divide up. I'll go home, but you might as well stay, you seem to think that everything here is completely amazing. Everything is so fucking *wow*. You probably fit in better with Dad than I do."

Maddy turned and left, then started to jog out of the room. I heard her steps going away through the hall. Away along the corridor.

It was over. It was all over.

I was standing in the bathroom again, in front of the mirror, with a big lump in my stomach. I felt nauseated and weak in the knees.

So this was what it was like to break up.

I regretted so much of what I'd said. The accusations, the paranoid questions. That business that Maddy would fit in better with Dad. Implying that she was some kind of gold digger. It was just mean. I had grasped for the nearest weapon and pounded away for all it was worth.

But above all I regretted that I had exposed myself. I had let Maddy look into my head, and she had drawn the right conclusion. *He's completely messed up.*

Why couldn't I have just held it inside me?

I picked up the toothbrush and squeezed a string of toothpaste on it. Started brushing. Maddy was the best thing in my life and now I'd thrown it away. But the biggest sorrow was that somewhere I'd known the whole time that this would happen. No one who really got to know me would want me. I was too damaged.

I started crying. Spit out the toothpaste and supported myself against the sink. Sobbed like a little child.

I heard steps out in the hall and stopped abruptly. I had nothing to lose any longer, but it was ingrained in me: What would Maddy think if she saw me standing here sniveling in front of the mirror? Felt an impulse to take a few quick steps over to the door and lock it, but realized that she would hear the knob being turned, and that would also tell her something.

The steps continued into the exhibition room. I didn't need to be worried.

That Maddy was back meant that I pulled myself together anyway. I finished brushing my teeth and rinsed off the toothbrush. Took off my clothes, stepped into the shower, turned on the faucet. Looked up and closed my eyes and let the water spray over my face.

I shuddered to think of being eye to eye with Maddy again. Maybe the quarrel would start up again. I knew that I should apologize, but I also resisted that. Why I didn't really understand. Was it because it was unpleasant to be reminded of what an idiot I was? Or was I afraid to appear weak?

I stepped out of the shower and dried myself carefully. The mirror had fogged up. Wrapped the towel around my waist, opened the door and went out in the hall. Tiptoed with damp soles across the floor, into the exhibition room. The lights were off. I went up to the bed, where Maddy was lying on her side, turned away from me, with her knees pulled up against her belly, almost in a fetal position. She didn't move and I didn't say anything, simply started rooting as quietly as possible in my bag for clean underwear. I found what I was looking for and started tiptoeing back toward the hall.

"Are you just going to leave?" Maddy said without moving. Her voice was little and thin; she sounded sad.

I stopped and turned around. Something was still in the balance between us. There was silence for a moment.

"I don't know what to say," I said at last. "You're right, I'm disturbed."

New long silence. Maddy lay motionless in the bed. I stood as if frozen to the floor, hardly dared breathe. My eyes started to get used to the darkness in the room. I heard Maddy's quiet voice from the bed.

"I don't think you're disturbed. I just got so damned angry."

I took a deep breath.

Slowly I sank down on the edge of the bed.

"You know, I… I did say that my mom and dad died in a fire. But I was there too." My voice didn't really hold, but I ignored that. "It was in Grandpa's summer house. I was close to dying. And I had a little sister who was three who died."

I sat with my back toward Maddy but I heard that she turned around in the bed, turned toward me.

And then I started telling her.

About Dad, who was still in Stockholm when the fire happened. Who had a breakdown and wasn't able to take care of me. About the move to Grandpa and Grandma's in Småland, about starting from zero in a new town, in a new class where I didn't know anyone, and not having any friends either, because I was so strange and kept to myself all the time. All the drawings of burning houses. The games of make-believe outside, on the playground, where I was a fireman dragging hoses because there was a fire in the playhouse, and all the other kids played around me, on the same playground, but they still weren't really there, they weren't really real, because they didn't see that there was a fire, and I saw it.

Welcome to the class, "fireman."

"Come," Maddy said quietly behind my back. I turned my head. She was lying with her hand stretched out toward me.

I lay down beside her and she crept close to me, burrowed her face into my neck, put her arms around me.

I told about the child psychologists, one after the other, year in and year out. About Grandpa, who was the only one who could get the fire inside me to calm down.

And I told about Dad, who started to use the fire in his art. He painted big, frightening pictures, resembling the one we'd seen in the restaurant the night before, but even bigger, even more violent, even more unpleasant, even more beautiful. He had a breakthrough with those pictures; that was how he made a name for himself. Dad used my trauma and got filthy rich in the bargain.

"He never got in touch with me. Not a single time. Yes, once. When I was thirteen, when he showed up at a soccer match. Then he disappeared again."

Maddy and I were lying with our faces close, so close together, our noses grazed each other. She looked me deep in the eyes and stroked my cheek.

"God...sorry. I didn't know," she whispered.

"You couldn't have," I mumbled.

"So Anders adopted you?"

"Yes."

We lay silent for a while.

I had just been dead sure that all was lost, and here I was a short time later, enclosed in this enormous love and closeness. The quarrel had split us, but then melted us together into one.

Maddy turned, I put my arms around her and we spooned, me in just my underwear and Maddy still dressed. She hadn't showered but that didn't matter; she didn't smell bad, only more of her own special aroma. More Maddy.

"I want to explain that thing with the faucet," said Maddy.

"You don't need to," I said, hugging her and kissing her neck.

"Yes, but I want to," she continued. "We have one just like it at the summer house."

And the summer house, it was in a luxurious little resort town on the French Riviera; that much she'd already told me. It was a townhouse with direct access to a private beach. All the houses were equipped with just such a little nozzle, powered by a photocell, that rinsed the sand off your feet before you stepped up on the patio.

We lay quietly a moment. Then she said, "I'm trying to get you to take your dad's outstretched hand…but I don't know if I would be able to do that if my mother extended hers."

"No."

I had understood that Maddy had a bad relationship with her mother. But now she told me a little more.

"She doesn't like me. I've known that since I was little."

Maddy brought her hand to her face, wiped away a tear under her eyes.

"You," I said, hugging her.

"Yes, it's true," said Maddy and laughed, quietly and self-consciously. "I don't know why I'm crying. Most people have had a worse childhood than me. I'm really privileged, I know that."

I thought that few things are probably worse for a child than to feel that your mother or father doesn't like you. It's all the same even if you get to spend holidays in a fancy house on the Riviera. But I didn't say anything, just held her and stroked her hair.

Gradually Maddy pulled herself out of my embrace and padded out to the bathroom to take a shower. I heard the water start streaming. Didn't know if I could stay awake until she came back. Once again I had that thought that the wooden statues were only waiting for me to close my eyes to start sneaking up closer to the bed. But, I thought, now I had set out the CDs. That thought calmed me.

I must have dozed off, because suddenly Maddy was standing by the bed again. She dried her wet hair and smelled freshly showered. Looked at the old gods.

"They're a little spooky."

"Yes. I had a really creepy dream last night."

It was just an impulse, that I should tell her my dream, because we were on the subject anyway. And I gave in to it. It was no doubt a sign that we'd come closer to each other that night. I told that I'd woken up and that the statues had gathered around the bed. She giggled.

"God…my hair stands on end when you say that."

"You haven't heard the strangest thing yet."

I told that I'd found a little round disk in my bag in the morning, and that it belonged on one of the statues. How it had ended up in my bag was a mystery. Unless…

"It must have come from the mask," said Maddy.

I hadn't even thought about that. Maddy had tried on a big bird mask, and it had also been sitting on the bed for a while.

"But I found the exact same disks on one of the statues. There weren't any like that on the bird mask from what I saw."

Maddy wanted to see the little disk. She seemed enlivened by the whole story. She turned on the ceiling light. I showed her the disk and she took it and went over to the bird mask.

"Yes, there are disks on this too," she said. "Come and check."

I went over to her, and she pointed at the beak. On the one side, halfway between the tip and the head, was a little black disk, which was probably supposed to indicate the hole that many birds seem to have on their beaks. The disk didn't look exactly like the one I found in my bag. The shape wasn't quite the same and it seemed to be made of a different material. But the same place on the other side of the beak was empty. It might very well be that the disk I found in my bag had sat there.

It seemed as if the mystery was solved.

Maddy turned off the ceiling light, and we went to bed. Soon I heard from her calm breathing that she had fallen asleep.

But I thought about Grandpa, and about the CDs, and about how all that had started.

The ravens were my first major terror as a child. That happened even before the accident, before the fire. They lived in the forest around the summer house. Big, black, unafraid, brazen even. They quickly figured out that where there were people there was something for them. Sometimes when Klara and I were swimming they hopped around on the shore, just a few steps away. They cocked their heads and looked sternly at me with their cold eyes.

The accident, and what happened afterward, didn't exactly reduce my fear of ravens.

The summer after the fire I'd moved down to live with Grandpa and Grandma. Grandpa and I were often at the lot by the lake to clean up after the burned-down house. As soon as I caught a glimpse of a raven I ran in panic to the car and locked myself in. It was enough that they flew high over the lot, crossing from spruce top to spruce top. Then Grandpa hung up old CDs in trees and bushes. He told me that the ravens didn't like it when they shone and flashed in the sunlight; the CDs kept them away.

And it really worked. They stopped hopping around in the yard. I got calmer. They probably still flew over our heads but it no longer aroused the same terror in me. I felt that they wouldn't dare come really close. The flashing disks protected us.

I kept having a lot of nightmares. One day I asked Grandpa if we could set up CDs in my bedroom too. Maybe they could chase away bad dreams, just as well as ravens. Grandpa thought it was worth a try. He went and got some of his discs, Dire Straits and Imperiet and Monica Z and Miles Davis, and placed them out in each corner of the bedroom. He told me that he'd read in the newspaper, just the other day, that Dire Straits CDs in particular were extragood for nightmares. I wondered if that could be true, but Grandpa looked quite serious, so I assumed he wasn't making it up. He wouldn't lie about such a thing.

I still remember that I woke up the next morning, and realized that I'd slept the whole night without interruption. The disks had worked! It was like magic.

The nightmares didn't stop completely of course. I had bad nights after that too, but they came less often. Then, when I was seven years old, I was quite sure that it was thanks to the disks. Now I guess maybe it coincided with my starting to recover a little after the accident. Things were moving in the right direction for me anyway, with or without CDs. But they helped me break a thought pattern, an important step.

Brothers in Arms with Dire Straits. *Blue Heaven Blues* with Imperiet, *Waltz for Debby* with Monica Z, *Milestones* with Miles Davis. Those were the four CDs that were now set out in each corner in the room where Maddy and I slept. They were what kept the wooden gods in place.

I was lying there thinking about such things with Maddy sleeping beside me. That, and food.

I've never been able to fall asleep hungry. It becomes like an obsessive thought. Now I started to think about what was in the refrigerator in the kitchen. Ice-cold orange juice. Butter, liver sausage, cheese, marmalade. And in a bread box or drawer that light sourdough bread we'd had for breakfast the morning before. Nothing remarkable, but my desire for them lying there in bed couldn't be talked away. This wouldn't go away; on the contrary, it would just get worse.

Quietly I pulled aside the covers and got out of bed. Maddy slept on with calm, deep breaths.

I padded barefoot out of the room with a T-shirt in hand,

pulling it over my head as I passed the hall under the threatening storm cloud of the sofa. Felt that I relaxed when I came out in the corridor and started making my way to the kitchen.

Gray daylight seeped down from the skylights. My eyes were used to the dark now and I didn't turn on any lights. I came up to the entry to the corridor with the guest rooms, the one that was covered with plastic barriers, and stopped.

Should I take the opportunity to take a look for myself?

True, I was hungry, but the kitchen wasn't going anywhere. This night when I alone was awake in the big house gave me a strange feeling of freedom. Have you ever felt that way? I could move in my little corner of the world without being seen and without having to explain myself to anyone.

I loosened the duct tape and squeezed past the plastic barriers.

The corridor resembled the one I'd just come from. Here too were small niches and differences in level and skylights that let in the morning light. On both sides were doors that I assumed led to the guest rooms. They were placed irregularly.

In the corridor there wasn't the slightest trace of any water damage. Everything looked clean and fresh. It even smelled a little new in a way that I hadn't sensed in the rest of the house.

I don't really know what I'd expected. Big dripping damp stains in the ceiling with half-full buckets below? No. But at least some signs of construction activity. Plastic on the floor, a small ladder, a construction fan, that sort of thing.

None of that was there.

I looked into some of the rooms too. Slightly different sizes, those that were bigger had more beds. Elegant and austere furnishings. I got a bit of a *Star Trek* feeling. Here lived the crew, all dressed in identical uniforms.

Not the slightest trace of any water damage in the bedrooms either.

Either I didn't understand a thing about what water damage looks like, which of course was quite possible. Maybe the fact that no traces were visible had to do with that superadvanced construction Dad had talked about.

Or else Dad didn't want us to sleep in the guest rooms.

I squeezed past the plastic barriers and carefully closed the opening behind me with tape.

The kitchen was quiet. The first light of dawn fell in through the big glass sections out toward the patio, but it only reached a short ways in, farther away from the windows the kitchen was in darkness.

I quickly found what I was looking for, in the refrigerator and in the bread box, and made myself a cheese sandwich with marmalade. Decided against orange juice and had a glass of cold two-percent milk instead.

The sandwich tasted just as amazing as I'd imagined. Is there anything better than a night sandwich?

I ate the sandwich standing up, too agitated to sit down. Didn't feel tired at all—on the contrary, I was exhilarated somehow. Everything had worked out so well with Maddy, the sandwich was so good and I knew that I would sleep well when I returned satisfied to bed.

I went up to the big sliding glass door out toward the patio, looked down toward the sea. A ribbon of light at the horizon.

Tomorrow I would sleep in a long time. What would we do later? Stay or go home? I didn't know. But regardless of that, Maddy and I would do it together, and that was the important thing.

I stuffed the rest of the sandwich in my mouth and turned in toward the house again to make another. My gaze swept across the darkened kitchen, and I noticed the outline of a piece of furniture I hadn't seen the day before. It stood at the far end of the kitchen, far from the windows, where the darkness was deepest.

At first I thought it was a big charcoal grill, you know, like a

Weber, with a cover over it that hung down to the floor. That was roughly the shape.

I stared into the darkness.

It was no grill. It was Barbro who was squatting there, with her arms around her knees and her head bowed to the side, away from me.

She sat absolutely stock-still. It looked like she was asleep.

Per gives me the glass and the tablet. I set it on my tongue, take a sip of water and tip my neck back. Puff my cheek out a little, just enough so that the tablet could glide down on the outside of the lower jaw, squeezed firmly by my cheek. I swallow and give Per a grateful look. Open wide on my own and show that I don't have anything under my tongue.

I'm starting to get so good at this.

Or am I?

Per looks searchingly at me.

I look puzzled, hold out my hand.

"Shall we take the next one, or what?"

"Listen," he says. Not unpleasantly or irritated, just a statement.

Knock it off. I know what you're up to.

I look at him sheepishly. Can't think of anything to say.

He taps my cheek with the tip of his index finger, far down on the chin bone, almost exactly where I'd hidden the tablet.

Damn it.

Resigned, I poke out the tablet with my tongue, take a little more water and swallow it.

Per keeps looking at me.

"Don't you think I've seen that before?"

"Worth a try," I mumble.

"It will be really hard on me if you were to succeed. I have a little responsibility for you, you know."

"Hmm."

"So can't we decide to forget that kind of nonsense during the time you're here? Then I would sleep better at night."

"Sure."

He gives me the next tablet. It's round and white and harmless, for stomach problems.

"I get that you think your life is over. But there is a way forward for you too. I promise. I've seen that many times."

A little later I'm lying on my cot, in the dark, waiting for the tablet to carry me away from this world, into unconsciousness.

Just away.

I wonder if Per believes in God. Admittedly he swears a bit, but much of what he says sounds suspiciously like grace, even if he doesn't use that word.

I'm starting to feel foggy, my brain more and more sluggish. It's nice.

They're so nice, Per and Soraya. Almost as if I were worth just as much as them. As if I were a completely normal person.

That goodness only makes me even sadder somehow.

I haven't earned it.

I'm not a person; I'm a monster.

A completely ordinary monster.

I am wakened by Maddy standing by the side of the bed, poking at me.

"Up and at 'em!" She smiled, leaned down and kissed me. "Are you hungry for breakfast?"

"Yeah."

I yawned, stretched, got up on one elbow.

"But you? I still want to go home today."

Maddy became silent. She looked surprised. And a little disappointed—she couldn't hide that, even though she tried. At last she nodded.

"Okay."

"I just... Well, that didn't feel cool yesterday."

Maddy sank down on the edge of the bed.

"No."

"And I understand that it's more about me than about Dad. I understand that he wants to reconcile, and all that. That's fine. But I don't think that..." I fell silent, wondering how to put it. Maddy waited for me continue. "It tears up so much shit inside me just seeing him, and being here. I really can't take it."

"No, I understand." Maddy reached across the bed and took my hand. "Then let's go home."

I slept really poorly after my nighttime outing to the kitchen. The discovery that Barbro was sitting on her haunches asleep in a corner almost scared the daylights out of me. I slipped away from there as quietly as I could, but then I lay in bed and tried to figure out what it was I'd actually seen. Was there some possibility I'd seen wrong? Who goes to sleep squatting, fully clothed?

And then there was the collision that I couldn't let go of either. That horrid thud was still ringing in my ears. I saw the fluttering summer dress before me.

I didn't intend to tell Maddy about Barbro. We were in a good place now. We'd gotten through our quarrel, I'd told about my paranoia and nightmares, now she knew who I was but we'd kept on going, it felt like. Should I present her with the next sick thing already the next morning?

By the way. I made a sandwich last night and then Barbro was sitting in a corner, sleeping.

Not a chance. Maddy would lose faith in me again. Lose faith in us.

It was almost ten when we headed for the kitchen. The weather was just as amazing today too.

Dad had already made breakfast. Or else it was Barbro. I cast a quick glance at the corner where she'd been sitting last night.

No one was there. Dad was pacing around on the patio talking on his phone in English. I poured a glass of smoothie, pink colored and creamy. Made a few open-faced sandwiches and added cucumber slices and pepper rings. Filled a mug with coffee and balanced it all in my arms out to the patio. Sat down at a table under a parasol. Maddy followed me.

Dad noticed that we'd come and ended his call. Then he came up to us and sat down at the same table.

"Hi. How are you doing?"

"Good," Maddy said curtly, taking a bite of her sandwich.

Dad truly looked worn out. His posture was different. Every movement looked like an exertion.

I took a big sip of smoothie and swallowed. Collected myself. Then I said, "We're planning to go home today."

Dad collapsed a little more, leaning with his elbows on the table. He had sunglasses on but it was easy to see that he was sad.

"Isak," he said at last, almost imploringly.

I didn't wait for him to continue. Instead I repeated more or less what I'd said to Maddy on the bed. That I wasn't angry at him, but that I wasn't ready to dig into the past either, it tore me up too much.

It was a half-truth, that I wasn't angry at him. Or more correctly a bit of a lie. I thought he'd acted out of control the night before. But there was no reason to explain that to a person I would never have any contact with again.

While I talked Dad took off his sunglasses. His face looked saggy now, the wrinkles in his skin deeper, the circles under his eyes bigger and darker. If he'd looked younger than his true age when we met him the first day, now on the contrary he looked older. An old, distressed person.

"I apologize for yesterday," he said, and his voice was a little hoarse. "I drank too much. And then I take pain relievers for the cancer. Not a good combination."

Maddy was sitting beside me. She stroked my back lightly, but didn't say anything.

Dad continued. "But… I thought it was a pleasant day…up until…"

His voice died away, and then he looked straight at me.

"I have so much I want to say to you."

I really wanted to get up and leave, get in our old car and drive away, anywhere at all, away from Ajkeshorn and Dad and Mom and Klara and the person I was when I was little. Away from the fireman.

"Such as forgive me," Dad continued. "And then I don't mean for yesterday."

There was silence. Both Dad and Maddy expected me to say something. I felt it like a hot spotlight against my face. I squirmed.

"Hmm. Like I said, I… I forgive you. But…for me that's enough."

I turned to Maddy.

"Maybe we should check when the ferries depart?"

"Hmm," she said, taking out her phone and starting to search.

Dad looked out over the sea, put on his sunglasses again.

"You're going to Oskarshamn, right?"

"Yes."

"There's a four, a seven-fifteen and an eleven-fifty."

There was silence for a moment. Maddy googled on Destination Gotland. I took a bite of my cheese sandwich with pepper rings, tried to chew as quietly as possible.

"The Lamborghini is yours in any event," Dad said quietly. "Regardless of what you think about it."

That fucking car.

"Give the money to charity instead," I said.

Maddy quickly determined that the four was fully booked, but that there was space on the seven-fifteen, in the cabin. I told her to make a reservation.

Dad took off his sunglasses again. It was apparent that he was thinking about something. At last he said, "Seven-fifteen, then you still have the whole day here on Gotland."

"That's right."

"There's one thing in particular that I've planned for us to do today. And we would still have time for that."

"Okay," I said, guardedly.

"You'll be back well in time before the boat departs. I guarantee it."

Why did he say "you"? Wouldn't Maddy be along? I didn't say anything, felt hesitant.

"Please," said Dad. "I beg you."

A couple of hours later we were approaching Visby Airport. I had a bad feeling in my gut.

Maddy was behind the wheel of our Nissan Micra, I was in the passenger seat and Dad had squeezed into the little back seat. We had packed up all our things and carried the bags out to the car. Maddy would spend the day in Visby while Dad and I made our "outing," as he called it. She had accepted without grumbling that Dad and I would be doing this on our own. Maybe she thought it would be nice to have a whole day in Visby to herself.

Dad hadn't said what we would do, but he recommended that I dress up a little, if I had that kind of clothing with me. So I put on a pair of light chinos and a short-sleeved, dark brown shirt with a collar, like a tennis shirt but in thin lambswool and with a short zipper in front. I felt like an Italian beach bum in that shirt. Not quite comfortable. But Maddy thought I was handsome in it. Along with dress sneakers in light brown leather. Dad had on a tight black T-shirt, black linen trousers and black linen jacket, plus some kind of basketball sneakers, in bright colors, yellow and green and violet and pink. They really drew your eyes to them, which was probably the idea.

Now the terminal building was in sight. Dad leaned up between the seats and pointed.

"Continue past the terminal. And then drive up to the gate over there."

Maddy did as he said. The airfield was surrounded by a high barbed wire fence. The gate was video monitored and had a little telephone alongside. Maddy stopped in front of it. Dad put his hand on my shoulder.

"Go to the phone and say that Freddy is here."

I didn't move.

"Listen," Dad said after a moment. He squeezed my shoulder lightly.

"If we don't get back when the boat is leaving..."

"We will. We will. I guarantee it, Isak."

I looked at Maddy. She smiled at me.

"There's plenty of time."

I sighed, opened the door and got out of the car. Went up to the gate phone and pressed on a button.

"Freddy is here."

There was a crackling sound. Then the big gate started to slowly roll to the side. I went back to the car and jumped in. Maddy drove through the opening.

Dad pointed to the left on the airfield.

A private jet was parked there.

We sat across from each other in the little cabin. I was facing forward, Dad backward. On the other side of a narrow aisle were another two facing seats. I looked out the window. Far below us the Baltic glistened dark blue. When I looked ahead I could see right into the cabin where the pilot, a man in his forties, was guiding the plane.

"Cheers," said Dad, loud enough to be heard over the engine sound, and raised his glass to me. He was drinking champagne from a crystal glass, I had asked for a Coke instead. I raised my glass in response and took a deep gulp. It was cold and good.

"Is this your plane?"

"No." Dad shook his head. "A friend who runs a computer company on Gotland. But I get to borrow the plane if it's available. In exchange for him getting to go to London on a gallery round a few times a year."

I nodded. This plane was pretty far from the private jets you see on TV and in movies. It was small and noisy and wasn't brand-new—that was apparent. The light beige leather seats were a bit compressed and shiny where people had sat. The safety belts didn't appear to be the absolute latest model. Nonetheless an extremely luxurious feeling, riding in your own jet plane. A feeling I was careful to keep to myself. I understood of course that this flight was yet another attempt from Dad's side to impress me, to please me. It wouldn't succeed; I had decided that.

The flight attendant, a rather short and slender woman my age, came with a tray for each of us. A piece of meat, a few dollops of swirled potatoes, broccoli crowns, a little package of sauce. For dessert a plastic-wrapped cube of carrot cake or the like. It didn't look all that inspiring but I hadn't eaten since breakfast and started shoveling it in. Roughly the same time as I was peeling off the plastic from the carrot cake the noise from the engines quieted a little, and the plane quietly descended. I looked out the window; we were already flying over land.

"Where are we?" I asked.

"We're going to Riga."

The plane touched down just as I was finishing the last bit of cake. Dad applauded sarcastically and laughed. The pilot raised his right arm in the air and displayed his middle finger, without taking his eyes off the runway. Soon the plane stopped moving and ground personnel rolled a stairway toward us. Dad exchanged a few words with the pilot. They seemed to know each other well.

I smiled at the stewardess, bent down to come out through the doorway. The sun was burning just as much here as on

Gotland, and hot winds chased across the open field. I took the stairs down and stood on the runway. Soon Dad followed. The engines were still running and it smelled of jet fuel.

Nearby a taxi was waiting, a late-model electric Mercedes with tinted windows. A well-groomed man in his thirties waved to us. He was wearing a dark suit, white shirt and tie. We walked over.

"Mr. Barzal?"

"Yes."

"Welcome."

The guy opened a rear door for Dad, who climbed in and sat down. I got into the back seat from the other side. The chauffeur closed the door on Dad's side, rounded the car and got behind the wheel. When he closed the door with a plop there was complete silence and the world was closed out. Gently the car glided away, through a gate like the one in Visby, then a short time later out on a freeway.

It was cool and pleasant in the car with a smell of new leather. Small, concealed lamps discreetly lit up the handles on the rear doors in a cold blue color. I had plenty of leg room, even though I was sitting behind the driver. I leaned my head back against the neck rest and closed my eyes.

Suddenly I felt how incredibly tired I was. If I could spend the rest of my life in this car I would be content. Dad noticed that.

"We'll be driving about twenty minutes, so you'll have time to rest a little."

"Good," I mumbled.

I had no idea where we were going, but I couldn't care less. I took a deep breath and let my body sink down a little deeper in the seat.

I woke up with my mouth open and my neck at an uncomfortable angle. When I sat up straighter I had to work to get my head on an even keel, it felt like. Still a little dizzy, I looked out the tinted side window. It looked like a run-down suburb. Multistory buildings in gray, cracked concrete, flaking paint.

I had a sense of sitting in a hypermodern spaceship, on a visit to a strange, primitive planet.

"You're waking up at just the right time," said Dad.

The car turned into a big courtyard with multistory buildings on three sides. The buildings were dilapidated, but in the courtyard was a large playground with swings and jungle gyms in bright colors. Everything looked new. Small children played and shrieked. Staff in pink vests monitored the play. They all appeared to be women.

The car drove up to an entry and stopped. Another three women were waiting here, like a small reception committee. One of them was rather formally dressed in a dark suit. She smiled and waved at Dad. He waved back, opened the car door and turned toward me.

"Welcome to Skirotava."

Skirotava turned out to be an orphanage. The woman in the suit was named Galina and she was the director of this orphanage and several others too, if I understood correctly. The orphanages were run by the authorities in Latvia but with major contributions from Dad.

Galina showed Dad and me around and told about the operation in perfect English. The other women, whose names I heard when we shook hands but which I've forgotten, also followed along on the tour, like two silent shadows. They only opened their mouths when Galina asked them about something.

The very generous donations from Mr. Barzal had made it possible for the premises to be renovated, and to build the nice playground we passed on our way in, Galina told us.

I sneaked a glance at Dad. He didn't react at all when his name was mentioned; he didn't act as if he'd heard it at all. His face was serious, and he looked moved. But it was so constant, so totally without changes. I got the feeling that he'd put on a mask. What was really going on beneath it was hard to guess.

Dad lit up and went over to a girl with cerebral palsy in a wheelchair. She appeared to be in her early teens.

"*Sveiki*, Tatjana!" Dad said happily, and took her withered hand in his. She reacted with a moan. One of the silent women with us on the tour hurried up to the wheelchair and said something in Latvian to Tatjana.

"This girl is completely unbelievable," Dad said to me, still with Tatjana's hand in his. "She's the most amazing artist." He turned to Galina.

"Shall we go to the workshop?"

"Yes, a very good idea," said Galina. She gave a command in Latvian to the woman by the wheelchair, who nodded.

The workshop, or studio, was a fairly large room where you could draw and paint and clip and paste and build and work with clay. It was Dad's idea and his pet project, I understood. He took over from Galina and told about it himself. The idea was that even the children in this home needed to express themselves artistically, maybe especially them.

He showed some pictures that Tatjana had made, and explained that she used both the one hand and her mouth to guide the brush. I couldn't see that the pictures depicted anything; they were just an incoherent daub of colors. But that applied to most modern art, in my opinion. Tatjana was probably no worse than anyone else.

"Very nice," I said, smiling appreciatively at her. "That's amazing."

Dad explained that at every visit he selected a number of pictures which he then sold to his wealthy clients around the world. That brought in a good deal of money. Then he added just as much himself and sent it all to Galina.

After the guided tour she and the other women followed us out to the taxi. As we pulled away they stood there as if at attention and waved to us, until we turned the corner and they were out of sight.

Dad looked at his watch.

"It's only two thirty, or just past… I thought that we fly home at four, then we'll land in Visby two hours before the ferry leaves."

"Sure, that will be good."

"Shall we go into town and have a beer? Better than sitting around at the airport."

The closer we got to the city center, the cleaner and tidier the streets and buildings became, almost block by block. The taxi dropped us off at the end of a pedestrian street paved with cobblestones. Dad instructed the driver to wait nearby and then we would be back in an hour.

The sun had been blazing all day, and the whole town steamed from a dense heat. The buildings looked old but were newly plastered and recently painted. Like a fresher Gamla Stan in Stockholm, more or less. Tourists streamed in and out of souvenir shops, eating establishments and cafes.

Dad piloted us to a restaurant with outdoor seating on the shaded side of the street. He'd been there before. The special thing about this place, he explained, was that it had Riga's largest assortment of beer. Actually the biggest he'd encountered anywhere in the world. When I got a menu in my hand I understood that probably wasn't an exaggeration. Thirty-some different kinds of canned beer, hundreds of different kinds in bottles.

Dad recommended a German bottled beer he'd had there previously, Bock something, so we each ordered one. Soon the waiter came back with two half-liter bottles, two ice-cold tall glasses and a big plate of salted pretzels.

I tasted the beer.

Damn, it was good.

The cold filled my mouth, while the bubbles tickled and scratched in my throat.

A deep, full-bodied taste. Bitter, yes, but also a little sour and almost a tiny bit sweet. I'd never tasted a light beer that had so much flavor.

Damn, how good life was.

The beer was so good, the pretzels so salty and crispy. It was hot, but not too hot, when you sat quietly in the shade like we did. The tiredness had softened me up. Now when I was drinking the intoxication came almost with the first sip, a feeling of casting loose from existence. I hovered and floated; someone else could hold onto the rudder. A balloon on a string. All the anxiety and fear simply evaporated. I looked neither forward nor backward; I looked at the world exactly as it appeared right in front of my nose, just at this moment, and I felt that it was good and beautiful.

Dad ordered each of us another one of the same.

I asked Dad if he was involved in other charitable projects, other places in the world. He told me that he donated a painting or two to charity auctions now and then, but Skirotava was the biggest deal.

"Damn, I could really go for a cig now," he said. "You don't have any on you, do you?"

"No. But can't we buy some here? I wouldn't mind having one myself."

Dad called to the waiter and ordered a pack of cigarettes. Soon it was on the table, with a lighter and an ashtray beside it. Dad opened the pack and we each took one.

I took a deep drag. My completely perfect life just became a notch more perfect.

"The thing is..." said Dad, letting the smoke circle out of his mouth as he thoughtfully looked at the tourists streaming past us out on the street. "You do realize that this thing with charity, it's just another thing you do for the sake of your own enjoyment. It's like it's neither worse nor better than driving a Lamborghini."

"I don't think the children at that orphanage would agree."

"But the world is so complicated, you can't possibly know what effect your actions will have in the long run. This orphanage may be completely counterproductive. Maybe it will lead to more children being abandoned, because the possibility exists. More children having unhappy lives."

"I don't believe that."

"No, but you don't know. I don't either. I'm not going to stop with Skirotava—it makes me feel good, feeling respect and admiration for myself. I'm sure you noticed that when we were there."

"Yes." I thought about Dad's enthusiasm when he told about the studio.

"But I have no illusions about why I'm doing it. We humans are programmed to fit into the group. A thing like this makes other people think well of you, it benefits me and it feels good inside. So it's pure egoism."

I took a sip of my second beer, licked away the foam from my upper lip.

"Hmm," I said.

"I don't believe in good and evil," Dad continued. "It's an old superstition, like god and the devil. What I know is this: first there was the big bang, thirteen billion years passed and then I was born. Now I'll die soon. I get sixty years, more or less. Then I'll be dead for all eternity, an endless number of billions of years. Don't I have the right then to make the absolute best possible use of my life, this millisecond that I exist?"

"Hmm," I said again.

Dad's reasoning was starting to get a bit convoluted for me. He ran ahead so fast that I lost sight of him.

I also had to pee.

"I think so," said Dad. "I think it's my duty."

I thought that this kind of speculation probably comes up when you realize you have a short time left to live. Dad looked at me.

"Promise me that. Because that's what I've learned. When life invites you to dance, then you dance. Okay? Shall we shake on it?" Dad smiled and extended his hand to me, I reached out mine and then we shook hands.

When life invites you to dance. I didn't really know what that meant, but it sounded good anyway.

The taxi was parked where we left it. We jumped in. Dad sat in front this time.

My intoxication was absolutely world-class. A perfectly balanced tipsiness. I was longing for Maddy. In an hour or so I would be with her again. Maybe a little hangover would have started to set in then, I suspected. But we would drive on board the boat to Oskarshamn, go and have a bite to eat in the restaurant and then I would sleep well in the armchair in the cabin. My hand on Maddy's knee.

Soon we arrived at the airport. The chauffeur drove into the airfield by way of the steel gate. A man came walking on the road ahead of us. He was wearing a suit with a yellow safety vest over it. The taxi stopped, and Dad rolled down the window on his side. The man leaned down. He smiled amiably.

"Good day, Mr. Barzal, how are you today?"

"I'm fine, thank you."

"Good to hear. They are just preparing your plane for the flight back."

"We need to leave pretty soon."

"Yes…we just have some protocols we need to go through… some checks."

"So…is there a problem with the plane, or…?"

"No problem. No problem. But we just need to go through the protocol, because…yes."

The man was still smiling at Dad. Dad on the other hand wasn't smiling. He opened the door and got out of the car.

I checked my watch. Ten past four. We had plenty of time. Even if we took off an hour from now Maddy and I would make it to the boat to Oskarshamn in time.

The driver sighed and turned off the engine, which was only marked by one kind of discreet humming being replaced by another.

Dad and the man were having a discussion a short distance from the car. I could hear their voices but not what was being said. Dad sounded irritated, and the man tried to calm him.

I took a deep breath and sank deeper down in the seat. Looked out the dark-tinted side window. The runway was bathed in sunlight. The air was quivering over the asphalt.

The air conditioning came on. There was ringing in my ears.

"Isak? Isak?"

Dad had his hand on my shoulder, and he was shaking me lightly.

At first I didn't understand where I was but soon it all came back. I was still in the back seat of the taxi. Dad had opened the door on my side and tried to wake me.

I'd passed out. Oh God. I straightened up, and my neck was sore again. Gravel in my eyes, sandpaper in my mouth, I'd been sleeping with my mouth open.

Dad held his cellphone in his hand and handed it over to me.

"It's Maddy. She wants to talk with you."

"Yes, wait."

I got out of the taxi. My whole body was stiff. I had to move around to wake up. I stretched, arched my back, yawned. Then I took the phone.

"Hello?"

"Hi, darling...have you been sleeping?"

That voice, like vanilla, sweet and warm.

"Yeah."

"Fredrik says there's a problem with the airplane."

"Yeah."

"And that it will be hard for you to make it back in time for the boat."

Suddenly I was wide-awake.

How long had I been asleep, actually?

I looked at my watch. Ten past six. But what the hell. I stared at Dad.

"Why didn't you wake me?"

"The plane is still not ready."

"No?"

"I'm really sorry about this, Isak. I've argued like hell with them. I don't know if there really is something wrong with the plane or if they're just messing with me for some reason. Sorry."

I shook my head, clenched my teeth.

"You promised that we'd be back in time."

"I know. Sorry, I'm completely shattered. Nothing like this has ever happened to me before, I swear. So damned typical."

I heard Maddy's voice on the phone. She was trying to make contact with me again.

"Isak? Isak, listen..."

I brought the phone to my ear again, sighed.

"I'm getting so fucking tired of this."

"But listen, take it easy. These things happen. For my part there's no problem. One night more or less. Check into a hotel, get a good night's sleep, then we'll see each other tomorrow instead."

"But where will you sleep?"

"I'll probably drive up to Ajkeshorn again."

Maddy by herself in that screwed-up house, with the old wooden gods and the masks, and with Barbro. It felt unpleasant.

"Isn't there another boat, later tonight? Shouldn't we take that one?"

"It gets to Oskarshamn at like three o'clock and then we'd have to drive for a couple of hours. I can't deal with that."

"No."

"And you're probably really tired too. Seems like it."

Yes, I really was. My head was working in slow motion. My thoughts dragged their legs from one brain hemisphere to the other. My whole body longed to stretch out on a bed and sleep. I rubbed my eyes.

"Hmm."

"I can hear that, darling…go to a hotel and sleep. Your dad will surely arrange something good."

"Okay."

"Then I'll see you tomorrow instead, energetic and well-rested."

"Hmm. Maybe it's just as well."

"Shall we talk tonight?"

"Let's do that."

"Good. Love you."

"Love you too."

I ended the call and handed the phone back to Dad.

"Sorry about this," he said. "I'm embarrassed."

"We'll just have to stay here tonight then."

Dad nodded and started tapping on the phone.

"Yes. I'm on it."

We hopped into the taxi and drove into the city center again. The driver dropped us off in front of a well-kept building from the previous turn of the century. A porter in a dark green coat and tall hat welcomed us with a little bow. I followed Dad up the steps and we came into a luxurious hotel lobby. Thick wall-to-wall carpets, big couches, mirrors with gold frames, stucco like sprayed cream along pillars and walls.

Dad went up to the reception counter, where a pretty young woman welcomed us. She was wearing a uniform and a tasteful silk scarf with her dark brown hair gathered in a perfect bun. Dad said that he had reserved two rooms under the name Barzal. He also explained that we needed help getting a few things: toothbrushes, toothpaste, razor and shaving cream. A change of clothes for each with socks, underwear and T-shirt. Dad presented his requests as if this were the most natural thing in the world, and the receptionist nodded amiably; of course she would take care of it.

The world of the rich. No problems, no shame, only opportunities.

"What sizes do you want for the clothes?" the receptionist asked.

"For me large," said Dad. He looked at me. "For him…extra large?"

I nodded. The receptionist sized me up from top to toe, pursed her lips a little.

"Hmm, I would say extra extralarge." She was staring at her screen but I sensed the shadow of a smile on her mouth.

Our rooms were on the same corridor, on the second floor. Dad suggested that we meet in the lobby in a couple of hours, and I nodded silently without meeting his eyes. I was still angry at him.

I opened the door and stepped into the biggest hotel room I'd ever been in. Nothing was crowded here; the floor space was considerable. The decorative style from the lobby was repeated. Thick wall-to-wall carpet, furnishings in cream white, brown and gold. A gigantic double bed. Desk, a whole lounge suite. Big bathroom, completely tiled, with shower and bathtub, old-style sink and mixer. A little balcony out toward the street.

Sitting on the pillow was a small piece of dark chocolate. I put it in my mouth. But the urge for sweetness wouldn't let go. I found the minibar in one of the drawers on the desk. In a few minutes I'd stuffed a bag of salted cashew nuts, a Snickers and an orange-flavored San Pellegrino into me. Then I felt a little better.

I drew the heavy curtains, which immediately put the room into dense darkness. Stretched out on the bed. It was very nice, just firm enough. The pillow was high and broad but too soft. I folded it in half and put it under my head.

I closed my eyes. A life in luxury.

I woke up after an hour or so. Enjoyed lying there in the dark, gliding in and out of sleep. Listening to the muffled sounds from the life at the hotel, and life in the city. Someone walking in the corridor. Silence again. A door that opened and closed. Silence again. A Vespa drove past on the street outside the hotel. Silence again.

After a while I climbed out of bed and pulled back the curtains. In a thick leather folder on the desk I found the password for the WiFi. Surfed on both *Aftonbladet* and *Expressen* to see if they'd reported on a little girl who'd been run over or was missing. Also found the website helagotland.se with local news from Gotland, but there was nothing there either. I felt a little calmer.

I splashed water on my face and left the room. Took the stairs down to the lobby, where Dad was waiting for me. He asked if I was hungry.

"They have a pretty good bar menu here. You can get a burger or a steak. Whatever you want."

That sounded good, I thought. We went through a couple of glass double doors next to the reception counter and came into the bar area. One side faced toward the street. Along the windows were tall bar tables with stools and we sat down there. Menus were already on the table. I ordered a baconburger and a can of beer.

We hadn't been sitting very long before there was knocking on the window.

Outside two young women were standing who appeared to

come from another world. A fashion show in Paris or something. Both of them around twenty, slender and tall, the one with dark wavy hair that stood out to the sides as much as it hung down. The other with short blond hair, probably bleached, because I saw darker tresses under it. A perfect frame for a perfect face.

"Fredrik! Hi!" The girl with the dark bushy hair laughed with her whole face, her eyes became just two slits, and she waved energetically at Dad. She was the one who had knocked on the window. Dad looked happily surprised and waved back. Stood up from the table.

"Hi, Masha! Come on in!"

He gestured to the women. *Come in to us.*

I ask Soraya if she's heard anything more about the psychiatric evaluation, but she hasn't. I don't know yet if I need to go to Huddinge and do the big assessment.

Karin told me that the type of trauma I was subjected to when I was little can lead to dissociation, that you build up your own reality. And she talked about paranoia.

I could have told more about the outing to Riga, if I'd wanted to lead her onto that track.

The sweet, good beer that was so high in alcohol.

The airplane that didn't get permission to take off.

The women who happened to see us as they passed by outside the hotel.

All planned to the slightest detail.

And Karin would think that I was paranoid.

But if it turns out that you were right the whole time…? Is that still paranoia?

Masha and the blonde woman, whose name was Elena, greeted Dad. Masha was effusive; there were hugs and cheek kisses and shrieks and laughter, while Elena was more reserved.

The women looked like they were on their way to a super-exclusive party. Masha was wearing a tight white dress in some thin fabric, which clung to her body all the way down to her knees. It was held up by a ring of gold around her neck. Her golden brown arms and shoulders were bare. Elena had a black top with shoulder straps, and the tightest black jeans I'd ever seen. Sandalettes with sky-high heels. Her earrings glistened blue and accentuated her ice-blue gaze.

They sat down on stools at our table, Masha beside me and Elena beside Dad. He ordered champagne. Then he introduced me.

"This is Isak, my son."

"Really? You have a son?" Masha sounded as if it were the best news she'd ever heard. She laughed and extended her hand.

"So nice to meet you, Isak! I'm Masha."

"Hi, Masha, nice to meet you." I extended my hand to Elena.

"Hello. Isak."

"Elena. Nice to meet you." Elena's hand was cool. Her gaze on me was firm, she didn't look away. But the expression was hard to interpret. Shy, but curious. Challenging, but also inviting. I thought she smiled a little; it was as if she was inviting me to a mutual understanding, as if we both stood a little outside the situation we found ourselves in.

I know what's going on here. You know that too, right? Like that.

"So, what do you do?" asked Masha. "Are you an artist too?"

"No," I said. "I work with the... What do you say...care for old people."

"Oh, that's so nice! That's great!"

Masha leaned a little toward me and put her hand on my arm. Her curly hair grazed my cheek. She smelled marvelous, a deep and mysterious perfume.

Dad explained that Masha and Elena were art students in Riga and that he met them through Skirotava. They had interned at his studio on Fårö, so they were familiar with Ajkeshorn.

A waiter came with a bottle of champagne and four glasses. We toasted and drank. I didn't like it, but I put on a good face.

"You know, your father is a genius," said Masha.

"Okay," I said, rather neutrally, which made Elena burst out in a little laugh. There I revealed how little I know about art, I thought, but it was worth it to see Elena's warm smile. Masha continued.

"He is. I swear to God." She looked at Dad. "Some of the things he's painted…it's like the most profound experience I ever had."

"Yeah, yeah, that's enough," said Dad, raising his hand dismissively.

"I don't know much about art, I guess," I said.

"How do you like the sofa?" Elena asked. She fixed her eyes on me and sipped her champagne. I thought she looked a little mischievous behind the glass.

"The sofa at Ajkeshorn? The one going up in the…" I made a gesture to show how something puffed up to the ceiling.

"Yeah, yeah."

"Uh… I wouldn't want one at home."

"It's ugly, right?"

Dad looked at Elena.

"You think it's ugly?" Dad sounded offended, but I suspected that he was joking.

"Yes, Fredrik. It's ugly, and scary." Elena said it in a calm voice, as if she was stating an indescribable fact.

"That sofa cost me a fortune."

"I'm sorry, you're a genius, but it gives me the creeps."

Dad looked at me and shook his head.

"I hate art students that have their own opinions."

Elena looked at me too, and said, "It's scary, right?"

"Yes. Absolutely. I don't want to go under it."

Elena extended her glass toward me with a serious look, I extended mine, the glasses met and a light clink was heard, a seal to show that we thought alike.

★ ★ ★

Our food came to the table and we started to eat. I'd managed to get really hungry and a little dizzy besides from drinking beer and champagne on an empty stomach. The ladies had already eaten, and didn't want anything. They were actually on their way to a party but it didn't matter if they were a little late, Masha said, it was so nice to sit here and talk with me and "Frederic." The champagne was finished and Dad ordered another bottle.

Masha wanted to know what I thought of Riga. I explained that I hadn't seen too much of the city, but that what I'd seen looked nice. Masha's opinion was that Riga livened up at night. There were clubs that you otherwise only found in London or on Ibiza, she said.

The ladies went out on the sidewalk and smoked. I stole a glance at them standing outside the window. Elena looked at me, and our eyes met.

"Fine ladies, huh?" said Dad, looking at me with a little smile.

"Mmm," I said, and looked down at my plate. I'd finished the burger. All that was left were some rings of pickled red onion and a lettuce leaf, and some French fries at the bottom of a little steel basket. I fished out the remnants with my index finger and middle finger and stuffed them in my mouth.

Fine ladies.

Something in the way that Dad said that made me feel uncomfortable.

I checked the time. It was almost ten now and I thought I ought to give Maddy a call before it got too late. But soon Masha and Elena came in again, we kept talking and drinking and I forgot to call.

Neither Dad nor I wanted any dessert, but there was a little package on the menu with coffee, cognac and chocolate truffle that I thought would sit nicely. It would be the last order of the evening for me, I thought.

Dad ordered the same package as me. He gave his chocolate truffle to Elena. She opened her mouth, set the truffle on her tongue and bit. She probably didn't want to ruin her lipstick. I offered Masha my truffle, but she suggested that we share, and I said okay. She took it with thumb and index finger, brought it to her mouth, opened wide and sank her blindingly white teeth into it, biting it off in the middle.

"Mmm…" she said. "That's incredible." She chewed on the truffle.

Gradually as the evening had passed Masha ended up closer and closer to me. Now she was sitting so close that our bodies were touching all the time.

She held out the other half toward my mouth. The soft mass of chocolate had marks from her teeth. She leaned even closer, supporting herself with her hand on my thigh.

"Open your mouth. Be a good boy."

I opened wide and she stuffed the rest of the truffle in my mouth.

Her face was so close to mine.

I cast a glance across the table. Elena was looking at us, and I saw something in her eyes I hadn't seen before, something dark.

"Wait," said Masha. "You have a little…" She stroked my lower lip with the tip of her index finger.

Elena's gaze. Something that had flashed in her blue eyes. Desire.

He's mine.

Do you understand what that did to me?

I drank up the cognac, and when Dad and the ladies each wanted a drink and asked what I wanted, I didn't say, *Thank you, what a nice evening, now I'll say good night.* Instead I said, "Gin and tonic."

Masha sat close beside me, her hand stayed on my thigh under the table and Elena sought my gaze again and again. I don't remember what we talked about, but we laughed and we had fun. It felt as if I barely remembered when I was last completely sober—was it yesterday? The day before? But now the intoxication was at a perfect level again; I felt strong and handsome and sexy and fun.

We had more drinks. Caipirinhas and Moscow Mules and Snowballs. Elena's favorite, Black Russian. Vodka and coffee liqueur. The time simply disappeared, and it got dark outside.

I don't remember who first brought up the idea that we should move on. I only know that it wasn't me. But Dad, Masha and Elena were in agreement that it would be a scandal if I left Riga without getting to experience a little of the night life.

I checked the time. It was past midnight. For the first time in a long while I thought about my shipwrecked plan to go to bed fairly early. A diffuse feeling of shame and guilty conscience penetrated through the fog of alcohol. But I would be lying if I said that it was particularly strong.

"I don't know," I said.

Elena reached across the table and took my hand.

"Isak, you have to come. Please. You won't regret it."

That ice-blue gaze.

What was it Dad said?

When life invites you to dance.

I smiled at Elena.

"All right, just because you ask so nice," I said. "Let's go."

"Daugava, right?" said Dad, and looked searchingly at Masha and Elena. They nodded.

"Yeah. Definitely Daugava."

Dad called a taxi and soon we were cruising along the streets of Riga in the light summer night. The car we were in was a limousine, an extended variation where the seats were turned toward each other. There were a lot of people out, mostly young people, who staggered from place to place in various degrees of intoxication. But the sound hardly penetrated in to us in the car, and the windows were tinted. We could see out, but no one could see in. What was going on out there didn't concern us.

Masha pressed her body into mine and had my hand on her knee. Elena placed one leg over the other, and her bare foot in the sandalette rocked in the air over my outstretched legs. The stiletto heel scraped against my pants.

I had stopped wondering where this would end.

Dad had put his arm over Elena's shoulders, and she let it stay there.

After only a few minutes we had left Riga's presentable city center behind us and drove through rougher blocks. Worn apartment buildings alternated with vacant lots. Soon no apartment buildings were seen either. The streets were deserted and edged by small industries and dilapidated warehouses. The driver had to turn to the side sometimes because there were big holes in the asphalt.

"So...where is this place?" I asked. "Is it far?" Dad shook his head.

"No, we'll be there soon. Right away."

The taxi turned right, onto a slightly narrower road. It felt like we were on our way toward the heart of the run-down industrial area. But suddenly I could see other people along the street, dressed-up young people moving in the same direction as we were driving. We met a taxi, then another. More and more people, large groups talking and laughing but striding purposefully.

Now I saw the line. Or at least the end of it. More and more people joined it all the time. The driver reduced speed. The limousine cruised slowly up to where it started. I looked out the side window and saw several people stare back at me, with a mixture of respect and disdain. I knew they were staring at a black car window, that they couldn't see me. I was happy about that.

The ones that float on top. Now I was one of them.

The car stopped behind the red taillights of another taxi, which also let people out. Dad gave his card to the driver. The side door glided open on its own, and the pulse of the night struck us. Babble and laughter and shrieks from hundreds of people, rumbling car engines, smells of perfume and diesel and hot metal.

I got out and extended my hand to Masha, who also got out. Elena slid closer to the door, and I extended my other hand and helped her out of the limousine too.

The sky was deep blue now. Only at the horizon slightly lighter remnants of twilight were seen. Headlights and phone screens punctured the darkness. A night breeze fanned against my face and my bare forearms. It almost felt a little chilly.

The line ended by the end of a big dilapidated warehouse of corrugated sheet metal. A guy in his midtwenties dressed in a suit decided who got to come in and who had to stay outside. He had help from a couple of beefy security guards. The guy looked grim, but when he caught sight of Elena and Masha his facial expression changed in a moment. A big, warm, welcoming smile.

"Hey! Welcome!"

"Hi, Stani! Nice to see you!"

Cheek kisses, hugs, laughter. The guy squeezed my arm lightly, looked me deep in the eyes and smiled.

"Enjoy."

I felt noticed and welcome, and it was over in a second. What a pro. He let go of me and turned his eyes toward Dad, who caught up with us.

"Mr. Barzal! So welcome!"

"Long time no see, haha..."

We went into the old warehouse. Here it was dark; no lamps were on, only a little twilight that seeped in through narrow windows up by the ceiling. Our steps echoed. You felt more than saw that you were surrounded by a big space, like in a church.

Farther inside the warehouse I saw the outlines of a high overhead crane, almost up by the ceiling, like a massive dinosaur on four legs. Suddenly a pair of doors opened before us, light cut through the darkness of the warehouse and people walking ahead of us disappeared into an elevator.

I heard a pounding from the underground. A dull, dull bass.

The elevator doors closed, and once again it was dark in the warehouse. Now we had reached the doors. I saw that there was another pair of doors beside the first ones. Masha looked expectantly at me, and said, "Just wait and see. You'll like it."

"In the seventies the Russians started planning for a subway in Riga," said Dad. "They worked on it for over twenty years."

Now the other pair of doors opened. We stepped into the empty elevator along with four or five other guests who came after us. It was roomy and certainly could have held fifteen people. On the walls dark-tinted mirrors, gold and light panels. The contrast couldn't have been greater to the run-down warehouse we passed through.

"But there were problems in the eighties," Dad continued. "The bedrock under Riga proved to be difficult, and the Soviet Union ran out of money. So the whole project was shut down."

The pounding got stronger with every second that passed. Mother Earth's own heartbeat.

I nodded, and stole a glance at myself in the mirror, surrounded by Elena and Masha. So crazy good-looking we were, like on a movie poster. The light was so perfect.

"But," said Dad, "they actually managed to build one station. Daugava."

The elevator stopped. The doors opened. I simply gaped. Elena and Masha had to lead me out of the elevator.

In front of me an oblong space, with a high, arched ceiling. The old subway station. The floor packed with dancing people. Deafening sound, a bass that pounded deep inside your chest, like a tickling at your heart. And the light, the whole ceiling was one big light rig, with patterns and colors that rolled from one end of the room to the other. One moment the bow-shaped ceiling pulsed gently and glided seamlessly through the whole color spectrum, blue green yellow orange red violet blue again, to then suddenly turn completely black for several seconds—the drop in the music—and then explode in a freezing white stroboscope effect when the bass boomed again, two times per second.

The air was damp from all the warm bodies; it smelled of perfume, sweat and pyrotechnics.

The well-planned attack on all my senses short-circuited my brain, so I couldn't think. It was brutal. It was crazy. I didn't know if I'd ended up in heaven or in hell.

But I loved it.

I think that I actually started to giggle hysterically.

Elena took my hand and pulled me out on the dance floor, right into the sweaty, jumping mass of people. We raised our hands toward the ceiling and started dancing.

I'm not big on dancing actually, and the first few minutes I was self-conscious, as if I was seeing myself from outside. But soon my body took over. I had never experienced that before. I became one with the music, I didn't have a single thought and my body moved completely on its own.

Euphoria. Looked up, like a gaping, smiling fool. The arched ceiling high above, now a firework that exploded, the most beautiful thing I'd ever seen.

Lasers cut like knives through the darkness.

Masha took a firm hold on my neck, heaved herself up and kissed me. My hands on Elena's hips, our bodies tight together.

I never wanted to stop moving. Never. Let this go on the rest of my life, let me be in this moment forever, I felt.

Dad was gone for a moment. Didn't notice when he disappeared. But now he came back, put his hand on my shoulder, leaned forward and said something in my ear.

It was impossible to hear what.

"What?" I shouted, leaning my head down and turning my ear to him. Dad tried again, with more force.

"...room!" he shouted.

Still impossible to hear what he said. Dad saw my perplexed facial expression, held up two plastic cards and gestured with his thumb. *This way.*

He led the way through the jumping, bouncing sea of people, and we followed. Passed bars where guests almost climbed over each other to order, and a couple of pillars with a flat surface on top where scantily clad ladies and guys were dancing. Soon we had the worst crowding behind us. We were on the platform. On the tracks a row of older-model subway cars were lined up, four or five of them. They didn't look worn or shabby; on the contrary, they shone in black and gold. A couple of security guards monitored the traffic to and from the cars.

"The VIP rooms here aren't really like the ones at other places," Dad said. He gave me one plastic card and continued to walk toward the car farthest away. The one end disappeared into the darkness of the tunnel. How far did the tunnel actually go? How far did they get before the whole project was shut down? There was something fascinating, and a little creepy, about this finished station that had never been put to use.

We went toward the nearest end of the car. Dad tapped his card against a plate alongside the doors and they glided apart, like on any subway car.

In roughly half the car the original furnishings remained. An aisle, with seats on either side. But everything was of course pimped beyond recognition. All the steel tubes were gilded, and the seats and headrests had velvet padding in various subdued colors. Moss green, wine red, grayish blue. The floor was covered by a thick, black carpet. Discreet lighting. And then big green plants, enormous ficus and what looked like ivy, the vegetation climbed in through the windows and spread across the seats and floor.

Have you seen pictures from that city outside Chernobyl that was simply abandoned the minute the nuclear power accident happened? I got that feeling in that subway car. As if nature was in the process of retaking ground. How the plants could look so lively and lush despite the lack of sunlight I didn't understand. But maybe these plants got ultraviolet light when the club was closed, or else they were fake. In that case—a really really good fake.

The doors closed behind us and dampened the sound from the dance floor to a subdued, muffled rumble. Dad continued toward the far end of the car. He turned toward me.

"This car is ours, the whole night. Only you and I have the key." He held up the plastic card.

The far end was furnished with low sofas, or divans, around a coffee table. Was it the idea that you should lie down or sit? There were also lots of pillows in various sizes and a big mirror in the ceiling. A harem. Or the world's most exclusive pillow room. Heavy curtains in the same subdued colors as the rest of the interior concealed this end of the car from curious gazes from outside.

On the coffee table were ice buckets with champagne, vodka, beer bottles. Bowls with nuts and chocolate pieces and candy. Dad grasped the champagne bottle by the neck, started to pull off the metal around the cork. He nodded toward the bowl of candy and smiled.

"Do you see there? Do you see what that is?"

I looked. There were little red jelly monkeys.

"Is that Zoo?"

"Yes." Dad smiled. "It was your favorite when you were little, do you remember? Always Zoo on Friday nights."

"Mmm," I said, taking a fistful of the little red monkeys and stuffing them in my mouth.

"Isak loved those when he was a kid," Dad explained to Masha and Elena.

"Ah…that's so sweet," said Masha. She took a few and tasted, while Elena took champagne glasses from a shelf. Dad pressed the cork out of the bottle with a distinct pop. It bounced against the mirror in the ceiling and down into the pillows on the divan. He started pouring into the glasses. I was still sweating after the movement on the dance floor. Pulled my hand across my forehead, my fingers got wet.

"Uh..." I started. "I think I need to drink a little water."

"Sure," said Dad. He showed that there was a fridge full of mineral water and soda and juice. Anything you could desire. I took a bottle of mineral water, screwed off the cork and drank almost all of it in one big gulp. Like an ice-cold shredder through my throat, a stream that was felt all the way down in my stomach. Wonderful. I held the cold, empty glass bottle against my cheek and closed my eyes. Elena came up to me and gave me a glass of champagne.

"You poor thing," she said. "You're too hot."

She pulled the zipper on my tennis shirt down as far as it went. The fabric was glued to the skin between my pecs, it was dark from damp and sweat had run down in the gap. Elena took hold of the fabric and pulled it loose. Tugged on it to fan me.

She was standing so close now. I could look down at her side part, the dark roots in her blond hair. She bent her neck, looked up at me, so close that she couldn't look me in both eyes at the same time. Her gaze moved around between my eyes, my nose, my lips.

"Better?" She continued to fan with the shirt.

"Yeah. Please don't stop."

A drop of sweat crossed my jugular notch and stopped when it reached my sternum. Hesitated before continuing. Elena captured it with her index finger, put the finger in her mouth, sucked in the drop. Her other hand had glided in under the shirt and was now playing on my stomach, in the hair under my navel, right above the pants lining.

I got an erection. Elena's gaze was fixed on my lips.

"Cheers, everyone!" Dad's voice broke through Elena's and

my enchantment. He had raised his glass in the air and was smiling broadly. Masha too. Elena let go of me and took her glass from the coffee table. All four of us made a toast, to Riga, to Daugava, to new acquaintances and to a long night.

The champagne was cold and harsh and sour. I can't describe it any other way. The strange thing was that I thought it was really good.

There was knocking on the doors at the other end of the car, and Dad went over there.

My glass was already empty. I pulled the bottle out of the ice bucket and refilled. I also offered it to Elena and Masha, but they still had some.

The doors to the car slid open. Dad exchanged a few words with a person that I couldn't see. He extended his hand, and pulled it back. The doors closed again.

Dad came toward us with a triumphant smile. One hand closed. Then he opened it and held a couple of small bags with white powder up in the air. He smiled at me.

"Would you like some?"

"Is that cocaine?"

"Yes."

"Uh..."

Suddenly I felt much more sober.

"You're going to like it," said Dad. Masha took my free hand, the one that wasn't holding the champagne glass, in hers, squeezed it gently.

"It's great."

I was intensely aware that all three of them—Dad, Masha and Elena—were looking at me. There was an expectation.

"You know what?" I said. "I think I'll pass, but, you know... you go ahead."

Do you think I was dorky? Maybe I was. But I had never tried any kind of narcotics, not even smoked marijuana. It was a total no-no for me.

It wasn't that there hadn't been opportunities. Quite a lot of pot was smoked at parties even in my little town. And at our party trips in the summer, like to Antalya, my buddies used to smoke away. Sometimes they tried hash. I'd never been offered cocaine, but I was pretty sure it had been around at some of the parties I'd been to. Someone I'd never seen before shows up. Unnaturally long handshakes. The person disappears again. Three or four people go into the restroom and stay there a long time.

When narcotics crossed my path I always said no. It was so deep in my marrow—narcotics is "dope," and you use "dope" when you're a "dope addict." On the skids, down-and-out, the dregs of society.

I looked at myself with Grandpa's eyes. What if he found out that I'd tried dope, despite all the warnings, all his worry, over the years? We lived in a small town. Rumors traveled fast. Truth even faster. What frightened me wasn't that I would get a scolding; it was that I would disappoint him. His heart would break.

So: no narcotics. Not in any form. I'd promised myself that, again and again.

Dad looked at me. He looked happy and calm, loving. Took me gently by the arm. His voice subdued and secure.

"I understand that you think I'm a terrible drug addict." Now he was speaking in Swedish.

"No, no, it's not that..."

"Yes, but it's cool, it's cool, you don't need to explain."

"You don't either."

"Haha, no, that's nice...but I've used cocaine sometimes, not often, but at times, on special festive occasions. Maybe altogether—yes, what can it be?—seven or eight times."

"Okay."

"And... I'm just saying that, no matter what you've heard... you're not going to get hooked because you try it once. It doesn't work that way."

I sipped the champagne, squirmed a little. Now it had started, the persuasion campaign.

"No, sure."

Masha let go of my hand. She and Elena stood silently and listened to Dad's calm voice, a voice they didn't understand a word of. I assumed so anyway.

"As I said, I've taken it on festive occasions. And this evening is such an occasion," Dad continued. "A special occasion. Partly because we're together, and partly because..." Dad fell silent, looked me right in the eyes, not challenging but quietly. A slightly resigned, sad smile. "This is the last time I'll party. The last night out."

"Hmm." I didn't know what else to say.

"My brain tumor is roughly as big as a clementine." Dad's voice was darker now, more subdued. "And it's growing all the time. Any minute whatsoever I can go blind, or lose the ability to speak, or be paralyzed."

I put my hand on his shoulder.

"I understand. Truly. If you want to, then of course take it. I don't care about that. It doesn't bother me at all."

The last was perhaps not quite true. But you have the right to lie a little to a dying man, I think.

I reached for the candy bowl, fished up a few more Zoo. I turned to Masha and Elena and smiled a little apologetically.

"I'll just stick to champagne and these Zoo. Really good combination."

As soon as the words crossed my lips I regretted them. What kind of idiotic line is that? Neither Masha nor Elena, nor Dad for that matter, smiled.

I was such a farm boy. A first-class dork. I'd managed to maintain the illusion a good part of the evening, but now Masha and Elena understood who I really was. My cheeks burned with shame. I finished the champagne, tried to hide my face behind the glass.

Dad wasn't ready to give up yet.

"You know...this is actually a good opportunity to try it for the first time. You're surrounded by friends. If you want you can stay in here in the car."

"Sure. But... I'm good."

Dad nodded.

"I won't force you."

He turned to Masha and Elena, his voice more energetic and cheerful now.

"Who wants to go first?"

Masha laughed with her whole face.

"Me! Me! Me! Haha."

Dad leaned over the coffee table and carefully emptied out the contents of one of the bags. He took out the pass card for the VIP room and expertly arranged the cocaine in two neat lines. At the same time Masha took a bill out of her little handbag and rolled it up into a narrow tube. She got on her knees by the table, gathered up all her hair behind her neck with one hand, put the rolled-up bill in her nose with the other and bent down toward one of the white lines. Inhaled all of it in a single long drag.

"Oh my god...haha..."

Masha stood up, squeezed her nose and sniffed a little, making sure that she took in the rest of the cocaine. Elena took a step closer to me, leaned carefully toward my body. Tentatively.

Can we continue where we were?

Maybe the evening wasn't completely ruined anyway.

I put my arm around her, my hand on her hip, pulled her closer to me. She was soft and warm; it was as if we grew together again.

Dad looked like a believer in some Asian temple. Humble on his knees, his neck bowed, before the god he worshipped. I could see a big round area on his head that lacked hair, and realized that his back-combed hair was meant to conceal just that. And wasn't his hair dyed too?

Like Masha just now he leaned over the cocaine with the rolled-up bill stuck in his nose. A wheezing inhalation, a slight sideways movement of his head.

Elena's hand worked its way up to my neck, where it felt cool against my hot, damp skin. She spread out her fingers but still couldn't get hold of it all. She massaged my scalp, caressed the back of my head. Leaned her head against my shoulder, and whispered, "You know…it'll be the best sex you've ever had."

Dad stood up, laughed. Pinched his nose.

"Wow! Go to hell…now let's go! Haha!"

Elena mumbled in my ear, "And probably the best sex I've ever had too."

Dad gave me a sunny smile.

"You haven't changed your mind?"

Elena looked up at me.

When life invites you to dance.

We're on the dance floor again.

And everything is very clear to me now.

How unbelievably amazing the world is, and what an incredibly amazing life I have. And am going to have, for all eternity, forever and ever, amen.

How should I explain?

Maybe like this: my mobile phone camera has problems with focus sometimes, it zooms in and zooms out, but the image remains blurry. The only thing that works is to hit the phone properly, give it a tap on the side. Then, suddenly, the image is razor-sharp.

That's what the drug has done with me. Pounded my skull, so that I suddenly experience the world razor-sharp.

4K, baby.

I feel completely sober.

All the colors, all the sounds, all the smells. All at once. Fucking razor-sharp.

Hundreds of people on the dance floor, a rocking, rippling sea, but I see them all, every individual. I see you all! And you're beautiful! You are beautiful, you are beautiful, you are beautiful!

Most beautiful of all is Elena, who is dancing right in front of me with her arms draped around my neck.

And it's of course no accident that the most beautiful woman on the dance floor presses her body against mine, follows my slightest movement. Because I myself am so damned handsome and hot and dance so well.

I am the king and she's my queen, everyone in here is our subject and we will rule over them with great love and gentleness.

God, I could fuck all of them.

I am going to fuck all of them.

Guys, ladies, are you ready?

But of course!

The ceiling pulses yellow, orange, red. Waves from one end of the place to the other. Like the way the heart pumps blood down between my legs.

Elena and I kiss each other, we are deep inside each other's mouths, trying to swallow each other's tongues, and she tastes a little salty.

I have a world-class hard-on. Notice the admiring glances from those who are dancing around us. Cool! Appreciation is always cool, you know.

We are attached to one another at the mouth, suction cups that refuse to let go, I am her leech, she is mine. I take hold of her buttocks and raise her up in the air, she is light as a feather, I carry her through the crowd on one arm, move our subjects aside with the other, no one objects, everyone here worships us.

We come up to our car, I pull the pass card out of my pocket with one hand, still with Elena sitting on the other arm. The doors slide open and I carry her in, I almost stumble but manage to keep my balance, set Elena down on a seat right ahead, pull down and kick off my pants and shoes and underwear. Get on my knees and pull off her jeans and the black, silky panties, the string gets caught on the heel of one sandalette, but that doesn't matter, I let it hang. Bury my head between her legs.

Elena has a condom in her mouth, and she pulls it on. The best trick I've seen.

Dad waves new bags in the air. We get on our knees, one by one. Worship the same god now. And my faith is firm, the spirit is strong in me. Away with it, that I should betray! Not.

New misty ice buckets. The corks clatter on the ceiling mirror.

On the dance floor again. So fucking sharp, and smart, and happy, and sexy. Me, Elena, Masha, everyone in here. The ceiling light blue, like a summer sky. A black shadow spreads its wings and flies from one end to the other. Glides ahead, almost quietly, right out of my dreams.

My head has gotten a little foggy. Just barely, but I feel it. Too much champagne, no doubt. Want to return to that razor-sharp 4K feeling, ultra-HD, and I know what's needed. I ask Dad, he laughs and puts his hand on my shoulder.

"Nice and easy."

On my back in the lounge suite, naked. Masha is riding me; she is naked too. Elena behind her, caressing Masha's breasts and stomach.

What a great lover I am.

Just think that I had this in me.

★★★

Yes, there was one more bag.

The whole ceiling is burning, a sea of fire, and I know that it's only an image that rolls over thousands of diodes synchronized by a computer, with my razor-sharp mental acuity I think I see and feel how the processor itself is working, there's nothing strange there, everything is completely clear. But it looks just too real. It's as if the ceiling is burning for real. I have to look away.

The fatigue rolls in, like dark storm clouds toward a shore that is still bathing in sun. It comes slowly but isn't possible to stop. Elena gives me a bottle of mineral water from the fridge, and I chug it. On the table is a bowl with salted almonds—three fistfuls in my mouth then it's empty.

I waken, stand halfway up from the sofa, look up. Over there, by the seats, Dad is standing, taking someone from behind. I don't see who it is; she is on all fours on a seat. His hair is disheveled, the long strands that are usually combed back to cover the bald spot are hanging out at the side, his hands on her butt, but the posture—an old man holding onto the edge of the table so as not to fall down.

Dad is naked from the waist down. The buttocks like two shriveled balloons, forgotten under the table a week after the children's party.

The party is over. It is so fucking over, man.

I lie down again and close my eyes. That wasn't something I felt I needed to see. A minus when this night will be added up.

Maybe it's now that it turns. I'm starting to go back.

There is so much filth. I don't want to think about that.

Fire outside the car window. People gathered around an oil drum. No light diodes, real fire. Dad beside me in the back seat.

"You know...the world consists of the same basic elements as four billion years ago. What happened is that they've been rearranged and combined in new ways. Why should one way or the other matter? If certain hydrocarbons 'experience' a little more of what we call 'suffering'—and? Are you with me, Isak?"

No, I'm not with you.

On the beach below Ajkeshorn. The sun is broiling, the sand is too hot to walk on. I am lying stretched out on a towel. Masha and Elena are sitting beside me. Both have bird masks. I look toward the other end of the beach, over there is the group of surfers, they are beginners and fall off their boards all the time, everyone has bird masks, the instructor too.

Two small children are playing with a pail and spade at the water's edge. Both have bird masks.

Do I have a bird mask on too? I feel—no, my head and my face are exposed to the world.

I'm the only one who's not wearing a mask.

Masha has gone away somewhere, only Elena is still sitting by my side. She takes off the mask, it's not Elena, it's Maddy.

"Hi," I say, trying to make contact, but she doesn't seem to hear me, she simply looks thoughtfully out over the sea.

I feel very worried.

My back is cold. The damp from the moss has penetrated through the pajamas with the tractors. It's not morning yet, but not night either. Faint light between the spruce trees.

I hear a strange sound. Actually several different sounds, quiet small sounds, but intense. A picking. Something that resembles the sound when a cat shakes its fur, brief and intense. A wetter sound, splashing.

I sit up halfway, and something flaps behind my back. I get scared and twirl around.

The raven is already moving away, but it doesn't fly far, only to a boulder some ten meters away. Its claws tramp around in the moss. It stares at me with its head cocked, irritated that I've disturbed it. I see that it has something in its beak. A scrap of something bloody. It jerks its head and the scrap disappears into its mouth.

I am standing under one of the weeping willows in Herrmann's Park and vomit. Have never felt so bad in my whole life. It's New Year's Eve, the whole world is spinning and it just goes faster and faster, and I want to get off this fucking carousel now. Can hear firecrackers and rockets explode, the park is full of young people, but I've gone away from my buddies.

My feet are cold. My new Converse, which would be so perfect with the black jeans, are sopping wet, and my socks too of course. There is an inch of slush on the ground. Sleet too the whole evening. Around freezing.

I am seventeen years old and so miserable that I just want to die.

Grandpa thought that I should put on my boots, and then I could change into the Converse when I got to the party. Uh… no. Wouldn't think so.

When I'm done vomiting for this time I fish out the mobile phone and call him. He has said that I can call, whatever happens. And he has promised not to get angry.

He answers immediately.

"Hi…how's it going?"

"I don't feel good," I slur. "Really bad."

"Yes…you don't sound so good… Where are you? Shall I come and pick you up?"

"Yes… I'm in Herrmann's Park."

"I'm coming right away. Can you walk to the corner where Dressmann is?"

"Yes…can you bring a towel?"

"A towel?"

"I'm so wet… I don't wantto…get the seat wet."

"Son, it doesn't matter. Don't think about it. See you shortly."

Then I hear knocking.

When I woke up I didn't know where I was. The room was in darkness. Big curtains, from floor to ceiling, which were drawn. A broad bed with big pillows and cool sheets. Chairs and a table.

This was a hotel room, obviously. But which hotel room? Where?

There was knocking again. Exactly, over there was the door.

Riga. It was the hotel room in Riga.

I couldn't remember how I got there. The TV on the wall opposite the bed had a clock on the lower edge; the red numbers showed 10:24.

"Isak?" I heard Dad's voice outside the door. More knocking. "Are you awake?"

"I'm coming."

I pulled back the covers and rolled out of bed. My bare feet sank down in the wall-to-wall carpet as I padded over to the door and opened it. Dad and a hotel steward were standing outside. I squinted and blinked at the illuminated hotel corridor.

"Good morning," Dad said energetically.

"Good morning, sir," said the steward. "Would you like some breakfast?"

Now I saw that the steward had a rolling cart in front of him, with coffee, juice, bread, toppings, fruit salad and a couple of tin plates with a cover. It smelled like fried bacon.

"Uh...sure," I said, rubbing my eyes. Stepped to the side so that the steward could roll the cart in. Dad followed him. I let the door close. Dad went over to the curtains and pulled them apart. In my head it went from night to day in two seconds. The sun was reflected on the white facade on the other side of the street. It was so bright that I was forced to turn my eyes away.

The steward placed the cart by the lounge suite and bowed lightly.

"Enjoy, sir," he said and left the room.

Dad smiled at me.

"I'm sorry to wake you, but the plane back to Visby is ready and waiting. I thought you'd probably like to get back as soon as possible."

"Hmm," I said.

Dad looked fresh and rested. His hair was as it should be, and his posture was athletic. There was an aroma of shaving cream and aftershave around him. He said, "How are you feeling otherwise?"

Dad collapsed on a black velvet subway seat. Half-closed eyelids, no pupils that peek out. A string of saliva from the corner of his mouth. A syringe in the crook of his arm.

Had I really seen that?

"How am I feeling?"

"Yes? Are you hungover?"

I had to think about it. I felt a little tired, could have easily slept a while longer. But I wasn't exactly hungover. No headache.

"No… I feel completely okay."

"Haha, you sound almost surprised. But that's how it is with coke. One of many advantages."

I was still standing there just in my underwear, and now I looked around for my tennis shirt. On the desk I discovered a neatly folded pile with a white T-shirt, underwear and a pair of socks. They were the clothes Dad had ordered in reception the day before.

"And thanks for yesterday," said Dad. "That was a real good time. As I said, a special night for me. I'm so happy I got to share it with you."

I nodded but didn't say anything. Pulled on the clean T-shirt and sank down in one of the armchairs. Poured coffee in a cup. Raised one of the tin lids—oh my, there was bacon and scrambled eggs—put some on a plate and started eating. The food fed my hunger rather than stilling it.

"I think that...maybe you don't want to tell Maddy all the details about last night," said Dad.

The drugs. Elena, Masha and I naked on the sofas. Suddenly I thought that I reeked of sweat and sex, that the whole hotel room stank. A wave of shame washed over me, I tumbled around under the surface and it short-circuited my brain and my body. I felt like I was going to faint. I set the fork down on the plate and moaned lightly.

Maddy.

"Listen," said Dad, and now his voice was rather firm, as if he really wanted me to take in what he was saying. "You have nothing to be ashamed of. You helped yourself to life yesterday. Be proud instead."

I sighed, rubbed my face.

"What you did last night didn't hurt a single person," Dad continued, and now he was smiling. "On the contrary, from what I could see you made both Elena and Masha very happy... So the thing is that if you tell this to Maddy, that's when you're hurting someone. That's what you should be ashamed about."

Dad fell silent again. He probably wanted me to interject something, agree or argue. But I had nothing to add. My head was empty.

"I'll let you eat breakfast in peace and quiet," Dad said at last. "But we'll meet in the lobby after that?"

"Yes," I said.

Dad disappeared through the door, which slowly and solemnly closed behind him. A discreet sound was heard as it closed the corridor out.

I was alone again with my thoughts.

Strange that the last thing I'd dreamed about was Grandpa, and that New Year's Eve when I drank alcohol for the first time. The memory had come back as I was lying in bed gliding in and out of sleep. Incredibly realistic.

Anxiety. But not for any particular, concrete things I'd done the night before, like it usually is when you've had too much alcohol. This was something much bigger. A feeling that the ground below me was cracking. That I risked being sucked down into a big, black hole.

I set down the fork and leaned back in the chair. Unable to eat any more.

Disgusted with myself.

The airplane shook and rumbled and picked up speed. Soon we lifted off the ground. It was fairly windy, and it tugged and pulled on the aircraft body. Sure, it felt luxurious to fly in a private jet, but it was clearly more sensitive to turbulence; the plane was small and more exposed to the forces of nature. On this trip there was no stewardess. Nothing would be served, no champagne or coffee. It was just Dad, the pilot and me.

The weather was clear. I looked out the window and saw central Riga below and behind me, bathing in sunlight. Somewhere down there were Elena and Masha. I thought about Elena's look across the table when we were still sitting in the bar at the hotel, when everything was ahead of us. The desire.

Hands off. He's mine.

We would surely never meet again.

And I thought about Daugava, about the ceiling that exploded in colors, about the luxury in our own subway car, about the champagne, about the cocaine, about the feeling of razor-sharp joy and reckless lust, about the feeling of owning the world.

Did I truly regret that I simply hadn't finished my burger at the hotel and then gone to bed early?

Yes. When I thought about Maddy and about Grandpa I did.

"You look like you've got something on your mind," Dad shouted to be heard over the engine noise. He was sitting across from me.

"Yes… I was thinking that it feels like you're constantly trying to manipulate me to do things that I really don't want to,"

I said. My mouth moved, I was too tired to filter, could no longer bear to keep the cards close to my chest.

Dad looked back at me, and there was a lot of love and warmth in his eyes.

"I'm sorry if you feel that way," he said, "but it's actually the other way around. I'm trying to get you to do things that you really want to do. I'm guessing that when you think about yesterday, there's a part of you that regrets it, and another part that would like to do the same thing tonight, if it were possible."

He looked at me to get a reaction, but I didn't give him any. So he continued.

"I know that Anders means a great deal to you. And I understand that. But what you're experiencing...when you have regrets, then you see yourself with Anders's eyes. When you want to do it again this evening, then you're listening to yourself."

Dad leaned back in the seat and let this sink in.

I looked out the window. Now we were over the Baltic.

The last thing he said didn't feel true. It was really me that had regrets. I couldn't understand that I'd risked everything Maddy and I had together, the best thing that happened to me, for a crazy night out. What the hell was I thinking?

And yet. I could still feel the bass line tickling around my heart. My body one with the music. Elena, who captured a drop of sweat on my jugular notch.

Far below us the sea was dark blue like a wrinkled sheet. A sailboat was so small that I could barely make it out. In the distance I saw a cargo ship with a red-and-gray hull.

Dad started speaking again.

"You've heard the fairy tale about Rapunzel, haven't you? Who is confined in a high tower by an old witch."

"Hmm."

"The thing is...today we've reversed that fairy tale. Rapunzel wants to stay in the tower where it is secure and safe. The witch is God, who protects Rapunzel against all the evil out there. The prince, who wants to rescue Rapunzel from imprisonment, is evil. He's the tempter, he's the devil."

I didn't say anything, just tried to look neutral. Dad took a deep breath, then he continued.

"I am the prince who wants to rescue you from the tower. Liberate you. Get you to live life fully. I want to give you the world, Isak."

"I see."

"You won't be my heir. You know that."

"Yes."

"Because Anders adopted you."

"Yes."

"But I want to leave my fortune to you. It's upward of a hundred million."

I stared at Dad, wondered if I'd heard right. My head was just spinning.

"If you stay a few more days, then we'll be able to spend a little more time together. Are you up for that?"

A hundred million.

"Say that you stay for three days, for example," Dad continued. "Then you'll earn thirty-three million a day. That's decent payment, isn't it?"

I put my hands in front of my face. Slowly shook my head.

"Or what? What do you earn in the home health service? Maybe it's about that much, with overtime and all?"

This was too sick to take in. I started to laugh, still with my hands before my face, from pure shock I think. It was not from joy in any event. I actually felt more like crying. But I laughed and laughed.

"I'm completely serious," said Dad.

"Yes, sorry," I said, taking a deep breath. "Sorry…it's just… it got to be too much."

"But then you'll stay a few more days?"

Should I check with Maddy first?

"Yes," I said. "Sure, I'll stay."

She would understand.

A hundred million.

Not much more was said during the short flight. I saw the pilot moving up in the cockpit and Dad asked if I wanted to try flying. He'd done it one time, he said, and it was a powerful feeling. I declined. I'd had enough powerful feelings for a while. Just wanted to sit quietly in my seat, with a firm grip on the armrests, and try to get the dizziness to settle down. Like when you're standing at the foot of a really tall building and look up.

But when I closed my eyes I saw myself in the pilot's seat of the airplane, with a firm grip on the steering wheel, I pulled it toward me and the nose pointed upward, right up into the sky. We left the earth behind us and flew right into the sun. As we approached I had to evade solar flares, gigantic cascades of burning helium hundreds of miles up in the air. Our whole field of vision was filled with boiling yellow and orange, and then we crashed into the sea of fire and were annihilated in a moment.

The taxi drove into the turnaround in front of Ajkeshorn and stopped in front of the entry. Dad and I got out. I had my dirty clothes from yesterday in a plastic bag from the hotel. As we came in through the door Dad extended his hand toward me.

"Give me those," he said. "Barbro can wash them."

Did they smell of an unknown woman's perfume? Was that what he was thinking? It hadn't even occurred to me that it could create problems.

Dad truly thought of everything.

I handed the bag over to him.

We continued through the house, to the kitchen, where Barbro was preparing lunch. Dad had called from the airport and said that we were on our way.

"*Hola*, Barbro," he said, went up to her and placed his hand gently on her back. She did not reply, was fully occupied with whisking up a dressing. Only made her usual tic and bent her head back.

We went out on the patio, where a table was set in the shade of a couple of parasols. Maddy was sitting slouched in a chair turned toward the sea. She was wearing sunglasses. When she heard our steps she turned her head.

"Hi, darling," I said and smiled.

Maddy. It felt like coming home. Only now did I realize how much I'd missed her.

"Hi," she said in response, rather neutrally, with a smile that didn't look particularly enthusiastic.

"Sorry about this," I said, leaning down and kissing her.

She responded to the kiss.

"It's cool," she said. "I said so."

But she didn't take off her sunglasses. I sat down beside her, Dad on the other side of the table. There was a big glass bottle of mineral water on the table. Dad poured for all three of us.

Maddy said, "So, what did you do last night? Did you think of anything fun?"

There was silence a moment. Dad and I looked at each other. I wished I'd put sunglasses on too.

"No, but…we checked into the hotel, and then we just went and ate in the bar."

"Uh-huh," Maddy said, looking at me.

I bit my lip.

"Exactly," I said. I was about to say *and then we went to bed, we were a little tired since yesterday*, but Dad got there first.

"Then a couple of friends of mine came by, and they wanted to go to a club, so we tagged along."

"I see."

"It's a place I've been to before, pretty cool, actually, a closed subway station. Or to be more precise it was never put into use. But it's… Yes, there's good ventilation there."

I felt cold sweat break out on my scalp and neck. What was Dad up to? Would he tell everything?

"There was probably some champagne," Dad continued, smiling wryly.

"So, who were these friends?" Maddy's question sounded unconcerned. A little too unconcerned.

"A Latvian artist I know, Andreis," said Dad. "And his boyfriend. Real party animals. They did coke and everything imaginable. But we stuck to champagne."

At the same moment I heard Barbro come out of the kitchen. She set out a big bowl of Caesar salad on the table, and a basket of sliced sourdough baguette.

I helped myself to the salad and relaxed, felt how my shoulders lowered a few centimeters. What a master Dad was at lying. Personally I would have wanted to stay as far away from the truth as possible. But Dad knew that the most credible lie, the one that's the easiest to stick to, is the one that's closest to the truth. And the way he presented it. A hundred percent believable. Dad finished chewing, then he said, "Mmm… Isak has decided to stay a few more days."

He speared a new piece of chicken on his fork and put it in his mouth.

"If that works for you, that is," I hastened to add with a look at Maddy. I felt a sting of irritation at Dad. Why couldn't he have let me bring this up with Maddy myself?

She didn't answer at once. Chewed, poked at her salad, drank a little water.

"I know I should have called and checked with you, sorry," I continued.

"No, no, it's cool."

"But we… Dad suggested it when we were on the plane here."

"Really, it's cool." Maddy sounded dismissive and didn't look at me. The salad was clearly more interesting than me.

She was annoyed, no doubt about it. I guessed that it was

more about my not checking in with her than with the decision itself. And I understood her. We hadn't come home from Riga when we said and now I suddenly wanted to stay a few more days. Things had changed with short notice.

Dad set his silverware down on the plate and wiped his mouth with a linen napkin. He looked at me.

"This afternoon I thought we should take the bull by the horns."

I suspected what he was referring to and felt a lump of discomfort in my stomach.

An hour later we were walking through the forest by the shore, along the same path we'd taken to the treehouse that first evening. The sun was still almost at zenith and the air was motionless. There was an odor of warm bark from the knotty pines. Grasshoppers jumped away from the path as we approached. Sometimes the sea was visible between the pines but you could barely hear it.

We passed where the path that led up to the treehouse branched off, and now I saw the studio between the trees. A rather small, oblong structure, painted white like the main building. It wasn't placed parallel to the shore but at a right angle to it. The end closest to the water was made of glass and in the roof there were also large windows.

Dad bent down toward a big pot with a little olive tree, tipped it and fished a key out from under it. He unlocked a simple door in the middle of the long side. We stepped into the studio.

"Damn, it's hot," Dad said. "I'd better open some windows."

It was truly like a sauna in the room, which was seven or eight meters long, and maybe four meters wide. The glass wall toward the sea was divided in two, and high up on each half was a horizontal oblong window. Dad opened both. The door we'd come in through he also left open.

Daylight flooded into the studio. Along the walls were benches and shelves with paint cans, brushes and tools. The floor was covered with paper with lots of paint stains. Everything was messy and untidy. On a desk was a steel thermos; it too was stained with paint. It smelled of paint and solvent and something else. It was familiar but I couldn't put my finger on what it was. Dad smiled and inhaled through his nose.

"Do you sense it? Coal. Charcoal. Love that smell."

Exactly. It smelled like charcoal briquettes.

Leaning against the opposite short wall, where the sunlight didn't quite reach, was a big painting, several meters tall and several meters wide. It covered almost the entire wall. I assumed it was a painting anyway—it was covered with some old bedspreads so it wasn't possible to see what it depicted.

Something stirred deep inside me when I saw that covered painting leaning against the wall. A feeling of distaste. Something dark that didn't want to come out into the daylight.

"This is my playroom," said Dad. "Not even my assistants are allowed in here. If we need to do some bigger things when we're here then we use the exhibition room, where you're sleeping."

Dad explained that his big studio in London was always full of people and full of activity. It wasn't just art that would be planned and realized; there was also a lot of administration to be done. Visits from clients, budget meetings, staff meetings, hours in front of the computer answering emails.

"So I started to associate that studio with all the other things that go into being an artist at this level. I mean, it's wonderful to direct gifted young people and all that—that's creative too—but I wanted to find my way back to that feeling I had when I was little and sat in my room and fooled around, forgot the world, the hours simply passed..."

He went over to the desk and picked up a model car from a kit. It was plastic and depicted an older-model Porsche, from the seventies. The car was white and "Carrera" was written in red on the lower part of the doors. It wasn't particularly neatly constructed. Hardened glue ran out here and there and the lights were a little crooked.

"I built this when I was seven years old, I think. I only need to see this, then...it puts me in a particular mood. Do you understand?"

I nodded. Sure, I understood. When I was little I had a black-and-blue plastic ball. I loved that ball. Since then I've always liked blue and black together. There are no better-looking football jerseys than Inter Milan's, for example. Just seeing those blue and black stripes gives me a warm feeling in my chest.

On the table was a little statuette. It appeared to be made of stone, or maybe clay, and resembled the sculptures in the exhibition room, although in miniature format. It was maybe fifteen centimeters tall. The head was triangular with crooked eyes and its hands were at its sides, like a strict mother who comes into the children's room late in the evening and says that now it's time to go to sleep. On the stomach and chest there were strange signs and symbols.

I recognized them. They were the same as what Dad had tattooed on his forearm.

And I recognized the little sculpture.

"I didn't think that I would work here at all," Dad continued. "It was just for relaxation. But it has turned out that I get a hell of a lot of ideas when I'm here."

There was silence for a moment. I couldn't take my eyes off the statuette. Dad saw that. He went over and picked it up.

"Do you recognize this? I had it in my old studio in Stockholm. When you were little."

I nodded but didn't say anything.

"It was the first little idol I acquired. It's about six thousand years old. Isn't that incredible?"

"Mmm."

"Archaeologists think it's an image of a fire god. You see the signs here on the front side...according to one theory they should be interpreted as 'Me fire big big big.' Now their language didn't have the same structure as ours, so if you were to translate this it would mean roughly 'My fire is the greatest.' I thought that was pretty cool. So I had it tattooed on my arm." He held out his right arm to show.

My fire is the greatest. I didn't understand what was amusing about that. The heat in the studio was almost unbearable. Opening the windows hadn't helped because the air was still outside too. Dad set the figure back on the desk again.

"But I actually brought you here with me to show you this," Dad said, nodding toward the big, covered painting. He went over and pressed a light switch next to the door. Spotlights came on in the ceiling. In the darker end of the room where the painting was it made a difference.

"That is the first painting I did of the fire. I have never sold it."

I suspected that. In some way I'd had a feeling about it. My stomach churned.

"You decide for yourself if you want to see it. We can forget about it if you want."

I'd seen a photo of one of those images on the Internet some time when I was a teenager, and I almost fainted.

How would it feel to see the picture in reality, in this giant format?

I didn't want to show Dad how upset I was. Tried to keep my breathing under control. Didn't dare turn my gaze toward him, so I stared at the covered painting, or rather at the floor right in front of it, and said, "Why do you want to show it to me?"

"Because it stands between us. I sense what you're thinking about these paintings. But I want to hear you say it. And then I want to tell you how I look at them."

There was a long silence. I tried to breathe through my nose, thought that if I started breathing through my mouth it was going to reveal the emotional storm inside me, but that was absurd. My breath hissed through my nostrils like an air conditioning unit set on high. I gave up and opened my mouth.

"But you don't have to see the painting," Dad said at last. "We can talk about it anyway."

I could no longer stand still, walked around in place, a tickling sensation in my gut, like when you know you're going to vomit. You hesitate but you also want to get it over with. Damn, how tough this was. A goddamned attack from Dad's side.

"Isak..."

"You left me."

Suddenly it just came out. I heard myself say it, and knew that I'd gone directly to the core. There was a lot to say about the paintings, but this of course was what was important.

He had left me.

So simple, actually.

"Yes. I left you."

"I was six years old, I'd lost my mother, and my little sister. You were all I had left."

"I had a break..."

"But you never showed up."

"I'm sorry about that. But I wasn't strong enough. I couldn't take care of you."

"I asked Grandpa every day when you would be coming back. Every morning, every evening. 'When is he coming?' And Grandpa said that you were sick. But do you know what I thought?"

Now I was staring at Dad. Didn't care if he saw how upset and sad I was. Or on the contrary even—it was good if he saw that. I wanted him to understand a little of the pain I felt. Dad looked back at me. His gaze firm, but his jaws clenched.

"I thought that you were angry with me. That that was why you didn't come back. Because I hadn't rescued Mom and Klara. Because that's how I felt. It was my fault that they died. And for that reason you didn't want to even see me, because you were so angry."

"It wasn't like that. Of course."

"And you couldn't at least have called me?"

"Isak, I..."

"If you had just called and said, 'This isn't your fault, I'm not mad at you, but right now I'm feeling so bad that I can't take care of you.' But you couldn't even manage that."

"Listen..."

"I was a child! You were an ADULT, damn it! Then you better pull yourself together a little!"

"But I did that, I called. Many times. But Anders wouldn't let me talk with you."

I just stared at him.

He looked at me without turning his eyes away.

"It's true," he said at last. "I promise. You can ask Anders about it."

Could that be right?

I really wanted to believe that he was lying. I really wanted to believe that.

It felt as if I'd lost balance. I was shoved off course. Turned my eyes away and rubbed my face.

"My God," I mumbled.

"I was very angry at Anders then," Dad continued. "But when I look back on it now I can understand him. He knew that I wasn't able to take care of you. So maybe it was best to cut the ties completely. So that you could move on."

I didn't say anything, just stared down at the floor. My fury at Dad had subsided; it felt as if there was an empty echo inside me. A vacated warehouse.

"Anders and I don't get along well," said Dad. "And I knew that from the first time we met. He simply doesn't like me. It's just that way. And I think he prevents you from living your best life. Getting the most out of your short time on earth. But... I also know that he did what he did because he believed it was the best for you."

The best for me, I thought. How could it be the best for me not to get to talk with my father?

My unseeing eyes had fastened on the covered painting without my having thought about it. Dad followed my gaze.

"What do you want to do? Do you want to see it?"

Now you're surely going to think that I'm a weak bastard.

But I was badly shaken up. This going back in time had reminded me of my vulnerability and despair when I was little; it had brought my anger at Dad to life, everything that had been hidden inside me. And then added to that finding this out about Grandpa, that he'd prevented Dad from talking with me when I was little, if that was even true—that was what had hit me the hardest.

I'd been afraid of Dad's pictures of the fire for so many years. In my mind they had almost acquired magical powers.

So no, I didn't feel that I was strong enough to see the painting.

I shook my head quietly and left the studio.

There was quiet rustling in the crowns of the pines, or else it was just in my ears. From the shore a laughing child's voice was heard.

Dad turned off the lights, stepped out of the door too and locked up behind him. We started to take the path back to the house.

"You and Madeleine will probably want to have a little time to yourselves now," said Dad. "But we can meet about six or so. On the patio."

I nodded silently.

The painting leaned against the wall, hidden by the bedspread.

It stirred up something inside me but I couldn't get ahold of what.

★ ★ ★

I'm lying on my back on the cot, daydreaming.

My restrictions have been lifted, and Per says that there's someone who wants to meet me, someone who has longed for me for many years, and I don't understand who that can be, but deep down I hope of course, and when I come into the visitor's room she's sitting at a table, our eyes meet and she stands up with tears running down her cheeks, she looks older but not all that much, and we reunite in a hug.

"Isak…beloved Isak… I have longed so…but now everything is fine. Everything is fine again."

I wonder if the chance for me to meet Mom again is greater in this life, or in the next?

It's probably more or less fifty-fifty.

I found Maddy down on the shore. She had placed the towel close to the water's edge, just out of reach of the waves. A day as hot as this one you wanted to be close to the cooling water.

The beach was deserted, except for a family with children fifty-some meters away. It was probably one of their kids I'd heard laughing earlier.

Maddy was lying on her back in her bikini. One knee was pulled up so that her leg was at an angle, one arm over her head. Sunglasses on.

"Hi," I said, spreading out my towel alongside hers. She took a deep breath and changed position with sluggish movements. Maybe she'd been asleep. She looked at me and smiled, without taking off her sunglasses.

"Hi."

"Were you sleeping?"

"Maybe I dozed off a little."

I looked out over the sea. No waves, but small ripples were moving on the surface.

"I have to start by taking a dip, I think. Do you want to join me?"

Maddy turned on her side toward me, resting her head on one elbow.

"Maybe."

I glanced over toward the family with children. Would I be able to cover myself when I changed to bathing trunks? No. No one would care. I pulled off the white T-shirt, undid my pants and kicked them off, pulled down my underwear, stepped out of them too. I turned my rear end toward the family as I unfolded the bathing trunks to step into them.

Maddy looked inscrutable behind her sunglasses.

"I didn't know this was a nude beach."

"Ah," I said, nodding toward the family. "That kid over there is running around naked. I guess I can too."

"He's three years old, Isak."

"Whatever." I held up the bathing trunks and put my first foot through the opening, wobbling on my other leg.

"I never get used to how fine your body is."

"Haha, stop."

"No, but really. You have such a fucking Michelangelo body."

"Come on now."

The bathing trunks were on. I extended my hand to Maddy, she took it and then we walked together out into the water. Maybe it wasn't quite as cold as on the first day but it still felt shockingly cold against my shins. Then gradually, after we'd dipped our bodies a couple of times, it felt nice. We hugged and I said I was sorry because I hadn't checked on the change in plans with her. Maddy said that she understood, it didn't matter, the important thing for her was that we were together, and Ajkeshorn was a fine place to do that, be together that is… The hug became a kiss.

Did I use a condom? Every time? The whole night?

My body stiffened with shame, and the kiss became unfocused.

I didn't remember anything else. But on the other hand I didn't remember the whole night. I had memory gaps. Didn't know how I got back to the hotel, for example.

I couldn't be sure.

"You… What is it?" Maddy noticed that my thoughts were elsewhere.

"Nothing," I said. "I love you so much."

I told myself that Elena and Masha had been less affected than me, and more careful, and presumably they weren't carrying anything anyway.

When life invites you to dance. That's how I thought. But worry and a guilty conscience took a firm hold.

The lie had sneaked in like a curious neighbor cat. I could have chased it out of the house, but I picked it up on my lap instead. It purred, closed its eyes, rubbed its head against my cheek.

A little later we were lying on our towels drying out in the sun, Maddy's hand in mine. The loveliest moment, when the cold of the sea still lingers on your skin and meets the heat of the sun. The movement from cold to warm.

"He says he wants to will his fortune to me."

Maddy turned her head, lifting it from the towel.

"What?"

"A hundred million. More or less."

She took off her sunglasses and looked searchingly at me, uncertain whether I was joking. She looked so shocked that I started to laugh.

"Haha…it's true."

"No. You're joking."

"That's what he said."

Maddy's head sank down on the towel again. She took a deep breath.

"It's incomprehensible," she said at last, rather quietly.

"No. It's a crazy lot of money."

I told her that Dad wanted us to spend a little more time together; that was why I'd agreed to stay a few more days. Maddy guessed that this was what Dad had in mind the whole time. It explained why he'd been so persistent that I should come and visit him.

I was a little surprised at her reaction. Thought that she would be happy for my sake, for our sake. Imagined to myself how she lit up, let out a shriek and threw herself around my neck. I know, it was silly to think that way. But that was why I'd waited to tell her. I wanted to savor the moment, find the perfect occasion.

But it was almost the other way around. She fell silent and looked thoughtful, as if she'd gotten bad news. I couldn't help but feel a little disappointed.

"Your life is going to change completely," she said.

"Yes," I said. After a while I added, "But it's probably up to me too."

Maddy lay on her back, looking up at the sky. She'd put on her sunglasses again. At last she said, "Am I going to be a part of that life, do you think?"

"Darling, stop," I said, edging myself over to her towel. I put my arm around her. "It's obvious I wouldn't be here if it weren't for you. I didn't want anything to do with him."

"That's easy to say now."

"Half of that money is, like, yours," I said, because I felt it sounded good in the moment, and maybe it would put Maddy in a good mood. But I regretted it the moment those words passed my lips. It was an exaggeration; it was going too far. Would I have to eat those words sometime in the future?

That thought glided over me, briefly shadowed my mind.

Maddy turned toward me, curled up against my chest. She

was here in my arms, and I loved her. That was the only important thing.

It was, wasn't it?

Soon we started talking about what it would mean in practical terms for me to inherit Dad's fortune. Or actually it was probably Maddy who did most of the talking and I was the one who listened. It would be my job, basically, to manage his art, to safeguard his name. I would have to get involved in this world he lived in. Take care of his properties, maybe, the studios and residences in London and Stockholm. And Ajkeshorn. Many people would surely show up and maintain that they were close to Dad, that they would gladly help manage the inheritance for reasonable compensation, Maddy thought. It was a big cake to divide up and everyone would want their part. By the way, did I know whether Dad had any other children? Had we talked about that?

No, we hadn't, of course.

I must have looked a little pale, because Maddy stroked my cheek.

"Sorry. I didn't mean to frighten you."

"No, it's cool. You're right. Haven't had time to think that much about it yet."

"Of course."

"But… I mean, Dad must understand that this isn't all that easy for me. I think he's probably trying to put as much as possible in order before he dies."

"Mmm."

What would Grandpa think about all this? Would the fortune drive a wedge between us?

The ground rocked beneath me, and I got back that feeling I'd had that morning, that I was about to be consumed by a big, black hole. Felt an impulse to say to Dad, *Thanks, but no thanks. That money, that world, is not for me.*

Why did I tell Maddy before I'd thought this through properly? Yet another mistake.

"But of course it's like you said," said Maddy. "Your dad has obviously thought through everything. He doesn't seem to be the type who leaves things to chance."

She pointed out that I would have the opportunity to live anywhere at all in the world. I didn't need to keep living in darkest Småland.

But I like darkest Småland, I was about to say.

I'd read somewhere that people who won enormous sums on betting or the lottery often said afterward that money didn't make them happier. More like the opposite. I already thought I understood why. All the choices you're suddenly faced with. That freedom could become a burden.

At the same time: getting up at five o'clock on a pitch-black Monday in November, getting in an ice-cold car and driving your rounds, eight hours of changing diapers and pissed-on sheets. Days when winter was at the door and somehow dragged the whole world down, days that never became other than dark gray even at lunchtime.

I could probably manage to live without that.

"It wouldn't be bad to live in Thailand during the winter," I said. "Never been there but it seems nice. Thirty degrees Celsius in February or whatever it is."

Maddy joined in and painted the picture for me. A deluxe bungalow on the beach, with several rooms. Running and yoga before breakfast. Then an outing, maybe by boat or kayak. Siesta during the noon hours. We would wake up together, make love before we got up and each made a chai latte.

I nodded.

"But I think...somehow you have to find a purpose in life."

"Yes."

"It wouldn't feel right to just live in luxury."

Maddy thought that was the least problem if you had a fortune of a hundred million, finding a purpose in life. Doing good was a child's game. I could for example finance some enterprise like Dad did with the orphanage in Riga. Something with a connection to Dad's art. Or, if I thought that was too much work, donate eighty million to the Red Cross and live well on the twenty million I had left. Then I would still have done much, much more good for the world than most other people.

It didn't sound too bad, when she presented it that way.

"That thing about doing good, you can leave that to the money," said Maddy. "Your job will be to learn to enjoy life."

Maybe she was right, I thought, and the first thing that passed through my head was that I would buy myself a new rainsuit.

Isn't that crazy? A rainsuit.

But for a long time I'd been pining to buy one of those really nice suits, in some expensive material that resisted rain but still breathed. Jacket and pants. Watertight zippers on the pockets. Sturdy straps. Slits that could be opened if you wanted to make the jacket airier. Norröna, Haglöfs or even Arcteryx. Those rainsuits could cost up to ten thousand kronor. Maybe even twelve. Completely out of reach for me. Until now.

A new rainsuit. Talk about enjoying life.

After a while we went back to our room, showered the sand off that had stuck to our skin and lay down to take a nap. My hand rested on Maddy's stomach. I fell asleep like a child.

When I woke up the light fell at an even lower angle and had lost a bit of its sharpness. I realized that it must be early evening. It was like I was still numbed by fatigue. Last night had finally caught up with me. But I realized that it was high time to have dinner, and that Maddy and Dad were presumably waiting for me out on the patio. I got out of bed, pulled on a clean, dark blue tennis shirt and a pair of beige linen shorts.

★ ★ ★

They were sitting at the same table where we'd had lunch under the parasol, which actually was unnecessary—at this time of day the patio was shaded by the house itself. Maddy had a glass of white wine in front of her on the table, Dad a drink that appeared to be straight whiskey or cognac with some ice cubes in it. On the table were some bowls with various nuts.

"Sorry," I said. "I slept a little longer than I intended."

Dad didn't say anything, hardly seemed to notice that I arrived. He had sunglasses on and his face was turned down toward the shore. I pulled out a chair and sat down next to Maddy.

"What would you like to drink?" Dad asked without turning his gaze toward me. I heard him breathing, short and shallow, almost as if he were out of breath.

"Uh…a beer, if there is any."

"Barbro! A beer!" Dad shouted right out, with his face still turned toward the sea.

Someone was evidently not in their sunniest mood. Maddy and I exchanged a look.

Suddenly I understood.

"You're in pain, right?"

Dad didn't reply at first. Just sat silently and took his short, shallow breaths.

"Dad?"

"Yes, I'm in pain." He grasped his drinking glass and took a big gulp. "I didn't take my extended-release tablets yesterday. You don't notice until the following day. Now it's too awful. Just too awful. I've taken them now, and a few fast-acting ones too. But nothing is happening."

Dad changed position in his chair, leaned forward, rubbed his forehead with one hand. His face wasn't turned toward us but I sensed that it was twisted in a grimace.

I thought silently to myself that maybe it wasn't a good idea to drink whiskey and take two different kinds of strong pain relievers at the same time, but I didn't say anything.

"Are you able to eat dinner?" I asked. "Don't you want to go lie down instead?"

"No, I'll manage."

Barbro came out from the kitchen with a bottle of beer and a glass on a tray.

"What a fucking long time that took," said Dad.

Maddy sighed and squirmed. That was enough for him to turn toward her instead.

"What?" He sounded angry, as if he was fishing for a quarrel. "It damned well shouldn't take fifteen minutes to bring a beer, should it?"

"It didn't either."

Barbro placed the glass and the bottle on the table in front of me without a sound. I looked up at her, smiled and said thanks. Not a movement in her stone face. Dad looked at her and said, very clear and categorically, "Barbro, you are completely fucking worthless. I don't get why I still let you work for me."

A quick smile, cold as steel.

"But..." I said. "Seriously."

If Barbro was offended by Dad's words she didn't show it. Simply bent her head to the side as usual. But perhaps that was the reaction, I thought.

"You are no damned fun to be with when you're like this," said Maddy, raising her wineglass and taking a big sip.

Dad was breathing heavily.

I was a little shocked that she had said that. The fact is that a part of me—a part that I wasn't particularly proud of—was ashamed. She didn't know Dad, had only known him a couple of evenings, and that was an extremely direct thing to say.

Another part of me was proud. Maddy had said what I myself hadn't dared to.

But I also felt a different shame. He had snared me so quickly,

Dad had. I'd already thrown the ambition to keep my distance from him overboard.

Was it in reality because I didn't want to make Dad annoyed, and that there were a hundred million reasons for that?

Dad turned his head toward Maddy, stared at her. Suddenly he started laughing.

"Point taken…haha."

"No, but seriously. How are you behaving?"

"Haha…"

He was laughing hysterically and couldn't stop himself for quite some time. I tasted the beer. The bitterness contributed to the harsh sensation in my mouth and throat. A rasp that removed my thirst.

Dad collected himself at last.

"Haha…ah…well then, cheers."

He raised his glass toward me and Maddy and I answered the gesture. All three of us drank. Dad set his glass down on the table and shook his finger at Maddy.

"I like you. You're funny." He took out a pack of cigarettes, shook one out and put it between his lips. He lit it at the same as he said, "Can you help me with something, Isak? With the food?"

Dad went ahead of me and Barbro through the long, winding corridor. He had his usual clothes on, but also a big, black leather apron, you know, the kind you find in the finer kitchen stores. It was just that this apron looked a hundred years old, as if it had been passed down in a family of butchers, more or less. It was worn and spotted and looked like it could fall to pieces at any time. Before we reached the hall with the overgrown sofa Dad opened a door on the left side, and we came into a room that served as a storage area. Here were things having to do with the cars, like plastic bottles of oil and extra wiper blades, and various machines and tools to keep the yard in shape. Trimmer, hedge shears, crowbar and spades of different sizes. Dad walked right through the room and opened the next door, we followed and then we were in the garage.

The lights were turned off but I still perceived a large space. Considering the heat outside it was almost strangely cool. I sensed an odor of cellar and damp concrete.

A lamb bleated from the darkness.

Dad turned on the light. Fluorescent lights blinked to life and soon the garage was bathed in a cold, blueish light.

The one wall was covered by two identical garage doors, and a regular door. Outside was the turnaround, I assumed.

In the middle of the floor stood what appeared to be a portable workbench for an outdoor kitchen, of stainless steel with a pair of wheels at one end. On the bench was a large bowl, also of stainless steel, and a butcher's knife. One of Dad's painter's coats was hanging over a handle. From the ceiling a meat hook was hanging, covered with dried blood.

Next to the workbench stood a cage made of wooden slats, and in it was a lamb. It had no wool but was totally clean-shaven. The ribs were visible on the sides of the stomach, and the neck was sinewy and a little wrinkled. It bleated heartrendingly and paced around inside the cage. The hooves slid on the concrete floor.

Dad went over to the workbench and the cage.

"We'll have grilled whole lamb this evening," said Dad. "So I need a little help here."

My mouth was completely dry. I had difficulty forcing out the words.

"So, I... I don't know anything about such things."

"No, no," Dad said soothingly. "Barbro will take it out and flay it and all that. The only thing you need to do is to cut its throat."

★ ★ ★

The lamb stuck its little nose out between the slats, flaring its nostrils. Maybe it sensed the smell of death. Shrieked for its mama with eyes wide open.

No. Never.

I shook my head.

"I don't want to do that."

"No?"

"Sorry."

Dad sighed tiredly.

"I beg you, Isak."

"No."

"Someone has to do it. This is our food tonight. Now I'm asking you for help, because I'm in pain, and I'm tired, and this lamb must weigh thirty kilos, if not more. It's a heavy job before the blood runs out and it's hanging on the hook...but you don't feel like helping out?"

He was staring at me, waiting for a reply, but I didn't know what I should say. At last he continued.

"Do you think this is unpleasant?"

"Yes, of course it is."

"Have you ever eaten lamb?"

I stared at the lamb which was moving around in the cage.

"Isak?"

"Yes. Sure."

"How do you think those lambs died, then?"

I took a deep breath, simply shook my head.

"Most have lived a much worse life than this lamb, and they've died in a much worse way. If you were vegan, absolutely, then I would understand. But if you eat meat...at least have the backbone to do what's required."

I had no arguments to present, stood quietly like a fool. Felt little, weak and dumb.

The garage echoed from the lamb's hooves against the floor.

In the corner of my eye I saw Barbro twist her head to the side. Then back.

Dad went up to the workbench, took the painter's coat, turned toward me and held it up. He was smiling.

"Put this on." His voice was gentler now. "You know, when you've done it, and stand there with the knife in your hand… I promise that you're going to have a powerful feeling. You'll see."

I stood as if frozen to the floor, couldn't move; my body had locked up. Wanted to run away from there but my legs wouldn't obey.

Dad's smile fell from his face, like a mask. He took a half step toward me and the light from the fluorescent fixtures now fell from overhead. The furrows and cavities in his face were emphasized, and his eyes suddenly looked like two big black wells. His voice was rough and commanding.

"Now you do this. I demand it, Isak. If you want my money. That's not much to ask."

The lamb shrieked.

I felt weak in the knees.

Fifty million to the Red Cross.

Barbro went up and picked the steel bowl in her arms.

The winter months on a beach in Thailand.

The blade of the knife shone on the workbench.

The nostrils that fluttered, the panic-stricken eyes.

A rainsuit from Arcteryx, with concealed zippers.

I took a step forward and put my right arm into the painter's coat. Then the left arm. Dad helped me button it.

I went up to the workbench and took hold of the big knife.

Dad opened the cage by raising one end. The lamb tried to slip away, but Dad caught hold of its withers with both hands and raised it in the air. He carried it up to me and handed it over in my arms.

"Hold your hand under the chin so you can bend the head

backward." Dad was out of breath, and I understood why; the lamb felt heavier than I'd thought.

It bleated and thrashed in my arms but Dad didn't let go. He helped me hold it tight. Barbro came up to us with the big steel bowl in her arms. We stood close together, all three of us; our bodies almost touched each other, united by our task. Between us the lamb tried in vain to squirm out of our grip. Maybe it sensed what was going on.

I let one hand glide up along the lamb's neck, to the underside of the jaw.

"You cut along the whole jaw line, from one side to the other," said Dad. He sounded a little excited. Or else it was just the exertion.

I squeezed the knife shaft. Brought the edge toward the lamb's throat. I was a little out of breath too now from holding the lamb still. Breathed through my mouth.

Dad looked at the knife, and then at the lamb's throat. He grinned.

"It looks like the neck on an old man."

The lamb bleated, then I bent its head back further, stretched the skin on the throat, leaned the side of the knife blade against the end of the lower jaw and pulled.

The knife was so sharp.

The edge cut through the skin without effort. I pulled and pressed at the same time, and it sank deeper in through tendons and cartilage and muscles. The blood sprayed out over the knife and over my hand. It was quite warm, and it ran down into Barbro's hair and face. She made a strange sound, like hissing, or else it came from the lamb. Anyway I continued pulling the whole way across to the other side, almost behind the ear.

The blood poured out, down over the lamb's stomach, down into the bowl. The wound in its neck was gaping. A few more strokes with the knife and I could have separated the body from the head completely.

"There now," said Dad, looking triumphantly at me. A little blood had splashed across his face too.

The lamb's movements quickly became more feeble. The body slackened. A final kick with a rear leg, then the lamb hung quietly in my arms.

The adrenaline rushed in my veins. I was aroused, excited.

I had taken a life. It had been so easy.

Barbro placed the bowl with the blood down on the floor and I set the lifeless body alongside, with the opening in the throat over the edge. The blood continued to run but already more quietly.

Dad gave me a pat on the arm, and at the same moment the sound of an engine was heard from the turnaround outside. Crunching of car tires over gravel. Dad looked up and appeared surprised, wiped away the blood on his cheek with his palm.

The crunching stopped, and the engine fell silent.

Dad went toward the door out to the turnaround.

Barbro crouched beside the metal bowl. The blood was still body temperature and steaming. She dipped a finger in it, then put the finger in her mouth.

A car door opened out there. At the same time Dad opened the door to the turnaround and went out to look.

"Hello," he said, and his voice sounded both surprised and semihostile.

"Hello," the person out there answered, and I felt a cold wave through my body; my heart stopped.

Barbro had stood up and was holding the lamb's body by the rear legs over the bowl. A thin trickle of blood was still running out of its throat.

"Come," said Dad. "Isak is in here."

My heart started beating again, with a few extrastrong strokes to make up for lost ground.

Dad came back into the garage. I was still standing with the bloody knife in my hand, I hurried over to put it back on the workbench and just as I let go of the shaft Grandpa came in through the door.

His look, as he tried to take in the whole scene there in the garage. Barbro, who was holding the dead lamb over the bowl. All the blood that had splashed out on the floor. Me in my bloody painter's coat.

"You will stay for dinner, won't you?" said Dad. "Isak has just butchered a lamb."

PART THREE

If you stare too long down into the abyss,
the abyss will stare back at you.

Friedrich Nietzsche

"I WANT TO TALK WITH YOU," SAID GRANDPA. HIS VOICE SOUNDED hoarse and a little breathless. His gaze wandered around, from the bowl with blood, to the knife on the workbench, to my bloodied hands.

"Yeah...sure. But..." I didn't finish the sentence, started unbuttoning the painter's coat.

"Wait," said Dad. "I'll help you." He came up to me and started undoing the buttons. Probably didn't want me to touch my own clothes with bloody fingers. Grandpa looked at us standing there close together. His gaze dark and worried. Dad said, unconcerned, without looking at Grandpa, "What do you want, Anders? To what do we owe this honor?"

"I want to talk with Isak."

Dad undid the last button and helped me take off the painter's coat, as if he were my servant or something. Then I followed Grandpa out of the garage. I squinted at the sunlight reflected in the white gravel on the turnaround. We walked over to Grandpa's car, a Ford Mondeo station wagon that had seen better days. He had on a short-sleeved checked shirt and three-quarter-length pants with many pockets, both garments heavily wrinkled. Sandals and short socks.

Grandpa turned toward me, and only now did I notice how tired he looked. His face was shiny and his hair stood up in sweaty shocks around his head. Red-rimmed eyes, with big, dark circles below. He looked thinner and more hunched up than usual, I thought. He looked at me seriously.

"You called me last night."

"What?"

"You don't remember that?"

"No."

I didn't understand what Grandpa was talking about.

"Yes, you called me and you were quite desperate."

"So, wait...when was this? What time of night?"

"About four or so. Quarter to four maybe."

I had absolutely no memory of this. It was unpleasant. I swallowed, stared off into the forest that surrounded the turnaround.

"We talked for over half an hour. You don't remember?"

"No."

"You were almost in a panic. Like when you were little. You talked about bird masks, and that there was fire. You said something about a fire in the ceiling, but you couldn't explain where...it was as if you had night terrors."

The dreams I'd had late in the morning before I woke up. I had only extremely blurry memories of them.

"You finally calmed down anyway, or else you woke up so that you understood you were just dreaming."

"Hmm."

"I got really worried about you."

"I understand that. I'm really sorry."

"Then I've tried to call you today. Lots of times. But you haven't answered."

With every new thing that Grandpa told me I felt guiltier and guiltier.

"No. Uh...my phone died yesterday, then it's been charging all day today."

"Yes, yes."

"I am truly really sorry about this. It was absolutely not the idea to make you worried."

He looked searchingly at me.

"What did you do yesterday?"

I squirmed a little, rubbing my eye with my palm.

"Uh… Dad and I were in Riga. In Latvia. He wanted to show me an orphanage that he sponsors."

"I see…so what did you do later?"

I realized that Grandpa only wished me well, but this was starting to resemble an interrogation.

"Yes…we…we went out."

"Did you take anything?"

"Did I take anything?"

"I'm sorry that I'm asking, Isak, but you said yesterday that you'd taken something."

"Okay…"

"It sounded like that anyway. I'm not completely certain."

"No, I didn't take anything," I said. "But we mixed wine and beer and drinks. So it got to be a little too much."

How good I was starting to get at this. I stood and lied right to Grandpa's face without blinking. I remembered Dad's words, that the truth causes pain, so it's the one who tells it who should feel guilty. Or however it was he expressed it.

Grandpa took a deep breath. He looked like he was ready to collapse. The tension had probably lightened a little and then the fatigue washed over him even stronger. He ran one hand through his hair. I put my hand on his arm.

"Are you okay?"

"No, it's… I'm a little tired." He laughed ironically and smiled joylessly. "I couldn't fall asleep after we'd hung up."

"No, I understand."

"And then I tried to call you, and you didn't answer… I tried to call Maddy, she didn't answer either…so I felt that I had to come here, I had to get hold of you." Grandpa closed his eyes and rubbed the bridge of his nose with thumb and index finger.

"Yes… I'm super sorry, but you don't need to worry, everything's fine."

Grandpa looked away toward the door into the garage. Dad was leaning against the doorpost squinting toward the sun. Observing us. Behind him, from inside the garage, Barbro was heard making noise. Metal against concrete, a singing sound, a creaking hook.

"That then?" he said with a gesture toward the garage. "What was that?"

He turned his gaze back toward me and now it was searching again. The gentle, slightly apologetic look was gone.

I stood quietly, didn't really know what I should say. How could I explain what I didn't understand myself?

"Dad needed help. He was in pain."

He called to us from over by the door.

"Hello? Shall we go in and have something to drink?"

"We're not finished!" Grandpa sounded aggressive and angry. I didn't really recognize his voice.

Dad raised his hands in the air in a dismissive gesture. Grandpa turned to me again.

"And then he wanted you to butcher the lamb? Don't you think that's strange?"

I had no reply to that. Found myself between two worlds. Grandpa's and Dad's. One foot in each world.

Grandpa rubbed his face again, as if he was trying to waken himself from a nightmare. At last he said, subdued so that Dad wouldn't hear, "Let's get out of here, Isak."

"Now, do you mean?"

"Yes. We'll take my car. You can come back and get your things later." He spoke quickly and intensely, almost sounded imploring.

"No, but that's not possible."

"There's something very wrong here. I sense it."

Sure, I sensed it too. But not in the way that Grandpa meant.

"Well… I can't just run away from Maddy."

"Get her then."

"No… I'm sorry, it's not possible."

That Grandpa was tired and worn-out after a night without sleep, and a whole day of traveling besides—that I understood, it was nothing strange. But now I started to realize that it had affected his psyche too. He wasn't thinking clearly. What he proposed was a little crazy. What would Dad think if we just jumped into Grandpa's car and drove away?

"We're going to have dinner here this evening. We've made plans."

"He isn't good for you. You shouldn't be together with him anymore."

Not your decision, I was eager to say. *I'm grown up now. Dad wants to work things out before he dies, there's nothing wrong with that. He wants to give me all his money. Nothing wrong with that either.*

"Hello?" Dad called from the door again. "I won't disturb you, you can talk as much as you want…but you don't need to stand out here in the sun, do you? Come in and we'll have something to drink."

I put my hand on Grandpa's arm.

"Let's do that. We'll go in, so we can finish talking."

He looked irresolute but didn't say anything.

"You can get a cup of coffee. Sit down a little in the shade."

Something in our relationship was changed now. I felt it so clearly, and I think he felt it too. A different balance of power. For me it felt good and right. But I don't think it felt that way to him.

A few minutes later I was back in the exhibition room. The phone was fully charged now and I turned it on. Five missed calls during the day, all from Grandpa. Checked the call list. Yes, there it was. From 03:51 to 04:33. Forty-two minutes that I didn't remember a trace of. Forty-two minutes that had turned Grandpa's life upside down. Bird masks and burning roofs.

I went into the bathroom, washed my hands, splashed my face and neck with cold water. Heard steps from the hallway outside. Then Maddy came into the bathroom.

"Hi," she said, looking at me a little worriedly. "What's going on?"

I turned off the faucet and sighed.

"Yes, well…what isn't going on?"

I told what Dad wanted help with, to butcher a lamb for tonight's dinner. And then Grandpa showed up.

"Apparently I talked on the phone with him last night. I have no memory at all of that."

"No…he seems worked up."

Dad and Grandpa had come out on the patio where Maddy was waiting. Dad offered him something to drink but he didn't want anything. Maddy tried to get him to sit down in the shade and rest a little, but he refused. He paced around in the sun as if he had ants in his legs. And then he'd asked Maddy why she didn't answer the phone. He must have called five times during the day, he maintained.

"You know, he was so…almost aggressive," said Maddy. "I've never seen him that way before."

I dried my face, hid it in the towel.

"No," I said right into the cloth.

"I mean, I don't check my phone all the time. Today I've mostly been lying on the beach."

"Yes, yes, sure."

"You wonder a little about his state of mind."

Barbro was standing by the kitchen island preparing tonight's dinner. Dad was nowhere to be seen. I saw that Grandpa had sat down on a chair out on the patio, under a parasol. Always something. I took a big glass from a cupboard, filled it with cold water from the tap and went out to him. Maddy followed me.

"Here," I said. "Drink this."

Grandpa stood up, took the glass and drank in big gulps. His face was red, his forehead and neck shiny with sweat.

"Thanks," he said and wiped his mouth. He cast a glance toward Barbro. "Who is that?"

"Barbro," I said. "She's mute."

Grandpa kept staring at her as he set the glass down on the table. He looked seriously at me and Maddy.

"I think we should leave here."

I took a step closer to him and placed my hand on his shoulder. He reeked of sweat and needed to take a shower. I made my voice gentle.

"But listen," I said. "We have to eat anyway. Stay and have dinner with us, then we can talk more about it later."

Dad joined us, and then we had a drink on the patio before dinner. His bad mood, the touchiness that I assumed had to do with his pain, had vanished. Grandpa's arrival had altered the circumstances. Or else it was the tablets and the alcohol in combination that had started to work. In any event he was a polite and charming host, to Grandpa too. Grandpa on the other hand was taciturn and contrary. He didn't let us forget for a second that he had stayed under protest. He didn't want to have anything to drink other than tap water.

It was almost eight o'clock and the air had cooled a bit. As usual you could hear the waves more toward twilight. A light breeze made the treetops murmur.

Barbro stood in the doorway to the kitchen and looked at Dad. He nodded.

"Well then...shall we go in and sit down?"

Maddy took the lead and I followed. One end of the big dining room table was set. The appetizer was already on the plates, a small toast with some kind of shrimp mixture. Several open bottles of wine were also set out on the table, both red and white. There was an aroma of grilled meat, oven-roasted peppers, garlic and potatoes and cream, charred sprigs of thyme and rosemary. Suddenly I felt very hungry.

Maddy went around the table, to a seat so that she had a view toward the patio and the sea. My first impulse was to follow her and sit down beside her, but then Grandpa and Dad would end up next to each other. So I took the chair opposite Maddy instead. She gave me a little questioning look, but didn't say anything. Grandpa stood beside me. Dad rounded the table and pulled the chair out for Maddy.

"Help yourselves."

We sat down and started to eat.

Maddy and I continued with white wine, and Dad kept us company. Grandpa sipped his tap water and ate tiny, tiny bites of the toast.

"Damn, this is good," Maddy mumbled in the middle of a big bite. "Sorry for swearing with my mouth full."

Dad laughed and took another bite. He glanced at Grandpa and at his place, whose toast was almost untouched.

"What do you think, Anders?"

"I'm not that hungry."

Brief silence. We continued eating. At least the three of us. Dad drank from his wineglass.

"But…you seemed to like fish and seafood a lot before. If I remember right?"

Grandpa stuck his fork in a sticky shrimp and stuffed it in his mouth.

"Mmm."

"Didn't you fish a lot there in Lunnen? Both nets and those, what are they called…?"

Dad fell silent, left the field open for Grandpa to fill in. But he didn't intend to let himself be lured into a conversation. He stared at his plate, chewed on the shrimp, looked angry and dismissive.

Grandpa. Here he sat in his wrinkled shirt and his wrinkled pants, his sandals with socks, far forward on the chair, a little hunched up as if he were on tenterhooks. Shiny face, hair in disarray. Irascible. Resentful. Need for control. A desire to rule over me.

And a lack of manners. Yes, really. He had shown up at Dad's house, without any notice whatsoever, and Dad had invited him to dinner, a really nice dinner with supergood food and supergood wines, and Grandpa couldn't even make himself say thanks or make some appreciative comments.

Regardless of what had happened in the past between them, to dig in so totally to his antipathy for Dad, or whether I would even call it hatred… I didn't like that.

And I thought that maybe it was true that Grandpa only fit into the little world he had created around himself at home in Småland; as soon as he came out in the big world it became obvious that it wasn't for him.

In contrast to me. I had progressed to the next level. Grandpa hadn't progressed.

Dad still looked questioningly and invitingly at Grandpa, who was staring down at his plate.

"Longline," I said, looking at Grandpa. "That's what it's called, right?"

No response.

When the toast was eaten up Barbro took away our small plates. Dad served red wine. Grandpa said no, thanks, of course, but Maddy and I accepted. We toasted and tasted. Barbro brought out au gratin potatoes from the oven and set it right on the table, the cream still bubbling at the edges. Oven-roasted vegetables. Bowls with a couple of different sauces. And then a plate with slices of grilled lamb, crisp and dark on the surface, perfectly pink in the middle, dotted with garlic and rosemary. We dug in and started to eat. The wine expanded in our mouths; new tastes showed up with every sip. My glass was already empty and Dad poured more.

A quick glance from Grandpa, not at me but at the glass. Disapproving. He thought I was drinking too much.

"You're really missing something," I said, raising the glass and taking a sip. "Sure you don't want a taste?"

Grandpa didn't even answer. Dad made a silent grimace—oops, that was no doubt sensitive. The gleam in his eyes I recognized from the night before. Probably starting to get a little tipsy. Like myself.

While we ate I told Grandpa more about what we'd been doing since we came to Ajkeshorn. Maddy and Dad filled in. I described the magnificent beach and the cold water. The late evening in the treehouse. The outing with the sports cars, the restaurant by the sea.

"Isak is now the lucky owner of a Lamborghini," Dad interjected.

"Hello, I haven't said that I want it," I protested.

Dad grimaced.

"Bah. You're just quibbling a little. You know that you really want it."

Grandpa set down his knife and fork. He hadn't put much on his plate, but almost all of it was still there; he had only poked at the food. Maddy gave him a searching look.

Barbro filled the plate with more slices of the grilled whole lamb and Dad encouraged us to take more. But I had already had seconds, so I couldn't take another bite. Maddy explained that she too was stuffed.

"This was probably the best lamb I've ever eaten," she said, breathing out contentedly.

Dad raised his glass to me, smiled so that his eyes glistened and said, "Yes, what you did was damned good. You're a natural."

I felt a little cocky. As if my capable way of cutting the throat of the lamb truly had contributed to it tasting so good.

I know. Completely sick. The wine had probably started to go to my head.

"Although this can't be the lamb that Isak butchered."

Grandpa's words came through clenched lips. Rather quiet, but intense. His voice trembled a little.

There was silence around the table. Dad's eyes sought the sea; he seemed to gaze toward the horizon. His good-natured expression had become a bit stiff.

I probably should have asked what Grandpa meant, but I remained silent too. Hoped that what he'd said would stay hanging in the air between us for a moment, to then dissolve in empty space like a soap bubble.

Maddy reached for the wine bottle.

"This wine is really incredible."

"Drink," said Dad. "Drink as long as it lasts. Then we'll open another."

"Right, Fredrik?" said Grandpa, and now he raised his eyes toward Dad. "It can't be that lamb."

I squirmed uncomfortably, glanced at Grandpa. He grasped the edge of the table with both hands, as if he was forced to hold on. You could hear that he was trying to keep his voice steady, that was probably why he spoke rather quietly, but it didn't succeed, it was as if he spit out the words. His whole body was shaking.

"I've grilled whole lamb many times—we've done it with the orienteering club—and it takes five hours, at least, before it's completely done. And you have to stand and rotate it the whole time. And I came here maybe two hours ago, or two and a half, and then the lamb wasn't even flayed..."

"Yes, yes," said Maddy, trying to stop Grandpa. "We get it..."

But he didn't let himself be stopped.

"So it doesn't make sense at all… Why are you trying to make us think that?"

Grandpa nailed Dad firmly with his gaze. His body was shaking, as if he had chills. Dad looked up, met Grandpa's gaze, firm and steady.

My head was spinning, and it wasn't just the wine. Once again I was about to be cut in two. One part that was ashamed of Grandpa because he ruined the atmosphere around the table. And another part that thought there was something in what he said, a part that tried to figure it out purely logically, but couldn't get ahold of it.

Dad's facial expression softened. He smiled, indulgently and considerately, at Grandpa.

"Are you cold, Anders? Should we close the glass door?"

"Just answer the question. Why are you pretending that Isak butchered this lamb?"

"You're shaking," said Dad, getting up from the table. "Shall I get a blanket? Or do you want to borrow a fleece?" Dad went to the glass wall and closed it.

Barbro stood by the kitchen counter, staring blankly ahead. Of course she heard and saw everything, but it was as if she wasn't taking it in. What was happening in the kitchen did not affect her in the least; she was in a completely different world.

Was she not only mute, but deaf too? Was that what it was about?

Now she drew her head to the side, turned her face away for a moment. Then back. The same neutral expression. As if she was thinking of something else.

Don't really know why I noticed this. Maybe because I myself experienced the mood around the table as so unpleasant that I simply wanted to flee. But I thought Barbro looked creepy.

Grandpa had Dad behind his back now, and that seemed to make him ill at ease, as he turned in the chair to keep him in sight. Dad went up to Grandpa, put his hand on his shoulder.

"My friend…listen…"

Grandpa shoved away his hand and hissed angrily.

"Don't you touch me!"

"Grandpa, calm down," I said and put my hand on his arm, while Dad went around the table and sat down again.

Maddy was biting her lip but didn't say anything.

"No, I don't intend to calm down!" Grandpa said in a loud voice. He no longer cared to seem collected and restrained—maybe it was his shout when Dad touched him that had freed him in some way.

"Why should he butcher a lamb? Why did you want that?"

Dad met his gaze and sounded peaceful, almost mournful, when he answered.

"Because I'm sick and tired and can't do it myself."

"That's just silliness," Grandpa snorted. He meant to say something else but Dad raised his voice and interrupted.

"Yes, but then I would like to ask you something, Anders," said Dad. "The only thing I want is a couple of days alone with my son. Before I die. Why can't you—"

Grandpa interrupted him.

"And what are you doing with these days? Yes, you drive race cars and go to Riga and drink."

Grandpa's voice was full of sarcasm and distaste. He truly looked down on what we'd done those days. But those weren't the only things we'd done, I thought; we'd talked too. The one thing didn't rule out the other. On the contrary, the fact that we'd done fun things together had opened a path between us. And that was probably Dad's intention from the beginning.

"Actually you don't care about Isak. You want to have control over him," said Dad.

Grandpa shook his head, with a bitter little smile.

"Oh…that was…that was nervy coming from you. That I don't care about Isak."

"Listen, it's completely meaningless to keep on discussing this," I said.

Rapunzel. Confined in the tower.

"Yes," Maddy interjected. "Just drop it now, both of you."

But neither of them seemed to hear us. Dad smiled when he said, "There's nothing I can do to change what you think of me, is there?"

"Now there probably isn't, no. Too many years have passed. I have…"

"You think I'm a bad person, and you've thought that since we met the first time."

Grandpa shook his head.

"No. That was the first time we'd met. I didn't know you."

Maddy sighed, got up from the table as if in protest, left the kitchen. Maybe she was just going to the bathroom. I was still upset and wanted this duel to end. But part of me had also perked up its ears when Dad mentioned the first time they met.

"But you didn't like me."

Grandpa was silent, looked down at the table, sipped the water in his glass to gain time. It was a telling silence. Dad stared at him, smiled coldly.

"You can say it, Anders. I know that you actually want to. You like judging people."

"I thought you were strange. Agneta thought so too."

"Strange? How so, what do you mean?" Dad sounded genuinely interested.

"You were completely uninterested in Agneta and me," said Grandpa. "It was so glaringly obvious. We lived in a hole in the countryside—who were we to care about? You couldn't even make yourself pretend."

"You don't think it may have been the case that you actually were a wee bit uninteresting?"

"Sure, of course."

"And that maybe you are a bit easily offended?"

"But we saw in Linn that this was extremely important for her. That we should like you, and that you should like us. But you didn't notice any of that. In any event you didn't care about that."

Dad didn't say anything. He simply drank a little more wine and then turned his gaze to Grandpa again. Encouraged him silently to keep talking.

"And then we thought…or in any case I did…that you didn't care about Linn either. Not for real. Because then you would have understood that this made her sad."

"And then you had the picture clear. He's bad for my daughter. He's a bad person."

I stole a glance toward Barbro over by the counter, who seemed completely unmoved by the conflict that was playing out two meters away. She looked down at a glass that she had in her hand. In the glass something white and slimy and bloody could be seen.

"No. But you asked about my first impression."

"He's evil."

"No, not evil…"

"Yes."

Barbro leaned her head back and emptied the glass into her mouth. I have never seen a person gape so wide as she had at that moment. It looked grotesque. An eyeball, because now I saw that's what it was, slid down onto Barbro's tongue.

"No, but I will say what I thought," Grandpa continued. "There's something that's lacking in him. Something that other people have."

I barely heard any longer what he was saying. I was still staring at Barbro.

She's eating the lamb's eyes, I thought.

"Empathy, perhaps."

"A person without empathy, isn't that an evil person? According to your way of seeing things?"

"I believe that we all have both good and bad in us…but I also think that most people know the difference."

The other eye had stuck firmly at the bottom of the glass. Barbro shook the glass so that it would come loose. And it was a shake that didn't resemble anything I'd seen before either. Or to say it more correctly, it did, just nothing I'd seen a person do.

You know how cats and dogs can shake a paw, quick quick, like a rapid trembling? Or when they scratch themselves behind the ear? The paw moves so fast that you can't see it.

I got that feeling when Barbro shook the glass. First once, then again. The eye released and fell down on her tongue.

"You believe that." I registered Dad's sarcastic voice as if from far away.

"Yes. If you have empathy, if you can picture for yourself what it's like for another person, then it's rather simple."

"Okay."

Barbro jerked her neck violently a few times, as if she was throwing her head backward. Swallowed. I got the feeling that the eyes slid down whole. She then turned around and set the glass down on the kitchen counter.

"Isak definitely knows that. He's a good person."

I heard my name mentioned, tore my gaze from Barbro and noticed that Grandpa was looking at me. Didn't know what to say, if I should say anything. My thoughts were still on Barbro and the eyes. At the same time Maddy came back into the kitchen and sat down on the chair next to Dad.

"And what are you? Are you a good person?" Dad continued.

Maddy tiredly shook her head and reached for the wine bottle.

"God, are you still carrying on…? Then I must have more wine."

Barbro had eaten the eyes, with hanging bloody fibers and all. Was I the only one who'd seen that?

"No," said Grandpa. "I'm not. But I do the best I can."

"May I ask then, if you look out in the world, what do you see?"

"I'm starting to get in the mood for dessert," said Maddy.

"You are definitely among the richest ten percent on this planet," Dad continued. "Maybe the richest five percent, even. There are billions of people who are born poor in the world, and die poor. How do you think they look at you? 'He's so privileged, but he doesn't do anything about it, so he must think he has a right to it. That he's earned it.' Do you believe they think you have a lot of empathy? That you're a good person?"

Grandpa's voice was hoarse when he replied. The almost paralyzing indignation had come back. And it was that tone, just as much as what he said, that made me listen carefully.

"You ruined our lives."

Grandpa's voice was unsteady; his whole body was shaking. Dad again turned his gaze to Grandpa, still smiling.

"Sorry?"

"I know what you did."

Dad turned toward me, but made a gesture toward Grandpa.

"Yes, you hear. I am clearly the devil himself."

"He's not doing well from being with you."

"Do you agree? Are you feeling unwell from being with me?"

"He called me last night and was quite desperate."

"Yes, but you shouldn't worry about that, Anders, we had simply tried some drugs. It's completely normal for the first time."

Dad was the only one who managed to maintain a carefree tone. I felt cold sweat breaking out on my scalp and neck. Maddy looked worriedly at me.

Grandpa looked at me too, and he could read on my face that what Dad said was true. We had taken drugs. I had lied to him. He stiffened; it seemed as if he had stopped breathing. He was crushed. I was crushed.

"This isn't you, Isak..." he mumbled.

"Sorry," said Maddy, raising her hands in the air to indicate that she wanted to say something. "But like this… Isak tried drugs, and no, he didn't say anything about it to me either. Big deal."

Dad sat silently, but he looked satisfied. Leaned back, took a sip of wine.

"Isak has never lied to me before," said Grandpa.

"No… I don't really know how you can be certain of that, but sure," Maddy continued. "In any case, that you've never tried drugs a single time when you're twenty-five, that's almost abnormal. So… I don't know why you're making such a big deal of it."

Maddy had joined my side. And it felt nice. When I looked at myself with Grandpa's eyes I felt little and pathetic and worthless, like I'd done something unforgivable. But here came Maddy and toned down what I'd done. That was big of her. I needed that so much at that moment.

"You don't understand," Grandpa said to Maddy, his tone curt. "You don't know the whole story."

"That's right," I said. "That Dad called and wanted to talk with me when I was little, but that you didn't allow it?"

It just came out. I regretted it immediately. And at the next moment I didn't regret it.

Grandpa was silent, stared at me with mouth half-open. His face turned pale. Dad sank down deeper in the chair on the other side of the table, cocked his head and looked at him.

Grandpa had no response. Not at first anyway. He moved his lips silently as if to say something, but closed his mouth again. I saw how he suffered. But I actually didn't have a guilty conscience. Not at that moment. Grandpa had said that I'd lied to him, but what had he done himself? Why didn't he let me talk with my father when I was little? If that was a lie, why didn't he just say so?

There was dead silence. A silence that seemed to suck up all the oxygen in the room. When Grandpa started to speak again his voice was broken.

"We can…we can talk about it later."

So it was true then.

Grandpa took hold of the edge of the table and stood up slowly. He swayed a little, looked as if he was afraid of falling down. He looked at me with a gaze that was resigned and powerless and imploring.

Something squeezed around my heart.

"I'll go now…but you can go with me. I beg you."

"Why should he do that?" said Maddy.

I raised my hand dismissively at her.

"But really, Anders," Maddy continued. "I think you, like… and I know that I don't have the whole picture, I haven't been there from the beginning, sorry, but Isak has spent his whole life with you, can't you just let him be with his father a couple of days?"

I leaned my elbows on the table, put my hands in front of my face.

"Maddy, you don't need to—" She interrupted me.

"No, I know that I don't need to, but I must say this." And now she turned toward Grandpa again. "Don't you see how bad he's feeling from this? The two of you evidently hate each other and Isak is torn between you—didn't you get that it would be that way when you came here?"

Grandpa seemed to be searching for something more to say. His gaze wandered and his lips moved, but he remained silent. Nodded at last, pushed in his chair and started walking toward the door. Hunched up and staggering.

My heart tightened up further in my chest.

"Grandpa…" I said, and was on the verge of getting up, but Maddy leaned over the table and took my hand in both of hers and gave me a look full of tenderness and sympathy.

Let him go. It's for the best.

And Grandpa left. I heard his quiet steps die away through the corridor.

I had a storm of emotions inside.

Grandpa wanted me to do something, Maddy wanted me to do something else and Dad wanted me to do a third thing. All three important persons in my life that I cared about—yes, that probably also applied to Dad after these intense days. They all wanted me to do something. But what did I myself want?

It was like thunder in my head; I couldn't think clearly, couldn't feel. A noise that cut off contact with myself.

Dad took a sip of wine, let it roll around in his mouth. He looked so unmoved, so content. He swallowed, and then he called after Grandpa.

"Anders, do you want dessert in a doggy bag? It will be panna cotta!"

He had won this evening, but he couldn't simply be satisfied with that; he had to twist the knife. Humiliate.

Nothing was heard from the darkness of the corridor. Perhaps Grandpa hadn't heard Dad call. Dad made a face toward me and Maddy, the same face that he'd made once earlier in the evening.

Oops. Someone got mad.

And then I saw it so clearly.

You are a fucking bully, I thought.

I knew of course that I was the most important thing in life for Grandpa, that I always had been. He'd come all the way here, to Dad's country place, even though he knew he wouldn't be welcome. He knew that Dad would be hostile. Maybe me too. But he was willing to expose himself to that because he was terribly worried about me. Because he loved me.

What Dad did now, pressing a little more even though he'd already walked away with the victory, simply because he could, that's something Grandpa would never do. He doesn't have that meanness in him. And Dad could talk all he wanted about how good and evil are only constructions and that everything simply flowed on if you just looked at it more closely, the truth was that good and evil really did exist, and it was empathy that was decisive. I felt that in my heart.

Dad was a bully, he'd gotten Maddy over on his side, me too, and all three of us had attacked Grandpa, who only meant well but was old and tired and unable to resist.

Beloved Grandpa. What had I done?

I felt like a wave inside that simply grew and grew when what had been hanging in the balance tipped over in one direction, and I was about to drown in a vortex of despair and shame.

I pushed the chair out and stood up, mumbling, "No… I have to…"

Maddy kept her hold on my hand across the table.

"Isak…take it easy."

"I have to speak with him."

I tried to pull myself loose, but Maddy's grip hardened. I pulled back hard and my hands were free at last. Rounded the table and headed for the corridor that Grandpa had just passed through, but Maddy stood up too. She took a few steps to the side and placed herself in my way.

"Listen! Let him go… You can talk tomorrow…"

"No…stop…"

Maddy took hold of my body as if she wanted to be hugged, put her arms around me. And now Dad had also placed himself between me and the entry to the corridor, like a gatekeeper.

"Calm down, Isak, there's no point."

Dad put his hand on my shoulder and took hold of my arm.

What was this? What were they doing?

"Just let go of me, damn it!" I shouted, pulling Maddy's arm loose and shoving her to the side with such force that she stumbled backward. I pushed Dad aside too and my one shoulder struck his face pretty hard, but it wasn't my damned fault, why didn't he listen to me, and not Maddy either?

I thought I heard a hissing sound from Barbro over by the counter. Started walking quickly through the corridor. Picked up speed—I was running now, and finally I'd reached the entry hall. I almost slid on my soles up to the door, tore it open and heaved myself out on the turnaround.

It was twilight. The sun had gone down but its rays were still reflected in the wispy clouds that showed up in the sky, pink- and peach-colored veils that gave a special luster to the white gravel. It almost looked luminescent. The trunks of the pines glowed red, and the crowns looked more black than green.

The turnaround was deserted.

Two red taillights disappeared just behind the first bend in the road.

The sound of an engine mixed with the murmur of the forest, like a drop of blood in the sea. Soon it was heard no more.

I ran back to the kitchen.

Damn, damn, damn.

I met Maddy in the corridor.

"Listen," she said and reached for me, but I only hurried past her. I had to call Grandpa, right now. Didn't have my phone on me so it must still be in the kitchen.

Dad was standing with his hands in his pockets and looked at me when I came back. The phone wasn't at my place at the table. I checked on the chair and floor too.

"Where's my phone?" I asked.

Dad raised his shoulders.

"I don't know."

Could I have set it down on the patio when we were having drinks before dinner? I opened the glass wall and ran out and looked, both by the table where we'd been sitting and by the low lounge furniture, although why would it have ended up there?

Nothing.

I rushed in again. Now Maddy had also come back to the kitchen.

"So, I must have left it here," I said. "What's going on?"

Dad looked away, stroked his mouth, pinched himself on the tip of his nose. Then I saw the outline of a phone through the fabric of his trousers.

"Give me yours," I said to Dad, taking a step toward him and reaching out my hand.

"Drop this now," he said. "You can call him tomorrow."

I took another step toward him.

"Give it to me."

It wasn't a request; it was an order. I had raised my voice.

Dad took a cautious step back, without taking his gaze off me. There was something guarded and sharp in his eyes.

"No, I want you to calm down..."

I rushed toward him. Maddy didn't have a chance to stop me. I reached for his pants pocket and he tried to twist away and stop my hands, but I was much stronger than him.

"Isak...control yourself!" he roared.

Dad and I pulled and tore at each other. But doggedly and deliberately I forced my hand down into his pocket and pulled up the phone.

It was mine.

I took a few steps away from Dad, staring wildly at him. Dad stared back. He didn't look exactly scared, but worried; he realized that something was about to go very wrong between us.

"You... I can..."

"Are you completely out of your mind?"

I almost ran out of the kitchen with the phone in my hand.

"Isak!" I heard Maddy call after me.

Fuck her, fuck Dad, fuck this whole fucking place.

Brought up the contact list in passing and called Grandpa.

No answer.

I was connected to voicemail.

"Hi, Grandpa, this is Isak, I'm really sorry that things turned out the way they did... Call me as soon as you can. I'll gladly leave here with you, if you… I mean, if you can bear to drive back, otherwise we can meet tomorrow instead. There's no rush, like, but…call me. I'm really sorry."

When I'd finished talking I had come to Maddy's and my part of the house. The hall was in darkness, and the grotesque sofa brooded like a storm cloud over it. I turned on the ceiling lights. Switched on a floor lamp that was in a corner too. Continued into the exhibition room, turned on the ceiling light there too. All the fluorescent lights. And both bedside lamps. I simply felt that I must have light around me, as much light as possible.

Sank down on the bed and called Grandpa again. No answer now either.

Now I heard steps approaching through the hall. I still had the phone by my ear, ringtone after ringtone without any answer. Maddy went up to me, looked searchingly at me, but didn't say anything.

Voicemail started up again. I clicked it off. No sense in leaving another message.

"Doesn't he answer?"

"No."

Maddy sighed and sank down on the edge of the bed beside me. Reached for my hand, but I pulled it away. She remained sitting turned toward me, with her open hand in her lap, her whole body shaped into a question that didn't need to be expressed.

We sat silently a moment. Then I turned and looked at her.

"Why didn't you say that Dad took my phone?"

"I didn't know!" She drew up her shoulders and threw out her hands. "I ran after you!" She sounded desperate.

I turned my eyes away but soon I heard a sob.

Sure, she was right.

"Sorry," I said. My voice was thin and brittle.

Maddy quietly wiped away a tear that ran down her cheek.

"Why can't you understand that I'm on your side."

"Because I'm an idiot."

I reached out my arms toward Maddy. It took a moment, but then she leaned toward me and I could put my arms around her.

We sat like that, a long time, quietly rocking from side to side.

The summer night was at its darkest point. All the lights were turned off. A diffuse frame was visible around the edges of the drawn curtains, but otherwise the room was dark.

Maddy was sleeping on her side, turned away from me.

I lay there, staring up at the ceiling.

Three more times I'd tried to call Grandpa, but he didn't answer. That made me worried. But I told myself that he probably hadn't charged the phone yesterday.

I had said to Maddy, as we sat there on the edge of the bed, that if I hadn't had so much to drink I would have gotten in the car and driven away from there at once. Dad and I were done with each other. I didn't want his damned money. He soiled everything he came in contact with. Maybe he was a genius, like people said, but he was also completely messed up.

Maddy nodded and said that the only important thing for her was that we were together. She suggested that we pack up and leave right after breakfast the next day.

That, however, wasn't what I was thinking about.

It was something that Grandpa had said.

I know what you did.

What did he mean by that?

I know what you did.

Those words implied that Dad had gotten away with something. It was something that Grandpa knew that Dad had done that he hadn't been held accountable for. So it couldn't refer to the fact that he'd failed his responsibility as a parent and disappeared from my life. That was no secret; it wasn't a truth that was waiting to be revealed.

It must be something else. Something bigger.

You ruined our lives.

And suddenly I realized what it was I'd seen in the studio that was important. What had just fluttered past without my grasping it.

It's strange how a memory can be resting deep down in us, like the muck on a lakebed. Then you move around down there and something releases, rises to the surface.

Now I remembered. My heart was pounding violently in my chest.

I must go to the studio again.

I'm in the laundry room. Remove the correctional service's washed-out cotton clothing, pants and collarless shirts from a washing machine and dump it all into a big wire basket with wheels on it.

Yes. I ended up here anyway.

Roll the basket over to the dryer, open the hatch and start loading the damp rags. All the machines are like twice as big as in an ordinary laundry room. Real industrial machines. It's warm and smells good from fabric softener. Enormous dust bunnies chase each other along the tile floor.

Soraya kept nagging at me until I agreed to come here for an hour yesterday. It probably says something about the monotony in the cell that I wanted to come here again today anyway.

I no longer want to live but I don't want it to be more boring than necessary either.

When I've loaded all the laundry into the dryer I pull out the filter from the inside of the hatch to see if it needs to be cleaned. The plastic filter is completely covered with dust and lint; it looks like a dark gray wool blanket. I start pulling off the lint from the filter. It's pretty satisfying. Try it yourself some time if you don't believe me.

As I'm standing there, with one hand full of lint, I hear steps behind my back. I think that it's someone from the staff and turn around. But there stands a rather short and broad guy, dressed in correctional system clothing. He has almost comically big muscles on his upper body. His arms stand out a little. His neck is like a bull's. His short legs also look enormously beefy. He is tattooed all over his arms, up on his throat and half his face. Shaved on the sides of his head, thick black hair above that sits in a charming wave on his forehead. Arabic descent, I think, maybe Turkish.

"Hi," he says. "Brother, can you help me with something?"

His tone is pleasant, the question feels open, but I sense that this guy isn't used to getting no in response when he asks for something.

"Do you work here?" I say.

He grins.

"Haha, no, I don't work here."

"Okay."

"Do I look like I work here?"

"Don't know."

"Do you work here?"

"Right now I do."

"But you're in jail, huh?"

The guy looks genuinely surprised.

"You don't think I'm allowed to be here?"

"No."

Surprised, and interested. He takes a few steps toward me.

"Why don't you think so?"

"Because I'm not allowed to meet other prisoners. That's why I'm in the laundry room."

Now he smiles, and takes a few more steps toward me.

"But we don't care about that, do we? We're tough guys, aren't we?"

He is standing right in front of me. Looks up in my face. We stare silently at each other a while.

I clench my right hand.

Just then I hear Per's voice behind my back.

"Abbe? I've been looking for you."

"Is that so?" the guy whose name is evidently Abbe says, without taking his eyes off me.

"Come on. We're going to play cards now." Per steps between us, shoves Abbe toward the door with mild force. The enchantment is broken. The who-can-stare-the-longest competition ends undecided.

"Who is that fucking clown?" Abbe wants to know.

"You don't need to bother with him," Per says. "He's from Småland."

In the evening I lie on my cot in the cell and look at the ceiling and think about how close I was to taking a swing at Abbe in the laundry room. If that had happened, what would Dad have said about it?

That was one hell of a right hook you got in.

He would have been proud. That makes me worried.

I went to Fårö and became a different person.

Or is it as Dad said, that this really is me?

In the glow of the cellphone light it was easy to follow the path through the dark forest. The murmur in the pine trees rose and sank, rose and sank. Down from the shore the waves were heard rolling in almost unnaturally loud. It sounded like they were only a few steps away.

Soon I saw the dark silhouette of the studio a short distance ahead of me. I tipped the pot with the olive tree and retrieved the key. Stood up, unlocked the door and went in.

The smell of paint and charcoal was almost even more pronounced than when Dad and I were here together. Maybe because it was dark. The sense of smell didn't need to compete with sight. I didn't dare turn on the light, didn't know if it would be seen over at the house. Dad might be up, or Maddy, or Barbro.

Was she squatting asleep in a corner of the kitchen tonight too?

The room felt smaller now in the darkness. I shone with the phone, turned it first here, then there. Everything seemed to be in the same place as the day before. The little statuette on the desk stared into the light without blinking. It looked strangely alive. I thought, *As soon as I turn the light away it's going to blink, it's just trying to hold out so that I can't see it.*

I let the phone light linger on the figure a moment. That little statuette scared me almost more than all the big statues in the room where we slept. But it didn't blink. I shivered involuntarily.

And then I aimed the beam of light toward the big painting. After all that was why I'd gotten up in the middle of the night and come here.

There it stood, leaning against the short wall with the sheet over it.

I'd seen it standing just like that once before. Many years ago, in a completely different place.

Klara, Mom and I were on a visit to Dad in the studio he had in Stockholm at that time. I was six and Klara was three. It was in the summer, and Mom was on vacation. The following day we would drive down to Grandpa and Grandma in Småland without Dad. We would leave early, so this was our chance to say goodbye to him.

The studio was an exciting place to be, with a high ceiling and big windows through which the light flooded in. Here were benches and shelves with paint cans and brushes and tools that Dad used when he painted. The floor was covered with protection paper, and the paper was full of paint stains.

Dad was always in a good mood in the studio. At home his mind often seemed to be elsewhere. Even when the whole family was doing something fun together, such as going to a bakery for pastries or to the beach, it felt like he wasn't really there. I remember that I thought about that when I was little: Dad seemed to like being in the studio more than being together with me, Klara and Mom. And that was probably why Mom seemed sad sometimes, although she tried to hide it from me and Klara.

So I was always cheerful. It was up to me to keep my mood up; I understood that. Klara was too little to take responsibility for something like that.

I will paint the whole world, dear Mom.

Mom probably thought that we would have a quick coffee and then drive back to the apartment and keep packing. But Dad had other plans. Klara and I would paint! We had painting clothes hanging in a closet so we started by putting them on. We each got paint and brushes and a big sheet of paper and then Dad told us to splash away just as much as we wanted.

Dad was in a good mood. An extremely good mood. Almost too good a mood.

"Splash more! Lay it on properly now! Haha!" He laughed loudly, and his eyes shone. Paint flew through the air, onto and outside the sheets of paper.

Klara was really content but I soon got a little knot of worry in my gut. There was something that didn't really add up. I saw it in Mom's eyes too. Maybe above all there. She was on tenterhooks.

I tried to show Dad that I thought it was fun to paint so that he wouldn't be disappointed, while I didn't want to seem too happy, because then Mom might think I was completely spellbound by Dad and that she'd lost control over me and Klara, which would make her even more worried. *You decide*, I tried to signal with looks and expressions. *If you want to leave then we'll leave.*

I was a hypersensitive little measuring device when I was young. Kept track of all the moods in the room, with every person. It was a lot of work I daresay.

There was a small kitchen that was part of the studio and while we painted, Mom put on coffee. When the coffee maker stopped sputtering she said that we should come and have a pastry. We sat down on stools around a little table. On a shelf over the kitchen counter the little stone figure with the crooked eyes was standing. I hadn't seen it before. I remember that it scared me. In some way I connected it with the fact that Dad was wound up, so exaggerated.

He took out a Festis each for me and Klara and opened a roll of Ballerina biscuits, not just at one end—instead he split open the paper along the whole length of the roll.

"Just help yourself! Eat, eat!"

Klara looked at Dad with surprise and helped herself. Dad nabbed three at a time with thumb and index finger and started eating them.

"One biscuit at a time," Mom reprimanded him. "You'll get a stomachache otherwise."

"My studio, my rules," said Dad. "Here you can take just as many biscuits as you want." He smiled broadly at Klara, leaned forward and winked exaggeratedly with one eye.

I took a biscuit and started nibbling at it with small, small bites.

The little stone figure stood with its hands at its sides and stared sternly straight ahead.

In the middle of the studio, on the biggest work surface, a painting was leaning against the wall. It was the biggest one I'd seen. Just as tall as a grown-up, and even wider. It was draped in old bedspreads so it wasn't possible to see what it depicted. When Klara had finished her Festis she jumped down from the stool and went over to the big painting, stopped and looked at it. Curiosity took over. She went over and raised the bedspread a little, down in one corner.

I got a little glimpse. Saw something red and orange. Thick with paint.

"Klara," said Dad. "Leave that alone."

I heard something very definite in his voice but Klara didn't notice it. Mom said, "Klara? Come here."

Klara took a firmer hold on the bedspread and started to pull. The fabric slid slowly over the upper edge of the painting. Soon it would fall off completely and we would see what the painting depicted.

Dad flew up from his seat, as if shot from a spring, and with three long strides he reached Klara, tore her hand away from the bedspread and with a hold around her stomach he picked up her and away from the painting.

It all happened in a few seconds.

I was a little shocked. Had no idea Dad could move so fast.

He didn't shout, he didn't scold, but the intensity in his movements was frightening. He had reacted as if Klara was in mortal danger.

She looked surprised at first, then her face was distorted, her lower lip starting quivering and she burst into tears.

"Mama!" Klara called, from where she was hanging over Dad's arm. "Mama..." The cry turned into sobs.

Mom was already by them, and she reached for Klara.

"Come. Come, honey."

Dad handed her over to Mom, almost absent-mindedly, as if she was a bag of groceries. He was completely concentrated on checking that the bedspread was still hanging over the painting. Yes, it didn't seem about to fall off. He stuck his hand in behind the cloth and pulled it down so that it hung securely over the canvas.

"There now, it's all right," Mom consoled Klara. Then she said that it was time for us to go home and keep packing. She sounded very determined.

I felt relieved. There was an unpleasant tension in the air between Mom and Dad. It seemed best that they weren't in the same room.

Klara and I each got a hug from Dad.

"I'll see you when I see you," he said. "It's not certain that I'll be coming down to Småland this summer."

But I looked over toward the monumental painting and wondered what it depicted.

And now I was standing here, in the little studio at Ajkeshorn, in front of the same painting, with the same question.

For it must well be the same painting...?

I aimed the phone lamp toward the big, covered canvas.

Maybe it looked somewhat smaller than I remembered. But that wasn't so strange; the last time I saw it I was only six, so it was much bigger then in relation to me.

Some bedspreads were hanging over it, just like then. Were they even the same ones?

My heart was pounding, I felt out of breath and my mouth was dry.

I went up and raised the cloth a little in the lower right corner, just like Klara had done almost twenty years ago.

The phone light fell on shades of red and orange. Thick with paint.

I let go of the bedspread and took a few steps back.

Yes. I recognized it. It was the same painting, the one whose motif Dad absolutely did not want us to see.

I was taking short, jagged breaths but still didn't get enough air. I felt dizzy and nauseated, and my heart was pounding and pounding.

I know what you did.

Yesterday Dad had said that this was the first painting he'd done of the fire that killed Mom and Klara. The depiction of his trauma. The turning point in his career.

It was just that, back then in the studio, when Klara was about to pull the bedspread off the painting, the fire hadn't happened yet. The next day Klara, Mom and I went down to Småland, we would stay in the summer house while Grandpa and Grandma remained in town and a week or so later that terrible thing happened.

You ruined our lives.

Dad had painted a picture of a fire that hadn't happened yet.

It was impossible. But it had happened.

Thoughts buzzed like wasps in my head.

I must tell this to Maddy. Would she believe me? Should I call Grandpa?

I couldn't make sense of it. Everything accelerated, the swarm of thoughts was like a ball of moths under a streetlight, round and round they turned. I was about to lose control.

Without really thinking about what I was doing I went up to the painting and pulled off the bedspreads, first one, then the other. It happened as if mechanical somehow, like when you're in the middle of an important phone call and you turn the coffee maker on at the same time. My thoughts were aimed in one direction, in toward myself, and I tried to slow them down, felt that I was on the verge of fainting.

I dropped the bedspreads to the floor. Took a few steps away from the painting, shone at it with the phone.

The effect was immediate.

Everything disappeared, except the painting.

It took me back.

I'm dreaming that I'm asleep in my bed in Grandpa's summer house, and the ceiling light in the hall shines so bright that it wakens me. There's something wrong with the lamp because the light isn't steady, It's like it's flickering, a little like the light from the TV when you're watching a movie. It sounds scary besides, several sounds at the same time; it's crackling light and crispy as if the lamp is about to break, while a dull rumbling is heard beneath it all.

Klara's and my bedroom is on the top floor in the summer house. Mom is sleeping in the bedroom on the ground floor.

I can't move. I would really like to get out of bed to go and see what's happening in the hall, but my body doesn't obey and this is just happening in a dream, right? I can't be awake in any event. I am lying as if paralyzed in the bed and the ceiling light in the hall shines brighter and brighter and it's thundering louder and louder and now I detect a smell besides, like when you're grilling, yes it's smoke I smell, and something else besides that I've never sensed before—it smells strong and sweet and sickening at the same time.

Now I even feel the heat on my cheek, like when you make a big bonfire and your face gets hot while the back of your neck is cold. What kind of dream is this? It can be seen, it can be heard, it has smells, it can even be felt.

At last my body obeys. I put my hands against the mattress and press myself to a half-sitting position, wide awake. Then the shock.

There's a fire in the hall. The door is ajar and I see the flames, I hear the rumbling and I can smell it. Smoke pours into the bedroom, as if running up and down through the door, and flows out across the ceiling.

I fly out of bed, wild with panic, and howl, "MOM! MOOOOOM!"

Mom doesn't answer. But this is my only thought: *Mom must come and rescue us.* There is nothing else, so I keep screaming.

"MOOOOOM!"

Klara wakes up in her bed, to a world that has gone crazy. She sits up and after a few seconds she screams and cries too at the top of her lungs.

Her screams do something to me. I'm not just a helpless, terrified six-year-old. I'm also a big brother, so much bigger and stronger than my three-year-old little sister. I know and can do so much more.

It's up to me to get us out of here.

I go up to the door and peek out. The heat is frightful; you can't turn your face toward the fire more than a second before it's too painful. The fury of the flames is completely incredible. I've seen big bonfires outdoors and always thought there's something exciting about mighty flames spraying glowing flakes toward the evening sky. But when I see the same violent fire burning indoors, in a narrow little hall in an old cottage, then I just feel terror.

The strange odor, so different, heavy and cloying, that fills your lungs. The flames seem to be howling louder with every second that passes.

I go back to Klara, take her hand and draw her toward the door, but she resists, sits on her heels and screams even louder. With all her being she senses that it's wrong to move toward the fire and the smoke and the rumbling; she wants to get away from that.

"STOP!" I scream to be heard over the flames. "WE HAVE TO GET OUT!"

Klara is hysterical.

"NOOOO! NOOOO!"

"COME NOW!"

I pull on her hand as hard as I can, and she stumbles and falls to the floor. I let go of her, go up to the doorway and look out, but quickly pull back my head. It's burning even faster and more intensely now. From wall to wall, from floor to ceiling, only whirling flames. It's as if the fire wants to put an end to the house and to me and Klara as fast as possible. It howls in my ear that I'm going to die.

If we were to each wrap ourselves in a blanket, I think. That ought to give a little protection. And then run just as fast as we can. Jump through the fire, toward the stairs.

"Klara," I say and take hold of her shoulders. Must talk loudly to be heard over the rumbling but still try to sound calm. But Klara isn't listening; she just screams and cries, shrill and heart-rending.

"MAMMAAAA!"

This won't work, we don't have time, we're going to die. I shake her forcefully, in a panic.

"LISTEN UP!" I scream desperately, and I'm crying too. A big part of me wants to do just like Klara, just stand there and scream at Mom and then whatever happens will happen. But the big brother in me wants something else.

And Klara actually falls silent. Maybe it's the shock. I have never been this rough with her before.

"We have to run through the hall," I say. "We'll each put a blanket around us."

I take Klara's blanket from her bed, tie it around her as fast as I can and show where she should hold on so it won't fall off. Klara is still sobbing but takes hold of the edge of the blanket with both hands so that her knuckles whiten. I take my own blanket and wrap it around me. Hurry over to the door and open it—it's barely possible to touch the handle any longer because it's so hot—retreat quickly a few steps into the room again.

Klara and I stand beside each other in the bedroom with the blankets wrapped around us. The smoke whirls. My eyes sting.

I take hold of Klara's blanket and pull it over her head, like a scarf.

"Run!" I shout. "Run to the stairs and jump!"

Klara obeys and starts pattering with her little feet toward the door, the blanket dragging on the floor behind her. I have to wait so I won't step on it. I pace impatiently in place.

The murderous heat in the doorway makes Klara hesitate. I howl, "RUN NOW!"

Klara screams her shrillest scream as she runs right out into the burning hall. I pull my own blanket over my head and rush after, unable to wait any longer, and I step on Klara's blanket as I throw myself right out into the sea of fire. It feels as if I'll burn up immediately. I'm dying now, can't see anything but rush in the direction where I know the stairs are, feel that I'm stumbling over something but just keep moving forward, two more big steps and then my foot steps into the air. I fall headlong, turn a somersault and don't understand what happened until I'm lying on the floor at the foot of the stairs.

The wind has been knocked out of me.

But I'm alive.

In the downstairs hall the fire isn't burning as violently. The heat is strong, the smoke stings my throat and my eyes, but being here isn't the same as dying. Not yet.

I crawl up to a sitting position, still wrapped in the blanket.

Where is Klara?

She's nowhere to be seen.

Did she already make it out of the house?

No, impossible.

I know the answer.

She's still in the upstairs hall. In hell.

I stepped on her blanket, and she must have fallen down; it was her body that I stumbled over when I rushed toward the stairs. But I didn't stop and help her up because I didn't want to die.

"KLARA!" I howl desperately. "KLARA!!!"

No answer.

I get up and leave the blanket behind on the floor, take a few quick steps up to the stairs, but the heat forces me down again. I am coughing violently from the smoke.

She's going to die, I think.

And then I see a little figure creep up to the top stair step, engulfed in flames, crawl over the edge and then tumble headlong down the stairs.

It's Klara. She remains lying on a stair step halfway down, halfway toward rescue.

"Klara!" I say again with a sob, but the fear is now mixed with a little hope. I fly up the stairs again and the heat doesn't bother me at all. I take hold under her arms and drag her down the stairs, away from the fire, through the now-almost-smoke-filled lower hall, place her on the doormat while I open the front door and then continue dragging her out of the house, down the two steps and out on the lawn, which is damp with dew. Away from the burning house.

On my back I can still feel the heat from the fire, but on my face which is turned toward the lake the summer night is cooling. And it's marvelously dark. Dark is life for me now. Light means death.

I set Klara down on the ground and sink down by her side.

"Klara? Klara?"

I look a little closer at my little sister, lying in the warm glow of the flames. She looks pretty awful; it can't be denied. Her hair is burned off on half her head, her ear and cheek and forehead black on that side, besides a red cut below her eye where the skin has cracked. Klara smells of smoke and burnt hair.

She appears to be sleeping.

"Klara?" I say, carefully now. I take her hand and squeeze it.

Klara opens her eyes and gives me a foggy look. Then she closes her eyes again; she seems to want to sleep. Even though she looks so terrible she has that facial expression that I love. Good-natured, trusting. As if she's sure that nothing bad can happen. That calms me too in some way.

Her pajamas are in tatters; one sleeve is burned away and the chubby little arm is also black and cracked. What is inside the arm, muscles and tendons and blood, is visible. It shimmers dark red in the glow from the burning house. I understand that she needs help, that she's alive now but she can still die.

"HEEEELP!" I shout and now I'm a desperate six-year-old again who doesn't know which way to turn. "HEEEELP!"

No answer.

The burning summer house lights up the night. The rumble and the heat reach us on the grass, halfway down to the water's edge.

I get up and hurry a few steps closer to the house until the heat stops me.

"MOOOOOM! MOOOOOM!"

If Mom is still inside she's dead now.

I touch on that thought but push it away so that it isn't clearly spelled out for me. It's impossible; I can't manage it.

Mom probably got out, I think instead. *Yes, that's how it must be—she woke up and tried to make her way up to our bedroom to rescue us but it was already burning so much that she had to turn around. Maybe she thought that if she doesn't make it through the fire then she'll die and then all hope is gone for Isak and Klara too. She'll go get help instead.*

That's probably how Mom thought. She's still alive, and Klara is still alive, and everything can still be fine.

If Mom has run away to get help, then where did she go?

To Ingegerd and Kjell, of course.

Ingegerd and Kjell are the nearest neighbors. They live by the next bay, a short distance through the forest. They're even older than Grandpa and Grandma and really like children. Sitting on their porch, under a roof of semitransparent plastic as a summer rain patters, drinking homemade cherry juice and eating rolls and cookies until you almost choke is one of the coziest things I know.

Yes, Mom must have gone to Ingegerd and Kjell.

I have followed the path through the forest with Mom many times. It takes fifteen or twenty minutes. I believe that I'll find the way myself even if it's dark. The path follows the water line almost the entire way; you're just a few steps from the lake. Except at one place, where a promontory extends out in the water. There the path cuts across and you have spruce forest on all sides for a short distance. But then the shoreline shows up again and then you only have a few minutes left to Ingegerd and Kjell's house.

If I walk there then I can meet Mom halfway, I think, *she's probably already on her way back.*

I go back to Klara, who is lying motionless in the night-damp grass. I get scared again about how she looks, almost worse now than when I looked at her the first time. The burned-off hair, the black, cracked skin. The bare flesh that glistens. And then the other half of Klara, the other side of the face, the other arm—a perfect little three-year-old girl in a pair of washed-out pajamas with cars and buses. The contrast.

I sink down on my knees on the ground beside her, stroke her cheek which is whole and perfect.

"Klara?" I whisper. "Klara?"

Klara doesn't open her eyes, but she swallows and twists her head a little to the side.

Yes, she's alive.

And I realize that I can't leave her here. I must take her with me to Ingegerd and Kjell so that she can get help as quickly as possible.

Mom may be dead.

The abyss opens up in me.

It may be that no help is on the way, and then it's all up to me to rescue Klara, and what if I don't manage that?

Can the world really be so cruel? It's as if everything I thought I knew about life is in turmoil now.

Dad showed me a film clip on the computer once. It was a washing machine that jumped and moved around more and more, parts started to loosen and it was as if the washing machine had gone crazy. Everything simply accelerated and got worse beyond all repair, until it fell over on its side and continued floundering, like when Grandpa caught a pike and it floundered on the bottom of the rowboat.

Dad laughed. I was scared to death.

Now it feels as if the whole world is like that washing machine. Everything is about to fall apart, faster and faster, and soon it will be impossible to stop.

I push one arm in under Klara's neck and the other under her rump, and then I lift. Straighten out my legs, stagger a little. Klara's head falls backward over my arm in an awkward way, and her mouth opens a little. She's heavy, but not all that heavy; I will probably manage this.

I walk with Klara in my arms toward the spruce trees a short ways up from the water, where I know that the path over to Ingegerd and Kjell begins. The forest is lit up by the fire and almost looks unreal, like in an animated film. The glow helps me find the right way. I leave the yard behind me, make my way into the forest.

The path is narrow and winds ahead over roots and stones. The glow of the flames flickers over tree trunks and moss-covered boulders. The heat from the burning house doesn't reach here. The night air is cooling from all directions.

Klara feels heavy in my arms. Her head and arms and legs hang and dangle back and forth. My arms ache, my knees sag. I have to take a little break. Carefully I set Klara down on the ground, straighten up and swing my arms a little back and forth. It is only a few steps down to the water's edge. The odor of smoke is here too, but it mixes with that sweet-and-sour smell that I connect so strongly with summer and the lake by Grandpa and Grandma's summer place. Grandpa showed me at some point that it comes from a low grass that grows by the edge of the lake. He pinched off a blade and held it under my nose. Bog myrtle, I think it's called.

I look out over the lake. It is still, a black mirror for the massive fire that is the summer house. The glow even lights up the forest on the other side of the water. I look back, can barely glimpse our house between the tree trunks.

Only a minute or so has passed since I set Klara down on the ground but I must move on. There's still a long ways to go. In any event I got to straighten my back and move my arms. I bend down and pick her up. She already feels much heavier now than when I picked her up the first time, in the yard.

The panic that is constantly lurking. I'm never going to make it.

I stumble ahead with Klara in my arms, ever deeper into the

forest. The booming and the glow from the burning summer house gradually diminish, and the darkness gets denser between the trees. The night air no longer cools; it chills.

The path winds ahead, the root to an unusually sturdy spruce extends right across it, I don't pick my foot up high enough and I stumble.

No, no, no, I'm dropping her, I have time to think.

Somehow I manage to counter with a quick step anyway, so that I more sink toward the ground than fall. It almost feels like I carefully set Klara down in the moss by the side of the path. I get on my knees beside her. My heart is pounding in my chest so that it's heard all the way up in my head. I am breathing heavily and feel sweat over my face. My arms are shaking so much from the exertion, it almost hurts to straighten them out.

I turn around with great effort and sit on my rump instead. The forest is dark now, and silent. The spruce trees stand densely in all directions, here and there a pine. Moss and brush. I sit stock-still and stop breathing in order to listen. No, the lapping of the waves against the shore is no longer heard. I've come to that part of the path where it's a little farther to the lake, and that gives me courage and energy. From here it's not far to Ingegerd and Kjell. I should be able to walk the rest of the way without stopping. As I crouch down beside Klara and pick her up, I stare at her stomach to avoid seeing her injured face and arm.

Like that time when Grandpa grilled sausages and forgot to turn them; they were black and cracked from end to end.

I start walking toward rescue. Stagger step by step with my little sister in my arms, afraid of stumbling and falling again. Soon my heart is pounding violently in my chest again, not from panic now, but from exertion.

I am so tired, so out of breath and so sweaty and so thirsty that I have a hard time thinking clearly. But one thing I think is strange: from that place along the path where you don't see the lake it should only be a few minutes' walk until you're down by the water's edge again. And now I've been walking a bit anyway but the forest is still just as dense in every direction.

Admittedly I've been walking very slowly, I realize that of course.

But still.

It's completely dark around me, even blacker than before. The forest seems to have stuffed me down into its big sack of tree trunks and branches and moss and tied it up, so that no light comes in.

Can't bear to think anymore.

Soon I must take another break. And then another. The times when I force myself ahead with Klara in my arms become shorter and shorter, the breaks longer and longer. At some point the two meet and are equally long, like an equinox. Then the breaks get the upper hand. I sink down beside Klara, stretch out on the ground.

I fall asleep for the first time. Wake up with a jerk, and think I hear sirens far, far away. I pick Klara up and carry her a little farther. I am thirsty and I feel dizzy. There is hissing and wheezing in my chest when I breathe. By the side of the path is a section with fairly even ground and thick moss. I set her down there, and then sink down beside her. The moss is damp and cold but nice against my body. And the air feels so clear in my nose here. No odor of fire at all. This is a really good place to take a short break. Just a very short one. Then I'll carry Klara to Ingegerd and Kjell, and Mom will be there. She'll start to cry from relief when she sees us again—I can picture it. She has already called the ambulance; help is on its way. Ingegerd brings out washcloths and bandages and Mom takes care of Klara's injured face and arm. Kjell gets juice and sets a tin of cookies out on the table.

Everything is going to be fine.

When I wake up the second time I'm shivering. The dampness from the moss has penetrated my clothes. My skin feels cold and wet. I shiver lying there with my cheek against the ground. Raise my head very briefly, but am so dazed that I immediately set my head back down on the moss again. I simply must sleep a tiny bit longer.

But I see that the forest is no longer really as black. Dawn comes sneaking between the tree trunks.

The next time I waken from a sound I don't recognize. Or actually there are several different sounds. Fairly quiet small sounds. Something like picking. Something that's like the sound my friend Axel's cat makes when she shakes her fur, brief and intense. Something that sounds a little moister, almost like smacking.

But they aren't loud. They are small sounds, almost shy, but still intense.

My awareness is a submarine that rises to the surface, and this time it doesn't turn back down into the unconscious. It's not morning yet, but no longer night either. Last night everything was various shades of black, but now the forest is putting on its usual colors. Green and brown and gray.

But that sound. What is it?

I sit up halfway with one palm deep in the moss, still dazed. Something flaps behind my back. I get scared and turn around. The big black bird is already in the air, but it doesn't fly far, only to a boulder maybe ten meters away. Its claws tramp around in the moss. It stares at me with its head cocked, irritated at having been disturbed.

I see that it has something in its beak. A scrap of something bloody. Now it quickly jerks its head backward and the scrap disappears into its mouth. The bird swallows.

I look at Klara who is lying beside me on the ground.

She has no eyes left.

Two empty, bloody sockets gape toward me. And the wound on her cheek has gotten much bigger; the flesh looks torn, a flap hangs down toward her chin. There's an opening straight through. I can see her tongue in there, and the little baby teeth.

The bird has eaten from Klara.

I moan and fall backward in the moss, brace myself with my feet and push myself away from Klara, in total terror and panic. Get to my feet, can't stand still, I start running around Klara in small circles, without looking at her. Sniffle and sob and scream.

"MOOOOOM!!! MOOOOOM!!!"

The bird spreads out its shining, blue-black wings, flaps and rises from the stone. For a second I think it's going to attack me. But it sets down high in a spruce instead, still with a view of Klara.

It feels like I'm going to fall apart inside. I must keep moving all the time, otherwise I'm going to explode—that's how it feels.

Morning comes. The first rays of sun cut between the tree trunks. Birdsong is heard. At last I feel calmer. Sink down on the ground. Sit on my rump, put my arms around my knees and bend my head down. I don't want to see or hear any more of the world. Something is about to come loose and fall apart inside me; it just picks up speed constantly, beyond all control. Like a washing machine in a dance of death.

If you imagine the absolute worst thing that can happen, then the world is still going to think of something even worse, something so horrid and frightful that it's impossible to grasp.

That morning in the forest, as I'm sitting with my head bent down and my arms around my knees, beside my dead little sister, and the birds are singing, this becomes my firm conviction about what the world is like deep down. Here I throw in my anchor; I moor myself. I am stuck at the bottom of the lake.

The sun rises in the sky, it beams down from straight above now and the light is filtered through the crowns of the trees.

Flies are buzzing around Klara's empty eye sockets.

Far away shouts are heard through the forest.

"Isak! Klara! Hello!"

Slowly the calls come closer. An hour or so later I am found. Unknown voices, someone puts their hand on my shoulder.

I remain sitting in the same position, with my head bent down between my knees and my arms around my legs. My body has locked up. I wouldn't be able to open it even if I wanted to.

More and more people arrive. I hear how differently they react when they catch sight of Klara. Some start crying and quickly hurry away, the blueberry branches rustling around their legs. Others moan or gasp, but stay. Crouch down beside me. Talk calmly and kindly, try to make contact.

Every time someone touches me I hug harder around my legs.

In my head the fire is still raging.

I had sunk down on my knees in front of the painting. Bowed my head toward the floor. All in order to get blood to my brain so that I wouldn't faint.

There was ringing in my ears, like when you're holding a big seashell over your outer ear. I also heard a shrill, straight tone that sounded almost electronic. Felt nauseated.

The phone was lying with the light facing down on the floor and the room was dark. Then gradually the wave of nausea ebbed and the ringing and beeping in my ears faded away. I dared to sit up on my knees. Small drops of cold sweat covered my face and neck. It felt as if someone had sprayed cold water on me with a spray bottle. I knew that my face was completely white.

I picked up the phone from the floor—the light had been on the whole time—and now I aimed it toward the painting again. It was roughly an arm's length in front of me, and I was sitting on the floor besides, so I couldn't perceive the image in its entirety. But I saw particulars, I saw brush strokes, I saw sections where the paint seemed to be applied with a knife and I got images in my head of Dad working in front of the canvas.

I saw the colors. The burning inferno.

The phone light moved across the canvas, lit up various sections.

I saw a big, black bird with outstretched wings. Gliding from treetop to treetop. Something was hanging from its beak.

In one place it looked as if Dad had squeezed out a whole tube of black paint. It formed a kind of river in the painting, that was raised up from the canvas. The paint had dried and cracked and down in the crack it was shiny and red.

It looked exactly like Klara's arm.

A pair of eyes stared at me without blinking.

It was the little god who was on the desk.

What was it doing in the painting?

Because weren't those the same eyes?

I stood up, went over to the desk and retrieved the little statuette. Shone on the painting from farther away, but when I saw it in its entirety I couldn't locate where it was I'd seen the eyes. I could no longer see them. That was strange. I looked for a long time but didn't find them.

At last I went closer and sank down on my knees again. Searched the canvas with the phone light, and soon I saw them again, the eyes. Held up the little figure alongside. Yes, sure. They were the same eyes.

Dad had painted the idol into the painting.

"Maddy? Maddy?"

I put my hand on her shoulder and shook her lightly. She twisted and whimpered a little.

"Mmm..."

"I've discovered something. You? Wake up."

At last she opened one eye and sat up in bed with great effort.

"What time is it?"

"Quarter past three."

I turned on the floor lamp that was on my side. For eyes that were used to the dark the light felt strong and flooding, for Maddy too, who was half-asleep. She turned her head away.

"But, please..."

"Dad painted a picture of the fire before it happened."

I sank down on the edge of the bed and told her from the beginning. That I couldn't fall asleep and that I'd started wondering about what Grandpa said: *I know what you did.* That it occurred to me that I'd seen that picture before. That I sneaked over to the studio to confirm that, and yes, it was the same picture; I was sure of it. Maddy tried to interrupt.

"Listen—"

"But wait, let me finish telling you... I saw a lot of other things in the painting too, things that happened the night the house burned but that I haven't told anyone else...well, maybe Grandpa, but he hasn't talked with Dad in all these years...so how could Dad know about it?"

I told about the big black bird and about Klara's arm and about the little god's eyes that I'd seen in the painting, and fortunately I'd thought to take pictures of it all with the phone, so that I could show Maddy as I explained.

Maddy rubbed her face.

"But Isak, wait a little," she said. "How do you know that it was the same painting you saw when you were little?"

"It was the same. It looked exactly alike."

"But you didn't see the whole painting when you were little. If I understood right? You saw just one corner?"

"Yes, but I recognized it right away. When I raised the bedspread."

Maddy sighed and shook her head, looked serious.

"No... I mean, I'm sorry..."

Maddy didn't believe me, and then I thought it was just as well to lay all the cards on the table and include all the details so that Maddy would truly understand that it wasn't some isolated little thing I'd gotten hung up on. Instead it was like I'd opened a door to a parallel world where everything was strange, and luckily I had evidence, I'd captured it in pictures, but this meant that my story got pretty long and at some point during my exposition Maddy stopped looking at the pictures in the camera and turned toward me instead.

She looked worried.

"You know," she said, and her voice was soft and tender. "I think you haven't been sleeping enough."

Well, of course I hadn't been sleeping enough. But what did that have to do with anything?

She asked how it felt to see the picture of the fire, and I said that I was completely knocked out; it felt like I was back in the burning summer house.

Maddy took my hand. I said that I almost fainted.

"I think we'll do like we said," she said. "We pack up and then we leave after breakfast. But now we have to try to get a little sleep."

"But don't you understand? We have to..."

I fell silent. Yes, what was it actually we had to do?

"But you have pictures of everything," said Maddy. "There's no hurry. You know... I'll go and see if I can find Fredrik. Then you can get some sedatives from him. You have to sleep now, baby."

I stood up from the edge of the bed, picked up the phone and called Grandpa.

"Isak, stop."

"I haven't got hold of Grandpa all evening."

"It's three thirty in the morning, for Pete's sake! You can't call him now!"

I let a number of ringtones go out but Grandpa didn't answer now either. Paced in circles, had a hard time sitting still. Maddy pulled on a T-shirt and sweat shorts.

"Can you manage on your own for a moment?" she asked.

"Yes, yes, yes."

She disappeared, walking quickly, as if it was urgent or something.

Part of me thought that she was probably right. I needed to sleep. My brain was running in high gear. It was still wound up and energetic, but it was like a thin casing, inside of which was a body that was deathly tired.

I wandered around aimlessly waiting for Maddy to come back. In constant motion, like that morning in the forest with Klara. I went out in the hall.

Grandpa's words ground in my head. *I know what you did. You ruined our lives.*

Without thinking I sat down at the only place in the hall where you could sit if you didn't want to sit on the floor.

The sofa with cancer.

The cloud of leather and padding arched over me.

The buttons. Where were they attached? I squinted in the gray dawn light.

Hadn't thought about that before. You didn't see it when you passed through the room, only when you sat right where I was sitting now, and looked upward.

The little idol's crooked eyes gazed down at me.

I flew up from the sofa, heard steps approaching. It was Maddy coming back. In her hand she had both a jar and a shiny silver blister pack of tablets.

"Now you'll see," she said. "Now you're going to sleep."

We went into the bathroom and she gave me a tablet from the jar and in addition pressed two out of the blister pack. I stuffed it all in my mouth and bent down under the faucet, slurped up the spraying water and straightened up again. I noticed a bitter taste at the back of my tongue before the tablets whirled down into my stomach.

Maddy looked up at me. Her gaze full of love.

"Come, now let's go and lie down."

I followed her to the bed. We undressed and lay down face to face, laced our bodies together and clung firmly to each other as if otherwise we risked blowing away.

A storm of fire inside me.

"Breathe," she whispered. "Draw the air all the way down into your stomach."

She demonstrated, and we breathed together, in time.

I closed my eyes but felt my eyelids twitching. My eyeballs moved around behind them.

"Feel that your body is getting heavy. Everything feels heavy."

I turned onto my back. Maddy still lay turned toward me, her arm over my chest.

And something in her warm embrace, her knowledge of the body, the love and consideration, reached in to me.

Long, deep breaths. My body heavy. It felt as if with every breath I was sinking deeper down into the mattress.

In my mind I saw one of those big prize wheels they have at amusement parks, that whirls and whirls but gradually slows down, the ticking sound when the metal strip moves over the spikes gets further and further apart, soon you hear every little tick by itself, you know that there are only a few left, maybe ten or twenty, but it whirls a little more, longer than you just thought, but you know it's going to stop soon, right away, now.

Maddy and I on the beach. Sun and sand. The waves rolling in. Eternity.

When I wake up I'm alone in the bed. Something isn't right. The room is darker than when I fell asleep. No longer any dawn light.

How long have I been out?

I'm naked and lying on my back and have no blanket over me. Feel a little cold.

I turn my eyes to the side and see that the wooden sculptures are again gathered around the bed. It's as if they are crowding forward. A silent and curious band. Their faces are turned toward me. I look in the other direction. Staring eyes, closed eyes. Gaping mouths that scream silently. Secretive smiles.

What do they hope to see? What are they waiting for?

A wave of terror rolls inside me, instinctively I want to fly up out of the bed, but nothing happens. I don't move an inch. Try by force of will. Turn my head, raise my arm, bend a knee, rise out of bed. But it's as if I'm paralyzed. My body is again a prison.

At the outer edge of my field of vision I sense that something is moving.

If I could only raise my head and see properly.

One of the sculptures seems to be climbing up into the bed.

My heart pounds violently in my chest. I take short, short breaths.

The figure is moving slowly toward me, growing in my field of vision, and now I see that it's not one of the idols.

It's Barbro.

She is crawling slowly and methodically up onto my body. She is heavy; it hurts. I scream out loud but the scream stays in my head. My tongue is like a chopped-up snail in my mouth.

Barbro is wearing her long black dress. Her hair in the same stern bun as always.

She doesn't look at me. Her face expresses no distaste or any other emotion. She is climbing up on me because it must be done.

Her hands grip my bare upper arms like claws. Then around my shoulders.

Now she is rising halfway up, leaning on her clawlike hands, and her head comes quite close to my face. Her unwashed, greasy hair is in my nose and my eye, a sour and heavy stench. I feel the soles of her shoes against my bare chest, first one, then the other. She lets go of my shoulders and slowly sits up.

Barbro is squatting on my chest. She is so heavy, so heavy. I can't breathe.

Now she bends her neck and looks down at me.

Her gaze cold and expressionless, like an animal.

She jerks her neck a little, leans her head to one side.

And then she blinks.

Her eyes are covered by a thin membrane, which moves from below and up.

Just like on a bird.

When I came to, the blanket was covering me. Barbro was gone. The wooden statues were no longer standing around the bed, instead as usual along the walls. The room was still just as dark.

It was raining. The drops pattered against the skylight. The wind pulled and tore at the house, and there was creaking in walls and roof. A big storm outside. And way off in the distance a dull rumble.

Thunder.

I lay on my side. Tried to move my arm. Yes, it worked. I was no longer paralyzed.

I turned onto my back, raised the covers a little so as not to get tangled. I was dead tired and just wanted to fall back asleep.

Then I discovered that Dad was sitting on a chair by the side of the bed. He looked at me.

"Hello," he said. His voice was calm and secure. In the darkness I sensed more than saw that his gaze was loving.

I rose laboriously up on one elbow.

"Lie down," said Dad. "Do you want to sleep more?"

I sank down on my back and closed my eyes. God how nice. I wasn't ready to wake up yet. I fell back asleep.

A thunderclap woke me. The rain changed in intensity with the gusts of wind. At times it pounded so hard against the skylight that the whole big room echoed.

Dad was still sitting on the chair beside the bed. Now he had the little statuette with the crooked eyes in one hand. A binder was on his lap.

I sat up. My hand in front of my mouth when I yawned.

"The thunder is coming closer and closer," said Dad.

I leaned forward and wrapped my arms around my knees, lacing my hands together.

"What do you want?"

"I know that you have many questions. I intend to give you some answers."

If I'd been wide-awake and alert maybe I could have said: *You know what, I'm not interested in your answers. It's too late for that. Get out of here so that I can get dressed and pack up my things, Maddy and I are leaving now. I don't want you in my life.*

But I still felt completely zonked and lightheaded, couldn't stop yawning. So I didn't have the fortitude at that moment.

I probably also felt something else that I have difficulty understanding, after the fact, and which is hard to admit.

It was a little cozy.

The darkness in the room, the rain and thunder outside that was heard so clearly but didn't reach in to us. The warm, nice bed. Dad by the bedside, his calm, secure voice. The scene touched something deep inside me.

A longing.

He started talking.

"Have you thought about what fire actually is? A dance of atoms. Like life. Fire and life resemble each other. Without fire, no life. If the sun didn't exist the Earth would be a cold, dead clump of dirt in space. And at the same time, if you get too close to the sun you'll die. It's an outburst of fury that lasts for billions of years. Fire keeps us alive. But can also kill."

Dad paused briefly. A drawn-out rumble was heard from outside, like an aftershock from the thunderclap that had wakened me. Light flickered around the skylight a few times, a reflection of lightning far away. I pictured the sea. Blue-gray and stormy.

"People can also be like that," Dad continued. "They can give life and meaning to millions. But be difficult to be close to. Too intense, too bright. You can't judge them by an ordinary measure. Should we demand of Mozart, or Picasso, that they change diapers and build Legos with their children? Instead of making art for humanity, for eternity? No. The only thing we can demand of Picasso is that he should be Picasso. Every second, every minute, every day, his whole life."

Dad let this sink in. Then he said, "You and I are such people, Isak."

I snorted, or maybe it was a giggle, sitting there with my head hanging over my knees. What Dad said was too ridiculous to be taken seriously.

"No," I mumbled, shaking my head tiredly.

"Yes. That's what I'm trying to get you to understand."

A squall whined through a ventilation duct somewhere, a whistling sound that rose and sank. The rain pattered against the windowpanes. A drumroll that never seemed to end.

Dad looked down at the stone figure, weighed it in his hand.

"I did say that this is an old fire god… Think about what fire meant to these people. It meant everything. It kept predators away, it meant they didn't freeze to death in the winter. It was the difference between life and death. Shamans were responsible for keeping the fire alive. I am a shaman, if you will. You too."

"Stop."

"I came across this twenty years ago, more or less. In strange ways. I paid much more for it than I could actually afford. Much, much more. But there was something about it that spoke to me. I was extremely unhappy then. Felt unfree, enclosed… I thought about committing suicide. Tried to think out the most spectacular way to die, so that my art would get attention… I know, it was silly. But this—" and now Dad turned the figure's face with the crooked eyes toward me "—this rescued me."

Dad sought my gaze; he wanted to be certain that I was listening and believed him. I looked away.

"It spoke to me, without words. It told me what I had to sacrifice in order to be free. In order to become my true self. And if I made that sacrifice everything I'd dreamed of would become reality."

He fell silent again. Let this sink in for me.

"You recognized the painting, right?" Dad continued. "You know what it means."

But I didn't want to know. I sat silently, quietly, curled up, a hardened body.

"I didn't depict the fire, I created it. I was forced to sacrifice you all, to kill someone I loved, to show that I was worthy, that my fire was the greatest. It was the idea that you should die too, Isak, but you didn't, you survived, and now I know that was the meaning the whole time. You have the fire in you, in the same way as me."

Dad reached out his arm and showed his tattoo.

Me fire big big big.

I think I moaned.

"Yes. There's no point in you denying it. I've noticed it just in these days we've been together now. This life which is within reach for you, that you didn't know existed. You want it. Deep down you want it. And do you know what's preventing you? You've been confined in a tower room like Rapunzel. For twenty years you've been brainwashed to believe that it's wrong, that you are bad to want it, to want to realize your full potential. But I'm telling you that's a lie. You aren't bad."

Dad made another short pause. My head was spinning.

"What is good and evil is always defined from outside a group, isn't it? The morals that are best suited for the masses, for group people, for those who follow the herd, that's what we call 'goodness.' Turn the other cheek, think first about your neighbor. It's egoism at a group level. And there's nothing wrong with that.

But those of us who aren't group people, who are unique and extraordinary, don't we have the right to be just as egoistic and choose the morals that suit *us* best?"

Dad had created the fire. He had intentionally made it so that Mom and Klara died. Something squeezed in my chest. I think it was sorrow.

"You loved driving the car. You loved Riga, the women, the drugs. You loved the knife against the lamb's throat. Trust that feeling. You only need to shift perspective a tiny, tiny bit, then you'll see everything in a new light. Think what life could be like. Never apologize for your power and your strength, your superiority. To go into the fray with life and lust, the battle for power and dominance, to be the alpha male. That's what you're made for. To live like that, that's to sanctify life. And you're going to feel that, once you've accepted who you really are. That you are living a true and full life, which you never have done before. Free to love, free to hate. Never a guilty conscience about anything. Everything is permitted. Imagine what a superpower! It has many names. Egoism, self-interest, ruthlessness, shamelessness. Haven't you ever dreamed of being a superhero? You have the chance to be that."

An image flickered inside me.

See everything in a new light. Change perspective.

The weight over my chest suddenly released. I felt the desire, the intoxication, the will to power, the life roaring in my veins.

Drop everything and let yourself go.

I saw an enchanted life, an enchanted world. So much bigger than the world I lived in.

It lasted only a second, if even that.

But it was wonderful, and it scared the shit out of me.

The fear gave me power. I looked up at Dad.

"You're insane."

"Presumably."

"Just because you don't know what good and evil are doesn't meant that it doesn't exist."

"Am I wrong? Is there anything in what I said that isn't correct?"

"There is goodness. There are good people. I don't want to live in your world. I want to live in Grandpa's world."

Those words made Dad stop. For the first time since I woke up I saw something like hesitation in his face. He squirmed. At last he said, "Anders is no longer alive."

I stared at Dad.

"I'm sorry, Isak. I know what he meant to you. But he died last night." Dad's voice was subdued and muted now. It was as if he was sorry to be telling me this.

I shook my head, bit my lip.

"You're lying."

"Have you tried calling him? Did he answer?"

I sat silently. Dad took a deep breath.

"He drove off the road last night. Not far from here. I heard on the local radio this morning that there'd been a car accident, so I called and asked a friend at the police. It was Anders. It hurts me to tell you this."

I simply wanted to wake up from this nightmare.

"Probably..." Dad started, but then he stopped himself. He was silent a moment before he continued. "He probably drove off the road when he tried to answer the phone. When you called."

Once many years ago I had realized how things actually stood with the world.

When everything was so terrible that you thought that now it can't get any worse, then the world thought of something that was even more terrible.

I had thrown my anchor in there. Then I'd forgotten it, or repressed it, but I actually knew it. Now I was swimming toward the bottom, following the anchor chain all the way down to the muck. There the anchor was buried in mud.

I cried, hunched up over my knees. My hands unusable, without will or power, on the covers.

Dad moved the chair closer to the bed, set the binder down on the covers. Reached forward and put his one hand gently on my arm.

"You know," he said, and his voice was gentle and smooth as velvet. "I think that somewhere you wanted him to die."

"No…no…" I sobbed.

"Yes. Because you wanted to be free. He was standing in your path. It was the only way."

Dad stroked my head, my cheek. Tenderly, lovingly.

"You are so close now. I saw a flash in your eyes just now. You want this. You really want this. The god has lived in me and shown me the way these twenty years, but now my body is too fragile a shell. He is seeking a new abode. You must simply show that you are worthy and ready and want this. That your fire is the greatest, that you are prepared to do anything to be free. You must do what I did. You must kill someone you love."

Dad set the statuette down on the floor and handed the binder over to me.

It was thin. There only seemed to be a few pages in the binder.

Dad turned on the bedside lamp and aimed it toward my lap.

I opened it.

It was an old-fashioned photo album, the kind they had at Grandpa's house. Photo prints glued on thick, dark sheets.

On the first page were two pictures. One depicted the beach promenade in Antalya. You saw a bit of the beach and the sea. The other was a selfie that Dad had taken. In the background I could see an alley from the old part of the city. Stands with bags and other leather goods, sunglasses and beach toys, extended out from the walls on both sides. Only a narrow passage in the middle was open.

I recognized the alley; I'd been there myself with Maddy.

A flash of lightning lit up the room. The masks glared at us. Suddenly black shadows on the walls behind the idols. Dark again. After that a sharp crack that made the windows rattle. The storm seemed to be almost right over us.

I didn't know if I wanted to see more.

Maybe better to guess than to know. Leave it open for another explanation.

I sat quietly for a moment with the binder on my lap without being able to decide. But the desire to know was too strong.

I turned pages.

The first picture my eyes landed on was also a selfie taken by Dad. But he wasn't by himself. He had his arm around Maddy. They sat close together, Dad held up the camera so that it looked down at them.

They looked happy.

I looked more closely. Thought I recognized the surroundings. They were sitting at a table at a restaurant, had wineglasses and used plates in front of them.

Yes. It was the same restaurant, and the same table, that Maddy had been sitting at when I met her that first evening.

The same place where I fell in love with her.

Other pictures. Dad and Maddy on the beach, her lying on her side in a bikini, he behind with his bare arm over her. Taken with the self-timer in the phone camera, presumably.

Dad in a lounge chair on an enormous, luxury balcony, with a view of the sea and the entire bay. The sky not quite clear, a little hazy but surely oppressively hot. The picture taken at eye level from behind, Dad turned backward toward the camera. He had sunglasses on. Smiled broadly.

Dad and Maddy in front of a large mirror. In a hall or the like. Dad had taken the picture; the camera hid his face. Maddy wearing makeup, dressed up, tight warm yellow summer dress, earrings and a necklace and sandalettes with high heels.

I remembered that she was dressed just like that the third

evening we met. We went to a bar, had drinks and a little finger food, then went back to my hotel, tightly intertwined. I remembered her scent, how soft the fabric in her dress was, how warm her body felt beneath.

The picture must have been taken only minutes before we would meet.

My eyes moved from picture to picture. Sat quietly with the album in my lap, in the wreckage of my life.

The foot shower by the patio that she used without thinking about it.

The waiter who recognized her.

The signs had been there, I'd seen them, but she had convinced me that I was just paranoid, that it was only delusions.

So easily fooled.

Dad leaned back in the chair and sighed deeply.

"I wanted to get to know you again," he said. "But I knew that Anders would never allow it. And you were still living at home with him. So I was forced to get help."

We sat silently a moment. Outside the storm raged.

"How did you know that I would be going to Antalya?"

"Oh, that was easy. Maddy monitored you on social media. Tracked your socializing. One of your friends posted a picture on Instagram of the screen when he booked the trip."

"But…the night we met."

"Yes? What?"

"She was sitting at that restaurant before we got there."

"Yes, that was a bit of luck. But we helped chance along. We knew which hotel you were staying at. It wasn't that unlikely that you would end up at that place. And this was early in the week. We had time. We had various scenarios for how you would meet. If chance hadn't helped us then she simply would have approached you at one of the clubs and gone home with you."

Something sour rose up from my stomach. It pulled and tightened in my throat, almost as if I had a cramp. I swallowed and swallowed.

Dad's voice had become livelier as he told about how he and Maddy had planned to bring us together. He almost sounded enthusiastic. Now he laughed a little.

"That loaded Englishman, who came onto her at the restaurant...we never would have thought of that. It was just too perfect. Damn, how we laughed about that when she came home."

The voice a little glossy, drenched in sunshine, as if it was hard for him to keep from laughing.

I shrank, sitting there on the bed. Soon I would disappear completely.

My nose was running, and maybe I cried.

"How...did you get her to move to Småland?"

"Hmm. Money can get people to do just about anything."

Dad leaned forward in the chair. His elbows on his knees, his hands laced under his chin. I didn't look up but felt his gaze on me.

The light in the room flickered. More lightning flashes, but not as sharp as earlier.

"You've come so far. You are so close now. I believe you feel yourself that there's no way back. Am I right?"

He made a short pause.

"If you turn around...what is left of the old life actually?"

Thunder came. Broad and deep, as if it swelled and rolled out, billowed into the room, into my ears. But it wasn't sharp and cutting. It receded again. The storm already seemed to be about to withdraw.

"Cut the last tie and feel how you float free. I promise, you're not going to regret it."

The promised land.

"But you must sacrifice her. You must show that your fire is the greatest. Then you'll get everything, Isak. Exactly everything."

It was as if all the pain, all the weight, all the darkness simply became too much. My brain turned off in some way. Grandpa's death, Maddy's betrayal. It was as if it didn't concern me at all.

A change of perspective.

Dad stood up. He put his one hand on my shoulder. I was still not looking up at him.

"You know how it's done, right? You've practiced. It's just a matter of bending the head back and then drawing the knife from ear to ear."

Dad raised his hand from my shoulder and left the room. I wanted to stop him, shout, *Don't leave me alone, I can deal with anything but not being alone.*

But I sat quietly. Dad placed the little fire god on the chair and left.

The binder lay open on my lap. The bedside lamp was still shining on it.

The storm slowly retreated. The rain quieted but didn't stop.

The pain returned. Again I was back in what was unbearable.

There was fire in all directions and from below and from above. A rage that would last for billions of years.

The washing machine was insane and dancing toward death.

I turned off the lamp.

For a long time I sat there. Alone in the dark.

Or was I alone?

No.

The idols were with me. Silent and discreet they stood along the walls. I had feared them and I had hated them but now I was happy that they were there.

And the fire god on the chair, with its crooked eyes.

They were all keeping me company. They wished me well.

I was free. Completely free.

Because what was left? What bound me to my old life?

Grandpa was dead.

Every minute I had spent with Maddy had been a lie.

Nothing meant anything.

What was it Dad said in Riga?

The world consists of the same basic elements as four billion years ago. What happened is that they've been rearranged and combined in new ways. Why should one way or the other matter? If certain hydrocarbons "experience" a little more of what we call "suffering"—and?

My pain didn't mean shit. It was nothing to worry about.

Not other people's pain either.

Cut the bonds. Float freely. Fly out over the world.

I got up from the bed. Left the room. Set out on the hunt.

I went through the corridor toward the kitchen. Passed the little courtyard with the hammock. It was still raining, splashing against the windows. There were big puddles on the ground. The summer night was like an afternoon in late November.

After sitting hunched up on the bed a long time it was nice to move around. I felt light and strong, looked positively at existence.

But where was she? Where was Maddy?

I was sure I would find her. But first I had to find the knife.

The kitchen was in darkness like the rest of the house. I looked around, squinted and peered into every corner and nook far from the glass walls out toward the patio. If Barbro was sitting somewhere asleep I wanted to know that at once.

But no. The kitchen was empty.

I didn't need to search for the knife because it was neatly set out on the table. It was the same one I'd used in the garage when I cut the throat of the lamb. Someone had taken care of it, cleaned it off and placed it conspicuously in the middle of the dining table. Probably Dad.

So considerate. He truly wanted to make things easy for me.

The pale light of the summer night glistened in the broad knife blade.

I took out a big drinking glass, turned on the faucet and held it under the stream. Took a few big gulps of water. I felt a cold current inside my body as it traveled through my throat and landed in my stomach. The taste was a little bit stale.

I went up to the big windows facing the patio with the glass in hand. The rain had let up a little now, but there was water all over the patio. The sky was reflected; everything was gray.

Now I saw that a body was stretched out on the lounge furniture. It was Dad. He was lying on his stomach. The low sofa was broad but Dad was lying close to the edge and one arm was hanging down, and the back side of his hand rested against the limestone.

Strange position to sleep in, I thought. But he was probably tired after watching over me the better part of the night. Probably hadn't gotten enough sleep. The enormous parasol protected him from the rain. I understood why he'd lain down there. Could have done so myself. It's cozy to be outside when it's raining in the summer, if you're under cover. The dripping, the splashing, the rippling. Those scents from the wet ground that you never notice otherwise.

I brought the glass to my mouth and took another sip and then I heard steps approaching the kitchen. I turned around. When she came in I stood facing her.

Maddy.

She saw me and was scared to death.

Shuddered and gasped for breath.

Maybe she didn't see who it was at first. A dark silhouette against the lighter window.

"God...you scared me," she said, breathing heavily. She went up to the kitchen counter and turned on the spotlights under the cupboards. She was wearing a camisole and sweat shorts. She looked at me again. Her gaze was guarded; she looked worried.

"What is it? Why aren't you wearing any clothes?"

I stood as if nailed to the floor. Stiff as a stick. I still had the glass in my hand, raised in front of my chest.

Maddy was right. I was naked of course, except for underwear.

Some kind of enchantment was broken.

"You lied about everything," I said, and my voice trembled.

I no longer felt light and free. Not at all actually.

It was probably the warm electric light. The practical everydayness of it, turning on a light in the kitchen. All that we humans have done to make life a little easier. Which also has made life a little more boring.

But the boring life was actually mine. That was where I belonged.

And then there was Maddy's gaze on me. Mostly that, I think.

I saw myself with her eyes, in the kitchen in the middle of the night in just underwear, my body tense as a spring, my shoulders hunched up, my elbows close to my side.

I heard myself. The thin, quivering voice.

That guy is completely desperate, I thought. *He is about to fall apart. Otherwise he wouldn't be standing here in the kitchen in the middle of the night like a mental case.*

"You lied about everything," I said again, and tried not to start crying. I stared at Maddy and she stared back and her eyes were filled with tears. She put her hand before her mouth as if she was going to vomit or something, and then she sobbed loudly.

"Sorry," she said, "sorry, sorry..." She sobbed and her breaths were short and agitated, as if she couldn't get air. "Oh god..."

It sounded like she was about to have a panic attack.

I sobbed too. Felt how my face was distorted.

"Did you intend to say something? Or...what...what were you thinking?"

She shook her head vigorously.

"I didn't think. I didn't think. Oh..."

She pulled out a chair, leaned her elbows against the tabletop and hid her face in her hands. Cried and whimpered and hyperventilated by turns.

If she was faking this, if she was just acting desperate and appealing to my sympathy, then she was doing it really well. What an actress.

Her gaze on me had brought me back to the world. I was no longer floating in space, I was not just any old atoms and molecules; I was Isak, and I had a girlfriend whose name was Maddy, and she had lied to me from the first moment.

In conspiracy with Dad.

Her betrayal was so monumental, too big to understand.

My pain meant something. A whole fucking lot.

So no, I didn't feel sorry for her sitting there crying and breathing fitfully at the kitchen table.

The knife lay between us.

"Please, Isak…may I tell you what it was like? From the beginning?"

She looked up at me, her eyes bathed in tears, her face red, shiny cheeks.

I didn't reply.

"I know that you hate me…you have every right to…but I can't just…" Her voice went up in falsetto and she couldn't finish the sentence. She put her hands in front of her face again and cried.

She was breathing a little more calmly.

My paralysis let go.

I let my shoulders sink down, lowered my hand with the glass. Took a few steps up to the table and stood there.

"I thought I was doing something good," Maddy said with a sob. "I was going to reunite a dying man with his son."

I pulled out a chair. Slowly sank down. Waited for her to continue.

Maddy was living in London when she met Dad.

She was an art student, shared a minimal apartment with two

other young women from the school and worked part-time as a bartender. Poor student, romantic, but a life from hand to mouth. She doubted herself and whether she had any business in the art world.

Then she and some other young women from the class were invited to a vernissage at a well-known gallery. The artist was a big name. Dad was there too and someone introduced Maddy and her friends to him. She was of course well aware of who he was. Fredrik Barzal, Sweden's internationally most successful artist since Anders Zorn. Before they parted Fredrik mentioned that he was looking for a new assistant for his London studio. They exchanged phone numbers.

"I was over the moon when I came home that evening," Maddy said. "Didn't sleep properly for two weeks. You must understand, this was a job that thousands of art students all over the world would kill to get. My girlfriends congratulated me, they were super happy for my sake. But I also understood that they were jealous."

Maddy started working for Fredrik in his studio in London. The days were long and poorly paid but Maddy thought she'd arrived in heaven. An intensely creative environment where anything seemed possible. And she felt right away that Fredrik trusted her. She quickly got her own responsibilities, sometimes tasks that she had no idea how to solve. Fredrik simply told her to take care of it. Many evenings she went to bed with a knot in her stomach. But somehow she always managed to execute what Fredrik assigned her. She grew, became increasingly self-confident. Felt that she really belonged.

The long hours in the studio affected her studies. She completed the semester a little half-heartedly but then she quit. Fredrik raised her salary and found an apartment for her. She got to go with to Gotland, to Ajkeshorn. He always wanted her near, it seemed.

Her rapid advancement in the team around Fredrik Barzal

raised some eyebrows. They thought it had happened a bit too easily. Suspect somehow. Grounds for jealousy.

"I realized that bad things were being said behind my back," Maddy said. "That I was sleeping with him and that. But I didn't care. I knew I was doing a good job."

"Were you?"

"What?"

"Sleeping with him."

Maddy looked at me seriously, looked wounded.

I didn't buy that.

"Don't give me that look," I said. "I have the right to ask."

"No. I didn't sleep with him."

We stared at each other for a while. Only the rain was heard, the dripping against the windows, the splashing, the rippling. Behind my back it was getting light.

My gaze wandered first.

Maddy continued her story. Because she was working so closely with Fredrik she noticed early on that something wasn't the same with him physically. He always drank more than what was healthy. Every evening a few beers or a glass of wine to wind down. Always a whiskey. Often alcohol with lunch too. But now he started to complain that he got hungover in a completely different way than before. Splitting headaches that could come on at any time of day. Even visual disturbances. He couldn't keep up the same pace as before. Often disappeared for a few hours during the day to rest.

Maddy talked discreetly about Fredrik's health with his closest collaborator, a woman who'd been with him for over fifteen years, almost since his breakthrough. But she didn't seem to have noticed that anything was wrong with him, and she didn't seem to care either.

"Suddenly I realized that I was the one who was closest to Fredrik. And I'd only known him a little more than a year. He was a very lonely person. Finally...yes, I took heart and asked how he was actually doing. He didn't get angry at all. He simply nodded and said, 'I have a brain tumor.' I see. Okay. Well, then we know."

Fredrik had known about his illness for several months. Maddy was the first one he told, and she had to swear not to tell anyone else about it.

Maddy fell silent, bit her lip. She had tears in her eyes again.

"And, uh…that was when he told me for the first time that he had a son. Whose name was Isak. And who lived in Småland. And he said that he didn't have any contact with this son, who was his only child, and that it was the most painful thing in his life. He'd had two children but one died in an accident, along with their mother. And after the accident he had a breakdown, which meant that he couldn't take care of his son. Who grew up with his grandfather instead. And this grandfather didn't let him see his son. Ever. And for that reason he needed my help."

When Maddy talked about Grandpa I was reminded of the unbearable fact that he was dead. It had already become a background factor for everything else I experienced. Like gravitation, or the changing of the seasons. But now the insight popped up in my mind again.

Exactly. Grandpa is dead.

I put my hand to my mouth. I think I moaned.

Maddy continued her story. Dad wanted to give her a special assignment. To help him make contact with his son again. But the son lived with his grandfather and for this to succeed they must be separated. Maddy said, "It felt so crazy. That I should seek you out, try to get together with you and then…that we would move in together. When I talk about it now, then… I get that you think it's hard to understand what I was thinking."

"Yes."

"But…"

"And you never thought, 'He's got a brain tumor and has gone crazy'?"

"No. Now I've thought that, these past few days. But not then."

"No."

"I'd been living in this bubble with him for a year, or a little more, and it was, like…there were other rules that applied in there. And it must be that way. We were creating art that would last and be admired and discussed for hundreds, maybe thousands of years. Like Giotto, Raphael, Velasquez. Nothing was so ugly in the circle around Fredrik as thinking conventionally. If someone said, 'that doesn't feel right in my gut,' or 'I can't get behind this,' then he went really crazy, then it was simply 'out of my house, right now.' It was like you were deported from the magic kingdom. And that job was everything for me. I lived for that. I'd lost contact with my old friends and with my father, they felt unimportant. And like I said, I thought I was doing a good thing."

She looked up at me.

"And I'm still not sure that it wasn't."

"Was what?"

"A good thing. Even if maybe it was a sick way in which to do it."

"He admitted that he killed my mother and my little sister. And he wanted to kill me too."

Maddy stared at me. The shock in her eyes looked completely genuine.

"How…? I don't understand."

"He didn't paint the fire. He created it."

New, brief silence. Maddy was trying to grasp the unthinkable.

"But…what do you mean, he set the fire?"

That wasn't how I had interpreted Dad. But I didn't say anything. We sat silent a moment. Maddy's gaze was lost in the distance.

"I've noticed since we came here that there's something different about Fredrik," she continued at last. "I don't recognize him. Like this thing that we should sleep in the exhibition room, what a strange thing. I asked him about it already the first day when you weren't around. What's the point of this? 'I have a plan,' he said. It would influence you, in some way, to sleep in the same room as the gods. Really screwy." She looked at me. "Can it be true, do you think? That he set the fire? Or is the brain tumor giving him delusions?"

"He believes he has a fire god inside him," I said. "And he wants it to have a place in me instead."

Maddy sighed.

"I guess we have our answer there, I assume… Anyway, what I meant was that maybe it was good that you got to see your father before he died. Even if you had to meet a lunatic who has done you very wrong. Maybe especially then. When you're older maybe you would have wondered why your grandfather didn't let you see him. Now you got to see for yourself. That's all I meant."

"Grandpa is dead."

Maddy stared at me again. But the shock in her eyes wasn't as strong now.

"How do you know that?"

"Dad told me. He was killed in a car accident after he left here."

My one leg was starting to bounce up and down; the heel was like a spring. I was breathing like a little rabbit. My weak little rabbit heart beat and beat but wasn't able to pump the blood out to my arms and legs and head, it started to tingle and my skin was crawling, on my neck and scalp, there was ringing in my ears and cold sweat beaded over my skin, like a rain shower from inside my body.

I bent my head down between my knees to get blood into it.

Heard Maddy push out the chair and round the table and I felt her soft hand on my shoulder, and it made me so damned mad. The lies and the manipulations never ended; now it would damned well be enough. I flew up from the chair and shoved her away and shouted, "LET GO! Don't you touch me!"

She tumbled back, took a couple of quick steps herself too. She wanted to get away; she wanted to have the table between us.

Maddy was afraid of me. And that felt good. At that moment I wanted it that way. The hatred and the anger. I was so dizzy that I was forced to support myself against the table.

"It's YOUR FUCKING FAULT that he's dead!" I shouted. "GODDAMN YOU!"

"Please, Isak…calm down…"

I reached out and grasped the knife with one hand, stabbed it deep down in the tabletop. The whole table wobbled, and the legs scraped against the floor. Maddy shuddered and moaned. I supported myself against the table with the other hand.

"Now you will damned well speak the truth," I said, and I wasn't shouting but my voice quavered with rage. "Did you sleep with him in Antalya?"

"No, you have to…"

"I've seen the pictures, Maddy. I'm not stupid."

"I swear, Isak…it was nothing like that. You know that I had a separate hotel room. I stayed there."

"You were lying on the beach, he had his arm around you."

"That's the way it is around Fredrik. He helps himself…you have to accept it. It's not just women, it's men too. He doesn't respect ordinary boundaries."

I thought about that evening at the restaurant south of Visby, when he wiped his sweaty face on the waitress's shirt.

"But it doesn't mean anything," Maddy continued.

I pulled the knife loose from the tabletop. Had to pull hard, as the blade had sunk deep down. Maddy stared at it. She exerted herself to make her voice sound calm.

"Set down the knife, Isak. Please."

"You deserve to die."

"And I haven't lied about everything. I fell in love with you for real."

"Stop, with your damned..."

"It's true, Isak! It's true! You must believe me. Do you think I could have handled moving in with you, living with you, if I hadn't been in love? For real?"

Maddy was talking so fast, the words seemed to be crowding to fall out of her mouth. She took her eyes off the knife and looked imploringly at me.

"He showed pictures of you, and I thought you were really handsome, to be honest. It was part of why I agreed to do this whole sick thing. I was curious about you before we met in Antalya. And I'd decided that I would try to make contact with you, as Fredrik wanted, and if it worked then we would hang out together down there, and then when I came home I could think in peace and quiet about whether I wanted to keep on with this business. I mean... I never would have gone to bed with you if I hadn't been attracted. You do understand that, don't you?"

Maddy stared at me. I stared back. My hand squeezed the shaft of the knife.

"No, I don't understand," I said.

"But... Isak..."

"You said that the job was your whole life. You wanted to stay in the bubble. I'm sure you did what Dad told you to."

Maddy shook her head firmly.

"No. Never anything like that. I do have that much self-respect. And Fredrik never told me that I should get involved with you. There was no such demand. He wanted us to establish contact, that was all. And then see how things developed. If you'd been a homely guy, then I would have said to Fredrik, 'Sorry, I don't want to see that idiot anymore. You can try to make contact with him yourself.' But you weren't a homely guy. You were nice, and considerate, and...the world's finest. I simply wanted to be with you all the time. And when I went home from Antalya I missed you so much that I thought I would go crazy. I missed your body, and...your warm, fine eyes. I was so in love with you, Isak."

Maddy made a little pause. Without my thinking about it my arm with the knife had straightened out and was now hanging limply along my side. But my hand was still locked around the shaft.

"I even think..." Maddy continued, but paused again. She appeared to be searching for words. "I mean, Fredrik was happy that we had good chemistry, that we'd found one another immediately. He said. But, to be honest, I think he got jealous too. Things between you and me were a little too good."

Dad's look at me and Maddy that evening at the restaurant. His bad mood, his bad behavior.

"I've noticed this too, since we came here," said Maddy. "That he's jealous of us."

"He wanted me to kill you," I said.

Maddy was silent. She stared at me, tried to see if I was lying to her.

"What?" came out of her at last. "No."

"Yes. I was supposed to cut your throat. It was a sacrifice I was forced to make."

Maddy understood that I was telling the truth. But she seemed to have difficulty taking it in. She stared silently ahead of her a moment.

"He truly is sick in the head," she mumbled at last. It sounded like she was talking to herself. "Completely sick. He wants to punish me because I chose you."

Dad had taken my mother from me, and Klara, and Grandpa.

He wanted to take Maddy from me too.

It wasn't the world that was evil. It was Dad. He had simply been such a big part of my world that everything else was overshadowed.

I had been shadowed by the sun. All the darkness in my life came from it.

I turned around, went up to the glass wall, took hold of the handle and pulled the whole big section to the side. The rain was still pouring down. I stepped out through the opening. The wet limestone felt cold against my bare feet.

I went over to Dad where he was lying facedown on the lounge furniture, bent down and took hold of the long strands of hair on his forehead. Pulled his head back and up. Set the knife against the stretched throat, pulled and pressed at the same time.

Exactly as he had shown me.

The edge cut through muscles and tendons and cartilage as if it were butter.

Behind my back I heard Maddy scream.

Warm blood sprayed out over my fingers and down on the light beige fabric.

I let go of Dad. He rolled off the sofa and landed with a thud on his back beside the coffee table. The back of his head struck the stone with a distinct sound, a clear crack. His legs fell toward mine as he was thrown off the sofa and I was about to fall over. I hopped on one leg and waved the knife in the air before I could take a step to one side and regain my balance.

His eyes were open and the gaze was as if they were made of glass.

I turned and walked away, toward the sea.

The hand with a grip around the knife shaft was cramping but I straightened my thumb and then the index finger and the ring finger and the other fingers and finally the knife fell out of my hand. It clattered against the limestone and soon lay still.

I sat down on the steps down toward the shore. It wasn't windy like before but looking at the sea it was apparent that there'd been a storm during the night. Mighty, blue-gray waves broke in high, white cascades down there.

Inside I felt calm. Something had quieted. I wasn't cold and barely felt the rain.

For a long time I sat in my own thoughts. Suddenly I heard a sound behind my back, as if Dad was moving over by the sofa. I turned around and looked.

Barbro was sitting by his head, bent over so deeply that I only saw her gray hair and the bun on her neck. His head was hidden but it looked as if she was holding it in her hands.

The bun on her neck wiggled and moved a little.

I turned toward the roaring sea again. For a long time I sat like that. Couldn't see enough.

Then by and by I heard sirens.

PART FOUR

Stop holding on to someone who just hurts you
Believe me, nothing's ever gonna work out
And I know I sound cynical but I promise you
I'm already dead and you don't want to be like me
This is gonna kill you, kill you

Daniela Rathana, "Wanted"

QUITE A FEW DAYS I'VE BEEN IN HERE NOW. IN MY LITTLE CELL. A week, maybe. The days are so alike that they run together.

The cell. The toilet. The interview room. The exercise yard. The sky.

This is my whole world.

I do understand that what my life has been like since I came here will be more or less the same for a long, long time to come.

I think about Grandpa, and I think about Maddy.

My life is over.

I must find a way out. Simply have to wait a little for Per's sake.

The sirens became louder and louder. Car engines in high gear through the forest. I understood that Maddy had called the police. Considered going to meet them but thought that maybe I would frighten them, if they came with guns drawn, nerves exposed. So I sat there.

I heard steps behind me. Several people approached. Someone shouted brusquely at me to sit still and show my hands. I raised them in the air. Rapid steps, boots against the limestone. Metal around one wrist, my arms pinned down behind my back, I understood what they wanted to do and willingly cooperated.

One of the police officers, a young guy it sounded like, took hold of my arm and told me to stand up. I obeyed. I still hadn't seen any of their faces. As we went toward the house I saw that two policemen were leaning over Dad's body.

Before I got into the police car they wrapped a blanket around me. I don't know if it was for my sake or because they didn't want the car seat to get wet. But it felt nice anyway and I was glad to get out of the rain.

At the police station I had to take off my underwear, then I was photographed. A doctor took blood samples and shone right into my eyes with a little flashlight. I was given clean, dry clothes and taken to my cell.

I gradually started to get warm inside but the cold lingered on my skin. I stretched out on the cot and pulled a blanket over me.

Now it came. The tiredness. I closed my eyes. If I could just sleep a while.

After what felt like ten seconds there was pounding on the door, and then it opened. A guard had come to get me. It was Per. I would be questioned, he told me.

I was still lying motionless on the cot with closed eyes. This was torture, waking me so soon.

"Listen," said Per, taking a few steps into the cell. "Wake up."

I took a deep breath and opened my eyes. Sat up laboriously. Collapsed with my elbows against my knees. But Per gave me a few minutes. There was no stress.

I understood immediately that he was a nice guy.

In the interview room a policeman was waiting. His name was Martin, he was in his forties and he looked physically fit. A faint aroma of aftershave was hanging in the air.

Martin explained that they hadn't found a defender for me yet, so it would be a short interview. He said that I was being held, suspected of having killed Fredrik Barzal, and asked what I thought about that suspicion.

"It's correct," I said.

Then it was over.

★ ★ ★

After that first interview I slept ten hours in a row or so. The whole day simply disappeared. I woke up, fell back asleep, woke up, fell back asleep.

Toward evening there was a knock on the cell door. The guard unlocked and let in an elegant woman in her fifties. It was Soraya.

She introduced herself and explained that she'd been appointed as my defender. Did I have any objections to that?

No. I didn't.

She said that according to the police I'd confessed that I'd killed my father, was that correct?

I said that was true.

Soraya looked at me thoughtfully. Nodded at last.

"You've been put on full restrictions. So you can't talk with anyone except me as long as the investigation is ongoing."

There was a new interview, now with Soraya present. Martin had also been joined by a colleague whose name was Agnes. A woman in her thirties.

Martin asked me to repeat what I'd said in the morning, that I confessed that I had killed Fredrik Barzal.

I did as he wanted.

Then he asked me to describe how I had proceeded.

"I took a knife from the kitchen, and then I went out and cut his throat," I said. "He was lying on his stomach on the sofa and I pulled up his head, I took hold of his hair and pulled, and then I cut, like from ear to ear, you know. He showed me how it's done."

"He showed you? Fredrik?"

"Yes. He wanted me to butcher a lamb the day before. Or maybe it was two days."

"And what kind of knife was it?"

"It was the one I used when I cut the throat of the lamb. Some kind...butcher's knife, I guess. I dropped it on the patio."

Martin paused briefly, looked down at the papers in front of him before he continued.

"So you cut his throat."

"Yes."

"Did you do anything else with the body?"

"No."

"You're sure of that?"

"Yes. Or...what do you mean?"

"The eyes were missing from the body when we got there."

Martin looked at me, waiting for me to say something. I understood at once what had happened.

"I see."

"But you have nothing to do with that?"

"No."

"Do you have any idea how that might have happened? That someone removed the eyes?"

"You don't need to answer that," said Soraya. "My client denies doing that. That's probably all you need to know."

But I was still light-headed from fatigue, even though I'd slept the whole day, and I wanted to put all the cards on the table, tell everything exactly as it was. So I said that it was Barbro who had taken the eyes.

Martin looked at me and asked who Barbro was.

I explained that she worked at Ajkeshorn, for my father. Described her age and appearance. I didn't go into who, or rather what, she really was.

"And why do you think this person took the eyes from your father's corpse?"

"I don't know who it would be otherwise."

"No."

I felt myself that maybe that wasn't a very convincing argument.

Martin and Agnes looked at me neutrally.

"This person you're describing, she wasn't at the scene when we got there."

"I see."

"Isn't it a little strange that she managed to slip away? Just before we arrived?"

I shrugged my shoulders. Soraya interjected again, her tone a little sharper now.

"You don't need to answer that either. My client is describing what he has experienced. If you haven't been able to find any traces of this person yet, that isn't something he needs to answer for. My client is very tired and is not going to manage a long interview, so I suggest that you stick to the essentials."

Martin did not comment on Soraya's objection. He looked down at his papers with jaw clenched. Then he told that a blood sample taken in connection with my arrest had shown high levels of sedatives, medications classified as narcotics. How did that happen?

I said that I got a couple of tablets from my girlfriend, Maddy, to be able to sleep that last night at Ajkeshorn.

Agnes made notes, even though the interview was being recorded. Then Martin asked about the motive. Why did I kill my father?

Yes, where the hell should I start? I thought. Then I said, "He wanted me to kill my girlfriend."

Martin looked down at his papers.

"And so that is... Madeleine Ström?"

"Yes."

"How did he go about that?"

Then I told them. That Dad described it as a sacrifice I had to make to get the power. Killing someone I loved. That was how I would earn total freedom by showing that I was prepared to do anything at all for it. I told about the little idol that was also in the painting and that there were images of it in my phone; they could see for themselves. Dad wanted the god to have a place in me, as it had a place in him. I mentioned the tattoo on the inside of his arm, the signs that were also on the little statuette.

Soraya interrupted me and asked if I wanted to take a break.

"No, it's cool," I said. "Not necessary."

I explained that the god had taken a place in Dad many years ago. That was why he could paint a picture of the fire that made it happen in reality so that Mom and Klara died and me too almost. We were his sacrifices. He loved us but he had to do that to be free. I survived however and now he had cancer, and then he wanted to transfer this god to me.

Martin asked many follow-up questions. I tried to explain it all just as clearly and coherently as possible. Soraya pointed out once again that if I felt tired I should just say so, and at last I actually felt that I was, that I couldn't take any more.

Soraya got a coffee for each of us. We talked a little while in the cell. She explained that there would be a detention hearing the following day, and I would probably be remanded for murder or manslaughter.

I got to see a doctor, who asked how I was feeling.

"I don't know," I said, because I didn't know.

I had such a strange feeling. It was like I was cut off from myself. Don't really know how to explain it. And I couldn't explain it to the doctor either.

In any case, he prescribed both sedatives and sleeping pills for me.

I dreamed that Mom visited me in the cell and told me that Grandpa had been in touch and that he was worried about me. Even in the dream I understood that it couldn't be true.

Mom had the same perfume as Soraya. A little sick.

If I hadn't killed Dad, could it have been me and Maddy then?

If I hadn't threatened her with the knife.

If I'd looked for her, that last night, with the binder in my hand, and said, *I'm really disappointed in you, because Dad showed me these pictures, but I'll give you a chance to explain. Talk, then I'll listen. Then I'll decide what I think about you.*

I know. Completely unrealistic. But anyway. If.

In the long run I think it probably wouldn't have mattered. Sure, we could have gotten through this, but sooner or later that damned washing machine would have come hopping and bouncing back into my life again and I would have been scared out of my wits and she would understand what a mental case I am.

We had a nice thing together but she never knew who I really was. Until at the end.

And then Grandpa, who's no longer alive.

That belongs to the part of myself that I can't make contact with.

I can think it, I can even say it out loud to myself, but it doesn't stick. It's like I can't get a grip on it.

When Dad told me I understood. And it was unbearable. The same pain as when Klara and Mom died, once again. So I think that my brain is protecting me, like a traffic cop at a car accident.

Back off. Nothing to see here. Move on.

I've been given a little respite.

It feels as if I'm standing on the beach below Ajkeshorn. The sun is still shining, but the light is whiter somehow, has lost its warm tone. It has started to get windy. Out over the sea it's cloudy and the clouds are moving toward land. By the horizon the sky is dark gray, almost black. Soundless lightning flashes zigzag down into the sea.

A dull, dull rumble is heard. It can barely be perceived. Yet.

Best to flee before the storm is over me.

I still haven't found out what assessment Karin has made of me. If I have to go to Huddinge for further evaluation.

I hear heels against the concrete in the corridor, energetic steps along with Per's more shuffling ones.

Soraya.

Per lets her in.

"Good morning," she says. "How's it going?"

"I'm tired."

"Then maybe I can perk you up a little. I've received new information this morning, which affects your situation a great deal."

Soraya smiles. Yes, she actually does. I didn't know that she could.

"You've probably already heard that you are no longer charged with murder, I'm guessing."

We are sitting in the interview room again. Martin looks down at his papers as he says this, as if his thoughts are already at the next step. Besides Martin only Soraya and I are in the room.

I nod.

"Yes."

"The autopsy has shown that Fredrik Barzal was already dead when you cut his throat."

"He was dead?"

"Yes. Presumably due to an overdose of heroin. But he had many other substances in his blood too."

I must think through this. Martin sits silently but observes me.

How can it not have occurred to me that maybe he was already dead?

I was so sure he was lying there asleep on the sofa. It looked that way. Admittedly I thought it was strange to lie down outdoors and go to sleep when the rain is pouring down. But it wasn't the strangest thing Dad had done or said during those days at Ajkeshorn.

I heave a deep sigh. So I'm not a murderer.

It's a bigger relief than I thought. I've come to the conclusion that I don't have anything left to live for. And then you might think that this shouldn't matter. But it does. I don't want to be a murderer.

"So the charge now is desecration of a corpse," Martin continues. "But I assume that you will admit responsibility for that? Because it's the same action that we talked about previously?"

"Yes, I admit responsibility," I say.

Martin nods.

"This is of course a less serious crime, so the restrictions are lifted now. You have the right to contact whoever you want."

Who? Who should I contact?

"Isak should be released immediately," Soraya says. "There is no reason at all that he should continue to be detained."

"We'll get to that," says Martin, and I sense a bit of irritation in his voice at Soraya's impatience. "But we want to question you about some things first… I'll tell you then that they have investigated Fredrik's eyes too. Or what's left of them. And it seems like it was an animal that poked out the eyes. Probably a bird."

So I was right, I think, but I don't say that.

"My client has made an effort the whole time to be transparent and tell the truth," Soraya interjects. "So it's gratifying that now it's in black and white that his information is correct."

Martin browses in his papers.

"Furthermore… I want to ask a little about this small figurine. The idol."

"Yes."

"We found it in the exhibition room. As you described."

"Yes."

"And…we've had it examined… I have to look in my papers here… So it concerns a so-called Vinca figurine, which originates from the Vinca culture in the Balkans… This is an artifact that is illegal to trade. Did your father say anything about how he acquired this figurine?"

"No. But he already had it nineteen years ago. When my grandfather's summer house burned."

Martin looks searchingly at me. I continue.

"And there are many more figures in the exhibition room. And masks. You must have seen that."

Martin nods.

"There are people who deal in such things. He probably acquired many of them illegally too."

Martin browses again in his papers. Sits silently a moment. Soraya stares at him, and then says, "Are we done?"

"No, we're not done… Isak, you said in one of the earlier interviews that your father caused the fire in your grandparents' summer house."

"Yes. That's what he said himself."

"What do you think he meant by that more specifically?"

I remain silent. Think a little while about how I should put this in words.

"He painted a picture of the fire. And then it happened in reality."

"Are you certain that was how he meant this?"

There is a new, brief silence. Certain?

"No."

"Can he have referred to the fact that in reality he set the fire?"

"That's very possible."

Martin wants to know what happened in the days before the fire. So I tell him. That Klara and I and Mom visited Dad in the studio in Stockholm. That we drove down to Småland without Dad the next day, and got settled in the summer house. About a week later the fire broke out. But it may also have been only four or five days—as a six-year-old I didn't keep track of the days.

Martin listens and asks follow-up questions.

"The fire was labeled an accident when it happened. But it doesn't seem to have been investigated that carefully. We're in the process of looking at it now. From what we've been able to see so far your father had no alibi for when the fire occurred."

I nod silently.

"Another detail which is interesting…he had a mental breakdown after the fire. Was admitted to the psychiatric clinic for a few months. But when we looked at this it turns out that he was in contact with psychiatric care already in the weeks before the fire. Several times even."

I think about what Grandpa said that evening a few weeks ago, when I visited him in the summer house.

The thing is that he was mentally unstable even before that.

"Do you have any recollections that your father behaved strangely before you went down to Småland?"

I nod and tell about Klara's and my visit in the studio, that he was so wound up that I thought it was unpleasant.

"And now, that last night at Ajkeshorn…he said that he'd thought about taking his own life. Then, twenty years ago. He described it as being him or us."

There is a brief silence. Then Martin sits up straighter in the chair, gathers his pile of papers, picks it up and taps the bottom edge a couple of times on the desktop. He looks at me.

"Thanks, Isak. You are free to go. If we need to get hold of you, how will we reach you?"

Soraya and I come out in the corridor outside the interview room. Martin stays behind.

I take a deep breath. Soraya takes me lightly by the arm and smiles.

"So, does it feel good now?"

She seems almost more relieved than me.

Yes, sure, I'm no longer locked up.

But the more life returns to normal, the harder it will be to keep the insight away that certain things will never be like before.

What should I do now? Go home to Småland, keep living in Maddy's and my apartment? Start working at the home health service again, as if nothing had happened?

"It's a little hard to grasp," I mumble.

"I understand that," Soraya says. "But you know what? I think you should call your grandfather now, at once. He's been really worried."

I look shocked. Soraya looks at me blankly.

"Is he alive?" I manage to say at last.

"Yes?"

Oh, God.

I sit down on a bench in the corridor.

Soraya sits down beside me, puts her hand on my shoulder.

"I told you that he'd been in touch."

I can't talk, hide my face in my hands.

"Don't you remember? It must have been...the second day you were jailed."

I shake my head. But then I remember the dream. Mom, who came to my cell and told that Grandpa was worried about me.

Mom, who had Soraya's perfume.

It was no dream; it was reality, I was simply too tired to understand that. Had too much medication in my body.

Soraya apologizes, but she didn't know that I thought Grandpa was dead. In that case naturally she would have cleared up the misunderstanding. She's been in contact with him several times.

Then she apologizes again. She's a little embarrassed, I think. Or maybe even a lot.

I still have my hands in front of my face. Sit there on the bench and cry, with Soraya beside me, for quite a while.

"Listen...shouldn't you call him?"

Soraya holds out her phone. I take it and think that I have to straighten up. Pull myself together. I close my eyes and take a deep breath. With trembling hands I enter Grandpa's number and bring the phone to my ear. Think that I should greet him happily, but not too casually. Dignified, like.

Grandpa answers immediately as if he's been sitting and waiting for the phone to ring.

"Hi," he says, and I hear by the tone that he doesn't expect it to be me at the other end; he thinks it's Soraya. Of course.

I didn't need to think about how to greet him—that was wasted time—because I don't manage to say a thing before I'm overcome by a new wave of unchecked crying. It starts hacking far down in my belly and chest and just wells out, completely unstoppable.

I sob loudly.

"Isak? Is that you?" So many emotions in his voice at the same time. Hope, relief, warmth, excitement.

"Yes," I whimper.

Grandpa is not a person who shows a lot of emotions. But now he's crying too.

We are both crying.

In the corner of my eye I see that Soraya opens her handbag and takes out a handkerchief.

I pick up my things. When I was brought to the police station all I had with me was my underwear. But the police have brought my bag, my clothes, my toiletry kit and my phone to Visby. Surely not for my sake—everything has probably been examined, I assume. But now they turn over a fully packed bag to me. I change into my own clothes.

Soraya tells me that Dad's death, and my arrest in connection with that, has received a lot of attention in the media. Journalists are besieging reception in the police station. A press spokesman just revealed that I will be released because the charges of murder or manslaughter no longer apply. So the journalists are definitely going to climb over each other to get a comment from me.

How does it feel?

Are you relieved?

What kind of relationship did you have with your father?

I can picture the scene.

For that reason Soraya is going to smuggle me out the back,

where Grandpa is waiting with the car. In the best case we can slip away unnoticed.

She shows the way through a corridor with offices on both sides. In the meantime she explains that it may take a month, or more, before my case comes up in court. It will be in Visby District Court and then I am expected to appear.

We go through a steel door and pass a stairwell before we come into an oblong trash room with big dark green wheeled containers on both sides. It smells sweetish and rotten. Soraya continues to walk but turns toward me.

"I don't dare promise that there won't be some journalists here too. So maybe you want to put on sunglasses?"

Sure. Sunglasses. I search for them in the bag. We stop in front of a steel door.

"We'll keep in touch the whole time," says Soraya. "If anything happens I'll call you. I have your number."

"Super. And thanks. For everything."

Soraya smiles and presses my arm lightly.

I put on the sunglasses, take hold of the door handle, set my body against it and heave open the steel door. The sun is shining, and a fresh breeze is blowing. The parking lot on the back side of the police station is asphalt and littered. No journalists are seen. I'm free—the world is mine.

Over there it's parked, Grandpa's old Mondeo. He is sitting behind the steering wheel and waves to me. I hurry over, open the door to the back seat and throw the bag in, round the car and hop into the passenger seat. Close the door.

We look at one another and smile. We've already done our crying on the phone. He puts his hand on my shoulder.

"Nice to see you."

"The same."

He starts the engine and looks down at the gearshift.

"It's probably best that we leave before anyone notices us."

"Yes."

"Are you hungry?"

"Yes. Actually."

The car takes off.

Grandpa. Always can be counted on.

I think a sense of duty is love that has hardened like cement.

Words and hugs are probably good. But you can build a life on a sense of duty.

I turn on the phone for the first time since I got it back. Dozens of missed calls, lots of voicemail. Loads of text messages. Many seem to be from journalists.

But nothing from Maddy.

Grandpa drives to Max and gets in the drive-through line. I order a combo, a double burger with avocado and bacon and extra everything, plus French fries and soda. Grandpa wonders if I shouldn't have dessert too.

Yes. Of course I should. I order a large chocolate milkshake.

Grandpa orders a Halloumi burger and a Sprite.

We get two paper bags with our food and our drinks in a holder, then we drive out of Visby. Soon we're in the countryside. It's harvest time and the farmers are working on their big fields. In meadows and pastures cows and horses are grazing.

Grandpa drives a short distance on the highway toward Fårösund, but then he turns right onto a smaller road. The villages are dense here. In one he turns left, at the next one he turns right and after a few kilometers with fields on both sides we are already at the next one.

In each village a stone church. Maybe Maddy and I drove here that night when I was supposed to take the Lamborghini up to Ajkeshorn.

Maddy. What is she doing now? Where is she? What does she think of me?

"I've had some time to kill," Grandpa says. "So I've explored

Gotland a little. In any event around Visby. And I've found a nice place where I think we'll be left alone."

He turns right again, onto a gravel road that leads through a patch of forest with alternating spruce and beech and oak. After some hundred meters the forest opens up, and there is the destination for our journey. A ruin of an old church. He parks the car by the low church wall and we get out with our food sacks and drinks in our hands.

There's no one here except us. The wind passes through the crowns of the trees, and birds sing. Otherwise it's completely silent.

The deserted church shines grayish white in all the greenery that surrounds it. The roof is long since gone, and much of the sides. The gables are what have managed best, but here are no sharp, straight angles; everything is worn down by weather and wind.

"What a place," I say.

"Isn't it special?" Grandpa says. "There's a bench over here."

We round the ruin and I can't tear my eyes from it. Have an urge to climb on the wall on the half-collapsed long side; it's almost like a stairway up. The old clock tower looks fairly well preserved. High up there is an opening.

"Is it possible to go up in the tower?"

"Yes. The stairs are still there."

We sit down on either end of the bench and set out the food between us. I take hold of my burger, unwrap the paper and sink my teeth in it. It tastes wonderful.

We eat in silence for a while. Then I say, "He told me that you'd died in a car accident."

Grandpa shakes his head but doesn't say anything. Stuffs a couple of French fries in his mouth.

"And that it was my fault. That you drove off the road when you were going to answer when I called."

I tell that I tried to call him when he'd driven away from Ajkeshorn, but that Dad had taken my phone. Grandpa explains that his phone had died, he drove back to Visby and slept at his hotel and the next morning he discovered all the calls I'd made. When he tried to call back I didn't answer. Toward evening he contacted the police and told that he was worried about me, but they said that the information he provided wasn't anything they could act on. He thought about driving up to Ajkeshorn again, but decided to sleep on the matter.

The next morning he heard on the local news that a murder had happened on Fårö and that a suspect was arrested. He got a terrible feeling that I was involved. And that maybe he could have prevented it if he'd gone there the night before.

I shake my head.

"No, you really did all you could. You mustn't blame yourself."

I tell him that Dad wanted me to kill Maddy.

"You are never going to hear this from me again," says Grandpa. His voice is a little unsteady. "But...if you had killed him... I wouldn't have held it against you. I've fantasized about it myself. Many times."

It does me good to hear this. Things are falling into place somehow. We eat in silence a while longer, then Grandpa says, "I've thought about whether maybe he wanted you to kill him."

"Do you think so?"

"This business of wasting away with cancer, like an ordinary mortal, that wasn't for Fredrik, I think. What would give the maximum attention? A family drama. To be murdered by your own son. There's something timeless about it. Something immortal. And that was all that meant anything to Fredrik. That he would become immortal through his art."

I take a paper napkin and wipe my fingers, while I think about what Grandpa is saying. Maybe he's right. Dad said himself that he'd had similar thoughts twenty years ago.

"It seems to have worked in that case," Grandpa continues. "I read on the Internet that the prices on his paintings have gone right through the roof."

"What did you mean when you said 'I know what you did' that evening?"

Grandpa sighs. He sits silently a moment, looks unseeing over toward the deserted church.

"I think he set the fire," he says at last. "He wasn't in his right mind in any event—that's quite certain."

"What made you think that?"

"When the three of you came down from Stockholm, a week before the fire, your grandmother and I both thought that your mother looked extremely tired and worn-out. We were worried. So when you and Klara had gone to bed I asked, a little carefully, if there was anything bothering her. She broke down and started weeping. It just came out, like a flash flood. And now you should keep in mind that she knew we had a rather negative opinion of Fredrik, so she never said a bad word about him to us, out of loyalty. On the contrary, she always emphasized his positive sides. But that evening there was no stop. She told us that Fredrik hadn't been sleeping properly for months, he was up at night and wandered around the apartment. He talked to himself. There was a work space in the hall, do you remember that?"

"Yes."

"The wastebasket there was full of crumpled papers one morning. So Linn took them out and unfolded them, and discovered that there were a lot of drawings of various ways to commit suicide."

I moan. Dad hadn't lied to me, at least not about that.

"She got him to go to the psychiatric clinic, but it didn't help. It just continued and got worse. Sometimes he was gone for days and didn't get in touch. She reported him as missing to the police. Then she discovered that their joint savings account was empty. Over a hundred thousand kronor was gone. It turns out that he'd bought a little stone figure with the money. A decimeter tall. Over a hundred thousand. She tried to get him to return it, but he refused... Your mother had a hell of a time. She was all done."

Mom. I see her before me. How she must have struggled to keep her tiredness and her worry hidden from me and Klara. I get tears in my eyes.

"So when the house burned," Grandpa continued, "I just felt that something wasn't right. I pressed the police and the fire department to investigate thoroughly, at the time it happened. But they didn't seem to care."

Silence again settles down over the deserted church. At last Grandpa says he has a suggestion.

"There's a night ferry to Oskarshamn at twelve thirty. Arrives approximately three thirty. Then we have a two-hour drive, but we could be back at the country house early tomorrow."

The summer house by the lake. The stillness and the isolation. Home. I long to be there so that my body almost aches.

"But we can also stay in Visby one night and sleep late if you want," says Grandpa.

"No, no. Let's leave tonight. That will be perfect."

"If we get a cabin we hardly need to see a single living soul on the way."

"Can you book online?"

"Yes, I think so."

I slurp up the last of my milkshake and take out my phone. Soon I've found the Destination Gotland site and booked the night ferry to Oskarshamn for us and the car.

It's a long day waiting for the ferry to depart, but at last it's late evening and we're in line to drive on board. The twilight falls so slowly that you hardly notice it, but the searchlights in the harbor area are clearly visible now.

I've been driving all day and I'm still behind the wheel. It may take a while longer before the line starts moving, so I read the news on my phone about Dad's death. All the major newspapers say something about the fact that the famous artist's son has been released today, because the charges of homicide or manslaughter no longer remain.

Somewhere Maddy is sitting and reading this news, I think. She must know now that I'm not a murderer.

But I also think that maybe it doesn't matter. That's not the point. She saw when I cut Dad's throat. She knows that I'm capable of killing another person in a very disgusting way.

The terror in her gaze when I grasped the knife in the kitchen. Then it felt good; I wanted her to be scared to death. Now it feels terrible to think about.

If you've felt such terror about your boyfriend, is it ever possible to repair?

I think about where she might be. Did she go home to her parents in Täby? Or is she still on Gotland? Can she even have gone back to our apartment in Småland?

My pulse rises a little when I think about the latter. It's actually not impossible. The apartment is her home anyway, even if it was part of the decor in a play she performed in, directed by Dad.

At last we drive on board. The ferry is far from full, but we still play it safe. I go out on deck, still with sunglasses and cap on, and wait while Grandpa goes to reception and gets the key to our cabin. Because I'm out there by myself I dare to take off the sunglasses. It's after midnight. The wind has died down. Visby's medieval buildings with their stepped gables brood in the darkness. But I hear a thumping bass, I hear laughter and talking and I see colored lights playing on a stone facade.

Get a text from Grandpa with our cabin number and make my way there. Knock on the door. Grandpa opens. The cabin is oblong, with a toilet to the left of the entrance and a cot along each wall. Grandpa immediately stretches out on one and I take the other. Lie on my back with the cap over my face and try to sleep a while.

When we drive ashore I'm behind the wheel again. Grandpa has offered to drive. He slept deeply for several hours and feels alert, he says. But I insist on continuing. Say that we can change along the way if I get tired, but it's mostly in order not to discuss it any more. I'm going to drive the whole way home to Grandpa's summer house; I know that. Because I want to.

There is a thud against the steel pier, and then we've landed in Oskarshamn. It's three thirty in the morning. The sun shines at a low angle over a sleeping city. The cars from the ferry cruise along the streets in the harbor in a long caravan, a caravan that gradually thins out. Some cars turn off already in the city, and when we come out to E22 half of the cars drive north and half south. Only a very few do like we do, continue straight along Route 47.

I've eaten my sandwich, I have yogurt in the holder in the car door and I have steaming-hot coffee in a mug with a plastic lid sitting between the seats.

I'm on my way home.

The road cuts through Småland's deep spruce forests, but here and there the landscape opens up with fields. Milky sheets of fog. Two deer with necks extended listen and sniff in the dawn light.

It is almost six o'clock when I meander along the last little stretch of the gravel road through the forest. I'm tired now, but my stomach is tingling with expectation. Soon.

Everything is the same. The house, the yard that slopes down toward the lake, the water. The tall spruce trees that frame it.

I stop the car and turn off the engine. The silence almost echoes in my ears. I touch Grandpa lightly on the arm.

"Grandpa…we're here."

He wakes up, looks half-asleep.

I get out of the car, stretch my body, which has gotten stiff from hunching over the steering wheel. Feel the fresh chill of the summer morning against my cheek. The night's dampness still lingers in the nearness of the forest.

Birdsong and a clicking car engine are all that's heard.

Must go down and look at the lake before I do anything else.

I round the house, follow the slope down toward the water's edge. It's calm. The lake is glossy. Water striders dart on the surface, and dragonflies chase each other nearby. Over in the reeds a fish strikes the surface of the water, then there is silence again.

This place. What Dad did nineteen years ago almost took it from me. But only almost.

We rest up. No one comes and disturbs us. I have my phone turned off most of the time. Every time I turn it on new calls and messages have arrived from unknown numbers. I turn it off again.

Grandpa drives into town to shop for groceries. I take a dip in the lake, and the water feels marvelously warm and smooth against my skin, such a contrast from the cold and biting sea by Ajkeshorn. I'm probably a lake person anyway.

We have *filmjölk* and cornflakes for lunch and in the evening we grill sausages on Grandpa's kettle grill. Have a light beer with it. An ice cream bar for dessert.

Then we sit on the wooden deck and look out over the lake. It's been a warm day, but now the air is starting to cool a little, and it's nice.

Grandpa holds one hand under his ice cream bar as he eats so that pieces of chocolate coating don't fall down on his lap.

"What do you intend to do with the apartment?" he says.

I think a little about what's implied in that question before I reply.

What he means more or less is that Maddy probably isn't coming back.

"I don't know," I say after a while.

"You can always move back in with me if you want. You know that."

"Yes, yes."

I think that I love Grandpa, but I'm not going to move back in with him. I'm a different person now.

Grandpa goes in to take care of the dishes and I stroll down the slope to the shore. Let the warm, almost hot water closest to land lap over my bare feet.

I think about the apartment and about the fact that Maddy might actually be there now, only half an hour by car from where I am, and suddenly I see the whole scene before me: I open the door and call to Maddy, she answers a little surprised from the living room, I step in just as she's coming into the hall from the other direction, she comes toward me with a slightly uncertain, guarded facial expression, but there is also longing and love and I open my arms and she comes toward me and we put our arms around each other, oh God, I feel her warmth and her scent.

The scene is so strong and alive that my mouth gets completely dry from longing.

This won't work. I have to call.

I have thought of course that I should let her contact me when she feels ready, considering what happened that last night, but what if she's thinking exactly the same?

I take out the phone, turn it on and call her. My heart is rushing so that it's pounding in my temples, and I think that if she answers now I'll hardly be able to talk. She's going to hear just how nervous and excited I am, but whatever, why the hell should I put on a facade?

Put the phone to my ear. Look out over the lake. Breathe with open mouth. Feel a little dizzy.

The ringtones go out. One. Two. Three. Four.

Click.

"Hi, you've reached Maddy. I can't talk right now, please leave a message or text me and I'll get back to you."

Beep.

"Uh…um…yeah, hi, it's me. I…uh… I'm home, at…at the summer house. I was released as perhaps you know. Give me a call."

Click.

Why didn't I say *miss you*, or *longing for you*, or *love you*?

Fuck. How hard can it be?

Yes, yes. I called anyway. *Don't be too hard on yourself now*, I think.

The phone call seems to have sapped my energy. It feels as if I'm going to fall asleep if I sit down.

Then the phone rings.

My heart starts galloping in my chest again, hop, hop, hop, more expectation than nervousness now—it has tipped over. The fact that she's calling right back must still be a good sign anyway…?

It must be.

I answer without even checking who's calling and hear the familiar voice.

Soraya's.

"Hi, Isak…am I calling at a bad time?"

I clear my throat and swallow. Try to catch my breath a little.

"Um…no."

"I just want to inform you that a will has been found up at Ajkeshorn."

Soraya tells me what is in the will.

Now I understand everything.

I press the doorbell by the front door to Ajkeshorn.

The wind tugs and tears in the treetops, and it feels like it could start raining at any moment. I only have a thin rain jacket over the hoodie and feel a little cold. Over one shoulder a backpack with toothpaste, toothbrush and a change of clothes. Expect to spent the night in Visby on the way home.

It's late September. Just over two months have passed since I was released from jail but it already feels distant, as if everything I experienced happened many years ago.

The Micra is still on the turnaround where we left it last summer. I'm here to retrieve it.

In any case that's my excuse.

I press the doorbell again.

There were almost no people on the Gotland boat. No lines in the restaurant, easy to get a table by the window. The ferry rocked a little from side to side but not so much that I got seasick. From Fårösund I had to take a taxi; the bus up to Fårö probably only runs in the summer. The summer places are silent and boarded up along the highway, abandoned like runaway summer cats. The whole island feels cold and colorless and turned away somehow. I walked the last stretch through the forest up to Ajkeshorn.

Press the doorbell again. Nothing is heard from inside the house. No one comes to open the door. There are no cars on the turnaround except for the Micra. But I'm pretty sure that Maddy is here. It must be that way.

Still no sound from inside the house. I lean toward the narrow, high window next to the front door, cup my hands around my face and peek in. Everything looks as usual.

I ring one last time but doubt that anyone will answer. Then I start walking around the house to get to the patio. Follow the facade to the right. Just as I'm about to round the first corner I hear the front door opening. I stop and turn around.

Maddy is standing in the doorway.

A thin blouse in some semitransparent fabric, with stripes of yellow, apricot, light brown and red. Tight white jeans. Big earrings. Elegant makeup.

She's crazy good-looking, but looks rather different than I'm used to. This only confirms what I already know. The Maddy that I was with was a role she played.

Is the real one standing in front of me now?

The pattern on the blouse looks like flames of fire. An elegant and comfortable fire, which is possible to be close to.

Nice detail there.

There is nothing welcoming or open in her gaze.

"You could have called and said that you were coming," she says.

"I did call," I say.

"But you didn't say you were on your way here."

"Would that have mattered?"

"What do you want?"

"To get the Micra. And talk a little."

I'm in front of her now, standing a short distance from the door. She has only opened it a foot or so approximately, as if I were a salesman she will immediately ask to leave.

"The police asked if I wanted a restraining order on you."

"My attorney told me about the will."

"I see."

Still the same hostile attitude.

"I only want to talk for five minutes."

At last Maddy opens the door and moves so that I can go in.

I follow her through the long corridor with the corroded, burnt wall lamps. We pass the courtyard, where Barbro is taking down the hammock. She looks the same. The gray hair in the same bun on her neck, the long, black dress.

"Who is she?" I ask.

"Don't know, but she's always been here."

Two months ago I was convinced that she was half bird and half human. Now I'm no longer as certain. The memory of her climbing up on my chest and blinking at me like a raven is just as crystal clear as before. It has the same quality as the memory of the cinnamon roll I had on the ferry a few hours ago. But I also know that the brain can create its own memories and images.

"What was it you gave me that last night, really?"

"When was that?" Maddy continues walking toward the kitchen but turns halfway around toward me.

"After the dinner with Grandpa."

"Well, it was a good little mixture. You needed to sleep."

Maybe it's as Soraya suggested, that Barbro is an undocumented migrant from the Balkans. Maybe they eat sheep's eyes there, if you were born in the countryside long ago.

"Would you like coffee?" Maddy asks when we come to the kitchen. "A glass of wine?"

"Thanks, I'm good. I won't stay long."

Just then rain starts to patter against the roof and against the stone flooring on the patio, heavy drops, a wall of rain that drives in from the sea.

"Damn," says Maddy, opening the sliding glass wall. "Help me."

We stow the cushions for the lounge furniture down in a big wooden box that is padded with plastic inside.

"You've bought new pillows, I see."

"Yes, it was just as well to replace everything. Picked dark blue instead. Cream white stains so easily."

Sure.

Maddy also folds up the big parasol and ties a ribbon around it so that the wind won't tear at it. The sea is roaring against the shore down there. Gray mountain chains of water that dissolve in white cascades.

We hurry into the kitchen again, Maddy closes the sliding wall. I ask, "What are you going to do with this place?"

"Don't know. Maybe a museum."

"And the staff?"

"Most will have to go, of course. But a few will remain. We'll try to take care of the inheritance."

"How long were you with him?"

"I told you that. Roughly a year, before I met you."

"Did you love him?"

Maddy is silent and looks out the window.

I don't really think she needs to think about the answer. But she is considering how much she should tell me. At last she says, "Yes, I loved him. A lot. He was everything to me. He believed in me, he trusted me. He gave me the world. Showed me what life could be. He was a genius and I got to be his. So absolutely, I loved him."

"Yet he wanted me to kill you."

Maddy took a deep breath through her nose, and her facial features became even tighter.

"He was also a jealous drug addict with a brain tumor. But that wasn't really him."

"You did it, right? You gave him the overdose?"

Maddy looks at me, her gaze more searching now. She doesn't say anything but looks thoughtful. As if she is thinking about how she should continue.

"Take off the backpack and your jacket," she says at last.

"Why is that?"

"Just do it."

Reluctantly, with slow movements, I do as she says. Place the backpack on a chair, hang the rain jacket over the back. She goes up to me and puts her arms around my body. Pulls me close to her. Spreads out her fingers across my shoulder blades.

I heave a deep sigh. God, how I've longed for her body against mine. I have told myself that this outing is about picking up the Micra, and maybe also to tell her that I've seen through her, I know what she's done, and when that's been confirmed I never want to see her again.

That's how I've thought. But my heart and my body say something else. I put my arms around her.

Her grip on me gets looser and her hands start moving. They feel my back, they feel my sides, move along my waist, down over my rear.

As if she's searching for something.

"What are you doing?" I ask.

"Have to check that you don't have any devices on you."

She bends down and feels with both hands along my one leg, crotch and backside, down over the knee and the shin bone, all the way down to my calf. Moves her hands to the other calf and follows the leg all the way up.

She suspects that I've been sent by the police to secretly record a confession.

I curse myself for feeling so disappointed.

She goes through my rain jacket too, feels in all the pockets and in the lining. Then the backpack. Opens it, looks and feels. Maddy would be a good customs official; she's quick and methodical.

At last she's done. She pulls out a chair, sinks down and looks at me with a firm gaze.

"Shoot," she says. "What do you want to know?"

I sit down too.

"You gave him the overdose, didn't you?"

"Yes. It was simple. He'd been drinking, he'd taken pain killers, sedatives…everything. He wasn't exactly on his guard."

"And the will? He didn't know about that, right?"

Maddy shakes her head.

"No. Do you remember that I took a trip up to Stockholm in April?"

"Hmm."

"That was when I arranged it. He was basically completely out of it but could sign his name anyway."

I nod and smile bitterly.

"Yes, it seemed pretty suspect that he would give everything to you. Dad only loved himself. No one else."

Maddy smiled a little, cocked her head.

"A few weeks ago you absolutely didn't want to meet your father. You didn't want anything to do with him. Now you're mad because you don't get an inheritance from him."

I shake my head.

"No. I don't want anything. All this is soiled by who Dad was."

"So why are you here?"

"I wanted to hear from you how it happened."

"No. You're here because you still love me. You want us to get together again."

What she says silences me. For a moment anyway.

"Who are you really? What you told about your parents…the summer house on the Riviera…"

"I'm from a suburb of Stockholm. Grew up with my mother in a two-room apartment. So when I came into this world, in Fredrik's world…of course I thought, *I want to stay here.* Who wouldn't have thought that?"

"Very few would have been prepared to murder for it."

"Says the man who cut his father's throat."

I fall silent again.

"He charmed me," Maddy continues. "And then when I noticed how lonely he was and that I was the closest to him of anyone, then I fell in love. I started thinking that we would spend the rest of our lives together. So when he told me that he had a son that he wanted to resume contact with…you understand that I didn't rejoice. You were a competitor."

"Why did you go along with this whole sick plan then? Why did you help him?"

"I already knew Fredrik well enough to know that if I didn't help him, he would find some other way to do it. If he'd decided on something he just did it. And he would be angry at me. Maybe even dump me. I couldn't take that risk. Better to do it myself and have control over how it developed."

"But I still don't get it. Like when Grandpa was at dinner, for example. When I wanted to run after him you helped Dad prevent me. Wouldn't it have been easier to let me leave? Dad couldn't very well have blamed you for that?"

Maddy shakes her head.

"I was playing a role. Then I had to go into it a hundred percent. If I were to try to evaluate every situation I ended up in, whether maybe it would be smarter to do it some other way, it wouldn't have worked. I couldn't have carried it off anyway."

She pauses briefly before continuing.

"But I must say one more thing… It wasn't a role that was hard to play, being your girlfriend. On the contrary. I liked it a lot. I liked you a lot, Isak."

"But you didn't love me."

"No. Do you know what I mainly got out of being with you? I noticed that Fredrik got jealous. And that was how I understood that he loved me too."

I already understood that, but it still hits me harder than I thought to hear Maddy say it flat out. I squirm in the chair and rub one hand around my mouth.

"You're fooling yourself so much," I say and try to keep my voice steady. "Don't you think that Dad slept with the other assistants? Of course he did. He wanted to own you, he wanted to have power over you. That's not love."

I wanted to hurt her, like she hurt me, but she doesn't seem to care.

"Was there anything else?"

"You made the sacrifice, Maddy. Didn't you? You killed someone you love. And now you've won everything. You own the world! You have superpowers! How does it feel?"

Maddy stands up.

"I don't want anything that's in the apartment. You can throw away everything you don't want yourself. I'll just get the keys to the car, then you can leave."

Maddy disappears from the kitchen. I remain seated. Look down toward the sea one last time. I'll probably never come back here to Ajkeshorn.

Right now I just feel empty. But the pain has strong legs and big lungs. I know that it's going to catch up with me.

When I hear Maddy's steps approaching again I stand up.

She reaches out her hand with the car keys toward me, but they're not the keys to the Micra; they're the keys to the Lamborghini.

"Fredrik wanted you to have it."

I see now that she has a new tattoo on the inside of her outstretched arm.

I recognize the sign.

Her fire is greater than mine anyway.

★★★★★